Angelee

A Coming of Age Story

By

Dalletta Olena Reed

In honor of my grandparent's generation.

Paternal Grandfather
Harley Shilkett 1897 – 1936

Paternal Grandmother -- "Granny"
Flossie Gregory Shilkett Hildebrand 1898 - 1996

Paternal Step-Grandfather – "Gramps"
The only grandfather I ever knew.
Harry Harm Hildebrand 1900 – 1978

Maternal Grandfather
Bert Cox 1902 – 1959

Maternal Grandmother -- "Grandma"
Mamie Deloris Boltz Cox 1901 - 1984

Character List By Family

Tilson

Angelee (Gee-Gee) Giselle	
Andrew Bartholomew Sr.	Angelee's Father
Emileah	Angelee's Mother
Andrew Bartholomew (Drew)	Angelee's Older Brother
Aimee (Mee-Mee) Paige	Angelee's Younger Sister
Alistair	Angelee's Younger Brother
Anastasia (Stacy)	Angelee's Baby Sister

Barnes

Grandy Barnes	Angelee's Maternal Grandfather
Grandma Barnes	Angelee's Maternal Grandmother
Millicent (Milly) O'Neal	Angelee's Aunt/Mommy's Twin

Biers

Olivia Annalise	Angelee's Best Friend
Papa	Olivia's Father
Mamma	Olivia's Mother
Opa	Olivia's Grandfather
Oma Biers	Olivia's Grandmother

Hanson

Jasper	Hanson
Eleanor "Nori"	Hanson
Bobby	Hanson
Jill	Hanson
Louis	Hanson
Bart Pickering	Nori's younger brother

Parkham

Marcheline	Parkham (Nee: Boyer)
Addison Campbell Boyer	Parkham--Mrs. Parkham's Nephew
Frances-Rae MacKinnon	Mrs. Parkham's Housekeeper

Other

Steffken Torrington	Family Friend / Aimee's Art Teacher

Table of Contents

Wednesday, July 4th, 1917--Afternoon and Evening Fireworks

Wednesday, July 4th, 1917--Feast of Light Dance

Thursday, July 5th, 1917--Making Peace

Saturday, July 7th, 1917--Driving Admission

Sunday, August 5th, 1917--A Birthday Announcement

Sunday, September 2nd, 1917--Sidewalk Sermon

Friday, September 7th, 1917--Reporting for Duty

Friday, October 5th, 1917--Distracting Concert

Tuesday, November 13th, 1917--Sunday School Request

Thursday, November 29th, 1917--Thanksgiving

Thursday, November 29th, 1917--Love Stories

Thursday, November 29th, 1917--Mrs. Parkham's Story

Wednesday, December 5th, 1917--The Army's Christmas Appeal

Monday, December 24th, 1917--Nativity Play

Tuesday, December 25th, 1917--Christmas Day

Tuesday, December 25th, 1917--Christmas Evening

Tuesday, December 25th, 1917--Unveiling

Wednesday, December 26th, 1917--An Admission

Wednesday, December 26th, 1917--Afternoon Pondering

Friday, January 18th, 1918... Children's Clothes and Toys

Saturday, January 26th, 1918--Let Go of The Fear

Saturday, February 16th, 1918--Pauley's Letter

Sunday, February 17th, 1918--Sunday Ponderings

Monday, February 18th, 1918--Monday Evening Conversation

Saturday Morning, February 23rd, 1918--That "T" Word Again

Saturday, February 23rd, 1918--Aimee's Impromptu Workshop

Saturday, March 16th, 1918--Alistair's Observation

Saturday, March 29th, 1918--An Easter Baby

Sunday, April 14th, 1918--A Question and A Hint

Friday evening, April 19th, 1918--Brownie Leader

Prologue

Seventeen-year-old Angelee Giselle Tilson loved her hometown. Nestled in a hollow of the rolling hills in the southern part of the state, about thirty-five miles southwest of Indianapolis, the large town of Martinsville, Indiana was not only well established, but thriving. The community, recognized as Morgan County's seat of government, was situated alongside the White River.

In 1917, the flourishing community boasted of several industries: including the Davis Cooperage Company-which produced barrels and smaller casks; A Van Camp tomato packing plant; the Old Hickory Chair Company. Eugene Shireman created an international market from swampland, the "World's Largest Goldfish Hatcheries."

Martinsville's moniker, "City of Mineral Water", came from its greatest claim to fame—the mineral springs. In 1888, while drilling for oil, Sulphur water was discovered. The first mineral springs resort was built by 1889. The reputed healing properties of the mineral waters were so famous, people came, not only from across the Midwest region but also from across the nation and even from foreign countries. By 1917, nearly thirty years later, the city boasted twelve mineral spring sanitariums.

Besides the grand sanitariums, this picturesque town, with its red brick Italianate courthouse, Carnegie library—constructed of locally quarried white limestone—and numerous, was home to the Tilson family. Angelee lived with her family on Washington street, across the street from the Home Lawn Sanitarium.

Angelee learned her family history during story-telling around the dinner table on Sunday afternoons, eating the large mid-day meal.

One of Angelee's favorite stories was how Daddy--Dr. Andrew Tilson—had brought his bride, Emileah, to the community in 1895. Managing to procure a consulting position at Home Lawn, Daddy joked that he was lured to Martinsville by the thought of multitudes of patients needing nothing more than being subscribed therapeutic baths and mineral water cocktails." Angelee was glad that her father had indeed treated many visitors who sought to partake of the waters at Home Lawn. But proud was the word she used when she thought of work in the community; providing free medical care to struggling families in poorer neighborhoods.

Mommy taught by example. Some of Angelee's earliest memories were of pretty ladies sitting in the parlor, enjoying Mommy's hospitality of tea, cakes and cookies. Before she was old enough to attend school, Angelee was allowed to sit quietly, listening to the ladies read from the Bible and pray.

A growing family did nothing to dampen Mommy's enthusiasm for serving the local population and supporting missionaries. Each child had been introduced to the practice of Christian faith, at home and with the church.

One of Angelee's favorite family stories involved Christmas 1897. Born on the 12th of December, the first Tilson child, Andrew Bartholomew, was cast in the role of baby Jesus in First Christian Church's annual nativity play. Now at twenty-years-old, Andrew—known as Drew—was too old to repeat the part. He had graduated from high school in 1916 and was studying science at Butler College.

Angelee had arrived in the world on the 6th of June, 1899. On that particular Tuesday, Mommy was so caught up with her own delivery process, she had no idea that her next-door neighbor was also in labor. Within a couple of hours, the residents of Washington Street had the birth of two healthy baby girls to celebrate; Angelee Giselle and Olivia Annalise Biers. It was no wonder that Angelee could never imagine life without her best friend. By sharing the same birthday, it was a bit like being twins.

It was twenty-two months later on 16th April 1901, that another girl joined the Tilson family—Aimee Rochelle. A baby with a bubbly personality, Aimee had grown into a kind-hearted, vivacious young lady. Angelee vacillated between wanting to smack her and wanting to hug her.

It was the delight of the Tilson children to enjoy spending at least two weeks of their summer vacation in Louisville, Kentucky. The family would make the trip by train to see Mommy's parents. After two or three weeks, Grandad and Grammy Barnes would travel back to Martinsville with the children.

When Angelee had turned eight years old, she became very worried about Mommy. In the early months of 1908, Mommy had been ill, often needing to eat dry toast and drink strong tea. As the months went on, Mommy had often been tired and resorted to taking naps—which was not normal for her mother. On a Sunday in March, while sitting around the dinner table, Daddy had told them that Mommy was going to have another baby. Angelee wasn't too sure how she felt about the idea of a baby in the house. She was a toddler herself been when Aimee was born, they grew up together. However, she did all she could to help her mother with cooking, cleaning and making sure Aimee stayed out of trouble.

The summer of 1908 was quite a memorable one. Instead of going to Louisville in June at the beginning of the school break, Mommy and Daddy decided that the trip would be made the last week of July. And instead of Mommy and Daddy taking them down, Grandad and Grammy would be coming up to collect them. Angelee thought it was going to be the best summer ever.

That summer's visit included incidents she would never forget. Among those moments that made an indelible impression was the first fifteen minutes of returning home.

Grandad and Grammy had awakened them early because the journey from Louisville to Martinsville would take the better part of a day. They took the train from downtown Louisville and arrived in Indianapolis, where they had to catch the next interurban. By the time the train arrived in Martinsville, Angelee and her siblings were tired, hungry, and overcome by the heat. Daddy met them at the station in the car. The cases were dropped on the floor of the car, and everyone piled in.

Once home, Daddy gave them instructions to wash their hands and face then join Mommy in the dining room for refreshments.

Having completed her cooling and refreshing, Angelee stopped in her tracks. Mommy sat at her usual place, a small bundle in her arms. Aimee ran forward to see the newest member of the family—Alistair John Luke, who had been born on the 5th of August. It suddenly made sense to her why the visit had been moved to later in the summer. Mommy wanted time to prepare better for the birth of the baby.

Angelee loved the tiny boy but always made sure that Mommy was close by. Angelee feared she would hurt the little one. At was nine years old, Alistair was the only sibling she had known as a baby. As he grew, her self-confidence around him grew. It was enjoyable watching the development of his boyish sturdiness and cleverness.

The year 1915 rolled around, bringing another change in the dynamics of the Tilson family. Mommy's twin sister, Millicent Barnes O'Neal came to live with them. For several years, along with her husband, Edwin O'Neil, she'd served as a missionary in Ecuador with the Christian and Missionary Alliance. A series of circumstances brought widowed Aunt Milly to Martinsville; heartsore, ill and unsure of her future. Needing to heal, Mommy had insisted Aunt Milly return home with them. Two years later, her health restored, Aunt Milly's life had become woven into the fabric of the Tilson family.

In her young life, Angelee had a vague memory of explorers reaching both the north and south poles, hearing of the sinking of a ship called the Titanic, and the war being started in Europe. Daily more automobiles were seen on the roads, quickly replacing horses and buggies.

Now the Spring of 1917 was toying with the residents of Martinsville. The weather would be cold one day with threats of rain; or hot the next, causing the crocus and daffodils to burst through the earth.

Angelee had hoped Easter weekend would be blessed with warming sun, clear skies and bold, riotous colors. Instead, the gray sky hid the sun, dampened the atmosphere and dark clouds threatened showers. But perhaps the dreary weather suited the day better. On Friday, April 6th, 1917, the Indianapolis Star and Martinsville Daily Reporter blasted headlines of the House of Representatives voting in favor of going to war.

Sunday--April 8th 1917
Easter Morning

Thinking it would be helpful if she could sit quietly, and ponder the future, seventeen-year-old Angelee Giselle Tilson once again ignored her questions and fears about the future. With pretended confidence, she stepped out from the church pew holding a woven, straw basket, decorated with variegated pastel ribbon.

Easter morning service at the First Christian Church had been a mixture of somber, prayerful moments and the joyous singing of Easter anthems. On Good Friday, April 6th, 1917, the newspapers had printed President Wilson's Pronouncement of War against Germany. Rev. Matthias's prayers and sermon addressed the gravity of this decision, the effect it was to have on the country, and the local community. But the minister had also emphasized the power of love, faith and hope

Looking around the sanctuary for her sister, Angelee took in the shining organ pipes resting on the polished wooden ledge. Matching hand-carved, polished, inlaid wood panels completed the chancel area. Cedar pews gave off the scent of wood wax from the previous day's rubbing.

She wondered where her sixteen-year-old sister, Aimee— "Mee-Mee"—had so quickly disappeared to. Her scanning was interrupted.

"Come on Gee-Gee!" Alistair, the youngest in the family, pulled her by her free hand, addressing her by her family nick-name. "I don't want to miss the start of the Easter Egg hunt!"

The day before, Alistair's unruly blond, curly tresses had been cropped close to his head. What remained had been tamed with tonic and a comb.

"Stop rushing Alistair! There are plenty of eggs for everyone. And these shoes are slippery!"

Resisting her nine-year-old brother's impatient tugging, she felt her new, smooth-bottomed shoes sliding.

"But I want to be at the front!" Alistair was adamant.

"Why are you being so greedy? You colored eggs at home yesterday. And helped make an Easter Cake." Angelee reasoned.

"That's not the same!" Alistair protested, insistently pulling Angelee up the aisle.

As if realizing Angelee was not going to rush, Alistair let go of her hand, with the door only two foot-falls away. He ran out the door and down the steps.

The frictionless soles of her soles slid, causing her to catch her foot on the threshold plate. Stumbling, she was thrown forward, her arms waving in an attempt to regain her balance. In those seconds she anticipated the painful smack of hitting the concrete and probably rolling down the steps.

At the next instant, she felt a pair of strong arms around her, breaking the fall. Swung up into those same, sinewy arms, Angelee she found herself face-to-face with Pauley Alexander Bannister. Tenderness and merriment danced in his turquoise eyes. A new straw hat balanced precariously on the back of his brown wavy hair. His lean frame bore a light beige linen jacket and vest.

As her older brother's best friend, Angelee had known Pauley most of her life. He had frequented the Tilson home many a day. With Pauley hanging around with Andrew Jr., better known as Drew, it felt as though she had two older brothers. She was accustomed to his teasing.

Seconds seemed like hours, and still, he held her like a rescued damsel, grinning at her like a pirate who'd absconded with a priceless treasure.

"Pauley, there's no doubt I appreciate your catching me," Angelee said. "But I would appreciate it very much if you would put me down. People are starting to stare."

"And here I thought you were throwing yourself at me. It only seemed right to snatch you up while I could." Pauley's blue eyes sparkled.

Angelee could never remember a previous time when she'd felt awkward being so physically close to Pauley. Today, the difference was the unrecognizable glint in his eyes, and the prolonged time in his arms.

"Well, your moment of heroism is now passed, so please put me on my feet."

"Are you sure you can trust those new shoes?" He mocked, letting her down gently. "You know, your big, brown eyes were filled with terror as you were trying to fly like a bird." He lifted his hand and gently pushed an escaped blond tendril behind her ear.

Swatting his hand away, Angelee rolled her eyes and shook her head. "I'll be fine!"

Though he'd set her on the steps, he'd left an arm around her waist.

"Now what are you doing?" Angelee snapped.

"Just making sure you get down the steps safely." Pauley shrugged.

Angelee's exasperated sigh made him chuckle.

"The handrail is more than enough support for me. Now please excuse me. I can't keep Alistair waiting any longer."

Children's laughter directed Angelee to the front yard of the Blackstone House, opposite the church. Sunday School teachers attempted to keep a modicum of order, organizing clusters of same-aged children in small groups. Angelee smiled at the younger children who appeared excited and confused by the unusual activity.

"I see you got stuck holding the basket." Olivia Biers quipped as she joined Angelee. Olivia, who lived a few doors down from the Tilson family, was Angelee's best friend. Olivia's raven-colored hair, braided and coiled into a tidy chignon, was a striking contrast to Angelee's blond tresses; as were Olivia's distinctive sapphire eyes to Angelee's deep brown eyes.

"Yes!" Angelee sighed. "Yet again, Mee-Mee has managed to 'magically' disappear." Angelee shook her head.

"It's because she knows you're a natural with children, while she is flummoxed by a group of five-year-olds." Olivia chuckled.

"Would you *please* stop telling me how great I am with kids!" Angelee protested. "I think they're cute and fun to be around. That does not mean I want to become a teacher or work with them," not wanting to rehash old arguments.

"You are so funny." Olivia gave an ironic laugh. "I never said anything about you becoming a child-care worker or a teacher. *You* brought that up!"

Angelee scowled at her friend. "But I know you were thinking it!"

"Looks like Alistair decided he didn't need your help after all," Olivia said.

A shrill blast from a brass whistle filled the air. Boys and girls over the age of ten ran from the starting place, scampering around the Blackstone House property, as well as the property of the library.

"I'm going to go shepherd that little troop over there," Angelee said, walking toward the young Hanson family.

"I'll see you later," Olivia said. "Oma is coming, and I want to be there when she arrives."

Angelee gave her friend a quick hug, before joining Nori Hanson, who was holding a baby, while also trying to manage two other egg-hunters. "Do you need some help?"

Four-year-old Bobby Hanson looked up at her. "I see an egg...but I can't reach it."

He pointed to a colored egg, hanging by a string, on a tree branch just above his reach. Angelee sat the basket on the ground, lifted Bobby so he could untie the string. He squealed with delight. As she sat him back onto the grass, he stuck the treasure into the pocket of his second-hand pants. He tugged her arm. When she leaned down, he kissed her on the cheek. "Tank You!" Bobby said.

"Help too?" Two-year-old Jill Hanson pleaded, her round blue eyes, filled with hope.

Angelee smiled. "Well of course! Show me."

Jill took Angelee's hand. Angelee grabbed her basket and followed the toddler to a bush. Jill looked like a princess, even though her dress was well-worn. She squatted down and pointed under a bush.

"Can't get...too dirty," Jill complained.

Angelee crouched down next to the shrub, reached the dyed object easily and handed it to Jill. Jill cupped the egg gingerly, intrigued by the pattern of the decoration, gently placing it in her basket.

"Look, Mommy!" Her cheeks flushed, excited by her success.

Angelee guided the Hanson children back to their mother, who was busy with the newest baby in the family.

"Oh Angelee, I do appreciate your assistance." Nori Hanson smiled broadly. "Jasper's overseeing the boys' Sunday School class on this egg adventure."

"He's got his hands full too, it sounds like." Angelee laughed. "It's good that Bart is starting to make friends."

"Your brother was the first one in the class to talk to Bart," Nori commented. "Jasper just couldn't stand the thought of Bart being stuck out on the farm with my mother's latest husband. That man is violent, and a drunk to boot!"

"It's good that you and Jasper talked your mother into having Bart come live with you."

"I convinced her Bart was missing too much school. In a way, I think she was relieved."

"Is Bart okay with the babies?" Angelee asked her.

"Bobby is old enough to play with, and Bart likes to show him things. Jillie, she's a bit of a conundrum. Bart can't understand why she doesn't like playing with marbles, balls, or looking for frogs. But he likes all her hugs, the way she always shares her cookies, things like that. As for Louis, well, Bart calls him a 'human puppy'."

Angelee shared laugher with Nori.

"I talked to his teacher last week. She says that all the upheaval at home has caused him to get pretty behind. She's thinking that she might hold Bart back and have him repeat third grade."

Angelee's heart hurt for Bart, and his troubles at such a young age.

"I have an idea. I know it's only about eight weeks left of school. That might be enough time to show Miss Washings that he could catch up. I'd be more than happy to tutor him on weekends."

"But we couldn't pay you," Nori said. "That wouldn't be fair."

"Non-sense it would be fun! We'll tell him we're going to play games and set it up as a competition between him and Alistair."

"I think he'd love that. Are you sure?"

"Sure, about what?" Jasper Hanson's voice broke in.

"Angelee has offered to tutor Bart, so he can catch up on his schoolwork."

"Hey! That's great!"

"What's great?" Alistair asked as he came charging up with Bart. "And why didn't you come to find me, Angelee?"

"What's great is that it hasn't rained during these festivities," Angelee replied, looking up at, the tall, blue-grey, black-bottomed clouds rain-laden billowing masses reached endlessly across the sky.

"You didn't need me to help you gather your plunder—you Greedy-Gus!" Angelee teased. Angelee ruffled his curls; his running and jumping had loosed from the effects of the tonic.

In the meantime, Alistair was busy emptying the contents of his pockets—pants and coat-into the basket.

"When can we start Bart's tutoring; this coming weekend?" Nori asked.

"Is ten o'clock okay?" Angelee inquired.

"Nine o'clock will be better."

"Okay, I'll see you then."

"Tutoring?" Alistair sounded incredulous. "You mean Angelee is playing teacher again?"

"NO!" Angelee protested. "I *am not* playing 'teacher' again. You and Bart are going to play some games which will help him with his school work."

"Me?!" Alistair whined. "Why do I have to do it?"

"Because Bart is your friend, and it will be good for you," Angelee explained.

"But you haven't asked Mommy!" Alistair argued his point.

"No, I haven't, that's true. But I am sure she will be all for it. And I know I can't make you do it. However, I promise to make it fun."

"I like playing games." Bart chimed in.

This earned him Alistair's scowl.

"Right." Alistair rolled his eyes, then acquiesced.

"This looks like a happy bunch!" Aimee half-skipped as she joined them. "I was sent to collect my brother and sister. Daddy says that if you want to ride home, you need to come now. Otherwise, you'll have to walk...but don't be late for Sunday dinner."

"We're coming," Angelee said. "Nori, if I find out this Saturday isn't good, I'll give a note to Alistair and he can give it to Bart to pass on."

"Great! We appreciate it all. Come, children, we'll have lunch when we get home." Nori shifted Louis in her arms and took Jill's hand as she turned to leave. Jasper stopped Nori, lifted Jill into his arms, and wrapped his other arm around Bart's shoulders. Bobby took advantage of Nori's available hand. They walked away, toward Bucktown.

With all his eggs in the basket, Alistair took the basket from Angelee. Drew walked up to the car from a different direction, arriving just as they did. Within a minute they had climbed into the 1914 Peerless touring car.

Frustration swirling in her soul, Angelee sat in the back seat of the car, arms folded across her chest and her ankles crossed, resenting that there was no time to sit and think. Suddenly, she regretted not taking advantage of the opportunity to walk home. Soon she would be graduating from high school; she wanted time to consider what she wanted to do with her life after that.

Despite the secret vexation with her life—an unclear direction for her future—a fleeting smile crossed her face when she remembered the excitement caused when Daddy drove the car home three years previously.

It wasn't just the war that made her anxious. Without provocation, thoughts of British and American women campaigning for the right to vote came to mind. Some girls at school had very strong opinions, eagerly supporting the suffragettes who were willing to publicly protest, march, be arrested, spend time in jail, undergo hunger strikes, even risk their lives. But did the simple act of voting truly warrant risking one's life? Ambivalence made Angelee feel guilty.

Pauley's irregular and unpredicted behavior at church this morning still baffled her as well.

"That was a big sigh," Aimee said, who was sitting next to her.

"Don't worry about it. We're almost home. This cold, grey day seems to be getting me down."

"But it's Easter! Jesus is alive! Isn't that amazing?" Aimee, who was perpetually cheery, was trying to cheer her up.

Angelee leaned over and put an arm around her sister. "Thanks for reminding me. My thoughts are running around in my head like a horse on a race track; chasing round and round without getting anywhere."

"We're home now," Aimee said as Daddy parked the car at the side of the house. "Think about something else—like Mr. Torrington coming for dinner," Aimee suggested.

Aimee referred to the family's friend, Mr. Steffken Torrington, a Belgium artist who had emigrated to America. Mr. Torrington's father was a British Civil Servant. While working as a clerk in the

Foreign Office in Brussels, he met a lovely local girl, Birgitta Leys and they had married. Steffken was born in 1890. When it became clear that the war was going to erupt between Germany and the rest of Europe, Mr. Torrington had taken Birgitta and Steffken back to his home in England.

As a child Steffken been involved with a horse-riding accent, breaking both hips and fracturing one of his legs. Out of the necessity to pursue quiet activities while he healed, Steffken began drawing. This eventually led to an interest in art, specifically portraiture. He'd developed a career as an artist. Unable to serve in the military, Steffken had traveled to America. Through his acquaintance with the socialites in Boston, he'd met Mrs. Parkham. It was his connection with her that Steffken had come to Martinsville to partake of the healing waters at Home Lawn.

"I hope he tells us more stories about Easter in Belgium." Angelee nodded.

"I think he's got a weird kind of accent! Since he's supposed to be English!" Alistair quipped.

"Alistair!" Aimee reprimanded. "He has a French accent because he's half Belgium. You shouldn't be so rude."

"He's not here to hear me say it!" Alistair defended himself, with a shrug.

"It doesn't matter if he's here or not. It's rude to say he has a weird accent!" Aimee re-joined. "I wonder if Mrs. Torrington's family in Belgium is safe."

"You'll have to ask him," Angelee said as they climbed out of the back seat of the car. "In the mean-time, I bet Mommy is thinking five steps ahead."

As they walked in through the kitchen door, Mommy said. "Girls, can you get some aprons on? We can have dinner on the table in about ten minutes."

The doorbell rang.

"I'll go!" Aimee called and bolted for the front door. "I'm sure it's Mr. Torrington.

"I'll help you, Mommy." Alistair swathed himself in an oversized apron. With the precision of a well-trained team, the table was quickly laden with the Easter Feast of ham, green beans, mashed potatoes, gravy, Coleslaw, and fresh bread rolls.

Gathered around the table, guests and family joined hands and sang:

"Praise God from Whom all blessings flow;
Praise Him all creatures here below.
Praise Him above ye heavenly hosts.
Praise Father, Son and Holy Ghost. Amen."

"I'm so glad you could join us for your second Easter here, Mr. Torrington," Mommy said.

"And I thank you for the invitation to spend it with your family again." Mr. Torrington replied.

"Drew, I saw you talking to Rev. Matthias this morning? What were you discussing with him?" Aimee blurted.

Angelee could only shake her head and smile. Aimee's habit of letting the first thought in her head come out of her mouth, unchecked, often got her into trouble. Aimee was never offensive, just overly curious. Keeping thoughts to herself was a lesson she had yet to learn.

Drew, who was pouring gravy over his vegetables, frowned at his youngest sister. "Mee-Mee, you are the snoopiest person that I know. But, since everyone else probably wants to know, I'll tell you. I wanted to know Rev. Matthias's opinion on conscientious objectors."

"Why? Are you going to be one?" Aimee, obviously un-thinkingly spouted.

"What's a conscientious objector?" Alistair asked.

"They are men who believe fighting and war is wrong." Daddy answered. "Most of them are men who have religious convictions—like the Quakers and the Amish. Other men believe it is morally wrong. In either case, they refuse to carry a gun or fight.

"Drew, I'm sure Rev. Matthias knew many people would be wondering what he thought." Daddy continued. "He was wise to remind us that Jesus told us to expect war, rumors of war, and nations rising against each other."

"I wasn't expecting him to say that each of us must individually use our conscience and personal understanding of the Bible to come to terms with the news of the war," Mommy said. "Now, please, remember our family rule—no talking about politics at the table. Today is Easter. We are all together—plus our lovely guest. The days ahead will be full of war talk. But today we need to think about positive things and enjoy our time before Drew goes back to college."

Angelee sighed with relief, thankful for Mommy's rule. The relief was short-lived with Mr. Torrington's next remark. At least for Angelee.

"I have received a letter from Mrs. Parkham. Her Easter visit to Boston, she has decided to cut short. And I have a note for Miss Angelee. She enclosed it with my letter."

"I bet she has a big, old list already for Gee-Gee!" Alistair said.

While Aimee was known for her cat-like curiosity and verbalized it, Alister was known for his direct and blunt opinions.

"Alistair." Daddy's voice held a warning. "I hope you don't mean Mrs. Parkham any disrespect."

Alistair looked down at his plate. "Sorry Daddy...but she is rather bossy and takes up a lot of Gee-Gee's time."

"She needs lots of help with her ideas," Angelee explained. "She's in a position to do a lot of helpful things for lots of people."

In truth, Angelee was conflicted about Mrs. Parkham's impending return to Martinsville. Her high school graduation, plus her eighteenth birthday loomed just eight weeks away. Angelee's gut instincts told her that Mrs. Parkham had filled the summer calendar with activities based on the presumption that Angelee would be her assistant again over the summer. Mrs. Parkham wasn't going to like the idea that Angelee didn't want to work for Mrs. Parkham this summer.

With an effort, Angelee squelched thoughts of Mrs. Parkham and focused on Mr. Torrington's stories.

"Do you know, I am suddenly reminded of a Gillis Van Tilborgh painting." Mr. Torrington remarked.

"Who was he?" Alistair asked.

"Mr. Van Tilborgh was born in Belgium, in the 1600's." Mr. Torrington began.

"Not another art lesson!" Alistair complained. "Why is it always school around here?"

"No, no, not to worry, my young friend." Mr. Torrington chuckled. "The gentleman was a painter who often painted family portraits, sometimes showing the dinner. I am remembering a painting entitled 'Elegant Company', which is one of his works."

"But why did you think of that?" Aimee said.

"Because I was thinking about how very picturesque this lovely family is. This room would be the right setting for a painting. You see, the beautiful blond curls of your mother and your aunt are inherited by the children of this home. Only Angelee has inherited her father's brown eyes and the rest of you have the blue eyes. Your father provides a wonderful contrast of dark hair."

"Maybe we should do a family portrait!" Aimee enthused.

"And I suppose you would offer to help him with the painting," Drew remarked drolly.

"What would be wrong with that?" Aimee snapped. "I've learned a lot since Mr. Torrington has been giving me lessons."

"Miss Aimee, she has a talent, and is a good student." Mr. Torrington added casually. "She has great potential."

"See!" Aimee remarked. "Thank you for saying so, Mr. Torrington."

"But it is only the truth." The Belgian replied, with a sweep of his hand.

"Changing the subject, who wants dessert?" Aunt Milly chimed in.

"Now that will be a work of art." Drew teased.

Laughter filled the room. Angelee and Aimee helped to clear the dirty dishes and empty serving bowls from the table while Aunt Milly busied herself with bringing out dessert dishes and a coconut cake with peaches. A pot of coffee served after the sweets made the feast replete.

Before Mr. Torrington left later that afternoon, he passed Mrs. Parkham's note to Angelee. She couldn't help but sigh.

Later, in the early evening, Angelee sat at her desk, looking across the street at the construction work being done to Home Lawn Sanitarium. Diplomats, retired politicians, entertainers, and highly successful business people came to seek the healing virtues of the waters. The addition of a new wing was in progress at the luxurious facility; to bring in and accommodate more clients. To that end, the property looked more like a construction site than a resort.

Mrs. Parkham's note on lie her desk. She sat, staring at the communique, procrastinating because she dreaded learning its content. Her thoughts drifted back in time.

Angelee first met Mrs. Marcheline Parkham on a summer day, in June 1915. Lumbago, bursitis in her shoulders and arthritic knees had brought her to Martinsville, and Home Lawn Sanitarium, specifically. That first summer Angelee had been impressed by the confident, ambitious, elegant lady from Boston.

Daddy had come home for lunch with news of his impressive new client. During the consultation, Mrs. Parkham—a Boston socialite—had expressed the need for an assistant to do errands. Daddy thought it would be a good experience for Angelee.

After lunch, Angelee changed into one of her Sunday dresses, brushed her unruly blond curls, and pinned them down before accompanying Daddy back to his Home Lawn office.

Leaving his valise in the office, he then led Angelee up to Mrs. Parkham's room. "Mrs. Parkham probably won't want to talk long. She likes to rest after lunch. But she was very eager to meet you."

Walking up the steps to the third floor, Daddy lay his hand on Angelee's arm. She stopped and looked at him.

"I've just realized what a lovely young lady you've turned into," Daddy smiled. Pride shone from his eyes. "I'm sure Mrs. Parkham is going to be impressed."

"Thank you, Daddy." Angelee felt herself blush.

"Now then, I think I should warn you, don't be fooled when you first see Mrs. Parkham." Daddy knocked on the door.

Before Angelee had time to ask "why?" the door opened. The diminutive woman wasn't even five feet tall. Her silver hair was parted in the middle and pulled back, away from her face. The black, raw silk dress made known her widowhood. Surely, she wasn't anything other than a sweet little lady?

"Mrs. Parkham, you mentioned that you would like an assistant. With this in mind, I've brought my daughter, Angelee, to meet you." Daddy gestured toward Angelee.

Angelee smiled and had a strange urge to curtsey, but she reframed and stifled a nervous giggle.

"My goodness, Dr. Tilson, I wasn't expecting such a prompt service." Mrs. Parkham enthused. She waved them into the room. "I made this trip without my usual assistant. She took it upon herself to get married and is now on her honeymoon. Since I had already made arrangements to come here, I decided to risk coming on my own and finding someone when I got here." Mrs. Parkham sat down in the nearest chair.

"Angelee is on her summer break from school." Daddy explained as he sat in the other chair.

Angelee remained standing, hands folded in front of her.

Mrs. Parkham scrutinized Angelee, starting at the top of her head and scanning down to her polished shoes. Her eyes had a teasing, mocking glint, while the tone of her voice was firm and mellow. Tilting her head, the widow asked. "How old are you, Miss Tilson?"

"I just turned sixteen," Angelee answered, with a level look.

"Do you know how to use a typewriter?" Mrs. Parkham's intense gaze demanded Angelee's full attention.

"Yes, Mrs. Parkham. I took classes last year at school." Angelee was beginning to see that the small woman possessed inner steel. Now she understood Daddy's warning, not to underestimate the small person interviewing her.

"Do you take dictation?" Mrs. Parkham continued the interview.

"I've never tried it, to be honest. But I am willing to try at least." Angelee replied.

"I warn you, Miss Tilson, I am a taskmaster. I have my preferred method of doing things and I expect those who work for me to adhere to those methods. If you do not think you can abide by that expectation, then I shall look for someone else."

"Yes, Mrs. Parkham. I may ask a lot of questions at the beginning—to make sure I understand the instructions."

Angelee knew that if she didn't have the needed skills, she would end the interview without the job. This employment opportunity had unexpectedly presented itself. If she didn't get it, there would be no disappointment for her.

"I appreciate honesty." The grey-haired lady nodded. "Well, it's only for a few weeks at most. When can you start?"

"Tomorrow—any time you desire," Angelee said. "I know you will want to make the most of your treatments."

"Good, I prefer that. Now then, I believe it best to discuss your salary with your father."

Start the next day Angelee did. The job was interesting, allowing Angelee to gain experience with administrative work. Daily, Mrs. Parkham required things from town, thus Angelee was kept busy at Home Lawn and in town.

Mrs. Parkham had made an initial plan for two weeks of treatment. Two weeks grew into fourteen weeks. For the formidable lady, the "City of Mineral Waters" was a true find—a place she could rest and recuperate. She determined she must acquire a house in Martinsville and did so. This would allow her to come and go back and forth between Boston and Martinsville as she desired. It also meant that she could invite and accommodate her friends and family from the east coast when they came to visit her.

In September Mrs. Parkham decided that she would return to Boston to organize the management of her many rental properties. She would return as soon as possible. While she was away, Angelee and Mrs. Parkham corresponded.

During summer 1916, Angelee's awe of Mrs. Parkham began to diminish. What Angelee had first attributed to confidence, she now regarded as forcefulness—edging toward dictatorial behavior. Mrs. Parkham was gracious, amusing, and even entertaining—which enabled her to lead people into plans. Angelee conceded that Mrs. Parkham was good-hearted, generous, and community-minded. Yet, Angelee had also seen the subtle, stubborn, dogged determination Mrs. Parkham used to achieve her goals. Angelee agreed with Alistair's definition of "bossy." Mrs. Parkham's petite stature and apparent frailness belied her iron will and insistence on getting her way—a force to be reckoned with.

Angelee collected her thoughts, sat up straight, and withdrew the letter opener from her top desk drawer. With a quick motion, she slit the envelope, then removed the note.

The scent from the stationary wafted upward, filling her nose. She recognized the pattern of the scalloped edges as stationery she'd purchased on behalf of Mrs. Parkham.

"My Dearest Angelee,

"Visiting my brother-in-law, and his family has been a sheer delight. Friends have been making the most of the opportunity to see me as well and I have accepted many invitations to luncheon and dinner. The business I needed to attend to has taken less time than anticipated and therefore I have decided to return to my Martinsville home. Therefore, I wanted to let you know about my current plans.

It is my hope that you will be available to meet my train at Union Station in Indianapolis on 21st April. Though fully aware that the 21st is a Friday, you should have sufficient time to make the journey after school, as my train is due about 6:15 pm. I am awaiting confirmation of reservations at the English Hotel and Opera House for that evening. I know I shall be tired by the time I arrive in Indianapolis. What a grand treat to have you join me for the evening, followed by a good night's sleep. I shall certainly be refreshed by Saturday morning; when we shall return to your town with those marvelous healing waters.

With great confidence I await your reply, confirming that I shall see your lovely, cheerful face upon my arrival on the Friday indicated above.

Most Sincerely,
Mrs. Marcheline A. Parkham.

Sighing deeply, Angelee shook her head. While the thought of a night at one of Indianapolis' finest hotels, located on the northwest corner of the circle, looking toward the beautiful Soldiers' and Sailors' monument, would be an opportunity envied by most of her friends, Angelee felt her heart sink.

Needing an outlet for her emotions, she took out the hard-bound journal. Black ink flowed across the lines.

NO! NO! NO! I do NOT want to work for Mrs. Parkham this summer. How dare she presume that I am automatically giving up my summer again to work for her this year! What do I do to stop this?! What if I want a different job? Even if I don't know what it is?

While her heart rebelled, her mind felt she had no recourse. Had Mrs. Parkham made the arrangements for a week-day, of course, her parents would have supported her refusal. But the plans were on a Friday night, with the promise of being treated to a grand hotel and a fine dinner.

Taking stationery from a desk drawer, she smoothed it out, pressing it hard onto the wooden top. She prayed. Conquering anger, frustration, and resentment presented a huge task at that moment. Determined to be mature, overcome her negative emotions, and serve with a Christian heart, Angelee penned a reply.

After thanking Mrs. Parkham for the information, Angelee advised her friend and employer that she was taking the initiative to invite Olivia to accompany her to Indianapolis. Taking the initiative was a quality that Mrs. Parkham regularly insisted that Angelee cultivate. Only time would tell if this was one instance in which Mrs. Parkham approved.

Saturday, April 14th, 1917
A Conversation About Mrs. Parkham

Just before the alarm went off, Angelee awakened to rain splashing on the window. She smiled, enjoying the pleasant patter of the spring showers against the glass pane. She stretched, sat up in bed, picked up the clock, and turned off the alarm before it rang, knowing Aimee would appreciate an un-interrupted Saturday morning sleep-in. Placing the alarm clock back onto the nightstand, she peeked behind the linen curtain and paper blind to see how heavy the rain was. Steady, soft droplets fell from the heavens, soaking the ground. It was a day for putting on galoshes, for certain.

Swinging her legs over the side of the bed and with pointed toes, searched below the edge of the bed for house slippers. Only one was in its correct position, causing a bit of squirming to locate the second one. She slid the rest of the way out of bed. Having selected her Saturday morning clothes the night previous, she now lifted them from her desk chair.

Her morning ablutions took only a few minutes and she let her mind wander as she dressed. Seven weeks remained in her high school career. It would be bittersweet. There was the sweetness of one season of life-ending, and a new season beginning with new challenges. There was the bitterness of no longer dealing with the familiar routine, of seeing good friends daily. There was the sweetness of the summer holidays to enjoy. There was the bitterness of knowing many of the young men from her community would be enlisting—or called up for service.

She thought of Mrs. Parkham's imminent arrival. She grimaced. Now was not the time to deal with such thoughts. Not before coffee. Not before breakfast. Not before prayer. She left the bathroom, carrying her shoes, and quietly made her way in stockinged feet to the dining room. She sat down at the table to put on her shoes.

The smell of coffee wafted from the kitchen and her stomach rumbled. Mommy's and Aunt Milly's conversation bounced back and forth like a tennis ball, and Angelee half-laughed as she recognized they were finishing each other's sentences.

Aunt Milly—Millicent O'Neal—was Mommy's identical twin sister. Though now single, she had not always been. Edmund Scott

O'Neal, a pediatrician, had persistently pursued her, overcoming Milly's determination to be a spinster missionary. Fully convinced that Edmund, "Ned" too had a genuine call to serve in foreign Christian missions, she had joyfully married him.

They heard of the Christian and Missionary Alliance's work with the Mapuche Indians in Chile. In 1904 they made their application to join the work. There were many aspects to the CMA team's work, including organizing and looking after orphanages, building and running schools, and of course establishing protestant churches. In 1905 the O'Neals arrived in Chile, quickly falling in love with people, and the country.

Chile was their home for ten years. Ned began to lose weight, and slow down his activities. He denied being ill, saying he just needed a good rest. After the insistence of their leaders, Ned had seen a doctor in Santiago, the capital city, with Milly accompanying him on the trip. The diagnosis shocked them—cancer. They needed to return to the United States.

The ship's route from Santiago to Ft. Lauderdale, Florida included a stop in Panama, where the work on the Panama Canal had recently been completed. Wanting to visit a local market, Milly had gotten off of the ship. All kinds of mosquitos had feasted on her fair skin—leaving her with countless red welts. In the final days of the trip, she began having headaches, backaches, and a loss of appetite. At night she would shiver—first feeling hot and then cold. The doctor onboard the ship wasn't sure whether she had acquired yellow fever or malaria. By the time they arrived in the United States, Milly was very ill with high fevers, sensitivity to light, and jaundice skin. Though rare, it seemed that she had contracted both yellow fever and malaria.

Through telegrams and letters, the family had learned of the couple's journey home. Mommy informed the family that she was not going to let her beloved twin sister and brother-in-law—both seriously sick—travel home from Florida alone. Before packing her bags, Mommy had organized for Grandma Barnes to come up to look after the rest of the family. Then she had boarded a train to bring the missionaries home.

Upon arrival in Indianapolis, Ned and Milly were immediately admitted to Methodist Episcopal Hospital. Ignoring his illness, therefore leaving his condition undiagnosed, cancer had ravished Ned's body. Treatment would have been ineffective. Milly, still weak and fighting malaria, sat by his bedside until the day he died. Arrangements were made to have his body transported to Louisville, Kentucky so that his body would be buried next to his parents.

An exhausted, heart-broken Milly was beyond making any decisions about her next step. Although returning to Louisville to stay with Grandy and Grandma Barnes was an option, it was the twin-bond that prevailed. Mommy insisted there was plenty of room in the house. The children unanimously agreed. Thankfully, Daddy was genuinely fond of Milly.

Now, almost three years later, Aunt Milly had recovered her health and kept her faith. Aunt Milly had become a mainstay to the family.

Having tied her shoes, Angelee stepped into the kitchen. "Any chance there is coffee ready?"

Mommy pulled a cup from the cupboard, and placed it on the worktop, while Aunt Milly picked up the coffee pot. Steam rose from the black liquid flowing into a heavy china cup.

"You're up early, for a Saturday," Mommy observed.

"Just wanted to review the games and flashcards I'm going to use with the boys." Angelee improvised.

Aunt Milly looked at Angelee, raising an eyebrow. Angelee rolled her eyes, admitting to herself that Aunt Milly knew her very well.

"Well, I do want to get things ready for the boys...but I'd also like to talk." Angelee admitted, then took a small sip of the coffee.

Mommy, standing by the stove, spooned bacon drippings into the skillet, before ladling pancake batter onto the hot service. "So, what's so intriguing that it is keeping you awake?"

"I have a feeling it's something bothersome—not exciting." Aunt Milly interjected. "And I have a feeling it has to do with Angelee's intrepid employer."

"If this were a game, that would be two points for Aunt Milly." Angelee quipped. "I've been thinking about remarks Mrs. Parkham has made during this past year; hinting at changes she has in mind for me."

Angelee sipped the strong brew and pondered how to continue. "Well, this morning it occurred to me again that it is very peculiar that Mrs. Parkham has *still* not found an acceptable replacement for Hortensia, her former assistant. It's probably just my imagination, but she seemed delighted with the idea of luring me to Boston after I finish high school."

"I do seem to remember her being quite taken with that idea when Aimee spouted out that idea. Did she say anything since that remark was made last year? Has she written anything in her letters?" Mommy inquired.

"Well, no...nothing I can remember. But see, I've spent so much time with her I know what she's like. Let me give you an example.

"Last summer Mrs. Parkham became acquainted with the Allerton family. Their son, Aaron, who graduated two years ago, had been working at one of the hotels, trying to save up money to go to college. Now he and Missy Hardean were seeing each other. Missy was due to graduate last year.

"While at church one Sunday Mrs. Parkham happened to overhear the Hardeans and the Allerton discussing the situation. Both sets of parents were worried that neither Aaron nor Missy would continue with education because they couldn't afford college. And while both families liked each other, they were afraid the young couple might sneak off and elope.

"The day following, Mrs. Parkham had me make a reservation for one of the private dining rooms at Home Lawn and order a three-course luncheon. Next, she wrote letters to the Allerton and the Hardeans informing them of this lunch date—on a Saturday, to make sure they could come.

"As Mrs. Parkham's assistant, I had to be there as well. During this meal, Mrs. Parkham informed them that she had overheard their conversation. They were embarrassed at first. But Mrs. Parkham used all her Socialite charm to allay their awkward feelings and soon had them engaged with a discussion about their respective children. Where did they want to study? What did they want to study? How serious were Aaron and Missy about each other? Did the parents think the children could be persuaded to wait until after college to marry if arrangements could be made for them to attend classes the next semester?

"Right after the meal, and as soon as we returned to her office, she had me taking dictation for Lain Business School in Indianapolis, and Purdue University. Did they provide any scholarships? When did the next term begin? What were the fees for tuition? Was there accommodation nearby?

Angelee sipped the lukewarm coffee, grimacing that it had cooled so quickly.

"Finally, Mrs. Parkham organized a 'round-the-dinner-table' meeting with both sets of parents, Aaron and Missy." Angelee continued. "Mrs. Parkham presented an offer to provide scholarships for Aaron, to Purdue University, and Missy, to Lain Business School in Indianapolis. Mrs. Parkham made it clear that this was not an attempt to part them, but to help them with their hopes and plans for the future. The couple had to guarantee to complete their courses of study. Since Aaron wanted to study mechanical engineering, his degree would take longer. Missy, whose course work would be much shorter, would have to work while Aaron finished his degree. This would allow her to save up for the expenses of a wedding and plan it. If either of them failed to complete their courses of study, then the families would have to repay Mrs. Parkham for what she has spent.

"All the involved parties were astounded by the windfall and in total agreement. So, for them, at least, it was happy-ever-after." Angelee sighed. "I do think it's amazing that Mrs. Parkham helps people because she can afford to. But I do find it unsettling that she is so…. I don't know…not quite intrusive…."

"Do you think she's presumptive?" Aunt Milly suggested. Aunt Milly's plate was now empty. She'd eaten her breakfast while listening patiently to Angelee's story.

"Yes. She has so much social polish, she seems so capable of finagling her way into a situation through the back door. I guess I've thought of it as interfering in business that isn't hers; that she makes other people's situations her business. I know she means well. I guess I find it brazen, even if it is done with good intentions."

Mommy placed a plate of pancakes and eggs in front of Angelee, to which she added butter and syrup.

"Do you feel Mrs. Parkham is interposing herself into other people's problems or concerns for selfish reasons?" Aunt Milly poured more coffee into her cup and took a sip.

"What bothers me is that she involves herself, whether they ask for help or not. From where I stand, it never seems to cross her mind that maybe her actions won't be appreciated. She seems impervious to the idea that her suggestions could be unwanted."

"Gee-Gee, sweetheart, when some people get accustomed to having power, influence, and money, they also get used to getting things done in their way, in their time—and without being questioned. Mrs. Parkham probably feels a great deal of responsibility that goes with having social standing and financial resources. And from knowing her myself, I am sure her heart is in the right place—even if her methods seem imperialistic."

"I agree, she does seem genuine in wanting to help. I guess I am just afraid that she's going to try to maneuver me into a position that makes *her* happy, but that I am not interested in." Angelee admitted.

Mommy, with her plate of pancakes, sat down across the table from Angelee. "I agree with you, Angelee. There is a fine line between wanting to help and downright meddling. Why this change of feelings about Mrs. Parkham? When she came three years ago, you were enthralled with the opportunity to work for her."

"That was three years ago. I'd never met anyone like her before. She looked so fragile. But as I worked for her, her iron-will razor-sharp mind became clear to me. She said she moved here so she could get treatment at Home Lawn whenever she wanted. I didn't doubt it at first. But now, I'm not so sure. I mean there is so much more in Boston, more hospitals, doctors, and her family business there. I can't help but wonder at times."

"You are fortunate," Mommy said. "You've already got a job after you graduate."

"I've been thinking about that, Mommy. I want to try something different."

The grandfather clock chimed the hour.

"Oh, goodness!" Angelee looked at the clock. "I'd better get my games and flashcards organized. The Hanson's are due here shortly." Angelee drained the last of the cold coffee from her cup, took it, along with her empty plate to the kitchen. She'd have to try to have that conversation about changing jobs another time.

An Unexpected Traveller

Angelee and Olivia climbed aboard the Indianapolis-bound Interurban, each carrying an overnight bag.

"I'm so glad we packed last night," Olivia remarked, sitting down by the window.

"It sure made it convenient to get out of the house quickly." Angelee concurred. "I've decided that I'm going to make the most of this trip to the city. After all, the Opera House is a beautiful place."

"So, is Mrs. Parkham arriving on an interurban, or by train?" Olivia asked.

"Her train comes in at Union Station. It's a good thing it's a short walk. And I'll have to find a taxi for us. I'm sure she'll have lots of luggage."

"I'm just glad there are porters there." Olivia quipped.

"Me too!" Angelee laughed.

The conductor closed the door to the interurban car, and the number 38 began its journey.

Angelee's eyes widened. "I just realized, this is the first time we've taken a trip into Indy, on the interurban by ourselves. We've always had an adult with us before."

Angelee watched Olivia's blue eyes sparkle. "Suddenly, this is very adventurous!"

The girls sat wordlessly, watching the scenery roll by.

"You know, this is probably the beginning of lots of trips on our own. We're only weeks away from graduation." Olivia remarked eventually.

"I envy you," Angelee confessed.

"Whatever for...why?"

"You seem to know what's next for you. All you've ever wanted to do is become a nurse. You signed up for chemistry, biology, Latin, algebra...all those courses to do with science. But I've never known what God has called me to do. I mean, I pray all the time. But nothing seems to be obvious...at least not to me." Angelee explained.

"Oh Angelee, I had no idea you felt that way." Olivia comforted her friend. "I wish I could help you. But I know that when the time is right, you will discover your gift."

"In the meantime, it seems I'm stuck with this work with Mrs. Parkham. It isn't boring, per se. But it doesn't have much room for being creative. Everything has to be done her way—no questions asked. Well, I can clarify something; but I can't try any new methods.

"I'm sure I'll use all the skills I've learned from her at some point. And I am thankful for the experience. But I find myself dreading my Saturday mornings with her. But I don't know what else to do."

The late afternoon sun shone through the window, casting a golden glow into the car. Though perplexed about the future, Angelee found solace in the rhythmic movement of the interurban.

"Did I tell you about a remark that someone made at school the other day?" Olivia suddenly asked.

"What does that have to do with Mrs. Parkham and my dilemma about the future?"

"Just listen a minute, and I'll tell you." Olivia crossed her legs.

"In biology lab last week, I was working with Henry Knells. We finished the dissection and I flippantly said, 'Thank you, doctor.' Of course, we laughed, and he shot back, 'Thank you, Nurse.' Then Beth-Anne Fallon turned the whole conversation on its head by saying; 'Olivia, you know *you* could be the doctor. Lots of women are studying for that now.'

"Well, that got me thinking about the difference between being a doctor and a nurse. I went home that night and told my parents. It was a quandary for me; I didn't know what to do. I was second-guessing my calling from God."

"My father very wisely told me that everyone has moments that they are confused. In those times, it is best to wait and let the Lord lead them, and confirmation will come." Olivia continued.

"So, you're telling me to just wait...do nothing?" Angelee sighed. "Don't you think I should have some clue as to what I should be doing with my life? What if I should go to college? That is something I've never planned on—never entertained the idea."

"It is probably right in front of you, but for some reason, you can't see it. And I don't mean you should sit around and do nothing. Papa said that what God wants for us to learn is how to walk with Him and to listen to His voice. Then he said something a bit puzzling. *'When you don't know what to do, do what you do know to do until you know what to do.'*"

Angelee shook her head, baffled by the idiom.

"Don't worry." Olivia laughed. "Papa had to explain it to me as well. Part one: *'When you don't know what to do…';* Those are times when a problem or opportunity presents itself. You need to make a decision regarding it, but don't know what is best.

"Part two: *'do what you know to do…'.* Get up each morning, do those things you normally do—like chores, school, homework, etc. It also means to keep growing in your relationship with God, with others in the tasks you do. Study the Bible; become a person who knows how to seek forgiveness and knows how to forgive others, be kind, gentle, patient, joyful. Be teachable, willing to learn from those around you. Through the everyday routines, you develop your character.

"Which leads to part three; *'Until you know what to do.'* That means that when the Father sees you are ready to know His purposes, His direction, and His will, He will reveal it."

The explanation made sense to Angelee, she was sure it would take time to ponder it and apply the wisdom of it.

Out the window, Angelee noticed houses organized next to roads and the car slowed. Within minutes the car pulled into the terminus.

"Do you think we should catch a taxi? They like to wait just outside the station." Olivia asked as they disembarked.

"No, we've got well over an hour. The walk will be just as quick." Angelee encouraged. Also stepping out of the car.

"I'm glad I didn't pack too much," Olivia said.

"After carrying books all day, this doesn't seem too bad. It's organized better as well." Angelee said.

The workday in Indy had finished and the streets were filled with folk glad for the weekend. The girls walked out of the terminal onto Illinois Street. Watching the traffic, they crossed Market Street walking south toward Union Station.

"I don't know about you, but I sure could use something to drink," Olivia said. "Lunch seems like a long time ago."

"Well and truly!" Angelee agreed. "It's only going on five o'clock now! We've got time to get something at the dining room once we're at Union Station."

"That sounds great! When is Mrs. Parkham's train due?"

"At six-fifteen. And who knows how long it will be before we get to have dinner."

"A snack at a café sounds even better now!" Olivia gushed.

They turned right onto Louisiana Street within steps of the main entrance of Union Station. As expected, taxis to downtown locations were parked along the street. Dusk had darkened the rose-patterned stained-glass window high above the floor. The hardwood floors shone and the brass fixtures glistened in the gas lights. They made a direct line to the dining room, enjoying the comfort of padded chairs and marble-topped tables.

"You know, I just don't understand why Mrs. Parkham felt is so important that I come up to the city to meet her. She usually makes arrangements to stay overnight and come back to Martinsville in the morning."

"Well, maybe she wanted to treat you—what's on at the opera house?"

"I don't know. It never occurred to me to look." Angelee bit into the cheese sandwich, savoring the mellow flavors enhanced by sweet pickles. "Hey! Maybe she wants to do some shopping at L. S. Ayres in the morning. Their new Spring line will be out."

"We will find out soon enough!" Olivia said, nodding toward the clock.

Finishing quickly, they left the dining room and consulted the arrivals board. Identifying the correct platform, the girls made their way to the meeting spot.

The train slowly chugged into the station, steam hissing, brakes squealing. Angelee studied the train's windows, observing the passengers and trying to catch a glimpse of Mrs. Parkham.

The uniformed conductor stepped down from the train, motioning to passengers to start disembarking.

On the way to the meeting place, Angelee had engaged a porter for the expected luggage. Angelee looked down the platform and noticed one of the station employees helping Mrs. Parkham down the steps of the train car. Motioning to the porter to follow, Angelee rushed toward Mrs. Parkham.

Genuine affection surged up in Angelee's heart and she greeted the diminutive lady with a hug and a kiss on the cheek. "Welcome back, Mrs. Parkham. I've got a porter and I've sent Olivia to get a taxi."

"Well done, My Dearest Angelee. I'm glad we spent the night in Chicago. We had a wonderful meal at a fine Italian restaurant."

"We?" Angelee questioned. "I thought I was meeting just you." Her hopes raised. Maybe Mrs. Parkham was referring to a new secretary/companion.

Just then she noticed a young man right behind Mrs. Parkham. He was taller by an inch than her brother and Pauley. A thatch of brassy red hair was matched by a mustache. Bespectacled, hazel eyes were observing her. The crinkles around those studied eyes hinted that he was also older than Drew and Pauley. A soft smile graced his full mouth. She's never seen an olive-complexioned red-head before, which made him even more striking.

"It was a last-minute decision dear." Mrs. Parkham explained, with a dismissive flick of her wrist. "Let me introduce to my nephew, Cameron Addison Boyer-Parkman. He's only just home from England. He's been flying for the British Army. I told him I was returning to my Indiana home, and he didn't want me to travel alone. So, he bought the ticket the day we left Boston."

The impeccably dressed young man offered his hand. "Very pleased to meet you, Miss Angelee Tilson."

Angelee stood, speechless, and continued to take in his handsome appearance.

Cameron turned to his aunt. "Is she always this quiet?"

Mrs. Parkham smiled, eyes twinkling. "It seems she must be in shock. Angelee isn't one for surprises."

"Aunt March tells me you are a very capable assistant. And that you brought a friend with you?"

Angelee shook his hand and let it go. She gave her thoughts a mental shake as well. "Oh yes, my best friend, Olivia. She's waiting for us by the taxies out front."

Cameron Addison Boyer-Parkham joined the porter and collected the luggage. Angelee led them through the vast station with its vaulted ceilings. Angelee could see that the taxi driver was engaged in a casual conversation with her unsuspecting friend.

Running ahead, Angelee had enough time to tell her friend. "She's just gone and brought her nephew with her! Why would he want to come here?!"

Saturday, April 21st, 1917
A Saturday Shopping Trip

After the taxi delivered them to English Hotel and Opera House on the circle, they had been shown to their rooms. A suite of rooms provided sleeping arrangements for Mrs. Parkham and the girls. Cameron Addison Boyer-Parkham was provided a double room.

Although Angelee had made the arrangements for an overnight stay in Indianapolis, she had not anticipated remaining in Indianapolis for the whole of Saturday. Learning of Mrs. Parkham's plans to go shopping during the morning and then have lunch at Ayres' Tea room meant her tutoring session with Bart must be canceled. That meant a phone call from the hotel. Since the shopping was her prerogative, she quickly authorized the phone call. The evening flew by with dinner and watching *Avery Hopwood's Volcano of Corinth* at the Opera House.

Saturday morning, the lavish hotel restaurant boasted its opulence with starched white table cloths and sparkling cutlery on the table. The Maître D' led them across the thick, red carpet and held the chair for each of them to be seated. Another waiter provided them with a menu, then offered coffee or tea. The hot drinks were brought and poured from a silver decanter into hand-painted china.

"So sorry to keep you waiting," Cameron said, as he joined them. He smiled, his eyes free from sarcasm or disdain. "I took a walk and got a bit turned around on the way back."

"A walk? Already?" Mrs. Parkham's eyebrows raised. "By the way, we ordered coffee for you. The waiter will be right back."

"It's the military life, Aunt Marcheline. I'm accustomed to being up by five-thirty every morning. So, after I awakened the room service attendant, I ordered coffee. I got dressed and went in search of a tobacconist. The concierge kindly directed me toward Illinois street."

"Cameron Addison! When did you start smoking?" Mrs. Parkham put on her interrogator's voice.

Cameron Addison Boyer-Parkham laughed. "Now don't start, Aunt Marcheline. I only smoke the occasional cigar. I enjoyed them with the other pilots in England."

The waiter arrived with the first course, fresh fruit salad. "I'll bring more coffee."

"Mr. Boyer-Parkham, when did you go over to fight in the war?" Angelee asked. My brother and his best friend will probably enlist when they finish this year of college. Our parents hope that they will wait until they are called up. But Drew and Pauley are anxious to do their bit."

"Please, Miss Tilson, you must call me Cameron. To answer your question, I went to England to study on a Rhodes Scholarship at Oxford. Let me see...that was in 1912. I finished that year and stayed on in England. Airplanes are fascinating and being smitten with all things aerodynamics, I managed to find a job with the British company, Airco. When the war started, I felt it my responsibility to use my knowledge to help Great Britain fight"

Angelee had finished the last of the oranges and banana and put her spoon down. She looked up at Olivia. With a glance, Olivia indicated that Angelee should look at Mrs. Parkham. Mrs. Parkham's eyes glimmered with satisfaction; her smile triumphant.

"Are you home on leave?" Olivia joined the conversation.

"Unfortunately, my flying days are over," Cameron replied.

The waiter came with their hot food and poured the steaming coffee into each cup. In the meantime, Cameron did not attempt to explain why he could no longer pilot planes.

"Right, my darling young people, enough talk of war. The objective of this morning's shopping adventure is the purchase of dresses for your birthdays and graduation, both just a few weeks away." Mrs. Parkham looked from one girl to the other, daring them to argue.

Angelee and Olivia exchanged looks. If spite of herself, Angelee began to laugh.

"Whatever is so funny?" Mrs. Parkham asked, a single eyebrow raised.

"I was just remembering our first shopping excursion in Martinsville, Mrs. Parkham. We went to Toners, with two floors. Then we stopped at Dickson's men's store, which had nothing you wanted. The final stop was Dessaur's Clothing store. When we'd exhausted that one you asked me where the next store was. You just couldn't believe that was it! Three stores in our town."

The memory had them all laughing.

"That is certainly not the case here in Indianapolis. However, would you prefer to shop on your own, Cameron?" Mrs. Parkham offered her nephew.

"By no means; this being my introduction to the 'Crossroads of America.' Finding an early morning cigar is one thing. But to find the best stores, two guides are invaluable."

The conversation during breakfast was taken up planning a strategy for the order in which shops would be visited, a list compiled so that nothing be forgotten.

Mrs. Parkham's energy was tempered by arthritis in her hips and bursitis in her shoulders. Angelee admired Mrs. Parkham's fortitude as they went from store to store, procuring underclothing, hosiery, hats and gloves, shoes, and the celebration dresses. By the time lunchtime arrived, Mrs. Parkham was showing signs of fatigue.

"Come, Aunt Marcheline, we need to stop for a rest," Cameron observed. "I can tell you're getting hungry."

"I know I am." Said Angelee, thirst parching her throat.

"And how can you tell I'm getting hungry?" Mrs. Parkham demanded of her nephew.

"You're getting crotchety. And you're limping." Cameron grinned affectionately at his Aunt.

"I am not getting crotchety!" the older woman protested. "But, I do confess, my hip is beginning to ache."

Cameron chuckled at his Aunt's simultaneous protestation and confession. "Now, where is this tea room or café you wanted to visit?" Cameron inquired of the girls, signaling his taking charge of the schedule.

"It's here, on the eighth floor," Angelee said. "And we can get the elevator over in that corner, she indicated by pointing.

"Angelee! Stop pointing…haven't you learned it's impolite." Mrs. Parkham scolded.

"I thought you said you weren't getting crotchety!" Olivia quipped.

"I am not!" Mrs. Parkham harrumphed. She claimed Cameron's offered arm.

Cameron, who grinned despite himself, provided the required support his aunt demanded.

Angelee mused, watching the tenderness between the duo. She felt leery of Mrs. Parkham's motivation in bringing him from Boston. Wouldn't it make more sense for him to stay in Boston and overlook her business there?

Angelee's suspicions made her want to find a reason not to like him. But his apparent devotion to his relative was difficult to dislike. Unless his deference and protection of Mrs. Parkham was a pretense or an act.

Giving a mental shrug, she shared a look with Olivia. They linked arms and followed the Bostonians to the elevator.

A white-aproned waitress showed them to a table for four next to a window. All packages had been checked into the cloakroom.

Sheer curtains hid the view from the floor-to-ceiling windows which were accentuated by golden brocade drapes, with swags at the top.

"Too bad it's overcast today. The view today would be great from up here." Cameron remarked.

"Yes, but I doubt they'd open the curtains just for us," Angelee observed.

"Do you ladies come here often?" Cameron asked, running his hand across the white linen table cloth. "If so, what do you recommend?"

"I'm having the chicken velvet soup," Olivia said.

"They have the best chicken pot pie," Angelee replied. "The crust is different than the kind Mommy makes."

"I shall have the honey-baked ham." Mrs. Parkham commented.

"Where's your favorite restaurant in Boston, Mr. Parkham?" Olivia asked.

"Well, I occasionally like to visit the Union Oyster House," Cameron remarked. "The Green Dragon Tavern is another good place to enjoy good company and good food."

The waitress arrived with glasses of water, and tall glasses of iced tea. Taking their order, she hurried away.

Angelee had made up her mind to keep her distance from the strikingly handsome man sitting at the table with them. Once again, the fine wrinkles around his eyes gave witness to a life lived in the wind and sun. But it also hinted that he was significantly older than, Drew, Pauley, Olivia, and herself.

Lost in childhood memories, Angelee smiled.

"And what's that smile all about, Miss Tilson?" Cameron's lyrical voice broke into her thoughts.

The grimace lasted only a flash; Angelee embarrassed that she'd been caught daydreaming. "Sorry, I was just thinking about Drew and Pauley. It's like they're one unit. Very rarely are they without each other. Just like Olivia and myself. Or like salt and pepper. It's been that way all our lives."

Cameron's grey eyes narrowed. "Drew and Pauley? You mean your brothers?"

Mrs. Parkham, beginning to revive from the tea and a rest, took control of the conversation. "Now Cameron, you know from my letters and conversations that Drew is Angelee's older brother. And Pauley is his best friend."

Cameron shot a reprimanding glance at his aunt. Looking back at Angelee, a subtle smile hinting at the true meaning of his question.

"When Pauley's around, Angelee feels like she has three brothers instead of two." Olivia chimed in. "Although, I must say, that Pauley has been acting a little differently when Angelee's around."

Cameron, who had been leaning forward, sat back in his chair and crossed his arms. He suddenly seemed very satisfied. "Ladies, there are times when over-familiarity causes us to be blind to what is in front of us."

The waitress, laden with a large circular tray, arrived. Adeptly she placed the food-laden china on the table, promising to return presently to refill their glasses.

Angelee bowed her head, saying a silent blessing over the meal. She looked up at Olivia, seeing her also finishing a silent prayer. They grinned at each other.

Angelee purposed to keep quiet during the rest of the meal and let the conversation flow by her. She had no intention of getting better acquainted with Cameron Addison Boyer-Parkham.

"Besides the obvious, your Aunt, Mr. Boyer-Parkham, what brings you to Indiana?" Oliva addressed Cameron.

He chuckled at Olivia's humor. "I suppose looking for new opportunities. I haven't been home long from the war. Rather than jump right into something, Aunt Marcheline suggested I take some time to regain not only my health but also regain some perspective about the future."

"So, you're going to be 'partaking of the healing waters' in Martinsville?" Olivia probed.

"Since so many have recommended the practice as being helpful, I decided it couldn't hurt anything," Cameron affirmed with a nod.

"Be pragmatic, Darling Boy, and tell them about your time in the war. You must know they are curious." Mrs. Parkham instructed.

Cameron sighed, reached across the table, and patted his aunt's hand. "It is so hard to deny this woman anything. So, explain I shall."

Angelee was honest enough with herself to admit her curiosity had been piqued. His turn of phrase had been influenced by his time in Great Britain. His mellow voice was like listening to a shallow stream pass over pebbles. During the meal, she'd allowed herself to notice the small scars along his hairline and across his chin.

"As I mentioned this morning, I was in England when the war broke out." Cameron's bright eyes darkened slightly with the memory. "I found employment as an engineer at the Royal Aircraft Factory in Farnborough, helping to design and build all kinds of aircraft. Anything from reconnaissance planes with cameras to bombers. They found I was a good test pilot, and I spent quite a bit of time in the air.

"Eventually, I joined the Royal Flying Corps as a cameraman on reconnaissance planes. Last August, we had finished our assignment and were on our way back to England. About half-way over the channel, we were attacked by German flyers. Taking a beating; the engine started smoking. The pilot did his best to control the landing, managing to clear the channel. However, the wind played havoc with the aircraft, causing us to bang down. The undercarriage buckled on one side, causing the plane to summersault and break apart. I was thrown out of the plane. My last memory is of me exiting the plane and flying through the air.

"I was in the hospital when I woke up, with the worst headache I can ever remember having. Besides a concussion from banging my head, I discovered I had landed on my right shoulder. My scapula and collar bone were broken, as well as a couple of ribs. One lung was punctured by the broken clavicle. Falling debris hit on my legs, breaking both of them just below the knee. I have residual headaches that affect my concentration and vision; which is why I was honorably discharged. Once I was out of the hospital, I came home, to Boston."

"So, you've been with your parents all this time." Angelee surmised, feeling compassion and respect develop toward this man who had arrived unexpectedly.

"Actually, Aunt Marcheline has been my guardian and parent since my parents passed away. I was eleven years old at the time."

Angelee gave Mrs. Parkham a wide-eyed stare. "You never told me that."

"Yes, but I have often mentioned my nephew." Mrs. Parkham smiled, ambiguously. "But yes, Cameron was with family in Boston."

"My cousin and her husband very kindly invited me to stay with them to further recuperate." Cameron offered. "Over the last few weeks, I have finally felt strong enough to join Aunt March."

They paused while the waitress served each of them a dish of ball-shaped vanilla ice cream covered in pecans, hot fudge, whipped cream, and a cherry on top.

"I've convinced him to stay at Home Lawn for two weeks, so he can make the most of the treatments." Mrs. Parkham said as the waitress departed.

Cameron reached into his vest pocket, pulled out a watch, and checked the time. He replaced the watch, dug into another pocket, and pulled out a tin pillbox. "Please excuse my rudeness, but I really must take some pain relief."

Angelee watched as Mrs. Parkham's brow furrowed, and her face softened as she reached across the table and covered Cameron's hand. "I'm sorry Cameron. You're overtired from all our shopping. When we finish here, we'll go back to the hotel. You can rest while the girls and I get our new purchases organized, along with the luggage."

As Mrs. Parkham's assistant and occasional secretary, Angelee had never seen Mrs. Parkham express maternal comforting or nurturing as she just had with Cameron. This new facet to Mrs. Parkham was a revelation to Angelee, and a bit confounding.

Declining coffee, they finished dessert and requested the bill. After paying it, and leaving a generous tip, the party of four left the restaurant to return to the hotel.

True to Mrs. Parkham's word, once back at the English Hotel and Opera House, Mrs. Parkham organized the girls, who in turn took responsibility for their luggage and purchases to be taken to the interurban station. With all the traveling paraphernalia sorted, they caught the later afternoon car home.

Angelee and Olivia took a seat at the back of the interurban car. Angelee was hoping she and her best friend would have some space to chat privately. But Cameron and his Aunt followed them, taking seats directly in front of them.

"I don't think the conductor is too happy with all this luggage we're bringing with us," Angelee said to Olivia. "I just hope that Daddy is going to meet us at the station with the car."

"I know what you mean. Mommy is going to be surprised to see how much stuff Mrs. Parkham has bought us." Olivia remarked about the new clothing and accessories.

"I hope Mommy isn't too disappointed that she didn't get to give me an opinion before we bought those new dresses," Angelee said.

Cameron turned, placing his arm across the seats. "Will it be long before you are to wear these new gowns?"

Angelee and Olivia exchanged a quick look.

"Not till June, when we graduate from high school and turn eighteen the same weekend," Angelee replied.

"Both of you?" Cameron's eyebrows lifted.

"Yes, we share the same birthday," Olivia said. "We've known each other all our lives. Almost like twins, but with different mothers."

"Fascinating. So, I suppose there will be a party—or two?"

"Oh yes!" Mrs. Parkham chimed in, turning in her seat as well. "I've asked your mother if I can assist in the arrangements. She's kindly said that I may contribute."

She knew of Mrs. Parkham's enthusiasm for choreographing events. Angelee hoped the plans made by her family and Olivia's, for a joint birthday/graduation party, didn't get commandeered by Mrs. Parkham's ambition.

"By the way, Mrs. Parkham, I've let Mommy know that Mr. Boyer-Parkham is also arriving with us."

"Now, Angelee, you really must call my nephew by his name, Cameron. I am hoping you two will become good friends." Mrs. Parkham gently reprimanded Angelee.

"If I didn't know better, I would think that Miss Tilson is trying to keep her distance," Cameron observed.

By the moment Angelee could feel the awkwardness rising within her. "I'm sorry." She apologized. But exactly why she felt the need to eluded her.

"Do you know Mr. Torrington?" Olivia asked, seeming to rescue Angelee. "We've known him for over two years, and we still call him Mr. Torrington. It does feel a bit soon to be referring to Mr. Boyer-Parkham as 'Cameron'."

"Oh, yes, I know Steffken." Cameron rejoined. "Aunt March commissioned portraits from him. He does good work. I think I'll talk to him about doing a portrait of the two of you together."

Both girls blushed at his admiring smile.

"Neither of you worry about calling me by my Christian name just yet. But please, don't be so formal. Just use Mr. Parkham."

Mrs. Parkham shifted, trying to get more comfortable. "Let me explain the Boyer-Parkham reference. Boyer is my maiden name. Cameron is the son of my older brother. When he and his wife were killed during a storm, it was our pleasure and privilege to take Cameron in. But I wanted him to keep his father's family name. Especially since my other siblings are girls. So, when we adopted him legally, he became a Boyer-Parkham."

With each new bit of information, Angelee realized that keeping Cameron at arm's length was going to be difficult. Each Saturday, when Angelee went to help Mrs. Parkham, he would be present. And after a few weeks in Martinsville, it would be impossible not to invite him to the birthday/graduation party.

"I'm sure you're looking forward to being finished with high school and turning eighteen. Aunt March sent me to England to study after high school. It was a great adventure. What will you girls be doing?"

"I am planning to study science at Butler University, up in Irvington. Then I am going to nursing school. I've always wanted to be a nurse." Olivia was replied.

Angelee realized that she could use this moment to tell Mrs. Parkham of her intention to quit working with her. But courage failed her, as she had no other plans or ideas about what to do instead. Nor had she told her parents her feelings. Fearful of causing a scene if she did indeed announce her intentions to work elsewhere, she shrugged and remained quiet.

"Angelee will be coming to work with me full-time after she graduates." Mrs. Parkham declared.

"How convenient for you, Aunt Marcheline." Cameron quipped. "But I thought you…"

Mrs. Parkham back-handed his arm, interrupting him.

Meanwhile, Angelee's stomach cramped, and she regretted her silence.

"Are you okay?" Olivia inquired, as she took in Angelee's face. "You've gone quite pale."

"I'm fine." Angelee fibbed. She refused to let her employer and the man, who was basically a stranger, know that the thought of graduation and working with Mrs. Parkham left her feeling anxious and frustrated. "You know how shopping wears me out."

Olivia took Angelee's hand, squeezing the message of understanding between them. "I'll be over tomorrow after church to study our Latin."

Angelee deciphered the code in her mind. They'd have a long talk before opening their textbooks.

"Look, Cameron." Mrs. Parkham instructed. "We are entering the delightful town of Martinsville."

The interurban glided into the station in the main square. Through the glass, Angelee saw her father waiting, standing next to the car. She would be glad to get home.

Sitting at her desk, looking out the window, Angelee let her mind wander through the events of the last few months. Changes, some more personal than others, had begun unfolding in April.

Newspaper headlines for Saturday, 28th April shouted the news that the Senate and House of Representatives in Washington D.C. had voted with an overwhelming majority, to institute a draft. America was going to war; an army was needed.

Upon the completion of their current semester at Butler College, which was in June, Drew and Pauley confirmed their intentions to enlist in the medical division of the Indiana National Guard. Angelee had no idea about whether or not her father would be affected by the legislation.

Typical spring weather presented a mixture of grey days with sporadic showers and sunny days. Leaves burst out on the trees. Crocus, daffodils, and tulips emerged, perfuming the air and creating quilt-like splashes of color in gardens and lawns.

After the Parkhams arrival in Martinsville, the remaining days of April and May elapsed, following the weekly rhythm of school during the week and church attendance on Sundays. Angelee spent Saturdays assisting Mrs. Parkham. Saturday evenings or Sunday afternoons Angelee spent tutoring Bart, with Alistair's assistance.

To explore the local area, Cameron purchased a new Ford Couplet, complete with a hard roof and glass windows. He often insisted on driving Angelee on errands. Unexpectedly, he'd offered to teach Angelee to drive.

Until his suggestion, Angelee had never considered the possibility of learning to drive. Pondering Cameron's offer she conceded that developing the skill to drive would provide a new opportunity. All the while, Angelee was dubious about Cameron's motive for wanting to provide the automobile tutelage. Was it just an excuse to spend more time with her? And if so, why?

Interaction with the Parkham's was limited to the Saturday mornings, for which Angelee was grateful. Her main priority focused on preparing for and taking her final exams at high school.

Graduation Day, Friday, June 1st arrived. Having completed exams the previous week, Olivia and Angelee, along with the other seniors had the morning off; although the senior class had a ceremony rehearsal scheduled for later in the afternoon.

Hopes for sleeping in were disappointed when Aimee's alarm went off. Her sister had smacked the alarm off. But it was too late, and Angelee was involuntarily awakened the same time as previous school days. Pulling the cover-up under her chin, Angelee let her eyelids drift closed, while she heard Aimee leave the room.

Hoping to drift back off to sleep, she laid in bed, relishing the spring smells of lilacs, wisteria, and newly mown grass wafting in on the breeze, through the open window. The future lay before Angelee; tonight, she, along with fifty-two others would celebrate their high school graduation. She felt herself drifting into sleep, only to be startled when the door swung open.

"Don't you just love riding in cars?" Aimee asked, waltzing into the bedroom.

"What? Don't talk to me! I'm trying to go back to sleep." Angelee blinked and shook her head.

Aimee laughed. "Too bad! I already know you're awake. Besides, I asked you, 'Don't you like riding in cars?'"

"Where did that come from? To answer your question, yes, I love riding in cars." Angelee remarked. "Now let me go back to sleep."

"Sorry, Mommy wants you downstairs for breakfast. I was sent to get you."

Angelee found her housecoat and joined the rest of the family at the table.

After breakfast, Angelee walked into town. She stopped at the post office to mail letters, as well as buy stamps for Mrs. Parkham. In anticipation of graduation and birthday gifts, she stopped in another shop to buy thank you notes. Seeing a box of candy, she bought it for Alistair and Aimee to share. Her final stop was to return books to the library.

Angelee was looking for a spark of inspiration, a clue to reveal the mystery of God's purpose for her life. She was adamant that she didn't want to become Mrs. Parkham's future, full-time assistant. But she couldn't seem to recognize any natural abilities within herself that would provide direction.

Notices, advertisements, and informational signs were a familiar sight on the windows of the library doors and the notice board in the foyer. A new one stopped Angelee as she placed her hand on the door. It read:

New Position Opening
Library Assistant
All interested parties please inquire at the front desk

Angelee's business at the library was going to take longer than she first anticipated. She made a bee-line for the check-out desk. Mrs. Johnstone provided a quick overview of the position and an application for the job. Angelee folded it, placing it in her bag. Time to prepare for the evening ceremony was running short, so she'd fill out the application later.

She was glad to find that lunch was ready when she got home, as she needed to get to the high school by two o'clock.

The songs of the evening's program played in Angelee's head as she and Olivia walked home after the practice. The principal had taken the class and performers through the ceremony's high points three times before pronouncing himself satisfied.

Once she returned home, she applied herself to the task of prepping her clothing for the evening. Made of emerald silk charmeuse, the dress's bodice had a square neckline, with draped angel-sleeves. The skirt had three layers. The bottom layer was ankle-length and had a straight hem. The second and third layer of the skirt, of matching emerald organza, had handkerchief hemlines, and created a soft fullness, gathered at the waist.

The first time Angelee had tried it on, she'd felt feminine and mature. The time had finally come to wear it. The dress, purchased two months previously, had been washed by hand and hung up to dry. It had hung in her closet, in preparation for the rite of passage. Today she would take her time, carefully ironing the delicate layers of dress.

Her afternoon included not only ironing her dress but also, polishing her shoes. She had worn the new ones just enough to break them in, making them comfortable for the evening's event.

After a quick bath and a rigorous shampoo, she'd left her hair wrapped in a towel, to absorb as much water as possible. Blond tresses drew up into even curls as it hung loose to dry.

Aimee had a knack for pinning the blond mane into beautiful arrangements, in a short amount of time. Just before time to eat, Aimee applied her skill.

Since the commencement ceremony began at eight o'clock Daddy had insisted on dinner at six o'clock, as usual.

Olivia's father had invited Angelee to join Olivia for a ride to the school. Daddy could focus on transporting the rest of the Tilson Clan.

Instructed to arrive an hour early, graduates were inspected to make sure all were properly attired in robes and mortarboards.   Waiting in the downstairs gymnasium until a few minutes before the procession Angelee and her classmates could hear the building fill with people.

Conversation buzzed amongst family and friends occupying every available seat in the auditorium and balcony. She was sure that parents compared notes, apprised each other about the origins of decorations, and festivities of the day.

At exactly eight o'clock, the principal's voice carried through the announcement system.

Angelee's heart fluttered. The choir, consisting of the junior, sophomore, and freshmen class members, came forward and took their allocated seats on the stage.

As the choir took their seats, the high school orchestra began playing "*Pomp and Circumstance*". On cue, the high school principal, Mr. Morris, stepped out, leading the green-robed young men down the north aisle while the young ladies, in white gowns, entered the south aisle. They marched up the steps, each stopping by appointed seats.

Superintendent of Schools, Mr. Tresler introduced the local Presbyterian pastor, Rev. Forest Taylor, who led the invocation. As the minister left the stage, the senior class seated themselves.

The orchestra and the choir performed "Battle Hymn of the Republic" before the Honorable Archibald M. Hall, of the Indiana State Board of Education, spoke. Angelee was grateful that Mr. Hall remembered it was already after eight o'clock in the evening and kept his address to ten minutes. Kathrine Collier, the valedictorian, challenged and encouraged her classmates, as well as entertained the congregation. Applause resounded in the auditorium following her inspiring words.

Diplomas, tied with green and white ribbons, laid stacked on a table next to the podium. Rising from their seats, the school superintendent and principal took center stage.

Releasing a deep sigh, Angelee suddenly relaxed. The tension of waiting was over, the moment to draw a line under her school days had come.

Voice booming, Mr. Tresler carefully announced each senior's name. When Olivia's name was called, Angelee's heart soared. She was so proud of her friend, who was close enough to be a sister.

The young man in front of her moved forward and Angelee rose from her seat. Joy bubbled up within her heart as if erupting from an uncapped well. The words from Psalm 31 resounded in her mind.

'But I trust in thee, O Jehovah: I said, Thou art my God. My times are in thy hand: '

"Angelee Giselle Tilson." Mr. Tresler announced.

Honorable Hall held out the vellum to her, and she firmly clasped it. Taking his other outstretched hand, she responded in kind to his congratulatory shake. Her cheeks hurt from the strength of her smile. She crossed across the stage, then made her way back to her seat.

Mr. Tresler's last words were to congratulate all those who had received their diplomas. Applause came from the audience giving a standing ovation. Principal Morris motioned with his hands to quieten the crowd.

"Please remain standing while the national anthem is played."

The swell of playing instruments and singing voices resounded in the school's theater. A John Philip Souza march followed, which allowed the graduates to exit from the stage, followed by the choir and the school officials.

Once in the hallway, several of the boys unzipped and pulled off their green silk gowns, trying to cool off. Pressing through the crowd, Angelee and Olivia met up.

Others seeking cooler air, flowed down the stairs, through all six doors at the main entrance which were propped open. Collecting in cliques and clans, they filled the drive and lawn.

"Let's go outside! I need some air!" Olivia suggested.

Angelee grabbed Olivia's hand and they skipped down the stairs.

"Hello! Angelee, you were beaming up there." Cameron Boyer-Parker greeted them, inadvertently twisting the end of his red mustache. "Well done, Olivia. You look lovely as well."

"I guess the realization of all I've accomplished just hit me." Angelee acknowledged. "And I was just so proud and happy for Olivia as well."

"I had no idea how relieved I would feel." Observed Oliva. "Just how many people were going to be here never occurred to me. I'm not one to perform in front of a crowd."

"Just think about Katrina!" Angelee said. "She had to make a speech. She didn't even look nervous."

"So, you two, what are your plans for tomorrow?" Cameron rubbed the back of his neck.

"I plan to sleep in! I'm not getting up until I wake up naturally!" Olivia punctuated this intention with a single, deep nod of her head.

"I'd love to do that!" Angelee lamented. "But I have a feeling that I'll get woken up by all the activity...again...just like this morning. Aimee isn't the quietest person when she gets up in the morning. Tomorrow night's party will require all-hands-on-deck...and that means being up early."

"Well, are you busy all day?" Cameron pressed his query. "I was wondering if you were still interested in driving."

"Oh my goodness! I've not had much chance to think about that between school, things at home, and working for your Aunt. I've been pretty stretched the last seven weeks."

"I can attest to that." Olivia verified. "If we didn't have the same classes and had to study together, I might not have seen her at all."

"Fair enough." Cameron conceded. "How about if we try to connect on Sunday, after church?"

"We'll have to see! My family might have plans. But I'm suddenly exhausted. It's been a busy day, and it's going on eleven o'clock. I'm ready to go home and wind down." Angelee said.

Alistair ran up, catching Angelee around the waist. "Daddy sent me to find you. He wants to know if you want to ride home with us, or if you're coming with Olivia's family."

Angelee pressed Alistair close to her for a moment, then looked down. "I'm going with Olivia."

"Okay. Mommy had a feeling; she says don't stay out too late. I'll see ya at home!" Alistair ran off toward the family car.

"So, you already have a ride home?" Cameron asked, seemingly disappointed.

"Yes, since our families are neighbors. We are always looking out for each other."

"Well, I'll see you at church then." Cameron shook hands with both girls as he bade them goodbye.

As he walked away, Olivia looked hard at Angelee. "What was that about driving?"

"Cameron has been driving me around town to do errands. He thought it would be fun to teach me to drive."

"Angelee! Are you crazy? YOU! Driving?" Olivia protested.

"But just think, Olivia. It's a great skill to have. I bet more and more women are going to be driving since the war has been declared. And just think about how independent it makes a person!"

"I hadn't thought about it before" Olivia chewed on her lower lip. "I suppose you're right. But there is another thing. You always seem so oblivious to guys. I think that guy likes you."

"Nonsense! He likes both of us. And if he didn't like me, he wouldn't have offered me driving lessons."

"Gee-Gee! You need to pay better attention! I think he might be attracted to you...like a man and womankind of thing!" Olivia warned.

Angelee exhaled heavily. "Listen, my brains are mashed potatoes now. I am physically spent. So, please, can we defer this conversation? I don't need a lecture now."

"You know what? I feel the same way. But I reserve the right to reprimand you at a later time." Olivia giggled, the tiredness taking over.

They walked to the Biers car. "All I ask is that you be careful...and don't spend too much time alone."

"Okay...Wait! I know...you can take driving lessons with him too! We do it together."

"We'll see." Olivia agreed, albeit vaguely.

The Biers' car stood with back doors open, waiting for them. Olivia's parents were in the front seat.

"Papa hired a taxi for Oma and Opa," Olivia answered before Angelee had a chance to ask. "They genuinely wanted to come but didn't want to hang about afterward. So, they left right after they saw me get my diploma."

"Good thinking! I know how close you are to them. They are so proud of you!" Angelee said.

Mr. Biers started the car and the girls settled back, chatting about the day's events. Mr. Biers stopped the car by Angelee's home.

"Thank you for the ride home, Papa Biers. I really must get to bed. I'm exhausted!" Angelee said, opening the door.

"I'm heading for bed too! See you tomorrow!"

Angelee climbed the steps to the brick house and found the door still unlocked. It was a relief not to dig to the bottom of her silk opera bag for the key. Especially since she was holding the diploma at the same time.

"Angelee, is that you?" Aunt Milly called from the dining room.

"Yes, just heading up, so I can go straight to bed. It's going to be an early morning."

"I just wanted to say how lovely you looked tonight. And how proud of you I am." Aunt Milly remarked. "But, there's a little surprise for you."

"But I'm so tired..." Angelee half-whined.

"Too tired to hug your big brother?" Drew's voice came from behind her. He put his hands on her shoulders and turned her.

Angelee's delighted squeal filled the room, as she threw herself into his arms and kissed his cheeks. "I didn't think you'd be home till tomorrow."

"Well, we managed to get away sooner."

"We?!" Angelee's eyes widened, staring into her brother's face.

He gave her a toothy grin, then started to laugh.

"Yes, we..." came Pauley's voice. "Am I going to get such an enthusiastic welcome?" His blue eyes twinkled and he held his arms open.

"Certainly, a hug anyway!" Angelee put her arms around his waist. She felt his arm tighten, and he held on longer than she expected. Leaning back, she asked, "When did you get here?"

"A few minutes after eight. We managed to see your class march in." Pauley said, releasing her.

"I just couldn't miss seeing my little sister get her high school diploma," Drew explained. "We had to miss our dinner to get here. But it was worth it. We're going to raid the kitchen. Want to come with us?"

"I'm sorry, but I'm exhausted," Angelee said. "You're home all weekend?"

"Yes, can't get rid of us too fast. After all, we can't miss your party tomorrow night." Drew replied.

Angelee gave them both another hug, excused herself, and went up the stairs. She'd leave Aunt Milly to look after "the boys".

Saturday, June 3rd, 1917
Birthday Morning

A cool breeze breathed softly, lifting the sheer curtain hanging next to Angelee's bed, the dancing floral lace brushing against her face. The fresh air, the tickling fabric gently called her from the land of dreams. Breathing in deeply, she rolled from her side onto her back. Pulling her bare arms out from underneath the covers, she rested them across her ribs.

She savored the luxury of awakening when she wanted to, for the first time in months.

Hearing the door latch, she lifted her head. Aimee, sticking her head through the opening between the door and its frame, waved.

"Come on in." Angelee invited.

"Happy Eighteenth Birthday! I'm the first one up and dressed. And how do you like that change?" Aimee charged into the room, flopped onto her sister's bed, and hugged her.

"If I didn't know any better, I'd think *you* were the one with everything to celebrate!"

"It's just that I know secrets!" Aimee teased.

Angelee laughed and stretched her arms over her head. She gently pushed Aimee off of the bed. Swinging her feet over the side of the bed she stood up and pulling on her robe. Angelee smoothed her hair back, clearing strands from her face. "I'm so hungry. I'm going to have breakfast in my nightgown!"

"I don't think that is such a good idea," Aimee warned, merriment twinkling in her eyes.

"Why not?" Angelee pouted. "My stomach is rumbling, and I feel almost queasy from it being empty."

"I'll go get you some apple juice. But get dressed before you come down. But that is ALL I'm saying."

With a sigh, Angelee harrumphed but went to the bathroom for a quick wash. Hot water melted the sleep from her eyes; pausing to enjoy the momentary bliss.

In her room, she took her favorite "Saturday at home" dress from the closet. Pulling it on, she heard the door open again.

"Here's the juice," Aimee said, coming into the room after a quick knock. You drink it and I'll do up your hair for you."

"I love it when you do my hair," Angelee said.

Aimee picked up the brush and started gently detangling the curls from the bottom. "Do you want a fish braid or a French braid?"

"Whichever is faster for you," Angelee said. "The sooner we're done, the sooner we can eat."

"Last night you looked so beautiful! Your face lit up as you walked across the stage and accepted your diploma. I can't wait for it to be my turn." Aimee's hands smoothed her sister's hair before parting it down the middle.

"I felt beautiful! I think all of the seniors felt humbled and amazed by fanfare made for us—the music, the decorations, and praise for our hard work."

Angelee sipped the juice, relishing the sensation of the liquid sliding down her throat and settling in her stomach.

Aimee's hands quickly twisted the strands of Angelee's tresses into braids starting at the front and down the side. When she completed the two braids, she wrapped the braids around the crown of Angelee's head. "You're done! So, what are you doing today while the rest of us prepare the church basement for your party?"

"That's a good question...it's been such an indulgence to sleep in this morning—if you call eight a.m. late! After breakfast, I'll probably come back up here and write thank you notes for the graduation gifts I've received."

"I guess that's as good a plan as any."

"I know it doesn't sound very celebratory, but I'm still a bit tired from all the excitement last night. And I want to reserve some energy for our party tonight."

"What's Olivia doing this morning?" Aimee wanted to know.

"You know, Opa and Oma Biers spent the night at Olivia's last night? Well, that's because Olivia is having a last-minute fitting of her traditional German dirndl. It's a special gift, because Oma made it, based on the village they came from in Germany. Oma has spent hours doing all the special embroidery."

"Is she going to wear it tonight?" Aimee asked. "What about the dress that Mrs. Parkham bought her?"

"Olivia figures that Mrs. Parkham needs a surprise or two herself!" Angelee grinned.

"Now what are you doing?" Aimee suddenly became impatient.

"Just tying my shoes!" Angelee said, her head over her knees as she worked with the laces.

Shoe tying completed, Angelee stood up! "I am so ready for some coffee…and whatever else there is to go with it."

Half-way down the stairs, Angelee was sure she heard a man's voice. But it was not her father's or Drew's. Angelee looked at her sister.

"Who's here?" Angelee stopped and stared at her sister. "That sounds like Grandpa's voice!"

Aimee just smiled, glee brimming from her eyes.

Angelee rushed down the rest of the stairs and into the dining room. At the head of the table sat a grey-haired man, with steel-grey eyes, shining with pride and joy. Next to him sat a lady, her blondish hair lightening to white, with a smooth complexion and pink cheeks. Her blue eyes reflected love and gentleness.

"Grandpa! Grandma!" Angelee exclaimed! As she came around the table, her grandfather stood and caught her into his embrace.

"Surprise Gee-Gee! Happy Birthday to you, my darling young lady." He smelled of fine cigars and bay rum. He had removed his jacket, rolled up his shirt sleeves up to his elbows, and was still stylish in his vest.

"I was so disappointed that you both couldn't come last night," Angelee said and leaned over to hug her grandmother, who was still sitting.

"We *were* there! We sat in the gallery. There was such a large audience. We made sure you didn't see us because we wanted to surprise you today. Your father got rooms for us across the way at the Home Lawn." Her grandmother told her.

Taking the seat next to her grandmother, Angelee grinned. "I'm so glad you did get to see me. Just thinking that you had been able to see Drew graduate but not me seemed so unfair. But now I know you were just hiding!"

"So were we!" Another male voice filled the air.

"Uncle Edward!" Angelee jerked around to see her mother's brother and his wife standing in the kitchen doorway. She stood, rushing around the table.

Hugging her uncle with pleasure, she was also worried. She had to find out.

Aimee, carrying a pot of coffee and a pitcher of milk nudged by them. "Hot coffee coming through! Food is following—better clear a path!"

Within minutes the sideboard was filled with bowls of scrambled eggs, baskets of freshly baked biscuits, and a large sour-cream coffee cake.

Aunt Milly came through the door and Angelee stood up to hug her. In Aunt Milly's ear, she whispered, "I need to see you in the kitchen."

"I forgot the melon!" Aunt Milly excused herself, turned back into the kitchen with Angelee following her.

"Is *SHE* here?" Angelee felt her heart racing.

"Mrs. Parkham isn't joining us, as this is a family breakfast if that's what you want to know."

"No, the --'Other She'—you know, his step-daughter. Since last I heard, she was living with Uncle Edward."

"Put your mind at rest, 'She', is not here either. Nor will 'she' be this weekend. Your mother and I made sure--in no uncertain terms--that the invitation was only for your Uncle Edward and Aunt Lavinia"

Angelee let out her breath. "For just a moment, I nearly lost my appetite. Which would have been sad since Grandpa and Grandma Barnes came up from Louisville."

Walking over to the cool box, Aunt Milly opened the door and took out a bowl of cubed cantaloupe. "Might look suspicious if I go in there without this."

They went back into the dining room. The doorbell rang.

"Angelee, I think that is probably for you. Go quickly, please." Mommy said as she was taking off her apron.

Angelee was still trying to calm her heart after the surprise of seeing her mother's parents, brother, and his wife. But she hurried to the front door to answer it.

"Welcome to Tilson's Hotel and Restaurant!" She quipped as she opened the door. "Grandy—Granny!" She embraced each in a tight hug. "Goodness—where is everyone going to sit?" She exclaimed as her father's parents came through the door. "I didn't think I'd see you until this afternoon at the party."

"Your mother said she was recruiting the whole family to decorate the church hall, and by way of payment she was providing breakfast." Granny Tilson said. "Even Grandy here is being dragged into preparation."

"Let's go through—we're just sitting down." Angelee led the way, taking her grandmother's hand.

Thirteen people crammed around the table. The conversation paused as Daddy said the blessing.

"Now then!" Mommy's quick burst caught everyone's attention. "Since today is a birthday, and a graduation celebration, I insist that there be absolutely no talk about politics, war, the draft, or such topics. I'm very proud of our Angelee and just want to say, 'You did us proud!' last night."

Conversation flowed around the table, as each person shared a favorite moment of the high school graduation observation, from funny little bumbles to the glorious music.

As they were about to finish the meal, Mommy began issuing orders. "Edward, would you mind staying here and helping Aimee and Alistair with the dishes? They can show you over to the church afterward."

"Sure, I guess a little dishwashing won't hurt me." Edward winked at his sister. Edward was as tall of his father, with the same steel-grey eyes. His once blond hair was showing signs of growing dark with maturity. His cheeks were well-tanned, as he traveled a lot as a salesman.

"Oh…and do NOT let Angelee help with anything. She is always helping everyone else or doing someone else's chores for them. So today is her day to be fancy-free."

"If you're finished, Angelee, off you go! Go back to bed, have a soak in the tub…whatever it is your heart desires. Maybe go off to the library to find another book to read."

"If I'd just graduated from school, looking for a book to read would be the last thing on my list." Aimee volunteered.

"We know, we know, you'd take your painting stuff and go paint in the country." Mocked Alistair.

"It's called 'En Plein Air', and yes, that is what I'd do." Aimee retorted.

Angelee rose from the table. "Thank you, Mommy and Aunt Milly, for the luscious breakfast. And thanks, everyone, for surprising me. I'll see you all later."

Saturday, June 3rd, 1917
Birthday Drive with Cameron

Angelee meandered onto the front porch and sat in the swing; setting the swing into a slow, steady rhythm. Progress was well underway at Home Lawn. It was becoming apparent that the new wing would be a mirror image of the original.

Angelee had expected to help with decorating at First Christian Church. After all, the party was for her and Olivia. But she had effectively been banned, as had Olivia.

The mid-morning sun cast shadows westward. The lilacs, their blossoms bursting on the bush, a honeysuckle vine replete with pollen-dusted flowers, growing up the trellis next to the porch, emanated their scent, creating a heady perfume. The too-tall grass would be given Alistair's attention, as part of his summer chores. Enjoying the unexpected gift of free time, she offered thanks. Having impromptu conversations with God was natural for Angelee.

"Heavenly Father, You've provided us with clear, blue skies, a sweet breeze, and all these beautiful blossoms. Jesus, I know it seems ridiculous to think that this beautiful day is Your birthday present to me and Olivia. But it is a nice idea."

She heard a car motor before she saw the car. Cameron's blue Ford pulled up in front of the house and stopped.

"Good Morning, this fine Saturday," Cameron said. "Aunt Marcheline learned of a local lady who sells honey from her hives; the bee-keeper over in Brooklyn. So, I thought I'd come by and see if you would like to take a ride? Rumor has it that you're banned from helping with any-and-all arrangements."

"It isn't a rumor—it's true!" Angelee stood up. "I'm presently at a loose end. Please come in and talk to Mommy while I go up and get my hat?"

Cameron followed her into the house. Angelee found her mother and left Cameron to apprise Mommy of their impromptu trip to the little town just north of Martinsville.

"You came at a very good time," Angelee remarked as they left the house. "I was wondering what I was going to do with the rest of this morning."

Cameron helped Angelee into the car, then climbed into the driver's side. He rested his hands on the steering wheel. "Before I forget to tell you, *'Bon Anniversaire'*; please excuse the accent." Cameron laughed.

"Is that French for something?" Angelee laughed with him.

"Yes, one of the few phrases I learned—Happy Birthday. But my accent was never very good."

Cameron started the car and drove toward Main Street. "What was interesting is that some of the fellas from Louisiana, with a Cajun background, seemed to pick it up pretty quick."

"It must be wonderful to learn a second language. My older brother has quite a knack for it. He's taking Greek, Latin, and Spanish. He says those are his fun courses. Aimee spends quite a bit of time with Mr. Torrington, so she is learning French and Flemish. As for Olivia, her grandparents came over from Germany— so she speaks German with them."

"A lot of German-Americans are getting nervous now with the President declaring war. Some are even forbidding their children from speaking German at home."

"I had no idea," Angelee said.

"You know what, let's not ruin this beautiful Spring day with talk of war. I've had enough war experience to last me for the rest of my life. So, are you still interested in having those driving lessons?" Cameron guided the car through town and toward Blue Bluff Road.

"Oh, absolutely! I was wondering, would you mind teaching Olivia as well? We kind of do everything together."

"Hmmm, I hadn't thought about that. But I suppose that it wouldn't be a bad idea. You know how people will gossip about things."

"Well, if anyone starts a rumor about us, I'll just say you were taking me out for a drive as a birthday present."

"Good thinking Girl! So, when do you want to start?" Cameron persisted.

"Next week, once I have a better idea about what your aunt is thinking! During the summer she's always let me have Saturdays off, so that might be the best day to try."

"May I ask you a personal question?" Cameron ventured.

Angelee turned her face away from his and stared ahead. "I suppose so."

"Do you enjoy working with Aunt Marcheline?"

Angelee took note of his intentional nonchalance when he asked her the question.

"Were you ever a spy in England, Mr. Parkham? For all your feigned lack-of-interest, I still feel the question is pertinent to your interests and purposes—if not your aunt's."

"Miss Tilson, you are a very observant young lady. But I also see that you are trying to avoid answering the question." Cameron parried.

"The answer might be more forthcoming if I understood your motive for asking." Angelee offered.

"Is it so hard to believe that one person would simply ask another person if she liked her work?"

"It is; when the person asking is related to the person who is employing me." Angelee

"Hmmm, looking at it from that angle, I suppose I can understand your suspicions." Cameron conceded. "The truth is, I wonder why you're willing to work for a strong-minded, mature woman when you clearly have a propensity for interacting well with children."

Angelee swung her head around, staring hard at his profile for any hints of mockery. "When have you ever seen me around children?" She demanded.

"At church on Sundays. I watch you when we're out doing errands. You seem to know a lot of the local children. When they see you, they always run up to say hello and chat with you." Cameron explained. "Your eyes light up; you become animated when you talk to them. And if you have any candy, well, you have to share it with them."

Angelee took in his words, pondering them.

"Don't you help some children with their school work, you know tutoring them?" Cameron pressed.

"Only Alistair's friend, Bart. He was behind with some of his homework assignments and needed some help in understanding things —because of family problems. I did help him, but so did Alistair; so Bart could pass to the next grade. I just tried to make things fun and interesting. It's easier to learn a new skill if it doesn't feel like hard work."

"I hope you don't mind if I'm candid with you. But you never look like you're having fun working for my aunt."

"Your aunt is very exacting in how she wants things done. She trusts me to do what she wants to be done; the way she wants it done. But what she doesn't allow for is any creativity or a change in the method of doing things. There are things I would like to try. But she's rejected all of them. Because she doesn't believe there are better ways to do things." Angelee replied honestly.

Cameron chortled, nodding knowingly. "Sorry, I can't help myself. I've been down that road with her several times on different matters myself."

"Tell, me, does she have *your* life all mapped out for you?" Angelee said.

Cameron tipped his head back, letting his amusement roll like a river when the dam is opened. "Oh, Miss Tilson, if you only knew!" Steering the car to the side of the road, he stopped. His laughter lasted several minutes until he wiped his eyes with his handkerchief.

"Thank you, Miss Tilson, for providing me with the best laugh I've had in...well since I can remember. I haven't scared you, have I?"

"No, not at all. But I do wish I knew what was going on in your mind." Angelee replied, feeling awkward, but not uncomfortable.

"Aunt Marcheline is such a paradox. She can get a vision for something, or someone, and she does all she can to see that grand idea come to fruition. She can get it wrong, but generally, she gets things correct, because she follows her heart and her intuition.

"But I've learned this; if she makes a mistake in judgment, while she may not verbally apologize, she does all she can to make things right. She takes time to find out what the situation or person requires—or desires—and does her best to implement the changes that need to take place for it to happen."

Angelee took this in. "Can you give me an example?"

Cameron restarted the car and pulled onto the road. "From the time I was a small boy, I was accustomed to spending time with Aunt Marcheline. She said I was very like my father, and there has always been a special bond between us. The year my parents died was very difficult for everyone. She was very relieved to find that my parents had made arrangements for her—and her husband—to become my legal guardians.

"I was attending boarding school when the accident happened. Aunt Marcheline came to the school to tell me and took me home with her. While some of the adults felt that I should not attend the funeral, she sensed that I needed to go. From that time forward, she has always, as they say in the boxing world, been in my corner.

"However, that first Christmas she thought I needed to go away, maybe to Atlanta, or New Orleans, so that I wouldn't have to be in the house without my parents. She was sure it would be easier for me. There were train tickets, and clothes bought—without my knowledge. When the school term ended, she told me all about this adventure that we were going to go on.

"Well, I burst into tears and ran up to my room. Aunt Marcheline was shocked. About an hour later she came up to my room and we discussed it. I didn't want to go away, because I didn't want to forget my parents. I wanted a quiet Christmas. On top of that, I told her that I didn't want to be at boarding school anymore. I wanted to be at home, and go to a local school. So, to her credit, she didn't make a fuss about the expense or the inconvenience.

"Aunt Marcheline did have other family members over on Christmas Day. In the evening, she took me into a small sitting room and we reminisced about my parents. She told me stories about my father—when he was a boy. She never apologized for 'thinking for me'. But her actions showed me that she understood."

"Does that mean she also brought you home from boarding school?" Angelee asked.

"Yes, I attended a private school in Boston. But I was home every night."

The Bee-keeper's place came into view and they stopped talking. Angelee had hoped to sit in the car while Cameron went and bought the honey. However, the woman insisted on showing both of them the hives in her back yard. She offered them a fresh sample, complete with the wax. Angelee passed on the offer. Finally, the golden, sticky liquid was purchased and they began the ride home.

As Cameron drove, he hummed. Angelee, lost in thought, enjoyed the rows of green corn stalks in the fields, the glittering light dancing on the White River, and the warmth of the sun. Once again, she found herself pondering life's purpose. It confounded her that Cameron, with whom she'd spent so little time, could tell that she wasn't content working for his aunt.

"What's going on in that head underneath those curls?" Cameron asked.

Angelee absently pulled at a tendril that had loosened from her hair-line. She collected her thoughts. "I feel like I keep riding on a merry-go-round. I start with the question, 'What's my destiny? What did God create me to do?' I don't want to be a secretary all my life—but I have no idea as to what I am supposed to do. What is exceptionally annoying is that I thought that by the time I was through high school, I'd have at least an idea as to what I'd be good at, what I'd want to do. I guess I've relied on my parent's direction too much. I thought if I just honored and obeyed them, it would produce some sort of inspiration. But here I am, a high school graduate and no idea as to how I can contribute to making the world a better place."

"Don't be too hard on yourself, Angelee. One thing I did learn in while fighting in Europe is to be thankful for today; what you do today will help you tomorrow. Think back to before that first day of high school; you didn't know what to expect. By the end of Day One you knew that you had to learn a new routine, get used to going from one classroom to the next for each subject, changing teachers each period. But you knew enough about school on that first day to know that at the end of four years, you would graduate--which happened last night. And today, you are meant to *enjoy* yourself. It's your birthday—and a Saturday at that. So, relax, keep taking in the scenery, and resume your daydream if you want. You have Sunday too. Let Monday be the day you start developing the plan for the future."

"I suppose you're right." Angelee sighed. She closed her eyes, drew in a deep breath, smelling the passing scent of wildflowers blooming, and the chirping of birdsong. Suddenly she laughed. "You know, you just told me to stop worrying. And that is good advice."

"Good, I want you to enjoy my company." Cameron chuckled, reaching over to pat her hand, which was lying in her lap.

"I am enjoying your company. Not to detract from your delightful camaraderie, I just wish Olivia could be enjoying this trip to Brooklyn with us."

"Yes, I noticed that to get Angelee, is to also get Olivia. Can you even remember when the two of you first met?" Cameron asked, turning the steering wheel, adjusting for the bumpiness of the oiled dirt road.

Angelee clapped her hands, laughing at the memories, and. "No, I don't remember. According to Mommy, our first meeting was on the sidewalk outside our homes, in our respective baby buggies. Living just a couple of doors down, our mothers often stopped to chat. Our mothers would babysit for each other. One day when they were sitting on the front porch my mother asked Mrs. Biers exactly how old Olivia was. That's when our mothers learned that we'd been born on the same day."

"So that explains the joint party for your graduation and birthdays," Cameron said, nodding his head.

"I can't remember ever having my own 'individual' birthday party. Since we lived right almost next door to each other, we attended the same schools—often in the same classroom. She's more like a sister than a friend."

"Do you realize how much of a gift it is to have such a life-long friend?"

"To be honest, I probably don't appreciate Olivia enough. It is easy to take for granted something—or someone—who has always been in your life. But what makes our relationship special is that we've chosen to be close friends. We even fight like siblings—usually over stupid stuff." Angelee giggled.

"Now I understand your laughter. Do you feel like Mrs. Biers is your second mother?"

"I hadn't thought of it before, but I suppose I treat her that way. I mean, I spend as much time at her house as I do mine; and vice-versa."

"Changing the subject, I have been thinking about those driving lessons," Cameron said, changing the car's gears. "You'll need to wear old, comfortable shoes so that if they get damaged, it won't matter much."

Angelee watched Cameron expertly operate the gear shift, the clutch and maneuver the car. Angelee was fascinated by the lifting of leavers, turning of wheels, and the constant turning of the head. "I'll keep that in mind."

"Mr. Parkham, about those driving lessons, would you keep them a secret? I want to surprise my parents."

"Well, you are officially old enough to decide for yourself. So, a secret it is." Cameron said, directing the car onto Main Street. "Let me know when you and Olivia are ready."

At the corner Main and Morgan, he turned east. "Since it's summer, let's invite your little brother as well. It will give him something to look forward to."

"I'm sure he'd love that!" Angelee agreed.

Turning onto Graham street, Cameron pulled up next to the house and stopped. "Shall I walk you to the door?"

"No need, thanks. I'm going over to Olivia's. I doubt anybody is home right now anyway." Angelee alighted from the car and stood in the yard.

"Okay, I'll see you this evening." Cameron put the car into gear and drove away.

Despite her determination to stay clear of Cameron, she was slowly discovering that he was certainly a man worth knowing.

Saturday Evening, June 3rd, 1917
Birthday Evening Party

After a short visit to the Biers home, to see Olivia's dress, Angelee returned to a quiet house, where she afforded herself the luxury of a bubble bath, washing away the grime from her ride in the country. The residue from the dusty car ride had left her neck and head with an itch. Since the day was warm, she didn't worry about how long it would take her tresses to dry. Clean from the soaking, soaping, shampooing, and a final hot rinse, she'd laid across her bed, wearing just her cotton housecoat. The extra time to dry meant an easier time dressing.

Hanging from the gaslight next to the door, the crimson dress for the evening revealed an attached note. Angelee left the bed and unpinned the paper from the soft, flowing material. The note explained Aunt Milly's administration of the iron.

Angelee smiled, first humming, and then singing as she dressed. She took the opportunity to put her favorite pocket-sized doll into the side-pocket. She was sure her miniature mascot would provide a calming effort during the emotional evening.

The screen door by the kitchen banging shut shattered the quiet as the family spilled into the house to wash and change for the evening.

Aimee charged into the room "Wow! Your hair is down; I thought you were going to wear it up." she blurted.

"Sorry to undo your masterpiece. But Mr. Parkham asked me to go with him while he was doing an errand for his aunt. We drove through the country to Brooklyn, so he could get honey from 'the Bee Lady'. I felt like I'd been powdered down with the road dust! Would you button me up?"

"So, no 'thank you' notes got written. I'd want a bath after a ride too." Aimee conceded, attending to the glass-inset fasteners. "There that's you done."

"So, should I leave my hair down or pin it up?" Angelee said, wanting her sister's opinion.

"Even though the windows are open, I'm sure it will get hot with all those people in the church hall. If I were you, I'd put it up."

Angelee sat down and began brushing her still-damp curls. If a few strands escaped around the front, they would curl nicely into soft accents around her face.

"Do you want me to do it?" Aimee offered, now dressed in her housecoat awaiting use of the bathroom.

"I was thinking in a Gibson Girl. But are you sure you have enough time? Get all yourself ready first." Angelee said.

Ignoring Angelee's instructions, Aimee came behind Angelee and took the comb from her hand. "The bathroom is occupied at the moment—I'll just put your hair up while I'm waiting. It won't take long. Open the pin box, please."

Angelee opened the simple wooden box with a hinged lid.

Angelee watched in the mirror as her sister combed up and collected the blond mass, twisted it, and pinned it securely. "Do you want me to do yours?" Angelee offered.

"Not today. I've got it all planned out—and I'm up next for the bathroom."

"I'll go see if Aunt Milly or Mommy need my help," Angelee said.

Angelee left her room and found Aunt Milly's room empty. As she stood in the hall, she heard her parents in their room and knew she wasn't needed there. Suddenly feeling thirsty, she went to the kitchen.

She poured a glass of water, wishing it was tea or lemonade. There would be enough of that at the party. She drained the glass in one go, surprised by her greediness. Thirst quenched; she went out to the porch. There she found Aunt Milly, sitting quietly, eyes closed.

"Catching a cat-nap?" Angelee teased, joining her Aunt on the swing.

"Uh-umm."

"Are you going to be too tired to enjoy the party?" Angelee made her voice soft.

"I'll be fine. As long as YOU enjoy the party, that's all I care about. This might be the last time most of your classmates will be together. So just savor the chaos!" Aunt Milly advised.

They sat quietly, slowly rocking, back-and-forth, back-and-forth. A breeze floated across the porch. "It feels like a kiss from the Holy Spirit, doesn't it?" Aunt Milly said.

Angelee smiled, cherishing a special moment with her treasured aunt.

"So peaceful." Angelee agreed.

"Almost too peaceful. It feels like the quiet before a storm." Aunt Milly observed.

"Guess what?" Angelee suddenly wanted to share her secret. "I'm making an announcement tonight."

Aunt Milly turned and looked Angelee in the eye, smiling encouragingly. "This sounds promising…"

"I'm applying for a job at the library. I turned in the application the other day. I spend so much time there, it just made sense to work there."

"Good, a step forward, in finding your 'place-in-the-world'." Aunt Milly reached over and squeezed her hand.

Moments passed in companionable silence.

Angelee eventually turned to her aunt. "What's going on in that mind of yours?

"I guess all these festivities are reminding me of my youth. Then the time afterward—Bible college, getting my teacher's license, moving to Costa Rica with Ned. I'm happy, but these memories are making me feel restless."

Alistair stuck his head out the door, the turned and yelled inside. "I found them; they're on the porch swing." At that point, Alistair came out of the house to join them. "I think everyone is ready to go."

"Goodness Alistair, did Mee-Mee put some tonic on your hair?" Angelee giggled.

"NO! She did not. It was Drew. And, so what if he did?!" Alistair challenged.

"Here comes that storm." Aunt Milly teased.

"And the car!" Aimee said as Daddy pulled the car to the front curb.

Everyone, except Drew, claimed a seat in the car. Drew, in his vehicle, and would drive over with Pauley, whom he was going to pick up.

As the Tilsons were climbing into their car, Angelee saw Mr. Biers drive around the corner on the way to the church.

Daddy followed his neighbor to the church parking next to the new library.

"Hang on Angelee," Mommy commanded. "Not so fast!" Mommy took a black scarf from her handbag and gave it to Angelee. "Now, tie that on over your eyes. Don't worry about your hair. We'll fix it, should it get messed."

Mommy turned to Olivia. "And here is one for you. Don't dawdle!"

The black silk scarf felt soft and smooth on her eyes and ears.

She felt someone next to her. "Now what?" she asked.

"Just take my arm and follow me. I'll go slowly." Daddy instructed.

Angelee could smell the Pinaud talc powder he'd used to freshen up. She held his elbow tightly, taking each step with caution.

"You're doing fine." Her father encouraged. "Now we're to the steps." He guided her up the steps, through the sanctuary, and then down the stairs to the basement. "We're here. At my count, both of you take off the blindfold. Three-two-one!"

"Glorious Benedictus!" breathed Angelee, as her vision clarified.

"Oh-My-Days!" exclaimed Olivia, blinking to focus.

Crape paper streamers of navy and rose hung from each corner of the room and met in the middle of the ceiling. Flower garlands were strung over the windows. Long tables, organized in rows, held china, crystal glasses, and stainless-steel cutlery. Napkins, folded in the shape of Birds-of-Paradise sat on each china plate. The centerpieces consisted of four candlesticks on a small candelabra, ornamented with fresh carnations, baby's breath, and laurel. At the back of the room, chafing dishes rested on serving tables.

"This room looks so different!" Angelee said.

"They have truly transformed it!" Olivia agreed.

"The string quartet just arrived, Daddy," Alistair announced. "Aimee is going to bring them down."

The musicians were led to the opposite end of the hall, away from the kitchen to set up.

"I'm just going to check with the caterers." Said Mrs. Biers.

Angelee excitedly hugged Olivia.

"Guess what? I was sitting on the porch this morning. Cameron Boyer-Parkham stopped by, on his way to Brooklyn to buy honey for Mrs. Parkham. He thought I might like to go. So, I did. I made sure he knew he was invited for tonight's soiree."

"Now Angelee, be careful. You don't want to give him the wrong impression."

"I know...but I did tell him that you and I both had discussed it and that the invitation was from both of us." Angelee protested. "However, I think you may be right."

Olivia's eyes widened. "Angelee! Why do you say that?"

Before Angelee could answer, Drew and Pauley walked up. "Hope you aren't interrupting." Said Pauley. "I must say, my two favorite girls, are looking stunning this evening. On second thought, let me say, my two favorite *young ladies,* are stunning. I left my two favorite *girls* at home today." Pauley referred to his two sisters.

For the first time in her life, Angelee found herself blushing at one of Pauley's compliments. She couldn't figure out this new feeling regarding him.

"I must admit, my little sister does scrub up well," Drew admitted. "And Miss Olivia, you're as remarkable as a Johannes Vermeer painting."

Angelee had never seen Drew look so admiringly at any girl before. He was gazing at her as if he had never seen her before. Olivia's complexion grew to a deep rosy color under his gaze.

A crash came from the kitchen and all four of the young people jumped. Laughter burst from the four-some as they realized the intensity of the moment.

"I hope that wasn't the main course!" Drew quipped.

"My mother will have someone's head if it is!" Olivia responded.

"Do we dare go find out?" Angelee asked.

"No, we can't do anything about it anyway. Let's leave it to the organizers!" Said Pauley.

"Oh look, we have guests. Isn't that Mrs. Parkham?" Drew asked.

"They're a bit early; it's only 5:15. The invitations instructed: *'Please arrive at 5:30 pm for a six o'clock start.'*"

"She is almost unrecognizable in that plum-colored dress," Olivia said.

"I didn't know she owned anything but black clothing!" Angelee said. "That must be Cameron's influence."

"My Delightful Hostesses, I believe you should go greet your guests." Pauley encouraged. "Don't worry, I shall rescue you shortly by delivering some punch." He walked toward the kitchen.

"Good Evening, Mrs. Parkham, Mr. Parkham. Welcome. You're our first guests. Why don't we find your seats?"

Drew led the little group to where the guest's seating arrangements were. The Parkham table was near the front of the room. Drew escorted the group to the allocated seats, where Cameron pulled the chair out for Mrs. Parkham.

Pauley arrived with a serving tray holding glass cups of punch; he set the first one in front of Mrs. Parkham.

The next one he handed to Angelee, smiling broadly. Why was it that his face was so familiar, but the twinkle wasn't? Throughout their growing up Angelee had seen mischief in those eyes, anger, frustration, amusement, and even guilt. But this expression was beyond merriment, deeper than anything she'd seen before. This 'new' Pauley puzzled her.

"Seeing as how I am well acquainted with the guests of honor, the waiter allowed me to bring your punch." Pauley nodded to Olivia and Angelee. "It seemed most appropriate to bring drinks to your guests as well."

"To Life's Miles Stones!" Pauley lifted his cup.

"Life's Mile Stones!" The others repeated, raising their cups of punch.

"What's in this?" Asked Olivia. "It's got quite a zing!"

"Neither Mommy nor Aunt Milly would tell me anything...so I'm of no help." Angelee replied.

"I believe it is a combination of orange juice, lemon juice, apple cider, and Canada Dry ginger ale." Mrs. Parkham volunteered. "A caterer in Boston sent me the recipe, just for tonight's happy celebration."

"Mrs. Parkham, your reputation for resourcefulness and generosity are truly in evidence this evening. I—we—sincerely appreciate your efforts." Angelee slipped her arm around the diminutive woman's shoulders and gave a gentle squeeze.

"Good evening everyone." Reverend Matthias greeted the group. "Miss Angelee, Miss Olivia. You both are looking bonny today. I must warn you; you're going to have a fair bit of male attention this evening when the tables are moved and the dancing begins."

"You're being very kind, Reverend Matthias," Olivia said. "But I have a feeling that two certain young men have gotten the mistaken idea that we need their services as protection officers. It's rough on them to stand down after a lifetime of habit!"

Drew and Pauley grinned.

"They will have to accept the inevitable someday!" The pastor quipped. "Now, I have a couple of small tokens for later. Where shall I put these gifts?"

Angelee scanned the room, saw Alistair, and waved him over.

Alistair worked his way around the tables to the group. "What's up, Angelee?"

"Mommy told me there is a table someplace for people to place gifts. Can you take Reverend Matthias's parcels over to the table? And make sure he gets a drink."

Meanwhile, Aimee was maximizing the employment of Daddy's new Kodak camera, intended to make a scrapbook for both Olivia and Angelee.

The stringed quartet played a fanfare to bring the guests' attention to the platform where Daddy and Mr. Biers stood.

"On behalf of our daughters, we welcome you." Mr. Biers announced.

Attendees who had been mingling took the cue and found their seats.

"We appreciate that you have all been able to join us for this joint celebration of their eighteenth birthdays and high school graduation."

"Before we eat this wonderful meal, a couple of announcements. First, thank you to the Home Lawn kitchen staff who have graciously cooked and are preparing to serve this lovely feast."

Applause filled the air.

"Next, we want to commend our wives, Mrs. Parkham, and Aimee who have worked together to plan and prepare this celebration." Mr. Biers read from a card.

"Yes, please let us hear your gratitude for the hours of discussion over menus, decorations, schedules, and clothing. Many a list has been written, abandoned, re-written, executed—and all without any executions!" Daddy continued with the narrative.

The clapping sounded like a rainstorm.

"Now, will Reverend Matthias join us here on the platform?" Mr. Biers invited the minister.

"Please, will you honor this afternoon's party by saying the grace?" Daddy added.

The crowd bowed their heads. Reverend Matthias used his best pulpit voice to invoke the peace of God over the proceedings and give thanks for the many provisions related to the event. At his "amen" all three men stepped off of the platform. The quartet began to play softly, so as not to play over the conversation.

As the guests of honor, Angelee and Olivia and the guests at the head table were served first. Angelee felt her stomach rumble, the smell of roasted meat wafting towards her.

Guests feasted on honey baked ham, freshly baked dinner rolls, sweet potatoes, mashed potatoes, sweet corn cooked with bell pepper and pimento, green beans with onions, creamed peas, and glazed carrots.

"I just love birthdays! It's an excuse to eat too much without the guilt!" Chuckled Olivia.

"But I'm not sure it's worth the suffering when the corset is too tight!" Angelee whispered in her best friend's ear.

Olivia laughed out loud. "Mommy said they asked the waitress to serve our grandparents and make sure the glasses were kept filled. It is so nice not to worry about them." Olivia commented, picking up the gravy boat and saturating the vegetables.

"Did your parents say anything about speeches?" Angelee asked.

"Not really—but Papa did say to expect some surprises. I hope they're good ones!" Olivia answered.

"The only thing that will surprise me right now is if I finish everything I've got on my plate." I'm going to give it my best shot—and hope I don't drop any of it on my dress."

"Exactly!" Olivia chimed in.

Aimee joined them at the table. As she sat down, she leaned close to Angelee's ear. "I'm so glad Grandy, Grandma, and Uncle Edward are here for this. But I'm equally glad that Hedda isn't here."

Angelee looked up into her sister's face, looked her in the eye, and nodded. She shuddered at the thought.

As Aimee looked around, she remarked; "I love this 'Ladies Only' head table."

"We discussed it and thought that Mommy and your Mom should be honored for all their hard work in organizing the party!" Olivia said. "And of course, Grandma Barnes, Aunt Milly, and Granny Tilson, and Oma Biers."

"Was Mrs. Parkham upset you didn't invite her?" Aimee asked.

"I think at first she was, but then I explained we wanted our family to sit with us," Angelee said.

Oma Biers, still very spry, joined the conversation. "Danke Schön, Mein Lieblings! Such a privilege to share this evening with *all my girls*." Oma Biers patted the young waitress's hand. "You are so kind."

The young girl sat the plate on the table, whispered her thanks, and retreated.

Oma Bier's masterful embroidery work on Olivia's dirndl was admired by the ladies at the table. Their conversation fell to reminiscing, the grandmothers telling about their lives as girls. Then the girlhoods of Angelee, Olivia, and Aimee were brought up—happy memories, embarrassing, silly stories, laughed about.

"Oh, Mommy! This is so wonderful!" Angelee gushed. "Thank you! And you too, Mommy Biers."

"I'm sure the night will have even more fun!" Commented Aunt Milly.

"I'm surprised Reverend Matthias said we could have dancing in the church." Observed Mrs. Biers.

"Well, to be honest, that topic was broached by Mrs. Parkham." Replied Mrs. Tilson. "I have no idea as to what she said to convince him, but she achieved her aim."

"You know she always does, Mommy," Angelee stated matter-of-factly. "She surely is a force with which to be reckoned."

Those around the table acquainted with Mrs. Parkham's reputation nodded their agreement.

Angelee looked around the room, taking the time to make mental notes of the many faces she recognized. Wishing she had time to sit with each guest for a personal conversation, she kept an eye out for those with whom she wanted to make a special point to talk to before the party ended.

"I think moving and mingling would be a good idea." Olivia moved her chair back and stood. "Please excuse us."

As they walked by tables, people interrupted them with a touch of the hand. They stopped a few minutes, chatting briefly before moving on. They managed to make their way to the table where Cameron was sitting with Drew, Pauley, and Alistair. Although the older three stood up, Alistair remained seated.

"Hey, show some manners! Stand up when ladies present themselves." Drew nudged his younger brother's shoulder.

"It's just Gee-Gee and Livy," Alistair complained, preoccupied with the food on his plate. But a second, harder, nudge caused him to put down his fork and stand up.

"Thank You!" Angelee and Olivia chorused together.

"By the way," Angelee tightened her lips; "I've told you not to call us by our nicknames in public."

Alistair just glared.

Angelee glared back at him.

"Please, sit back down gentlemen." Olivia encouraged. "We just wanted to come over and say hello."

"Are you enjoying yourself?" Angelee asked him.

"That is some dinner your parents put on," Cameron replied, patting his stomach.

"And there's cake to come." Supplied Alistair. "But I'm not allowed to say anything else."

"Then you'd better not." Pauley admonished. "Your Mom will have your skin-for-hide if you spoil all her hard work."

"I'm not worried about Mommy! Aunt Milly is the one that scares me." Alistair retorted.

They all laughed at Alistair's confession.

Resounding fanfare from the musicians caused the party-goers to shift their gaze to the dais where Reverend Matthias stood. He raised his arms, and the crowd grew quiet.

"The Tilsons and the Biers have asked me to call Olivia and Angelee up here." Reverend Mathias announced.

As the girls worked their way through the tables, Reverend Matthias went on with announcements.

"First of all, in a few moments, there is a matter of singing to be done; of which, I am sure, all of you can guess the title of the song. After that, there is dessert.

"It is true, there will be dancing, thanks to Mrs. Parkham's persuasive salesmanship. However, before dancing, there will be a couple of presentations."

Angelee and Olivia looked at each other, each girl's face mirroring the puzzlement of the other. "I suppose these presentations are part of the surprises," Olivia said in Angelee's ear.

"Just what I was thinking." Angelee lied to her friend. Truthfully, Angelee felt her stomach begin to churn. Being sung to, that was fine, to be expected even. But what if she had to be in the spotlight, as it were, for the presentations, the speeches? To have the attention of everyone in the room made her skin prickle.

Reverend Matthias looked to the back of the room. "Is the kitchen ready?" One of the cooks did a 'thumbs-up' signal. Reverend Matthias turned to the quartet, and with a nod, affirmed they were to start. The guests stood by their tables.

The strings resonated strongly, the first few notes inviting all those in the basement to join in a boisterous rendition of "Happy Birthday." Olivia couldn't help laughing through it; nor could Angelee. But Angelee's laughter was nervous—not joyful.

From the kitchen came a tea trolley, laden with a four-tiered cake. The Black-eyed Susans, Blue Asters, White Carnations, and green laurel sat around the base and on each tier. Black smoke from the flickering flames danced from the many birthday candles atop the first tier of the cake. The head chef brought the trolley to a stop in front of the girls.

Blowing simultaneously, Angelee and Olivia extinguished the flames in seconds. Clapping and whistling filled the room. Motioning for the applause to stop, Angelee and Olivia encouraged everyone to sit again. Together Angelee and Olivia took the cake-knife to make the first cut of the cake. Once again, their friends and families provided noisy appreciation.

Holding up her hands, Angelee said. "Please, please sit down. Olivia and I will cut the cake, and the waitresses will bring it to your tables. And thank you for joining us this evening."

Their guests obliged and the cake was promptly passed out.

The orange-essence and cinnamon flavored, yellow, sponge cake complimented the meal, adding another lovely memory to the day.

"Hello, Girls! Enjoying your cake, I see." Daddy leaned over and kissed the girls on their foreheads. "So, now that everyone has had cake, we'll have that lot play another attention-getter." He indicated the musicians. "So, try to think of what you'd like to say and be ready in a few minutes."

Angelee felt her eyes widen in disbelief. "Did you hear him say that *we* had to say something—besides thank you?"

Olivia's eyes were equally wide. "Which we've already said...several times."

"They know I hate being the center of attention. Why would they do this?" Angelee said, having lost all appetite for the special dessert.

They sat down by themselves. "Olivia, I'm feeling a bit sick."

Olivia patted Angelee's hand. "Take some deep breaths. That will help."

"Perhaps I should not say this, but I'm going to. It just feels like this night is about to become Mrs. Parkham's coup d'état."

The reverend stepped up on the platform. "Ladies, Gentlemen, Boys, Girls, the time has come for presentations, and surprises. Angelee and Olivia, would you and your parents join me?"

Angelee murmured to Olivia. "My feet are beginning to hurt with all this up-and-down business. Don't know what I'll do once the dancing starts! If I make it that long."

"I hope they open some doors. Even with the windows open, it's stuffy in here." Olivia replied.

Their parents took places at the side of the platform, while the girls were directed to join Rev. Matthias on the stage.

Daddy mounted the platform in a single step, as the pastor introduced him.

"Now then, we have been looking forward to this moment all evening." Daddy said. "To be honest, this is the part the girls had no idea about—which means they haven't been looking forward to it. Then again, they haven't, 'not' been looking forward to it either."

Free and easy laughter filled the room.

Dread, in the form of nausea, welled up in Angelee's stomach again.

"Olivia, would you come up here first?" Daddy said. "I think your father has something for you."

Olivia blushed as she came forward. Stepping up with the others, Mr. Biers met her and hugged her. "Olivia, you must know how very proud of you we are—your mother and I, your grandparents. Ever since you were a tiny girl, you have dreamed of being a nurse. You've studied hard to prepare for college. This is a gift to take with you, a tool to use as you pursue your calling."

Mr. Biers handed Olivia a small, wrapped gift. Shaking hands evidenced Olivia's excitement as she carefully ripped the paper from the box. The black satin, three-inch square box, shone in the light. Gingerly pulling up the lid, Olivia revealed a silver, Red-Cross nurses' fob watch. The cover was emblazed with a white enamel background and a crimson red cross.

"It's so beautiful!" Olivia exclaimed, throwing her arms around her father's neck, hugging him soundly, and repeating the embrace with her mother.

"Angelee, you're not forgotten." Mr. Biers said with a smile, his eyes twinkling.

Daddy reached behind to Mommy, who was pulling a small gift from her reticule.

Angelee fidgeted, rubbing the small glass doll in her pocket. She could feel her knees weaken. She thought to herself; *'You can get through this, just open the gift. Everything is okay.'*

"Angelee, we could not have asked for a gentler and more kind-hearted daughter. You've always surprised us with your creativity, your dedication, and obedience. You haven't said much about the future. But we are sure your dedication to Mrs. Parkham will continue for quite some time forward."

The words *'dedication to Mrs. Parkham for quite some time'* created an invisible cage, dropping over Angelee's heart and mind. She wanted to announce her desire, even her intentions to work find a new job—a different career.

Two things prevented her from refuting the announcement. The lack of insight into her plans prevented her from saying anything. It was embarrassing to feel so uninspired and directionless.

The second thing was her parent's expectations—not to mention Mrs. Parkham's.

"Your mother and I wanted you to remember your graduation and eighteenth birthday with a special token." Daddy's words distracted Angelee, and the queasy feeling that was beginning in her stomach settled a little.

She reached out, taking the present he held for her. The gift appeared to be about the same size as Olivia's, so she thought perhaps her gift would be a watch as well. Removing the embellishing paper, Angelee lifted the hinged-top of the highly-polished, wooden container. On a piece of velvet rested a locket attached to a broach. Intricately detailed flowers and leaves surrounded an "A" on the front, while the back was smooth. Very gently, Angelee prized open the locket, finding photographs of her parents inside.

For a moment the rest of the room faded away. As she looked at her father, he said. "We love you very much and are so proud of you. No matter where you go, no matter what you do, this little accessory will always remind you that we are with you in Spirit."

Angelee wrapped her arms around both her parents at once. The nervous tears flowed, as well as the happy ones. She hoped that the dancing would be announced and that she no longer had to be part of the spectacle at the forefront.

Turning, intending to go back to the head table, Angelee stepped off of the stage.

"Wait a minute, girls!" Reverend Matthias chimed.

Stopped in her tracks, Angelee felt the hairs on the back of her neck rise. Being stopped did not bode well in terms of the dancing being next.

As Mr. and Mrs. Biers joined Daddy and Mommy to return to their table, Angelee and Olivia were recalled to the stage.

"Are we going to introduce the dancing?" Olivia asked, taking Angelee's shaking hand.

"There's one more surprise for you two." The pastor replied. "Mrs. Parkham, we've come to the moment *you've* been waiting for."

Cameron offered his Aunt his arm and escorted her to the stage, carefully supporting her as they mounted the few steps.

"Good Evening, Ladies and Gentlemen." Mrs. Parkham's strong voice was belied by her fragile-looking frame. "When I came to Martinsville, I came to partake of the famous mineral waters. It was my good fortune to meet Dr. Tilson and thus meet Angelee.

"Angelee has been a stalwart assistant. Not just an assistant but a friend, a companion. Miss Biers has also become a friend because these two girls are as close as sisters."

Angelee felt nausea rising again. Anxious prickles tingled on her arms.

Over the next few minutes, Mrs. Parkham regaled her captive audience with unstinted praise of Angelee's loyalty, diligence, and genuine hospitality.

Angelee felt her face heat, as shame and guilt mounted in her mind. Of late she had done her work perfunctorily, with resignation, and even resentment. It wasn't just the pressure of being misrepresented that affected Angelee.

The pressure to perform, to conform to this image of Mrs. Parkham's description, mounted. A premonition hit her. Her history as Mrs. Parkham's efficient, trustworthy, adjunct had led to this moment; now that her high school requirements had finished, Angelee was to automatically commence as Mrs. Parkham's permanent protégé.

It was a position that she didn't want.

Listening to the older woman's ambling speech, anger joined the churning emotions in Angelee's soul. *No one had asked her what she wanted!*

Her heart began to pound as instinct told her that an announcement of explosive proportions was about to be made.

Directing her full attention to the girls, the 'Grand Dame of Boston' commanded the whole room's attention. "Now, Angelee, Olivia, I must say it has been an absolute pleasure to have been befriended by both of you. Intelligence, talent, creativity, and virtuous character are traits to be invested in, nurtured. That is why I've taken it upon myself to arrange for you deserving, beautiful, young women to attend college at Wellesley College, near my home in Boston. I just know you will fit in so nicely there, and become a tribute to Wellesley's reputation of educating women of fine character."

Once again whistles, cat-calls, and clapping thundered in the church basement.

Mrs. Parkham lifted her hands, like a conductor, directing the crowd to cease their enthusiastic reaction.

"Equally, I want to offer to pay for Olivia's further education at the Woman's Medical College of Pennsylvania; an institution renowned for their training of excellent women doctors. While we know that nurses are very important, I believe Olivia has the aptitude to become a highly-skilled, compassionate doctor."

Angelee reached for Olivia's hand, squeezed it, and then looked at her.

All the color had drained from Olivia's face, and her mouth was open. But clearly, she was speechless. Her eyes blinked and were filled with alarm. The barely discernible shaking 'no' of her head was perceived by Angelee.

"Angelee, I know you're delighted on your best friend's behalf. You and I have discussed Wellesley so often; it just seemed natural that you'd want to join the ranks of graduates from one of the nation's best women's colleges. Wellesley will provide unimaginable opportunities. I look forward to hosting you both in my home."

Angelee felt as though the air had been sucked from her lungs. Anger, so deep, so burning, coursed through her veins; for the first time in her life, she understood what it meant to see red. Yet, she willed herself to remain smiling. She fought the temptation to raise her hand and slap the smugness from Mrs. Parkham's face.

Not since she was a child of ten had she felt so betrayed, so manipulated by a person she trusted. It felt like these three adults had schemed together, forming a plan for her life, of which she wanted nothing to do. Believing her parents were complicit in the plan, the searing pain in her heart made it impossible to breathe. Now she could not escape; the deed was done in public. For a second time in her life, she was in an impossible situation. The anger kept her from thinking straight. The bile in her stomach churned, and she broke out in a sweat.

Suddenly, it was just too much to take in. She blinked tears, tried to inhale, to calm down. Fearing total embarrassment should she be violently ill in front of everyone, she scanned the crowd, looking for reinforcements.

Making eye contact with Aunt Milly, she transmitted an urgent request for help. Just like that day when she was only ten years old, Aunt Milly came to the rescue. Coming forward, Aunt Milly took Angelee and Olivia by their hands and quickly led them from the room.

Angry tears spilled down her cheeks as she allowed herself to be led from the church basement to the pavement outside the church. Once outside, she braced her arms against the church's brick wall. She vomited. When her stomach was empty, her shaking legs struggled to hold her weight.

She hadn't realized that Pauley had come to assist her as well. Pauley and Aunt Milly eased Angelee onto the steps of the church. The anger cooled, but hot tears still burned a trek down her cheeks. They scalded, as she sucked the cool night air into her lungs.

"It's Hedda all over again isn't it?" Aunt Milly said.

Angelee nodded, trembling with shock; drawing deep breaths, crying with gut-wrenching sobs. Nausea rose again, her empty stomach still producing acid. Pauley sat down next to her, put her arm around her, letting her feel the warmth from his body. Slowly, her sobs receded to quiet tears.

"How's Olivia? Who's with her?" Olivia asked, still shuddering with emotion.

"She's in shock too. Drew's with her."

Angelee heard Pauley's voice over her head. "Mrs. O'Neal, I think Angelee needs to go home now. That was pretty astounding stuff in there."

"Here's another little bird who needs to fly the coop!" Drew said, supporting Olivia, in an equal state of shock. He helped her sit down next to Angelee.

Aunt Milly rose from the steps and went back to the party. Angelee supposed it was to inform her parents of the situation.

Angelee couldn't stop shivering; from the upheaval in her soul. Bitter bile, in the back of her throat, burned. The beauty of a wonderful day had been decimated in a short, five-minute speech.

Pauley held her lightly, stroking her arms, trying to calm and warm her.

She closed her eyes, knowing that with Pauley she was safe.

"I think your father should let you have some whiskey when you get home," Pauley remarked before gently pressing his lips to her temple, for a sweet second. Angelee tried to ignore that different shiver that ran down her spine.

"I don't want to talk to him right now. I don't want to talk to Mommy either. How could they do that to me?" Angelee ignored his expression of affection. Besides, she knew Pauley wanted to comfort her, so she took the delicate kiss like that—comfort.

"I can understand that. You can deal with that tomorrow. Right now, just be still. Drew's gone to get his car, and we'll take both of you home."

"Thanks, Pauley."

"Something tells me your parents were not expecting the reactions they got." Aunt Milly said when she returned. "I've told them both girls are going home. This party won't be long before it breaks up."

"Drew will be right here in a moment. He's parked over on the square." Pauley said.

Olivia, you're staying with us until your parents get home." Aunt Milly said. "And I'm raiding my brother-in-law's medicinal whiskey stash when we get home."

"I'd rather have something to settle my stomach." Murmured Angelee.

"I think I'm going to be sick," Olivia said.

Pauley released Angelee into Aunt Milly's arms. Then helping Olivia over to the lawn, he steadied her until she had emptied the content of her stomach again.

"Right, whiskey, soda water, and saltine crackers." Aunt Milly said.

Drew pulled up in the car then, and both girls were bundled in for the short ride to the Tilson home.

Once home, Aunt Milly plied the girls with the warming alcohol, fizzy water, and starchy crackers. She got them upstairs to her room, helped them undress, get into nightgowns, and put them into her double bed. Even before she left the room, they'd fallen asleep.

Saturday Night, June 3rd, 1917
Angelee's Dream

The stress of the evening's shocking announcements had exhausted Angelee and Olivia. Nestled in Aunt Milly's bed, sleep overtook them without delay. The girls were unaware of the occasional waft of air that stirred the curtains. Nor were they aware that only Aunt Milly was at home. In the safety of slumber, the girls were unaware of how their unexpected reactions had baffled their guests. Nor could they know the speculation brought about by their abrupt departure. Their parents were left puzzled, and embarrassed, not knowing how to address the many questions other family members and friends asked.

As for Angelee, solace, comfort and hope came in from an unexpected source. She began to dream.

The sun was turning from rose to golden as the day dawned in her dream. In the middle of a field, filled with Black-eyed Susans, stood a train station. She stood alone on the platform of the depot. As she watched, smoke poured from the chimney of the engine, as it pulled into the station. There were only a few cars, with words on each one.

'DESTINY' was painted on the side of the engine. On the coal-car was painted "ABILITIES.' The passenger car was labeled 'OBEDIENCE'. The caboose was inscribed with 'TRUST.'

As she surveyed the station, she wondered why no other passengers were waiting for the train. There also appeared to be no other passengers already on the train. The station manager came out of the depot, so she asked him why she alone was waiting for the train.

"This is your special train, Miss Angelee. It's time for you to board." Said the man, dressed in a uniform of royal blue. But he seemed ethereal, with translucent skin, shining golden hair, and piercing blue eyes.

"But I don't understand. I don't know where I'm supposed to go." Angelee said.

Peace resonated from him, and Angelee couldn't help but soak it in.

"Not to worry Child. The Chief Engineers knows your destination; you just need to get on the train. You can ride the caboose, to begin with.

Angelee stared at the last car, suddenly grasping that she needed to start her journey with trust. Though she may not know the final result, she would at least be making a start.

"In time," The Station Master continued, "the Conductor will come back and let you know when to move into the next car. It never takes long...it just seems that way at times."

Shifting her gaze to the passenger car, she took in the word, *abilities*. She realized that as her confidence in the Chief Engineer grew, she would discover the innate talents that would enable her to accomplish her purpose.

"I understand. In time, when I've polished my skills, there will come a time I must choose to obey." Angelee pointed to the car behind the engine. *Obedience* was emblazoned on the side.

The Station Master nodded, then somberly explained; "If you choose not to obey, it means getting off of the train. That could mean delaying your arrival, nor never reaching where you are meant to be.

"However, the chief Engineer will always be waiting for you to return, and will gladly welcome you. But be encouraged, many have taken this train and remained faithful to the end of the line. The conductor will always be available to guide you."

"Won't I need luggage?"

"No, everything you'll need will be provided along the way."

"Then I'd best be on my way."

The Station Master followed her across the platform, helped her onto the caboose—taking the first step of trust. Before stepping inside the car, Angelee turned to thank him. He gave her hand a reassuring squeeze as he said,

"This trip may not always be easy, but it holds the greatest rewards along the way, as well as the end.

Angelee nodded, stepped inside and car, and settled herself. Only a minute later, the Chief Engineer sounded the whistle. As she felt the train lurch forward, the dream ended.

Sunday, June 4th, 1917
Exhaustion

Emotional and physical exhaustion rendered Angelee listless the next morning. Sleep had been interrupted by taunting dreams, in which she found herself either tied up and unable to escape, or standing naked in public. Distressed by each nightmare, Angelee startled awake. In so doing, she faced thoughts of the previous evening. Weeping softly, her prayers for help were formed as thoughts; hoping that her restlessness was not affecting Olivia's sleep. Soon grief's weariness would overtake her, as undeniable slumber claimed her again.

The bedroom door muted the sounds of the family having a conversation, doors opening, and closing, footsteps on bare wood. It was this resonance of daily family life, seeping through the cracks around the door that aroused Angelee. As she came fully awake, knew she had a fight on her hands. She had no idea as to how that fight would look, or how it would sound.

"I was ten years old the last time I felt this frightened, this frustrated." She reflected.

Someone knocked on the door. Olivia turned over and look at Angelee.

"Come on in, we're awake," Angelee answered.

The door opened, and Aunt Milly stuck her head around. "I'll be right back. Breakfast in bed this morning." The door closed.

As Aimee placed the tray of toast, boiled eggs, and a small pot of tea with cup and saucer, onto Olivia's lap she said, "Mommy B brought over some clothes for you this morning. I'll bring them in before we leave for church."

"How much trouble am I in?" Angelee asked as Aunt Milly positioned the breakfast tray on Angelee's lap.

"I wouldn't say it's trouble, so much as facing their consternation." Aunt Milly said. "But those dark shadows under your eyes tell me that you didn't sleep well." Aunt Milly looked over at Olivia. "Neither of you did. So, just eat your breakfast and go back to sleep if you can. I'll collect the trays later."

"Aunt Milly, I'm still very angry with them. Of course, even more angry with Mrs. Parkham." Angelee confessed. "Just as much for Olivia's sake as my own."

"I know, Gee-Gee, I know." Aunt Milly's tear-filled eyes softened with compassion.

"But why are..." Aimee blurted, then faltered mid-sentence as Aunt Milly frowned at her. At that point, Aimee scurried out of the room.

"Girls, last night was hard on everyone. I'm not defending your parents in any way. Nor am I condemning their choices about the party. However, what I do know is that all parents have only their children's best interests at heart. And that is your parents' motivation."

Angelee dropped her eyes and nodded.

"I guess that's why it hurts so much," Olivia said.

"The rest of us are off to church now. But we agreed that some time and space this morning would be beneficial to you."

"Thanks, Aunt Milly. For the use of your room, for breakfast, for everything. We do appreciate it."

"Your welcome." Aunt Milly smiled tenderly at them before she retrieved a pair of gloves and a handbag.

Aunt Milly pulled the door open revealing Aimee's standing there, fist raised indicating her intention to knock.

"Oh My!" Aimee yelped and jerked away.

"Oh, I'm so sorry!" Aunt Milly laughed nervously. "Didn't mean to scare you."

"I was just bringing Olivia's clothes."

"Good girl!" Aunt Milly praised her. "But, if you want to come to church with me, make it fast."

Aimee crossed the threshold and put the valise on the end of the bed. "Enjoy your breakfast! Gotta go!" She exited, making sure to pull the door closed behind her.

Olivia poured tea into her cup, adding one spoon of sugar. She lifted the cup to her lips, testing the temperature of the drink. "Ummm...still hot! Lovely tea!"

Pouring out the steaming beverage into her cup, she brought the china to her mouth, tipping the dark brown liquid into her mouth. She allowed the warmth to slide down her throat, warming her insides.

"You know of what this reminds me?" Angelee said after a minute. "Our first sleepover." A nostalgia-born smile crept across Angelee's face.

"You mean the ones in our cribs when we were babies?" Olivia laughed.

Angelee chortled. "No! When we had just turned eight years old." Angelee said. She cracked the boiled eggshell, peeled off the top, and scooped out a bite from the shell. "Remember when you came over on that 4th of July. Our parents took us to see the fireworks."

Olivia dunked a piece of toast in her tea. "We were supposed to go straight to sleep, but hid under the covers talking until very late."

"I think it was our giggles that tipped Mommy to the fact we were still awake," Angelee smirked. "She certainly got very strict! Threatening us with 'No more sleepovers—ever', unless we went to sleep immediately."

"We must have done it…. because here we are today." Olivia played with her knife, turning it over and over. "But why did you suddenly remember that?"

"Egg cups…remember? We had an 'Every-doll-invited' tea party the next day. You ran home and got your dolls, and I sat up a picnic on our floor. We *borrowed* Mommy's egg cups for fancy teacups. I'd made bread and jelly sandwiches, leaving a mess in the kitchen. When Aimee discovered what we were doing, she joined us and brought up the cookie jar! We pretended water was a very special tea and made all the dolls drink some."

"Yes, with a few disastrous results! It took a week for some of the dolls to dry out." Olivia reminisced.

"Do you remember the look on our mothers' faces when they found us in my room? I thought we were in real trouble then. But that was nothing compared to what happened last night." Angelee's light-hearted banter turned somber.

"Looking back, we did get off rather lightly," Olivia added poignantly.

"Last night's fiasco makes me think I never want to go to another party." Angelee suddenly declared.

"What in the world makes you say that?" Olivia raised an eyebrow at her friend.

Angelee crossed her arms. "Our dolly 'egg-cup' tea party was great fun until our moms discovered wet dolls, crumbs on the carpet, and all the pretty china at risk of breaking.

Last night certainly left a sour taste in my mouth. We were both pretty embarrassed by the turn of events.

"Finally, there is that summer, right after you and I turned ten. Aimee and I were on vacation at Grandma and Grandpa Barnes's house. Someone promised Aimee and me that we were going to attend a party."

Olivia nodded. "I've always wondered what happened that summer at your grandparents' house. When you came back home, you were so different. Before you went, you were always playing with the babies at church. When it was your turn to choose what we played, you wanted to play a teacher."

"And you always played nurse." Angelee countered, amused by the memory.

With a nod, Olivia concurred. "But it was strange, you wanted to stop playing school. You avoided little children and babies. Except for Alistair—because he was your new brother. But at church, or on the playground you shied away from the younger kids. When I asked about it, you said you couldn't talk about it. Whatever it was that happened, it upset you too much to think about, let alone talk about. So, I never broached it again. Over time it seemed like it didn't matter anymore." Olivia confessed.

Olivia finished the last of her toast, lifted the tray, and turned, climbing out of bed. After she shook out the nightdress, she'd borrowed from Angelee, she placed the trays in the hall. Walking back to the bed, she stretched, then crawled back into bed. "Tell me about it, please."

Angelee heaved a big sigh. "I'd been so excited that year. We were going to Grandpa and Grandma Barnes's for two weeks-- just Aimee and me. It was supposed to be such fun because Uncle Edward had a new wife."

"Oh, yes, I remember, you told me his first wife died. And this is the woman he's married to now?"

"Yes. Uncle Edward's new wife, Lavinia, had also been married previously. Before the incident, they seemed pretty pleased with themselves. Her daughter, Hedda, became my cousin when they got married."

Angelee shifted, stretching her legs under the covers. She toyed with the corner of a sheet as she proceeded with her narrative.

Louisville, Kentucky, a lush, green city, situated on the Falls of the Ohio River, was often humid in August, as indeed it was that summer of 1908. The limestone and red-brick buildings, many built near landscaped parks and cultivated boulevards, revealed a history of one-hundred-thirty-years. Creative society, culture, and educational opportunities abounded in Louisville. For Angelee, who was ten at the time and Aimee, aged eight, spending two weeks with Mommy's parents seemed a grand adventure. The girls were considered old enough to enjoy the museums, churches, and libraries.

Their Uncle, Edward Barnes, was newly married to Lavinia; a widow of two years, when Uncle Edward met her. After a whirlwind courtship, they had married just three months after meeting. Lavinia's daughter from her first marriage, Hedda Rodina O'Keefe, was sixteen-and-a-half-years old. Before marrying Edward, Lavinia had made it very clear that she, and she alone, was to discipline Hedda. Totally infatuated with Lavinia, Edward readily agreed.

However, it was clear to everyone, except Lavinia, that Hedda was a vain, spoilt young woman. Shrewd and calculating, the teenager easily concocted viable stories to get around her mother's rules. It was this conniving that led to a great trauma for Angelee and Aimee.

Hedda wove a story about an afternoon soiree at the home of Mr. and Mrs. Mr. Garvin, to which she wanted to take Angelee and Aimee. There would be a pianist to accompany the afternoon of singing, as well as a few solos for everyone's listening pleasure. Treats would include pink lemonade, ice cream, and strawberry shortcake. After reiterating that she and the girls had been specifically invited by the Garvins, permission was granted.

The Garvin home was located about a five-minute walk down the block and around the corner from the Grandy's and Grandma Barnes's home. In awe of Hedda, Angelee and Aimee tried to mimic Hedda's prim-and-proper behavior, even her quick, clipped steps down the street.

Affecting sophisticated mannerisms, Hedda rapped on the door frame with her gloved hand.

In less than a minute, Mrs. Garvin came to the door. "Miss O'Keefe, I'm so glad you're here." Mrs. Garvin pushed the screen door open, inviting the girls in. "And with your new cousins, I see. Mr. Garvin and I didn't know what we were going to do if we couldn't find someone to stay with the children. Thank you for coming to our aid!"

Hedda allowed Angelee and Aimee to enter the house first. Following Mrs. Garvin, they walked down a short hallway to a large parlor on the right side of the hall. Angelee noticed the hallway ended at a double door frame, which was the casing for hidden sliding doors.

"Go sit down for a few moments," Hedda commanded, suddenly very business-like. "Mrs. Garvin is going to show me where to find things for the children."

Neither Angelee nor Aimee spoke, as they sat, in wide-eyed wonder, on the antique horse-hair couch, admiring the pieces of opaque porcelain, rainbow-casting crystal ornaments, and paintings.

Mrs. Garvin came back with Hedda, holding the hands of two little boys with cinnamon-colored hair. Mrs. Garvin held up the arm of the boy who was obviously older. "This is Charles. He is five years old. He's allowed to play on the swing hanging on the tree in the back yard." She held up the arm of the younger child. "This one is Zachary. He's two-and-a-half and loves to run everywhere! He does try the patience! However, he is a sweet little boy."

Mrs. Garvin let go of the boys' hands. Zachary toddled over to where the girls sat, climbed up next to Angelee, and put his head on her shoulder. Angelee put her arm around him, smiling at his friendliness.

Mrs. Garvin walked over to a white, wicker baby bassinet. "This is little miss is Clarissa. She's ten months old. If she wakes up, just change her diaper and give her a bottle. That should calm her down."

"Mr. Garvin should be here momentarily." Mrs. Garvin said, looking around as if taking mental inventory. "Oh, Hedda—I must show you this. Mr. Garvin just acquired it in the shop a few days ago."

The homeowner held out a delicately painted Chinese vase. "It's worth several hundred dollars. I think it's been insured…. Mr. Garvin brings things home for me to see, to keep me in the loop as to what's going on in the shop. Then he'll take it back to the shop to sell. I sometimes worry, because with children things can get broken. We try to keep the antiques away from the children—you know high on a proper shelf."

A car horn blasted outside.

"That will be my husband." Mrs. Garvin sing-songed. "We'll be back in a couple of hours." Placing the vase back into the breakfront, she picked up her evening bag and walked back down the hall and out the door.

Hedda pointed at Aimee and demanded. "You play with the brats there."

"Now then, You." Hedda pointed at Angelee. "come with me."

Angelee turned, feeling alarmed by Hedda's sudden change of attitude, stayed close to Hedda; they went upstairs to the nursery to see baby clothes and toys.

As they were going back down the stairs, Angelee finally gave voice to her confusion.

"Hedda, what about the soiree? When is the piano player coming? Where are the other guests?"

"Surprise! No party for *You and Aimee*! *You and Aimee* are staying here to watch '*the precious children*.'" A sardonic smile matched a knowing twinkle in her eyes. "My escort—Mr. Marshall Garvin, who happens to be Mr. Garvin's nephew—will be here in a few minutes. I'm going to powder my nose." Hedda sashayed from the room, practicing her care-free and sophisticated pretense.

Angelee followed Hedda back into the parlor, where Aimee sat on the floor entertaining Charles and Zachery. For the life of her, this sudden turn of events left her baffled; she couldn't figure out what to do next. Should she refuse to stay and take Aimee home with her? Or, was it more important to make a good impression on Uncle Edward? Would he be disappointed if she and Aimee offended his new wife and her daughter? Even more important, she couldn't leave the tykes on their own. Perhaps she should send Aimee back to Grandma's house and ask for help.

Unfortunately, she didn't have time to decide. The doorbell rang. Hedda ran on tip-toes to the door.

"Do come in Marshall. I so appreciate you being willing to meet me here." Hedda cooed. "I'll get my bag and be right with you."

"But Hedda! But...you can't leave..." Angelee protested. "We've never done any babysitting before! I don't know where you're going to be. Tell me where you're going! We don't know how to get in touch with Mrs. Garvin. What if something happens?"

"Now listen, I refuse to stay here and I can't keep Marshall waiting." Hedda pouted. She drew her brows together in consternation, impatience flashing from her eyes. But her voice stayed sweet. "Oh Darlings, nothing will happen. They're perfect children. Now, I really must go."

"Well, at least tell me where the Garvins are," Angelee begged.

Hedda turned to look at Angelee. Distracted, she bumped into the end table next to the couch, stumbling. Just in time, Hedda caught a hand-painted Chinese vase.

"See what you made me do! This nearly broke." She haphazardly sat it back on the edge of the end table. "And if I had fallen it would have been your fault! Oh, I do wish they'd move this table. Last time I was here I did suggest it to them." Hedda complained as she refocused on Angelee. "Mr. and Mrs. Garvin are just down the street—at a Methodist Church. Some sort of benefit concert." She rubbed her leg again. "Now, I'm leaving."

At ten years old Angelee felt that she and Aimee were in deep water. Without any previous experience of any similar situation, questions rolled around in her mind.

"Can we go swing?" A small voice intruded on her thoughts.

"Well, Charles, you're Mommy did say you could. But you have to take Aimee with you. Show her the way."

Charles walked over to Aimee, who stood up and took his hand. They walked toward the kitchen.

"Aimee, make sure the kitchen door is open, in case you need to yell for help. Hopefully, I can hear you."

A white cat, with a flicking tail, pranced through the dining room and into the lounge. Zachary was captivated. Wobbly, toddling steps tried to keep up with the cat. The cat was too fast and hid under the coffee table in the center of the room. Zachary squatted down to watch the cat. The feline sat, swishing his tail, staring back at Zachary.

A sudden wail from the baby's buggy startled Angelee. She hurried to the side of the baby's bed, lifting an unhappy Clarissa out.

"What's wrong, Little Girl?" Angelee jiggled the wrestling child, trying to figure out what Clarissa needed.

The distinct smell of a dirty diaper clearly explained Clarissa's sudden fussiness. The small fist in her mouth indicated she was hungry.

"Ki-ki, come back! Ki-ki come here." Zachary cried.

Angelee turned to see what Zachary was doing. The cat scrambled from underneath the low table and marched by the sharp-cornered end table.

Having the bawling baby in her arms made it impossible to move quickly. It was only then that she saw the throw rug had been left askew by Hedda's misstep.

Hedda had unthinkingly left the expensive-looking vase sitting precariously on the table.

Chubby legs tried to run, to catch the teasing cat. Instead, tiny feet caught on the lifted rug. Nausea rose in Angelee's throat as she watched Zachary go down, first banging his forehead on the sharp point of the end table. As he hit the floor, the vase crashed down, breaking first on the toddler's head, then shattering completely on the parquet floor. As Zachary screamed, blood trickled from his head wounds. As he tried to push himself up, he cut the palm of his hand on the glass.

Angelee realized she was holding her breath. "Breathe, Angelee, breathe!" She told herself. Her father was a doctor! He had taught her basic first aid!

"Bleeding! I've got to stop the bleeding."

Angelee returned the crying baby to the wicker bassinette.

"Mee-Mee!" Angelee roared at the top of her lungs. "Aimeeee … come quick!! I need help."

Angry, her needs unmet, Clarissa squalled, at being put back into the basket.

Angelee swiftly crossed the room and picked up Zachary. Being careful of where she stepped, she carried the sobbing boy to the kitchen. As Angelee sat Zachary onto the butcher's block, Aimee came through the back door, Charles on her hip.

The screen door slammed shut; the smack of wood-on-wood barely audible as Zachary continued his wailing.

Aimee, stood, shocked by the bloodied, yelling boy.

"Quickly, get me some kitchen towels. Charles, can you show Aimee where to find some dish clothes?"

Charles fidgeted, and Aimee shook off the initial surprise of the situation.

Five-year-old Charles walked over to a drawer and pulled it open. His little hand, dirty from outside play, pointed. Aimee collected several pieces of cloth, ready to hand them to Angelee.

Angelee was busy trying to hold Zachary's hand open, to look for shards of colored glass. She wanted to place it under running water but thought he would be even more panicked. So, she gently stroked the tiny palm, lifting of the particles of glass that stuck in his flesh.

"Aimee wet down another towel for me. Make sure it's good and cold."

When Aimee had the cloth ready, she handed it over. Quickly administered to little Zachary's bleeding hand, the rag ends were tied into a knot.

"Now Zachary, leave this on. It will help to stop the bleeding."

"Aimee, please, leave the water running low, as I'll need it to keep rinsing these clothes." With the hand bandaged, she turned to Zachary's head. An egg-sized knot bruised blue, and bleeding from a cut made by the table corner had risen on his forehead. The cuts were still bleeding, and Zachary sobbed his misery. Angelee plied a cold cloth to his head, holding it firmly, to get the bleeding to stop.

"Aimee, go get Grandma, Aunt Milly...we need help.   Run fast. I'll keep the little ones here in the kitchen."

Aimee rushed through the lounge. Angelee heard the screen door slam close behind Aimee.

"Charles, I need you to be really brave, okay." Angelee swallowed the tears threatening to escape, and almost choked. With determination, feigning a calm she didn't feel, she instructed Charles. "Are you big enough to push the baby's buggy in here?"

Charles, wide-eyed, looked at Angelee. "Mommy lets me help sometimes."

"Good, now then, go roll the buggy in here. Then I need you to go upstairs and get a clean diaper for...eh....eh"

"Cla-issa." Charles supplied.

"Yes, Baby Clarissa. Quickly. I've got to keep helping Zachary."

The profuse bleeding slowed but required a frequent change of cloth for both his hand and head. Zachary's piercing screams had settled to soft blubbering.

Throughout it all, Angelee kept praying in her heart. *"Please help me, Jesus. Please help us, Jesus. Please let someone get here soon."*

Though awkwardly pushed, Charles maneuvered the baby buggy into the kitchen; Clarissa still protesting of soiled pants and an empty tummy.

"Can you find fresh clothes for Clarissa? I'll do my best to calm her down."

Angelee knew she was taking a risk in attending to a messy Clarissa. But keeping Charles busy meant he was distracted. She heard his footstep as he hurried off again, hearing his footsteps on the stairs.

Angelee wished she could warm the bottle, but she had no previous experience.

She hoped Clarissa would be hungry enough to drink the milk cold. Her fervent prayer was for help to arrive soon. Despite shaking hands and feeling weak-kneed, she spoke softly to the injured child.

"Now you stay still, Zachary. Can you just sit here while I change her? We're going to turn her from a cranky baby to a quiet baby...."

Zachary seemed to understand what was necessary and didn't move. Angelee half suspected that Zachary was going into shock.

Angelee, leaning over, lifted Clarissa's dress. The baby seemed to understand what was happening; her protesting cries changed to a whimper.

Angelee kept looking up to check on Zachary, who remained motionless. Clarissa fidgeted a bit, not liking her bottom exposed or being washed. Especially since the cloths Angelee used were wet and cold.

Charles arrived back with diapers and a baby dress. Angelee she made sure that the baby's fresh diaper was secure, lifting the baby straight upward to make sure it didn't fall off.

Once the dirty job was finished, Angelee looked at Charles. "Where are the bottles kept?"

"Mommy puts 'em in the box." He walked over to the icebox and pulled open the door, pointing at a shelf with a couple of milk-filled bottles with nipples on top. "She 'papares' 'em for 'eady when Cla-issa wants one."

Taking a fresh bottle from the icebox, she propped Clarissa up in the carriage, immediately giving the little one the bottle. Clarissa eagerly drank the cold milk.

At that moment, Aunt Milly walked in. Angelee sighed with relief, her knees going weak.

"Where's Aimee?" Angelee asked.

Aunt Milly washed her hands, then proceeded to examine Zachary. Zachary, scared of this new person with poking, probing fingers, protested with a wail.

Ignoring the toddler's fussing, Aunt Milly worked on. "Aimee is with Mom and they've gone to the Methodist church. Mom knew exactly where Aimee meant. I just hope Hedda told the truth about where the Garvins are. Angelee, go into the lounge and sit down; you're the color of wallpaper paste."

"But I can't leave the children alone!" she protested. Still in shock, and trying to suppress an overwhelming urge to cry, Angelee remained in the kitchen. However, she found a chair and sat down.

Aunt Milly lifted Zachery. "Now, young man, you have to stay awake for a while. I know your head hurts. But we don't want you to have a concussion."

Charles had followed Angelee, climbed up into her lap, and laid his head on her shoulder. "Thank you fo' letting me help with Cla-issa."

Angelee fought the urge to weep in front of Charles. The children had been upset enough already.

Hearing voices and the front door hinges squeak, Angelee and Aunt Milly turned to look toward the front door. Mrs. Garvin charged into the room, followed by Grandma Barnes and Aimee.

"Where are they? Where are my children?" Demanded Mrs. Garvin. "And where is Hedda?"

Grandma's arrival meant that the crisis was over. Angelee sagged as all the strength melted from her body; adrenaline dissolving from her system.

"Mrs. Garvin, I'm Millicent O'Neal; Angelee and Aimee's aunt. This is my mother, Mrs. Barnes. I'm afraid that Hedda has duped my nieces into babysitting while she went out to a party."

"Well, yes, that is what I was told on the way here." Mrs. Garvin remarked sharply. "Aimee explained that Hedda had left—

with my husband's oldest nephew. Unfortunately, I have no idea as to how they met."

Grandma Barnes stood behind Angelee, placing an arm around her shoulders. "Because of Hedda's irresponsibility, our children have been in the wars today"

Aunt Milly passed Zachery over to his mother. "These cuts on his head are seeping, I'm afraid. He probably needs stitches. Is your doctor's office nearby? "

"*Our* children? What do you mean, *our* children? Zachary is the one who is hurt!" Mrs. Garvin lamented. "Charles is scared half to death. And who knows if the baby is okay! Your girls haven't got cuts and bruises!"

"Maybe not cuts and bruises. However, the care of three small children is a lot of ask of a ten-year-old and an eight-year-old." Aunt Milly stated plainly. "Now, am I driving you and Zachary to the doctor's office?"

"Ten years old?" Mrs. Garvin glared at Angelee. "You're not old enough to be in charge of babies! You're no more than a child yourself."

Despite her best effort, tears rolled down Angelee's cheeks. Dropping her head, for the first time she noticed the front of her dress was blood-covered. She looked up at Aimee, who was looking at Mrs. Garvin through narrowed eyes.

"Stop picking on my sister!" Aimee commanded. "Angelee tried to stop Hedda, but she just walked out all hoity-toity. She promised us lemonade, ice cream, and finger sandwiches. *We* didn't lie about singing or listening to pretty music. We got this dumped on us."

"I apologize, Mrs. Garvin." Grandma Barnes said. "You see, my son, Edward, only met Lavinia…Lavinia O'Keefe…about three months ago. She so totally charmed him that he rushed to marry—only a few weeks ago. Lavinia introduced us to Hedda just a week before the wedding. Hedda's gracious invitation to Angelee and Aimee seemed so generous and authentic, we agreed to it. Had we known Hedda better, we would not have allowed her to involve our girls in such a fiasco."

Grandma Barnes's words worked to calm the environment. "You go with the lad to the doctor'', and I'll make sure the others are entertained."

"Don't worry about taking me to Dr. Montgomery's; he lives right across the street. Mr. Garvin has just gone across the street to see if he is home."

Mr. Garvin walked into the house and found everyone in the kitchen. "Hello, my Little Soldier." His tenor voice comforted his youngest boy. "You and I are going over to see Uncle Thomas. I bet he'll have a nice piece of candy for you when we're done."

Mr. Garvin nodded at the others, then walked out, making sure the cloth remained in place on Zachary's head.

"I apologize for being so snappy, so rude. Please, go into the living room, and I'll make us a pot of tea. It always seems to work for the English." Mrs. Garvin went towards the cupboard.

To Angelee's surprise, Charles snuggled closer and she put her arm around him. She found solace from this little person. She rose and carried him to the other room.

Aunt Milly, commandeering the wicker baby-buggy, followed close behind.

"Are you okay, Angelee? You're shaking." Aimee observed.

"I'll be okay. Everything just…happened…so quickly. I…could…couldn't stop him… from falling." Angelee's words betrayed her.

"Angelee, I know you probably don't believe this; but you handled the situation very well. You have nothing to be ashamed of."

"But Zachary got hurt!" Angelee explained Zachary's dash to catch the cat. "If I was a good babysitter, I could have prevented it."

"Angelee, you must not blame yourself. When there are children around, there will be accidents. Even parents can't prevent children from tripping, falling, or climbing up things they fall from. I'm sure Mrs. Garvin agrees."

Grandma Barnes and Mrs. Garvin were returning from the kitchen. There was a crunch underfoot, near the end table.

"My goodness, what's that?" Grandma Barnes looked down toward where the sound came from.

"I'm so sorry." Angelee looked up, another tear escaped down her face. "It's that vase from China. It fell off and broke. When Zachary went to get up, he cut his hand on it. I'm so sorry. I just haven't had time to clear it up." Angelee took her arm away from Charles and went to get up.

"The vase? That lovely china vase?" Mrs. Garvin's laughter surprised everyone. "I bought it at the dime store. It just looks like the expensive one Mr. Garvin brought home. He wanted to compare them. The good one is over there, behind glass in the breakfront. I'll clean it up. You stay where you are."

Mrs. Garvin reappeared after a moment with a dustpan and brush. While she swept up the broken china, Grandma Barnes poured the tea.

To Angelee's cup, she added three sugar cubes. "Drink it while it's hot! The sugar will help you get your energy back."

Still feeling weak and weepy, Angelee drained the cup in one go. She felt the warmth sink down her throat and spread through her body. The sugar revived her a bit, and the shaking receded some.

As she was setting the cup back on the coffee table, she heard giggling coming from the front door. She heard the spring on the screen door creak again, and a male voice joined in the laughter.

Hedda and Marshall stepped foot into the lounge--meeting Mrs. Garvin as she came in from the kitchen.

"Oh my Goodness! What's going on here?" Hedda quipped lightly. "I didn't think you were back until later this evening. You know, after you and Mr. Garvin had enjoyed dinner out?"

Every set of eyes were on Hedda and for a full minute, silence reigned.

"Mr. Garvin and I were compelled to return home early. He's is over at Dr. Montgomery's with Zachary. It transpires our youngest son needs stitches in his head, and maybe his hand."

"Really?" Hedda turned pale. "Well, mercy, how unfortunate. Really, Angelee, I did say if you thought it was too much, I would stay too."

"You're lying!" Aimee retorted. "You lured us here with the guarantee of music, fancy food, and drinks. Then you didn't even ask us if we wanted to help you. You just sashayed out the door like we were your slaves. All you cared about was seeing him!" Aimee pointed toward Marshall.

Marshall turned pale, running his finger around his shirt collar. "I had no idea about any of this."

Hedda broke into pretend tears, covering her face with her hands. "That poor boy. Do you think he'll have a scar?"

"Stop that nonsense!" Mrs. Garvin said, recognizing Hedda's amateur dramatics. "If he does, it will just give him character. He's a boy." Mrs. Garvin said, matter-of-factly; fire burning in her eyes.

"Well, Angelee always seems so responsible." Hedda defended her actions. "I had no idea that she couldn't be trusted on her own. And I let Aimee help. With two of them and only three babies, nothing should have gone wrong." Hedda objected. She wiped at theatrical tears.

"Hedda, the truth is that Angelee is a ten-year-old, and Aimee is eight." Grandma Barnes said. "You are sixteen-and-a-half. According to the girls, you were the one who made the arrangements to bring them here. That means it was your responsibility to make sure the youngest ones were safe. You didn't do that."

Hedda rolled her eyes, flung her hands outward as if shaking off unseen water. "But just last night Angelee told me that she loves being around little kids. She likes to play with them and read to them. So, I figured she would enjoy playing with these kids. Especially if Aimee came with her."

"Is that true?" Grandma Barnes asked Angelee.

"Yes, but she asked if I liked kids. I told her it was at church that I helped with the little kids. You know, during Sunday school. There are always adults around. I didn't know she was asking me to babysit today."

"Well, it's still not my fault!" Hedda whined. "I thought the babies would be asleep. I didn't know Angelee would let them get hurt."

"Mrs. Garvin, what, if anything, can Hedda do to make this right?" Grandma Barnes asked.

"You can't do that!" Hedda snapped.

"I can't do what?" Asked Grandma Barnes, staring Hedda in the eye.

"You have no authority over me. Only my mother does. She doesn't let anyone else—and I mean *anyone else*--discipline me. Don't try to make me apologize or enforce some sort of consequences. I won't have it."

Mrs. Garvin answered Hedda's challenge. "I may not be able to slap your face or restrict your social activities. But I can say who is allowed—even welcome—in this house. And from now on, Miss

Hedda O'Keefe, you are not welcome. I will not have you in this house.

"Marshall, albeit that you are my husband's nephew, if you chose to play naïve to manipulative, selfish young women, who are as seductive as snake charmers, you are no longer allowed to cross our threshold. I won't have you around to influence my sons. Do I make myself clear?"

Marshall dropped his gaze to the floor, abashed by his Aunt's tongue-lashing. "Yes, Ma'am"

Despite feeling shaky, Angelee spoke. "Mrs. Garvin, I am so sorry that Zachary got hurt. I just couldn't get to him in time. He was after your cat when his foot got caught up in that rug."

"I want to apologize too." Aimee volunteered. "Because you said it was okay, I went outside with Charles. He wanted to swing. We thought it would be okay. As soon as I heard yelling, I came running. I brought Charles with me, of course. He was very brave. He helped us as best he could."

"What do you mean?" The child's mother asked, leaning forward.

Angelee explained. "I took Zachary straight into the kitchen, so I could get him next to some cold water. We didn't know where to find things. Charles answered our questions and did the little errands we asked. Like rolling the baby buggy into the kitchen and getting her clean clothes. He was a calm little trooper! You should be very proud of him."

"It was good thinking of yours, to have all the children together while Aimee went for help." Aunt Milly said.

"Hedda, you think what you want." Grandma Barnes warned. "But I can assure you, at some point, your deceitful ways will catch up to you. Even if your mother accepts your explanation of events this time, at some point the truth will come out. We will have a family meeting—because you chose to involve Angelee and Aimee. But we have caused enough disruption to the Garvins for today. Millicent and I are driving the girls home. For your sins, you will have to walk home—not that it is far."

Angelee was very thirsty and wished for another cup of tea. But she managed to find the energy to stand up.

"Angelee, Aimee, I want you to know that I appreciate your apologies. However, there is nothing to forgive. I do not blame you for the accidents. Not many girls of ten and eight would have fared so well as you did today."

The screened front door squealed on its hinges again. Mr. Garvin walked into the room, carrying a sedate, tired toddler. Bandages swathed Zachary's little head and his injured hand. The sweet in his mouth drooled onto his chin.

"I'm glad you haven't left yet. Dr. Montgomery said that the person who treated Zachary did exactly the right thing. He double-checked for any glass in the hand, but it had been cleaned very well. That hand needed three stitches. The forehead got seven. The doctor said he should rest now—but not go to sleep for a couple of hours. We have to watch out for a concussion. He can, however, go to bed early. I want to thank you girls for acting so quickly."

Angelee nodded. "Daddy taught us first aid. I just did what he taught us." Angelee said.

Aunt Milly, Grandma Barnes, and the girls walked out the front door, saying good-bye as they went.

Once home, Angelee went upstairs to change her clothes. As she removed the dress, she was once again confronted by the blood that smeared the whole bodice of the garment. The blood had seeped through to her corset cover.

The whole incident replayed in her mind. Anxiety, inadequacy, and frustration rolled over her like an ocean wave. She collapsed onto the floor, sobbing. Her gut-wrenching sobs must have been heard; loving hands pulled her into comforting arms--Aunt Milly's. Angelee was changed into a nightgown and put to bed.

Shaken to her core, she vowed to never allow herself to be close to very young children again. She just knew they would get hurt. And she wouldn't be able to live with that.

Olivia reached across the bed and squeezed Angelee's hand. "My Dearest Friend of All Time, that explains why you distance yourself from the children at church and why you also look so longingly at them."

"I do enjoy watching them. Especially when they do the cutest things."

"Well, last night was not a cute thing," Olivia remarked. "It's left me with all kinds of questions. It's like somebody took their boulder-sized expectations and dropped them on my chest. Do my parents want me to become a doctor? Do *I* want to become a doctor? Is this a new direction from the Lord? Will I dishonor Him if I don't want to do this? I just don't know." Olivia sighed.

"Well, as much as I dread it, I know that talking with my parents is the only way to move forward." Angelee

"Before we think about forward, I have a question about backward. What happened with Hedda?" Olivia toyed with a strand of her waist-long hair that she'd pulled around.

"Grandma pretended that she had a special bit of news for the family. Calling us into the living room after dinner, Grandma provided a round of wine for the adults—even Hedda. But I think that was to lull Hedda into a false sense of security.

"Usually Aimee and I weren't included in these serious family meetings. Grandma insisted because we were directly affected by Hedda's behavior. Once settled in our seats Grandma Barnes laid everything out on the table.

"First, Hedda disguised her true intentions to us. Misrepresentation with ulterior motives is lying—and the Barnes Family could not and would not tolerate liars. The lies had led to a small child being critically injured, and put the lives of two other young children, besides Aimee and me, in harm's way. Grandma did not appreciate her grandchildren being in distress. For an elderly woman, this could cause a heart attack.

"Grandma said she resented being put into the position where she must reprimand not only a sixteen-year-old young woman for her irresponsible behavior but must also address the mother's obvious indulgence of the young lady. Therefore, Lavinia and Hedda should carefully consider how they were going to behave.

"Grandma said she did not believe in divorce. But she saw annulment as a viable option; such as in circumstances when a bride misrepresents herself and her family, to push for a hasty marriage. Everyone else just sat there, stunned. It seemed like a long time—but was probably only a few minutes. Finally, Uncle Edward apologized for his wife's behavior and the trouble Hedda had caused before he excused himself and Lavinia. Hedda went with them."

"Aimee and I were there for another week. During that time Hedda left us alone. Ironically, Mrs. Garvin invited Grandma, Aimee, and me over for strawberry shortcake, ice cream, and cherry cordial. We played with the little boys, pushed them on the swing in the back yard, and had a lovely afternoon."

"When we finished our two-week visit, Daddy came down to bring us home. We later learned that Lavinia had sent Hedda off to a boarding school. I have no idea where she went after that. But when I saw Uncle Edward and Lavinia here, I was worried that Hedda might be here too."

"So, what about Lavinia? How are things with her now?" Olivia got out of bed, opened her small suitcase, and pulled out her hairbrush. She climbed back into bed and began tending her tangled tresses.

"Now that is interesting. Aunt Milly was an agent of grace. Shortly after Daddy brought me and Aimee home, Aunt Milly's furlough ended. She went back to Costa Rica to work at the mission. She wrote to Lavinia. In her letters, Aunt Milly explained that to become part of a family, people needed to become acquainted with each other. The correspondence included family history-- growing up with Uncle Edward, and being twins with Mommy. Lavinia stopped avoiding Grandma Barnes and made a concerted effort to be a good wife to Uncle Edward.

"After a few months, Aunt Milly inquired about Lavinia's faith— did she have a personal belief in Jesus Christ? Those letters were a turning point with Lavinia and our family. Of course, I learned all this from the letters Mommy read to me from Aunt Milly."

"So, Lavinia is okay, but no one has any idea as to Hedda?" Olivia wanted to clarify.

"I think that sums it up nicely. Once Hedda turned eighteen, she left the school and went off on her own."

"It seems weird that you'd be worried about her showing up now. Wouldn't she be close to thirty now?" Olivia asked, bemused.

Angelee laughed at her own ridiculousness. She shrugged and nodded her head.

"Changing the subject, why don't you take a bath first?" Angelee suggested.

"That does sound good," Olivia remarked, tying off the end of her second braid.

Unspoken prayers and questions swirled in her mind as she made up the bed and moved into her own room. "God, I've believed in you since I was a child. The Bible says if I honor my parents, things will go well with me. But if I refuse to attend Wellesley, isn't that dishonoring them? I am just so confused."

Olivia came to Angelee's room to dress. Angelee hurried through her own bath.

"I love hot water. It's always so soothing." Angelee said.

"After a bath, I feel relaxed," Olivia said; tying her lace-up boots. "Since it's still quiet, I'm going home. It will be less awkward for everyone."

"So, you're forsaking me in my hour of need?" Angelee teased as she hastily dressed.

"I would hardly say that. After all, I have to face my parents. I could say that you are allowing me to face the judge and trial without support as well." Olivia remarked, with a half-grin.

"Point taken. Have you gotten everything? And are you sure you don't want to stay for dinner?" Angelee entreated.

Olivia's gaze took in the room, checking for things to take home. "Well, if I have forgotten anything it isn't like I'm going away to Siberia. Well, as of right now I'm not. The post-trial conversation will determine the verdict."

Despite herself, Angelee laughed out loud. "It's good to know we've still got our sense of humor. I'll walk you to the door." Dressed, but still barefoot, Angelee followed her best friend down the stairs.

Angelee stood on the porch, watching Olivia walk across the street between their homes. Angelee prayed that Olivia would have the wisdom to know what to say to her parents.

Back up in her room, Angelee took out the hard-backed journal. She needed to write down her thoughts, to organize her defense. The minutes sped by as her pencil recorded ideas and feeling spilling from her troubled mind.

Hearing the front door open and the family return, fear, and anger bubbled up. Angelee knew that the meal would be an uncomfortable ordeal, with so much unspoken. Yet, she knew their Sunday routine would be followed. Hiding in her room was cowardly and pointless.

Angelee came out of their room, meeting Aimee at the top of the stairs. To Angelee's surprise, Aimee pointed her finger toward the bedroom. Angelee retraced her few steps into the room, followed by Aimee, who shut the door behind her.

"Can you unbutton me?" Aimee blurted, turning her back to Angelee.

"Some greeting!" Angelee smirked. "So why did you head me off at the pass?"

"So, you could unbutton me, of course." Aimee giggled. "Well, that and to let you know how things went at church today. Everyone was wondering about you. It was a bit weird though; because Mrs. Parkham was not there either."

"Really? Last night I think she was expecting a jubilant expression of gratitude from Olivia and me."

"When you suddenly left, it not only ended the party but embarrassed Mrs. Parkham, the Biers and Mommy and Daddy. Do you think Olivia is in trouble too?" Aimee shucked off her Sunday-best dress, opened the closet, and took out an everyday dress.

"I hope not. Of course, she'll have to explain why she had such an intense reaction to Mrs. Parkham's offer. She's like me, afraid of hurting her parents' feelings. I do know she's confused by 'That Woman's' announcement.   Especially when she's never, ever, talked about becoming a doctor."

"Did she sneak home already?" Aimee asked.

"You could say that. But what about Mommy and Daddy?" Angelee probed.

"Nobody has said a word about it all day. At least not to each other. They just kept telling people at church that you had a bad reaction to something that you ate."

"Aimee, I'm truly sorry that they are upset. But I don't want to go to Massachusetts. "

"I don't want you to go either, truth be told."

"We'd better go down now. At least Alistair will be hungry. Oh, by the way, Pauley said he'd come over this evening. He thinks you might need cheering up." Hugging, the sisters reassured each other.

"Great! Good ole' Pauley!" Angelee mumbled.

They joined the family in the dining room. Aside from singing the doxology together, there was no conversation. The uncommon silence, broken by the sound of cutlery on plates, persisted through to dessert.

"Alistair, Mee-Mee, I know it is not your turns. But will you please help with dishes now?" Aunt Milly suggested as she finished a piece of cake from the previous evening.

Grumbling, Alistair excused himself from the table and headed toward the kitchen. "Can I wash?"

"Fine with me." Aimee stood and began collecting the half-empty serving bowls before going to the kitchen.

"It's time we talked about last night." Daddy said, looking at Angelee, hurt emanating from his eyes. "Let's go to my office."

Angelee looked at Drew, who was drinking coffee. His wink-and-a-nod encouraged her.

Following Daddy and Mommy into Daddy's home office, she felt unsettled, anxious--because she was angry with them. She could never remember a time when she'd felt negative feelings towards her parents. Her heart raced, and she trembled from the emotional storm brewing in her heart and mind.

Pulling the chair from behind the desk and placing it next to the chair used by patients, her father sat down. He crossed one leg over the other, then crossed his arms across his chest. Her mother sat erect, her hands folded in her lap, occupied the patient chair.

Angelee took the other, crossing her arms as if preparing for battle. She looked from her father to her mother. She felt the accusations from their expressions.

"We'd like you to explain to us what happened last night?" Daddy said, pursing his lips.

The overwhelming urge to cry swelled up, tightening her throat. Angelee cleared it and said, the first thing that came to her mind. "Me? I had no idea about that scheme! What did you expect me to do? Jump up and down like a five-year-old being told I'm going to Grandma's for a vacation?"

"Watch your tone, Angelee." Daddy cautioned. "You might have been surprised. But you certainly over-reacted."

Angelee clenched her teeth, trying to control the heat rising in her chest. "Overreacting? How can you call it over-reacting when someone--who is _only_ my employer--conspires behind my back with *my parents* to organize my life without even asking *ME*? And then announce it publicly—without so much as a hint to me. "

"Angelee Darling, we were led to believe that going to Boston and studying at Wellesley was something you wanted," Mommy explained gently.

"Well, then she only presented to you what she wants me to do." Angelee spat out. "Did it *not* occur to you that you should ask *me*? You know how much I hate situations that are 'bait and switch'. Especially when the result is that I'm misrepresented." Angelee could sit no longer, rising from the chair, she began pacing.

"How do you think she misrepresented the situation?" Daddy leaned forward in his chair.

"What precisely did Mrs. Parkham say to convince you both that I would want to go to Massachusetts?" Angelee parried.

"Mrs. Parkham came to us with a suggestion, relating that she'd had several conversations with you regarding Wellesley," Mommy said. "Your feedback made her believe that you would do very well there. You complimented the school saying 'It sounds like a beautiful place for women to study.' She observed that no matter what you were asked, you always agreed to it. She thought you were a wise young woman, deferring to the wisdom of her elders. Based on these observations, she was willing to sponsor your education at Wellesley. She said she wanted the best for you because you had proven to be so helpful to her."

Angelee resumed sitting and chewed her lower lip. "Mrs. Parkham brought up Wellesley every single day I met with her. Wellesley was the only women's college to raise sufficient money to buy an ambulance for the war effort. Wellesley is the Alma Mata of an architect, Eleanor Raymond; songwriter Katherine Lee Bates. Then there is Helen Barret Montgomery, the famous social activist and fund-raiser for foreign missions. How wonderful it would be if all young women could attend Wellesley. And of course, I had to reply to all her bragging. It didn't occur to me that she was trying to sell me on an idea. But she never once asked me if I was interested in attending."

"Mrs. Parkham is a passionate woman, Angelee. It only makes sense that she would want to recommend someplace that prepares young women to make a difference in the world. She sees you as someone with great possibilities and wants you to experience the highest level of instruction and training." Daddy reasoned with Angelee.

Instead of calming her, his words angered her more. "Right, and of course, all I have to do is overlook being betrayed by my parents, and manipulated by my employer."

"Angelee Giselle!" Her father barked. "How dare you accuse your mother and me of betraying you. How can you say Mrs. Parkham is guilty of manipulating you?"

"None of you…" Angelee paused and pointed a finger at her parents, "…none, took the time to talk to me, to ask ME what I wanted." She poked her chest for emphasis. "Was I interested in moving to the East Coast? Was studying at Wellesley an ambition of MINE? Did I want to become Mrs. Parkham's full-time assistant? No, it's such a wonderful idea that we'll surprise her and announce it to the whole world. And because it's in front of her friends and family, she won't say no. She's so compliant, just one little word from Mommy and Daddy, Angelee will be heading east— just because they say so." Tears rolled down her cheeks.

"I've been trying to figure out just want my life is supposed to be about—to find that 'I-was-born-to-do-this' purpose. …Only I haven't found it yet…. So, rather than allow me time… to explore…and discover…my parents made decisions for me. … How can I become an adult…learn to make my own decisions……if they won't ask me what I want? You would *never* have done that to Andrew Jr." She used Drew's full name to emphasize her point.

Her parents remained silent and looked at each other. They looked back at her, with sudden understanding in their eyes.

"Another thing…you asked me how Mrs. Parkham misrepresented things. She actually made you believe it was my idea to study in Massachusetts. It wasn't. And she has thrown Olivia into a tizzy as well. Why would she presume that Olivia should become a doctor?"

"When I was ten years old, Hedda O'Keefe enticed me, and Aimee, into going with her, based on false premises and empty promises. At ten you can be tempted with ice cream, cake, and cookies. Not only did we not get to attend the party, but we also had to contend with a dangerous situation. I haven't trusted myself to be around children on my own since." Angelee explained. "I know the circumstances are different. But this time I feel like those people who were supposed to support and protect me let me down. And not only that, my best friend got hurt by the fiasco."

Though no longer charged with anger, awkwardness filled the atmosphere. Angelee blew her nose, then found a spot on the floor at which to stare. She wanted her parents to understand and appreciate that her disappointment with them was based on treating her as though was still a child. She wanted to be guided into adulthood, not pushed into an untenable position.

"We're sorry, Angelee," Mommy spoke softly, breaking the silence.

"Daughter, Angelee," Daddy's voice deepened as he addressed her. "Your mother and I have always taught you to apologize when you're wrong. We've always taught you to tell the truth. Today you have. We see we were wrong to not consult with you—and Olivia— first. However, Mrs. Parkham thought it would be a wonderful surprise."

"Daddy, Mommy, I appreciate your apology. But one thing I know about Mrs. Parkham; she likes to be the Queen Bee. If she can do something that makes her look magnanimous to the public, she will. Yesterday was our graduation, our birthdays, our party. I thought it was generous of her to volunteer help for the party. Had Olivia and I reacted the way she wanted us to, all the attention would have been on Mrs. Parkham. *'Wow! What a fantastic woman she is!'* She hadn't reckoned on us having such a negative and dramatic reaction."

Daddy rose from his chair, walked over to Angelee, pulling her up from the chair. He wrapped an arm around her.

"When we called you up here, we expected an apology. After hearing your side of the equation, we understand how you and Olivia felt cornered. Once again, we are sorry." Daddy said.

Angelee leaned into her father. He was a man who was unafraid of confrontation. Equally, he was a man who valued and embraced reconciliation and peace. For this, she loved and respected him.

"After working with Mrs. Parkham for two summers, I know she means well. I know she's helped other people. I also know that not having children of her own was a disappointment for her. She talks a lot about leaving a legacy. But I am *your* daughter. And I already have 'two' mothers. I can't deal with the idea of another one. I hope you understand."

Mommy smiled at Angelee's reference to Millicent. "Yes, you do rather have two for the price of one with Aunt Milly here."

"What about tomorrow, Angelee?" Her father asked. "I think Mrs. Parkham is expecting you to start working with her tomorrow."

"I've already decided that I want to look for a local job. I've put in my application at the library. But I will go over tomorrow. But I am also going to let her know how angry I am with her—for all the good that may do."

"Angelee, I know how you feel about Wellesley." Her father began. "However, I do agree with Mrs. Parkham. That college has a fantastic reputation. I don't want you to discard the idea completely out-of-hand. This is June and the classes don't start until September. Leave your mind open to the possibility. We can't demand you to go. Just don't make a knee-jerk decision, there is the possibility that you'll regret it later."

Mommy came, placing her arm around Angelee's waist. "I agree with your father. I know that Mrs. Parkham regards you highly. My advice is that you tell her that you will think about it for a while and get back to her later."

Angelee thought about protesting but appreciated her parents were providing a sound reason. "But I have no idea as to what I would study. It just doesn't seem right to spend someone else's money if it is going to be wasted."

"Let it rest for now," Mommy said. "One more thing about last night."

Angelee looked up, alarmed with the idea of more unfortunate news.

"We had a table set up for gifts. The idea was that you would open them at the party so you could thank your guests immediately. We brought all the presents here. Go next door and tell Olivia. You'll want to open them and get your thank you notes done as soon as possible."

"Thanks, Mommy. I'm sorry things ended so abruptly. It was beautiful—the decorations, the food, the music. I do appreciate all the hard work."

"We should pray together." Daddy said.

Joining hands, they gave thanks for grace, forgiveness, and love. Her mother embraced her tightly, and as she wrapped her arms around her father's neck, she leaned into his chest. The tension lifted when Daddy encircled her waist, ad lifted her off of the floor. Angelee giggled, rejoicing in the playful affection.

Angelee left the room, looking forward to catching up with Olivia later in the evening. But she knew she still had to address Mrs. Parkham the next day; a task she did not relish.

After dinner, a much more convivial meal than lunch had been, Angelee sauntered onto the porch, gravitating toward the swing, like iron to a magnet, then eased onto the wooden resting place.

Hours from setting, the warm June sun remained bright. Pushing the swing, Angelee waited for Olivia to come over and report. Having forgotten to bring a book to read, and loathed to move, Angelee dismissed the idea of reading.

Instead, she watched robins swoop by. A couple of ruby-throated hummingbirds hovered by the bird feeder. An orange tabby cat, known to live down the street, sat in the middle of the sidewalk, grooming himself. The Winkelmanns, who lived across the street and four houses down, were also out on their porch. They returned Angelee's wave.

Through the open window, Angelee heard the grandfather clock strike six o'clock. Pauley pulled his Underslung Scout up next to the curb and parked. Preoccupied with thoughts of the meeting with her parents, Angelee had forgotten about Pauley's visit.

Weary from the emotional ups-and-downs of the past days, she didn't budge from the seat. Instead, she gave him a general wave. Pauley waved back, before extracting himself from the car. He leaned into the vehicle, picking up something, and hid it behind his back as he turned. A straw boater shielded his eyes from the sun. He'd rolled his shirt sleeves up to his elbows, relaxed and casual. With long strides he covered the distance of the sidewalk, disturbing the cat as he went.

Seeming pleased with the world, Pauley whistled a popular song. "Did Aimee tell you I was coming?"

"Yes, Mee-Mee did warn me of your intended arrival." Angelee grinned.

"I wanted to see how you're doing. I was very concerned when I left here last night."

"When help is needed, Aunt Milly is the best." Angelee cocked her head. "No teasing, jeering, or remonstrations?"

"Angelee," Pauley's spoke softly, reproachfully. "You know me better than that."

With a flourish, Pauley presented his colorful surprise, then settled on the porch swing beside her. "I thought these would cheer you up."

"Sorry, I do know you better." She acknowledged, regretting her gibe.

The bouquet of Black-eyed Susans brought a smile to her face.

"You've been bringing me these since I turned sixteen." She laid them on her lap. "Forgive me for the snipe; I'm feeling a bit defensive. I'm going to have to answer the same questions over and over and over again. Maybe I should just write an article for the Daily Reporter." Angelee quipped.

"So, who was the weaver of this net of humiliation for you— well actually for everyone?" Pauley invited Angelee to unburden herself.

Angelee reiterated the conversation she'd had with her parents. She could understand Mrs. Parkham's motivations were meant to be seen as kindness, generosity, and appreciation. Would her party guests consider her actions dramatic, attention-seeking? How would they know that she and Olivia had been taken totally unaware?

Pauley stopped the rocking and stretched his legs out, resting them on the Old Hickory footstool. Lacing his fingers, he rested his them on his stomach.

"My biggest concern is that Olivia and I are thought of as ungrateful," Angelee confessed. "I know Olivia is very confused. But we're not ungrateful."

"Should I imply at this point that you are ungrateful?" Pauley pressed gently.

"Ungrateful? Maybe…I don't know. Am I resentful? Let's say that I am choosing to forgive. After all, no one meant any harm. But to be honest, I'm still cross: cross with feeling exposed and vulnerable, cross with people presuming they can make decisions for me."

"Understandable and justifiable. Changing the subject, is there any of that cake left from last night?"

"I don't know. I'd say, 'let's go check' but I'm expecting Olivia over in a while."

"Oh yes, Olivia Biers-Tilson, who knows to come in, and more than likely where to find us." Pauley quipped.

Angelee gently back-handed him on the arm. "Why did you say Biers-Tilson?"

Pauley rolled his eyes, pretending exasperation. "Come on— you two are always together. If you aren't at her house, she's here. Of course, that makes you Angelee Tilson-Biers." Pauley laughed as she backhanded him again.

"The same could be said of you, Pauley Alexander Bannister. It's like having an extra brother in the house!" Angelee taunted.

"Touché!" Pauley said, reaching down, taking her hand pulled her up, making the swing undulate as he got up. "Come on, to the kitchen Little Miss!" He.

Knowing Pauley was correct about Olivia, she allowed herself to be navigated into the kitchen. Aunt Milly was already there, sitting at the small desk, reading a recipe book.

"Hello, Mrs. O'Neal. Finding another culinary temptation recipe for this bustling family?" Pauley quipped.

"Well, Pauley B! I'm glad to see that you survived last evening's hoopla." Aunt Milly replied. "Let me guess, here for cake?"

"She knows me too well!" Pauley jerked his thumb in Aunt Milly's direction.

"I am sure I will know you even better when you've done right by making me your Aunt as well!" Aunt Milly laughed.

"And how would I be going about making you *my* Aunt?" Pauley countered.

"I suppose you would have to marry one of my nieces." Aunt Milly looked meaningfully at Angelee.

"Technically and logically, that would work. …" Pauley dimpled, grinning with mischief. "But ideally—would that be wise? I mean, if Aimee and Angelee only see me as an extra brother, I am afraid your ulterior motives will be disappointed."

Angelee rolled her eyes, dropped her shoulders, and shook her head. "You two are just…just…ridiculous!"

Aunt Milly and Pauley laughed together as if they knew a secret.

"*IS THERE CAKE?*" Angelee persisted. "If so, where can I find it?"

"I'll get it." Aunt Milly rose from the desk and went into the pantry. She returned with a cake tin.

"I thought I'd find you here! Especially when I saw Pauley's car." Olivia entered the kitchen, still looking tired.

"Hey! Are you insinuating that all I care about is food?" Pauley pretended disgust, his hands resting on his lean hips.

"Well, you know what they say—if the fork accommodates, eat with it!" Olivia improvised.

"And here I thought the saying is 'The way to a man's heart is through his stomach.' I can see how Mrs. O'Neal caught her husband!" Pauley winked.

"You Young People!" Aunt Milly crowed. "I see trying to think about menus right now is pointless, so I will leave the kitchen to you. Aunt Milly hugged them on the way out.

Angelee Declares Independence

"Look, everyone! The first ones of the summer!" Alistair placed the white enamel basin stacked with cherry tomatoes in the center of the table.

"Those are lovely little additions to breakfast this morning," Mommy remarked, taking her place. "In another week or two we should have some large tomatoes big enough to go on bacon sandwiches."

The aroma of fried bacon and eggs, toast, and freshly brewed coffee had drawn the family to the table. Brightening sunlight poured through the sheer curtains. Walking into the dining room, Angelee pulled herself out of her reverie.

The eighteen-year-old had decided the night before she was going to make an announcement. Given the previous Saturday night's events, she was sure that the pleasant mood in the family would be quickly changed.

Filling her plate from the food on the sideboard, she sat down at the table. However, the mood was altered by the events of the outside world.

"I was reading this morning's front page before breakfast." Daddy said. "Drew, according to the paper, only men aged between 21 and 30 are required to register for the draft. That means you and Pauley are exempt."

Drew bit into his toast and nodded his head. Swallowing, he replied; "I know. But Pauley and I are thinking of enlisting to be in the medical corps."

"Don't be too hasty in making that decision, son."

"We've just thrown the idea around. We're back to Butler this morning for our last week of term." Drew asked, before taking a bite of eggs.

"Concentrate on that for the time being." Mommy encouraged. "Does that mean you're not going to work at Grassyfork this summer?

"Actually, no. Mr. Biers caught up with me Saturday night and told me he has a position for me over at the cooperage if I want it. But no decisions about anything else until next week."

"Mee-Mee, what are your plans for occupying yourself today?" Daddy directed.

"I thought I'd go over to the White Star café and see if Mrs. Davis needs some help this summer. I've been helping Aunt Milly with the baking. I might have enough skills to help Mrs. Davis. It would be mornings, so I'd have time in the afternoons to take more art lessons with Mr. Torrington."

Alistair laughed and nearly choked. Recovering from his sputtering, he quipped. "Mee-Mee up and alert in the morning! Now that would be miraculous!"

Everyone laughed, including Mee-Mee. "I know, but it's only for the summer."

"Give her credit for putting herself to the challenge." Aunt Milly encouraged.

"And Alistair, what is on the docket for you today?"

"Thanks to Aunt Milly, I've been volunteered to help Mrs. Schufflebarger weed her vegetable garden. After that, I thought I'd go over to Roy's house and see the puppies. Speaking of puppies, could I have one?"

Daddy looked at Mommy, raising his eyebrows. Mommy tilted her head and pursed her lips.

"Your mother and I will discuss it, and then let you know." Daddy hedged. "You're going to have to wait for an answer. But don't pester us, because that is a sure way for the answer to become 'no'."

Alistair dropped his shoulders and sighed. "Okay."

"Mommy, Daddy, there's something you should know," Angelee spoke up. "Last night I made a decision. I'm going to tell Mrs. Parkham that I am not working for her this summer. I'm going over after breakfast to let her know. Then I'm going to go look for a new job."

"What?" Mommy snapped. "Just like that?"

"Angelee, you have a commitment to her." Daddy remonstrated.

"Actually, all of you have just presumed that I would work for her this summer." Angelee countered. "No one seems to think I needed to be consulted about it. Her letters never *asked* me if I wanted to help her this summer. Nor did she write, asking me to confirm that I agreed to be her companion again. I want to look for a permanent job here in Martinsville. And this week is reserved by employers for recent graduates to apply for jobs. If I wait until the end of the summer, I may not be able to find a job here in town."

"Angelee, what about Wellesley? And getting further education?" Her father challenged. "I thought you said you would give it more thought."

"Excuse me. But I better get on with the dishes." Aunt Milly said. "Mee-Mee, Alistair, come help in the kitchen."

"I'm off too! I need to finish packing so I don't miss the interurban to Indy!" Drew stood and picked up his plate before leaving.

Angelee was now conspicuously alone with her parents.

"Daddy, we discussed this yesterday. I'm not interested in going to college. But even if I were, why would I want to go to Wellesley? There's Indiana University in Bloomington, and Indiana Central or Butler in Indianapolis. I'd want to stay close to home. But I don't want to waste money to pay for college when I have no idea as to what kind of degree I want. Another thing, wouldn't a college education a waste of money and time if I get married and have children?"

"Getting further education is never a waste." Mommy asserted. "And I believe you owe it to Mrs. Parkham to give her at least a couple of week's notice before you quit. She'll need to advertise and find a new secretary/companion." Mommy observed.

"I suppose to be fair, you're right. But I'm still quite cross with her." Angelee acquiesced.

"Remember, forgiveness is not about a feeling; it is a decision," Mommy said. "How do you expect her to cope without your help until she can get a replacement?"

"I hadn't thought that far," Angelee confessed and dropped her head. "But it is still my decision about where I work this summer."

"Girl-Number-One, I agree, it does need to be your decision— even if I don't agree with it." Daddy admonished. "However, out of respect to Mrs. Parkham, I expect you to be her assistant until you help her find a replacement. Just walking off would be childish."

Suddenly, Angelee dropped her head. "I'm sorry if I'm disappointing you."

As soon as the words left her mouth, a strong desire for independence surged up within her. Jerking her head up, she looked at each of her parents in the eye by turn. "I just can't be a little girl anymore, just doing what you tell me to do. I need to start making my own decisions. Right or wrong! I may not know what my calling is, but I want to try other things."

Mommy opened her mouth as if to say something. But she stopped when Daddy shook his head. His eyes reflected resignation and pride.

"Knowing what you don't want to do is just as important as finding what you do want to do. So, a stint in the kitchen at one of the sanitariums, or Home Lawn's laundry could be very educational. But in the meantime, the right thing to do is work for Mrs. Parkham until you procure other work."

Angelee stood, pushing her chair away from the table. "I'm due to see Mrs. Parkham at 10.00 o'clock. I'll go into town now and get her the newspaper."

After taking her dirty dishes to the kitchen, Angelee returned upstairs to collect her handbag and a sun hat. As she stepped onto the front porch, she realized Pauley was walking up the path.

"Go on in. Drew's probably expecting you. He's packing." Angelee offered forthrightly.

Pauley laughed as he stepped onto the porch. "Angeeleee, you used to be so gracious! What's with all this business-like brusqueness? I used to get at least a 'hello' and 'how-are-you?' Today it's an informational news blurb. And a presumptive one at that!"

Angelee adjusted her sun hat and stuck in a second hat pin. "Why is it presumptive?"

"Because honestly, I was coming to see you." Pauley leaned against the porch frame.

"About what?" Angelee took a step back, surprised by his remark.

"Where are you off to this morning? I'll walk with you."

"I'm going into town to buy the newspaper for Mrs. Parkham, and some stationary for myself. But you avoided my question."

"You have been on my mind—well, you're always on my mind. How are things settling down at home?"

"While I appreciate the concern, I don't want to talk about it. I just get too angry to think straight." Angelee walked down the steps and headed towards town.

Pauley nodded; a solemn expression fixed on his face. "I can appreciate that." He fell into step with her, matching his long stride to her shorter one.

"Are you going over to hide in the library later? I know you tend to gravitate to that place when you want some personal time."

Angelee stopped, looked up at Pauley, ready to give him a dressing-down if he was mocking her. Instead, she read kindness and compassion in his eyes. She couldn't understand her sudden urge to cry and jerked her gaze away. Pauley had always been like that with her—teasing one minute, kind when she needed support and sharp with her when she became pompous. It became clear just how well he knew her. In her mind, the years of growing up together crystallized the depth of friendship. A different feeling surfaced, a feeling so strong it confused, annoyed and frightened her. And she was loath to acknowledge it.

"That is a brilliant idea. But it will have to be after I finish work this afternoon. I have a feeling Mrs. Parkham and I are going to have quite an encounter." She turned and resumed walking toward town.

Thrusting his hands into his trouser pockets, Pauley resumed his casual stride. "Is that meant to be a 'happy, let's catch-up chatter' or an 'I-have-news-and-you-wouldn't-like-it' conversation?"

"You have always been an astute one, Mr. Bannister." Angelee grinned, despite herself. "Being very grown-up, I have decided to resign as Mrs. Parkham's assistant and find a job here in town. After what she did on Saturday night, I want her to know that my home is here, in Martinsville."

Pauley ran a hand across the back of his neck, seeming to ruminate on this bit of news. "Here's Phelps." He opened the door to the drug store.

Angelee walked in making quick work of selecting the stationary she required, as well as the newspaper. Pauley purchased a few items as well, including chewing gum.

"Pauley, when did you start chewing gum?" Angelee raised her eyebrows.

"Not for me! The girls wanted to try the spearmint this time. It seems that some of their school friends are totally taken by Juicy-Fruit flavor."

Pauley opened the door, and they exited out walked back onto the square. On their own again, Pauley said. "Angelee, I think Mrs.

Parkham underestimated you. I also think she did you a big disservice by not discussing her ideas with you."

"Thanks for saying that. She thought she could just get my parent's permission, and it would be all signed-sealed and delivered."

"I'm behind you one-hundred percent of the way. How's Olivia holding up?"

"Olivia has always been so sure of what she wants and of her plans. Nursing has always been her dream. Mrs. Parkham's offer to provide doctor's training—well it is a stunning proposal. It rather rattled Olivia and her parents."

"So, Olivia is considering it?"

They turned back onto Washington Street.

"I wouldn't say she's considering it, more like re-evaluating her original plans against a new possibility. She wants to make sure it's God's plan for her."

"It is wise, you know, when a circumstance suddenly presents itself—something that hasn't been considered before," Pauley remarked.

"That didn't take as long as I thought it would." Angelee nodded toward her home as they arrived at the concrete path. "Time to prepare for battle."

Pauley smiled down on her. He pushed her straw hat back and planted a little kiss on her forehead. "A little token to encourage your bravery."

"Thanks for not pulling my hat off, especially since I still have the hatpins in!" Angelee complained. "But, I do appreciate the moral support!"

"I'll be praying for you." Pauley supplied.

"Well, make sure you pray for Olivia as well. It's been an inglorious weekend in many ways!"

"Now that is a big word for a little girl." Pauley laughed. "But yes, I'd say prayers are needed all round."

Pauley strode away, whistling softly. Angelee scampered up the path and into the house. She wanted to organize her mind before her appointment with Mrs. Parkham.

Monday Morning, June 4th, 1917
Mrs. Parkham's Confrontation

Angelee rushed into the house, the screen door banging behind her. Upstairs she stowed the new stationery into a desk drawer, along with her wallet. She sat down on the bed and prayed for clear thoughts and the courage, to be honest with Mrs. Parkham.

Depositing the newspaper into her satchel, she skipped down the stairs and out of the house.

Living across the street from Home Lawn, Angelee easily recognized the daily progress made to the sanitarium. Construction workers and scaffolding didn't seem to diminish the popularity of the sanitarium. Granted, the noise ended in the evenings, so it would not affect the guests' sleep. The new wing was due to be finished by the end of the year. This meant there would be a big celebration in the guise of a Grand-reopening; something to look forward to.

On her twenty-minute-walk, Angelee inhaled scents of freshly mown grass of a neighbor's yard, the sweet perfume of wisteria and lilac bushes that she passed as she covered the six blocks to Mrs. Parkham's rented accommodation. Situated six blocks from her home, the red brick, eight-bedroom house on Harrison street sat away from the curb with young trees in the front yard.

Preparing for a battle of wills, Angelee squared her shoulders and marched up the steps. Trepidation churned with frustration and anger; an emotional concoction Angelee had never experienced before. While facing Mrs. Parkham's reaction made Angelee apprehensive, the fear of losing her temper and saying or doing something foolish equally alarmed her. Taking a deep breath, she summoned courage and prayed for calm.

Using her key, Angelee entered the house. "Hello, I'm here."

Mrs. Parkham greeted her warmly from the parlor. "Angelee, Dear Girl, do come in. I've got so much lined up to do today. And did you bring the newspaper?"

Angelee walked into the room. *'One would think nothing happened on Saturday!'* Angelee thought to herself.

"Let's have coffee before we go up to the office." Mrs. Parkham said. "Frances is preparing the tray as we speak."

Lowering onto the settee, Angelee took the newspaper from the satchel and passed it to Mrs. Parkham. Tempted to blurt out her intentions to quit, she pondered how to bring it up. At just that moment, deep within her heart, Angelee sensed that it would be better if she held her peace until the end of the day. She recognized the wisdom of God.

Frances-Raye MacKinnon, Mrs. Parkham's housekeeper-cook, carried the expected coffee tray into the room, setting it on the coffee table. Angelee silently poured the coffee into cups, adding milk and sugar to Mrs. Parkham's.

"I'm going to take mine up to the office," Angelee explained. "I want to start on the correspondence." Angelee stood, picked up the case, and carefully collected her cup and saucer.

"You're keen to get started this morning, Angelee." Mrs. Parkham raised her eyebrows. "That's one thing I've always liked about you, Angelee; not one to prattle with idle chatter. Since you seem to be such an eager beaver, are you available to meet Steffken?"

"You mean to meet him at the interurban station, the train station? What about Cameron? Isn't he here? And what time are you expecting Mr. Torrington?" Angelee hesitated.

"Cameron is in Indianapolis—left yesterday afternoon. As to Steffken, he is arriving here at the house, any time after three-thirty. I'm due for treatment at Home Lawn this afternoon."

"I suppose I can be around to welcome him home. Of course, Francis is here."

"Of course, she is, Dear. But Frances will be busy." Mrs. Parkham insisted.

Angelee retreated upstairs to the bedroom-turned-office. Looking out the window, she watched the leaves rustle in the breeze, and drank her lukewarm coffee. Porcelain didn't hold heat very long. Setting the empty cup aside, she collected the mail, sorting it into appropriate stacks.

Fifteen minutes later Mrs. Parkham arrived in the room.

Mrs. Parkham consulted the stack of letters and worked her way through the stack. Frances delivered a sandwich-centered lunch as the courthouse clock struck twelve o'clock. They interrupted the work long enough to eat and lunch was passed with perfunctory conversation—planning menus for the week, the progress of the workmen at the sanitarium, and the headlines in the *Daily Reporter* about the war.

By two o'clock the account books for Mrs. Parkham's businesses had been reconciled, cheques were written for accounts payable and correspondence was written. Angelee decided to broach the subject of finding a new job.

Breathing deeply, Angelee sat up straight. "Mrs. Parkham, I am going to look for a job here in town. As soon as I find one, I am going to resign as your assistant. I've already applied for a position at the library."

Mrs. Parkham removed her glasses and stared at Angelee. "You simply cannot do that!" Closing her eyes, she pinched the bridge of her nose "And what am I supposed to do?"

"You are going to have to place an advert in the *Reporter*," Angelee replied adamantly. "I will stay until a replacement has been found. I will even stay long enough to help train the person."

Mrs. Parkham's neck and cheeks flushed pink as she clenched her teeth. "Why are you doing this? I have been very patient with you, waiting for you to finish high school."

"And planning my future for me behind my back!" Angelee snapped. "After watching you orchestrate life for Aaron Burkhardt and Missy Harcourt, I should have realized you'd take liberties with me as well."

"How dare you question my motives and benevolence?!" Mrs. Parkham protested. "I only made the offer once I knew they were happy to consider the help."

"Right! You asked *them*, and their parents, what they wanted. You talked to them upfront. But you didn't do that with *me*. No one asked me about what MY thoughts or desires were."

Angelee heaved a sigh, forcing her voice to remain even, but firm. "Mrs. Parkham, you were presumptive to think I would fall in line with your plans, even if my parents agreed to it. I want you to know that I will not...not...be attending Wellesley in September."

"I never thought I'd see the day that *you* would be ungrateful. Especially since I've gone to so much effort." Fire flashed in Mrs. Parkham's eyes.

"Perhaps I am compliant. However, I think your plan is more about you than about me. Somehow, you took my approval of the Wellesley program as an actual interest in becoming a 'Wellesley Woman.' Maybe I haven't been forthcoming in terms of my own ideas and plans for my future. But that did not give you a license to enlist my parents in conspiring to organize my life."

"I would have never believed you could be guilty of such rudeness, Angelee." Mrs. Parkham had stood up and placed her hands on her hips. "How can you say my offer to pay your expenses to attend Wellesley is selfish on my part? I have always had your best interest at heart."

Shaking with emotions, Angelee remained seated. "Were you surprised by my reaction on Saturday night? Did you think I was overcome with joy and enraptured by your surprise announcement? Oh, I was overwhelmed alright! I was shocked and embarrassed. I felt I was being suffocated. I could not fathom the idea that you were telling everyone I was going to Massachusetts and making them believe it was my idea. How could my parents allow such a momentous announcement to be made *without* my knowledge of the scheme?"

"But that doesn't explain your implication of my selfishness." Mrs. Parkham rebuffed.

"It is selfish because;" Holding up her hand and lifting her index finger. "One, you never asked me what I wanted," Angelee added a second finger. "It was selfish because Wellesley is *your* choice, your alma mater. I am not sure I even want to go to college. But if I were, it would be close to home." She lifted her third finger. "If I remember correctly, you informed everyone that I would be your assistant after I graduated from college. *Really*?! I didn't know I'd applied for the position." The little finger rose to show point four. "Your Boston residence is supposed to be 'my home-away-from-home' during Wellesley school breaks—convenient for you. I'd want to visit my family during vacations—not hang around in Boston."

Mrs. Parkham grimaced and shifted her gaze above Angelee's head. "So, all this protestation is because I didn't talk to you about my idea?"

"In part," Angelee confirmed. "But it is also because you presupposed, I wouldn't find it a problem—that I would respond like a child when offered a prize at the fair. Put yourself in my position, Mrs. Parkham. A room filled with extended family and friends; someone you trust and appreciate stands up and says: 'Six weeks from now, Mrs. Parkham is going to China for three months!' It isn't anything you've ever voiced an interest in and not a place you'd consider going. Wouldn't you feel misrepresented, frustrated, stunned? And that's what you did to me."

Mrs. Parkham squared her shoulders and replaced her glasses. "Wellesley has an impeccable history, a wonderful reputation, and an excellent curriculum." Her voice was resolute. "You always responded so positively when I spoke of the place. I can't imagine anyone turning down an opportunity to study at such a remarkable college." Mrs. Parkham nodded just once. "You are right, my actions have always been dictated by my preferences and experience. You're being foolish to make such a quick decision about attending college in Boston. So, I am not going to accept your announcement as a final decision. I'm sure that once you give it more thought, you will come around."

"Mrs. Parkham, I warn you right now, I am not going to change my mind; not about Wellesley, or about finding another job." Angelee glanced at the clock. "It's after two-thirty. You'd better get ready for your appointment. The taxi is to arrive at a quarter to three."

"I take it you're going to stay on until Mr. Torrington arrives?" Mrs. Parkham reiterated their previous arrangement.

"Yes, I'll stay. I'm sure I'll find something to pass my time." Angelee turned her back until Mrs. Parkham left the room. She would attend to the hateful job of filing while she waited for Mr. Torrington's arrival.

Steffken Returns

At Mrs. Parkham's departure, Angelee relaxed. Deciding she wanted a glass of tea; she went to the kitchen.

Frances-Raye, a thirty-year-old working woman of Scottish descent rested her lean, five-feet-ten-inches tall form, next to the porcelain sink washing leaf lettuce. She turned and smiled at Angelee. Her spectacles laid on the shelf above the sink. "Afternoon Miss Angelee."

"How are you finding things here, Frances-Raye?" Angelee enquired, taking a glass from the glass-doored cupboard.

"I reckon I'm in a good place." Frances-Raye shook her bangs out of her face. "Mrs. Parkham knows just what she wants, and lets me know straight away if I get something wrong. But I don't mind that. Once she knows that I understand what it is she's asking for, she just leaves and lets me get on with things."

"Yes, she can be exacting—and often gets good results. But forget telling her she's wrong. She doesn't back down."

"Now Mr. Torrington, he also gets what he wants—but he's all charm and kindness." Frances-Raye smiled fondly, thinking of the Belgian.

"He is the epitome of politeness." Angelee agreed. "Do you think he comes across as insincere?"

"Oh no, not at all. I think he genuinely appreciates what people do for him."

Angelee took a pitcher from the icebox, poured tea into her glass. "I agree. My sister admires him a great deal. She chats non-stop about her lessons with him. He is due back any time now." Angelee checked the clock on the kitchen wall.

"You mark my words, Miss Angelee. Your little sister has her eye set on him—maybe even her heart."

"I sometimes think that myself. But I just pray she doesn't get too hurt if he ever leaves town. Or meets someone more his age."

"Well, for the moment, I've prepared something for his sweet tooth—got a lemon and ginger cake ready for when he gets in. He'll want that with some special coffee. Reckon he'll be bringing some special blend back from Boston."

"Frances-Raye, do you want some help?" Angelee finished her tea and set the glass down.

"Oh no, Miss Angelee. Everything is under control. You can keep me company, though."

Angelee leaned against the cabinets, chatting with about the young men reporting to the draft registration precincts, the gardens around town, and about people they knew.

"Frances-Raye, you are great company, but I want to check the 'Help Wanted' ads in the newspaper."

"Goodness, Miss Angelee, surely you aren't looking for another job? What about Mrs. P?"

"I never intended to work for her permanently; which she seems determined to believe I would. My home is here, Martinsville. My family is here, and my friends. So, I need to find a local job."

"You stick to your guns." Frances-Raye encouraged her.

Angelee thanked her and went back to the office. She laid out the newspaper on her desk, flipping to the classifieds in the back. There were several companies in Martinsville, Van Camp, Old Hickory Furniture, the local fisheries, as well as the sanatoriums. The problem was, Angelee had no idea about the kind of job she wanted. But maybe by reading the adverts, she'd figure it out.

A car horn broke the silence of the afternoon, startling Angelee. Jumping up, she crossed the room and looked out the window. A blue model Ford truck pulled into the driveway and parked. She couldn't believe that noise was Mr. Torrington's fault; it was so out of his nature.

Scampering down the steps, and out the front door, she stopped to stand on the front porch. The truck doors open. Mr. Torrington slowly exiting the truck and stood to stretch. As the horn blasted again, Angelee clasped her hand to her mouth, muffling a yelp. The driver's side door flew open and out stepped Cameron Boyer-Parkham.

"Welcome back! Did you have a good journey, Mr. Torrington?"

Mr. Torrington's broad smile and twinkling eyes revealed his genuine pleasure at seeing her. "Thank you, Mon Ami. A long, but enjoyable journey." Mr. Torrington took Angelee's hands, leaned forward, and kissed her cheeks in true French form. "Let me introduce you to my companion, Monsieur Cameron Addison Boyer-

Parkham. We met up in Indianapolis." Mr. Torrington waved his arm in the direction of the energetic stranger.

"Oh, but we've already met! He's been here since April!" Angelee refused to play along with the frivolity. However, she did laugh at their antics. "As well you both know!"

"Oui!" Laughed Mr. Torrington. "To be light-hearted on a sunny afternoon is refreshing—is it not?"

"Oh! most certainly!" Angelee giggled. "Especially after the weekend!"

"Most unfortunate end to a lovely day," Cameron remarked. "I'm sorry my Aunt Marcheline embarrassed you and Olivia. I had no inkling as to what she intended to do. If I had known, I would have done my best to prepare you. In the end, Aunt Marcheline was confounded and everyone else confused. I've been filling Steffken in on the fiasco."

"Then, I guess I had better let you two know that Mrs. Parkham and I are at odds. I told her today that I was going to look for a local job. She can't believe that I don't want to study at Wellesley or be her permanent assistant." Angelee warned.

Angelee looked from Cameron to Mr. Torrington. She suddenly felt guilty about causing them discomfort in their own home. "This is not the time or place for unhappy topics. Gentlemen, please get your luggage and come inside. I know Frances-Raye has baked something special."

"In Belgium, we would say 'Un Accueil beautiful Bienvenue!'" Mr. Torrington quipped.

"A beautiful Welcome Home indeed! Any idea what the edible goodie might be?" Cameron asked.

"I do know, but I'm not telling!" Angelee said as she helped collect the suitcases and art supplies from Mr. Torrington's truck. "Over Frances-Raye's refreshments, you can tell us about your trip to Boston," Angelee suggested.

The three left the yard and entered the house. In the back of her mind, Angelee thought she should probably go straight away. She wanted to avoid Mrs. Parkham—at least overnight.

Tuesday, June 12th, 1917
A Job Disappointment

A week had passed since the party and fall-out of the announcement. Breaking open the muffin she'd taken from the wicker bread basket, Angelee buttered it. Cool morning air blew into the dining room through open windows. This morning Aunt Milly had baked walnut-bran muffins, as well as boiled eggs to feed the family. As Angelee was pondering whether to add strawberry jam or not, there was a knock at the front door. She heard the screen door open and footsteps coming through the parlor.

"Good Morning All." Pauley sing-songed as he walked into the room.

"Pull up a chair." Mommy invited.

Pauley pulled up a chair and collected a cup of coffee.

"Thanks for the invite." Pauley grinned. He looked across the table and winked at Angelee.

Angelee half-shook her head, wondering what this new behavior from Pauley meant. Was he flirting? With her? She reached for the jam, spreading the sticky sweetness on top of the muffin. As she got some on her fingers, she licked it away.

"Why are you here?" Asked Alistair.

"Now that Drew and I have finished the year at Butler, we're going to go see Major Robinson. We want to discuss enlisting to work with the Medical Department of the National Guard." Pauley sipped the coffee.

"But you're not required by law to even sign up for the draft, let alone enlist. You and Drew are only twenty. The paper says those who must register are from twenty-one to thirty-one years old." Mommy protested.

"Mrs. Tilson, my mom said the same thing. But she also knows that if we enlist, we are more likely to get into a division to work as medics or ambulance drivers. That means we don't have to be in the infantry."

"I suppose I have to accept it, but that doesn't mean I like it," Mommy said, her eyebrows furrowed.

"Now Mommy, we know that every family in town, even the state, have young men all fired up to go fight." Daddy interjected, voicing his pride. "I heard the other day that boys of fifteen and sixteen are lying about their ages to sign up. Pauley here, and Drew, feel they have a responsibility to fight for American."

"Besides," Drew joined in. "Jesus said that when we hear of wars and rumors of war, we are not to be not terrified, because these things must come to pass. Pauley and I believe that we can best serve, by being ambulances drivers and providing help to the medical corps."

"Well, not being terrified for me is one thing," Mommy said. "But not being terrified for my son's life—and every mothers' son—is different." Mommy's eyes filled with tears. "While I will worry about you, I am proud of you both. I don't want you to violate your conscience to please me. You just have to contend with me praying more for you than I ever have before."

"I wouldn't expect anything less." Drew smiled at his mother tenderly.

"But doesn't Major Robinson work as the house doctor at the Colonial sanitarium?" Aimee asked.

"Yes, but the National Guard is like an auxiliary military force. Since war has been declared, the National Guard is now active, and he's been ordered to recruit interested young men." Pauley explained.

Drew added. "He knew we wanted to finish our course work at Butler. Even if we sign up today, we may not have to report until September for training. There seems to be a lack of supplies. Pauley and I are driving over to the Colonial, so we can go to work afterward."

"I was hoping for a lift to the studio since I've got stuff to take with me." Aimee chimed in. "Mr. Torrington says that we can have an early lesson since I'm out of school for summer vacation."

"What happened to your working at the White Star?" Alistair piped up. "I thought you were going to do lessons in the afternoon."

"She said she didn't need help right now. She hired a couple of girls who just graduated." Aimee shrugged.

"Do you want me to see about any openings in the catering department today?" Daddy offered.

"Sure! Why not?!" Aimee agreed congenially.

"I've just got to return books to the library before I 'show-up' for my duty with Mrs. Parkham," Angelee explained. But the whole truth was that she wanted to discuss the library job with the head librarian, Mrs. Johnstone.

"I'll drop you off, Mee-Mee," Drew said. "It isn't that far out of the way."

"Why don't I give you a lift Angelee?" Pauley volunteered. "Especially since we're going the same way; the Colonial is only a couple of blocks from the library."

Angelee considered a moment and decided a satchel full of books was sufficient reason to accept the offer of a lift. Popping the last bite of muffin into her mouth, and drinking the rest of her coffee she finished her meal.

"Give me a few minutes to get my stuff. I wasn't going to hurry, since the library doesn't open till eight-thirty. But it might be open already since draft registration started at seven o'clock. Come on Mee-Mee, we can't keep the guys waiting too long."

The five-minute drive to the library was extended as Pauley circled the block. Diagonally across from the library flats of red bricks laid stacked next to a building going up. Men in blue overalls and cambric work shirts mixed cement, consulted blueprints, and laid brick, guided by plumb lines.

"This construction work on the new City hall is sure making it a challenge to park today." He observed.

"There's a lot of building going on all over town," Angelee replied.

Pauley parallel-parked the car as close to the library as the construction project allowed.

"Looks like you'll have about fifteen minutes to wait for the library to open," Pauley said, checking his watch. "Are you sure you want to wait? I know how Mrs. Parkham is about punctuality."

"I told her that I was stopping by the library first. So, nothing to worry about." Angelee said, taking her satchel in one hand and her handbag in the other.

"Shall I wait here in the car?" Pauley asked. "I don't have anything to do in the library."

"You don't have to wait. Once I take out all the books, this satchel isn't heavy. It's not even half-a-mile to Mrs. Parkham's."

"Changed my mind." Pauley swung out of the car and took the satchel from Angelee.

"You don't need to do that. I'm not a weakling!" Angelee protested.

"Of course, you aren't! Not with carrying all these books. But I AM a gentleman, and like to behave in a chivalrous manner." Pauley smirked. "You wouldn't deny me that, would you?"

Angelee just shrugged and let him keep the case. They walked up the limestone steps. Mrs. Johnstone came to the door as they mounted the last step. The head librarian turned the sign to read "open" and unlocked the door.

"Well, Good Morning, Angelee!" Mrs. Johnstone chirped. "I was hoping I'd see you sometime today. Just meet me at the desk when you're finished. I've got to put these keys away." She turned and headed toward the office.

Pauley held the inner door open, allowing Angelee to go first. She crossed the floor, bathed in light from the rotunda above. Reclaiming the satchel from Pauley and she opened the clasps, unloading the books. "Well, I guess making this my first stop before going to work was a good idea."

He made a point of seeing her all the way to the front desk before he turned to go.

"I'll be outside, in the car…" Pauley said.

Mrs. Johnstone returned and began processing the books Angelee was returning.

"Mrs. Johnstone, as you know, I've been a secretary-cum-companion to Mrs. Parkham for the last two summers. But I've already told her that I'm going to look into finding another job here in town. I was wondering about the job here at the library."

The door opened and a young family came in. Mrs. Johnstone and Angelee greeted them as they crossed the circular room and into the side wings where the stacks stood.

"Leave those returns and come into my office for a few minutes." Mrs. Johnstone tilted her head toward the office door with its frosted pane.

Angelee reclaimed the satchel, flapping open, along with her purse, and followed the head librarian into the business office. Mrs. Johnstone closed the door; gesturing, to Angelee to take a chair and then sat down herself.

"Angelee, the library board met a few weeks ago. A new budget was approved, along with funds to hire another assistant. I'm so pleased that you are interested in it. However, the board insisted that the person hired must have a college degree in either Library Science or English."

Angelee stood up, collected her bags, and as she reached the door, she paused. "Thanks for being honest. I suppose it makes sense to hire a college graduate."

Dejected by the news that she wasn't qualified to do the job, Angelee left the librarian's office.

As she prepared to leave the library, Mrs. Johnstone hurried after her. "Angelee, please stop for a moment."

Angelee hesitated, the empty leather bag yawning open. Waiting politely, she waited for Mrs. Johnstone to continue.

"I can see you're disappointed about the librarian position. However, we are always looking for volunteers. We want to start our summer reading sessions for the children this next week. I've seen you with the children at church. You're very good with them. Would you consider being a reader for us? It would be on Saturday mornings."

"What would I have to do?" Angelee asked, doubtful at the prospect of interacting with the children.

"You'd pick a book each week to read aloud to the children. The children sit in a semi-circle around you while you read. The group meets down in the public room." Mrs. Johnstone explained. "After reading it, you could have a question time or craft time."

"I'm sorry Mrs. Johnstone, not if I have to handle a group of young children by myself."

"Oh no, the mothers will be in the room as well." Mrs. Johnstone reassured. "I don't need an answer right now. Actually, if you can come by this Saturday morning, about ten o'clock, you can observe while I do it. Then you can think about it and let me know what you think."

Now that she no longer had to work Saturday mornings for Mrs. Parkham, that time was available to her. "Okay...that's a fair enough suggestion. I'll be here Saturday morning. But I'd better get to work now."

"Thanks, Angelee. I'll see you then." Mrs. Johnstone smiled appreciatively.

Angelee couldn't seem to throw off the disappointment as she exited the front doors. Realizing that her satchel was still agape, she stopped on the steps, rested the satchel on the concrete plinths just long enough to fasten the clasps.

Pauley pulled the car up next to her and pushed the passenger door open.

"No thanks. I'd rather walk. I need to think." Angelee said.

"What happened?" Pauley persisted.

"The library board says the person for the job has to have a college degree." Angelee stood, holding handbag and satchel with both hands.

"Understood. Can you please close the door for me?" He indicated with a point toward the open car door.

Angelee suddenly acquiesced and climbed into the passenger seat, pulling the door behind her.

Wordlessly, Pauley put the car into gear and drove Angelee to her waiting responsibilities.

Sunday afternoon Angelee sauntered into the kitchen. After church, an irregular meal of sandwiches and fruit salad had been served. Late afternoon found Aunt Millie and Aimee occupying the kitchen.

"Hi! What can I do to help?" Angelee offered.

"Scoot! Out! Right now!" Aimee commanded.

"We're fine, Gee-Gee." Aunt Milly affirmed. "I have a surprise in store, so go entertain yourself till it's ready."

Retreating upstairs, she tapped softly on her parent's closed bedroom door. She waited for a response. A closed-door meant her parents wanted privacy. Her mother's voice invited her in.

"Is this a good time, Mommy?" Angelee opened the door far enough to stick her head around.

"I was just writing a letter to your Grandmother. I was banned from the kitchen."

"I was too. Very mysterious." Angelee smiled. "We really do have to watch those two!"

"Come on in, if you want to. I can finish this later."

Angelee entered and closed the door behind her. Sitting on the end of the bed, next to her mother's desk, she breathed in the peace.

"Goodness, Gee-Gee that is a deep sigh. What's on your mind?" Her mother screwed the lid back on her fountain pen and set it aside.

"When I come in here, it feels so peaceful. I wish I knew how to feel peaceful, no matter what's happening."

Mommy laughed. "So do I, but that just isn't normal. Our emotions can be as changeable as the weather on a spring day. What makes you say that?"

"Lots of things, to be honest. The war has been surreal because it's only been about Europe. At church this morning, seeing the men dressed in their Army uniforms made it feel tangible. Drew and Pauley enlisted on Friday. I'm afraid for them."

"I don't know anyone who isn't afraid of what this war means, Girl-Number-One. Drew and Pauley have always felt very strongly about fulfilling their responsibilities."

"Pauley asked me to join him for ice cream, this evening. He said there's something he wants to talk about. He didn't give me a clue as to what that would be. I'm just kind of intrigued."

"Just the two of you?" Mommy asked.

"Drew and Olivia are joining us."

"I guess you can go," Mommy said.

"Mommy, I'm eighteen now. When do I stop asking permission for these kinds of things and decide for myself? I know Drew is a guy, but you allowed him to make his own decisions when he was thirteen or fourteen."

Mommy looked down at her hands for a moment, then looked up at her daughter. "Things are always different for men and women. That's why women in Indianapolis and around the country are fighting for the right to vote, for equality. More women are going to college. As your parents, we feel that it is our responsibility to protect you. That's all we want to do—protect you."

"But Mommy, I need to make my own decisions. What if I never get married? I can't be expected to depend on you and Daddy the rest of my life."

"That is exactly why we want you to take advantage of Mrs. Parkham's offer to study at Wellesley. We know she would be nearby to look out for you. And Wellesley is one of the best women's colleges in the country."

Frustration rolled around Angelee's chest, tempting her to storm out of the room. "Mommy, please don't push it."

"Angelee, you do need to think about it," Mommy said gently.

"It's a sore point with me, right now. Can we just leave it?" Angelee slid off of the bed and walked to the door.

"Don't be late for 'the dinner'," Mommy replied.

Restlessness inspired an impromptu walk. Angelee found the pair of sneakers she'd purchased for herself as a graduation present. She pulled socks onto her bare feet, put on the rubber-bottomed shoes.

A couple of minutes later she ran up the steps at the Biers family home, where Olivia sat in a wicker chair on the front porch.

"Hi! Have a seat." Olivia indicated to the empty one next to the table.

Dropping down unceremoniously, Angelee replied. "Thanks! I suddenly find that I have time on my hands. Feel like joining me for a short walk?"

"Sure—why not! Trying out your new sneakers?" Olivia laughed gently.

"Yep! So, where should we go?" Angelee quipped.

"Let's walk over to the high school. Maybe there's a baseball game." Olivia suggested. "Be right with you!" She went into the house to get a hat and let her parents know about the walk.

When Olivia came back out, they skipped down the steps.

"Olivia, do you have to ask permission to go places and do things? Or do you just let your parents know what you're doing?"

"My Oma Biers thinks girls should always ask for permission to go to places and do things, while boys are allowed to go freely. 'They must become men, and be independent.' But my parents allow me a bit more freedom. I have to tell them where I'm going, when I'm going, when I expect to get back, and what the event is. They've always made it clear that if I lied to them, then they would become very strict."

"That's what I thought. You know my parents; they treat me like I'm still ten years old. Mommy says they are trying to shield me. Don't they trust me?"

"Gee-Gee, of course, they trust you."

"It sure doesn't feel like it." Angelee lamented. "Oh well, at least I know they care."

A group of children was playing pitch and hit, but there was no baseball game. The girls walked along Ohio street, waving to people sitting out on their porches. Youngsters played hide-and-seek or hop-scotch, their laughter and shouting carried along on the breeze. Finishing their stroll, Angelee left Olivia beside her home and jogged home.

"Did Pauley ask about going to the café tonight?" Drew asked as Angelee took her place at the table.

"Yes, and I've been over to ask Olivia as well. I reminded her we'd come by about seven-thirty."

"Good to know," Drew responded. He leaned toward Angelee. "Do you have any idea about this 'mystery meal' that Aunt Milly and Mee-Mee have cooked up?"

"Haven't got a clue," Angelee replied. "But I'm so hungry I'm sure it will taste good."

"I know what you mean," Drew said.

Aunt Milly came in bearing a large soup tureen. "Tonight, dear family, we are having a culinary adventure, by way of Brazil. It's known as *Feijoada* in Brazil; a simple but tasty concoction of black beans, cooked with beef and pork. I've added some onion and potatoes, for my touch. We've made some *Pão de Queijo*, in English, Brazilian cheese bread. And we will have traditional rice pudding for dessert."

"It smells GREAT." Alistair enthused. "Let's sing the blessing so we can eat!"

Everyone laughed, happily in agreement with him.

"So, Aunt Milly, how did you get these funny little beans?" Alistair asked.

"Last week I received a box from some friends who are working in Brazil. They thought I would enjoy the result of some of their hard work."

"I didn't know they grew black beans in Clay County!" Aimee said.

"Not Brazil, Indiana!" Aunt Milly chortled. "These beans were grown in the country of Brazil, South American. You've been cooking with me all afternoon and you thought we were preparing food from the city not far from here."

"Oops!" Aimee covered her mouth, feigning embarrassment. "So, when you said south, you meant really south!"

"Very much so!" Aunt Milly said. "But, Brazil, Indiana is west of us, not south."

"How am I supposed to know that? I've never been to either place." Aimee protested, shrugging her shoulders.

"In fairness, Brazil, Indiana was in fact named after the country," Drew said. "I studied that in history."

So, Millicent, why this international feast this evening?" Daddy asked.

"Recently our pastor was preaching from Romans and Corinthians." Aunt Milly began. "He reminded us that God's gift of grace is timeless and His callings on our lives, doesn't change because of circumstance.

"Suddenly I understood that my daydreams and memories of Costa Rica were homesickness. I know I've not shared much about South America, my time there. Sharing about my experiences there meant I had to talk about Ned. I've also realized that I was grieving the loss of my work, the loss of a home, as well as my husband. For the longest time, I was too ill to deal with my grief.

"Cooking this meal, with Aimee's help, lets me feel connected to Costa Rica. It is a way of sharing Ned's and my own experiences. I wanted to say thank you for taking me in when I was sick and heartsore, mentally, and spiritually weary. Now that I am well, I need to let you know that I am thinking about the future; how to reconnect with my calling."

"Does that mean you're leaving us?" Alistair moaned.

There was grumbling around the table.

"I don't know exactly what it means. Of course, I'll be praying about the situation. I need time to ask questions, find answers from mission organizations. This will probably take a while, so please don't worry. I'm in no rush." Aunt Milly reassured. "Be prepared for lots of stories about Costa Rica and my time there. This meal is a way of acknowledging where I've been. It is also the first step in seeking God's plan for my future."

Angelee quailed at the idea of losing Aunt Milly. It was another unanticipated change that she added to her unsettled mind. What more was she expected to deal with?

Afternoon eased into Sunday evening; the worst heat of the day had passed. Angelee stood at the Bier's front door, knocking on the hickory-framed screen door. She called through the fine wire mesh. "Hello! Can Olivia come out and play?"

"You're here early!" A laughing Olivia said, opening the screen door and coming out. They walked over to the wicker chairs situated next to a wicker table and sat down.

"Aunt Milly and Aimee created a South American feast and felt honor-bound to clean up the kitchen. So, I came over." Angelee explained.

"Look, there's Pauley." Olivia pointed. "Don't you want to call him over?"

"Nah! Drew's still home; so—Drew will bring him over." Angelee said. "Here they come now."

The girls stood up then ran down the steps to meet Drew and Pauley.

"I was just telling Pauley about our interesting dinner—South American soup and bread," Drew said. "But it was quite a shock to hear that Aunt Milly is thinking about leaving."

"Ann-gee-lee! Why didn't you tell me?" Olivia pouted.

Angelee linked arms with Olivia and headed towards town. Pauley and Drew sauntered behind.

"First of all, she's just questioning things right now. She's not made any decisions. But I was thinking of other things. Like, I was about to tell you that I can't find any other job here in town. I'm sincerely disappointed that the library board insisted that the new person have a college degree. Did I tell you that Mrs. Johnstone wants me to volunteer with the children's reading program?"

Olivia stopped to look directly at Angelee. "You don't say! So, what did you tell her?"

"I told Mrs. Johnstone I'd think about it; I'm still considering it. It is certainly very different than being Mrs. Parkham's personal secretary. It's only volunteering—not paid. Another thing I'm discovering about the job search; most of the factory jobs are already filled. And the ones that are now open, pay less than what

Mrs. Parkham is paying me. I don't want to cut off my nose to spite my face. So, for the time being, I stuck with the Parkhams."

As they neared the White Star Restaurant, Angelee brought the story to a close.

The full restaurant hummed with conversation as the group entered the establishment. The smell of cooking meat, vegetables, baked bread, and desserts wafted invitingly around the room. Although sated with the unusual dinner she'd eaten, Angelee knew she could be tempted with ice cream and maybe a slice of pie.

An empty table, capable of seating four, toward a back corner, was available. They wove through the occupied tables and chairs. Pauley pulled out a chair for Angelee, and Drew did service for Olivia. Just as they settled into the wooden chairs, the waitress arrived with glasses of water.

"Hi, Patty! Are you being run off your feet tonight?" Drew asked.

"No more than usual. We have daily specials, so you get the curious, besides the regulars. Have a look at the menus, while I get you some knives and forks. Mike just cleared the table, but I haven't had time to reset it."

Short and stocky, Patty moved agilely around the seated crowd, making her way toward the kitchen. The four looked over the selection of desserts listed on the back of the cardboard menu and decided.

Inspecting the contents of her purse, Angelee mulled over the options.

"I invited you, Gee-Gee. So, it's my pleasure to pay for it."

Looking up at him, Angelee observed his playful, smug grin. "I get it!" she mocked. "You're practicing your dating etiquette for when you go back to college."

Pauley blinked and drew back. "Goodness, is that jealousy I hear?"

Angelee snorted. "In your fondest dreams. Just remember, we've grown up together...I know the real you."

Patty came back, pulling a note pad and pencil from her white apron pocket. "Have you had enough time?"

"Olivia's having chocolate cake with ice cream. I'm having two scoops of peach ice cream." Drew replied.

"What pie do you have tonight?" Pauley asked.

"Apple, peach, cherry, and custard."

"I'd like apple pie and vanilla ice cream. I'd appreciate a cup of coffee to go with, please."

"I'd like a caramel pecan sundae," Angelee said.

Confirming their selections Patty hurried off to get their order.

They chatted about the local news since it was too crowded and noisy to consider any personal topics. Angelee began to wonder if just spending time was on Pauley's mind, or if he had a more serious matter to discuss.

With no need to rush, they dawdled eating their dessert, finishing just before the ice cream melted. Feeling hemmed in by the proximity of the other diners, the layers of conversations around them, and the growing stuffiness of the air, they decide to go walking. Leaving sufficient money to cover the bill and Patty's tip on the table, they walked out into the balmy June evening.

Pauley took Angelee's hand and placed it on his elbow. "Let's stroll over to the bandstand. I've had something on my mind for quite a while. But I just need some privacy. Drew said he'd see Olivia home."

The foursome walked the short block to the courthouse square. As they arrived at the bandstand, Drew and Olivia nonchalantly proceeded toward home. Pauley led Angelee to the giant gazebo and they both sat on the steps.

"I'm so glad it's clear out tonight. I don't know where we could have gone if the weather was bad."

"I can't think of anywhere else—at least where there wouldn't be lots of interruptions." Angelee conceded.

"Are you okay?" Pauley asked looking up in the pink and turquoise evening sky. The setting sun bathed the evening with a rosy hue.

"What do you mean?" Angelee hesitated, overcome by an inexplicable ambivalence. Should she open herself to Pauley? He was changing, from the 'boy from down the street' into a man. He was both a familiar friend and a stranger.

Pauley rubbed his hands together, then placed them palm down on his knees. "It just seems that you've been hit by one bucket of cold water after another; graduation, turning eighteen, Mrs. Parkham grandstanding at your party, the job disappointment and now your Aunt announcing that she is thinking about leaving the family—returning to missions. That's a lot to process two weeks."

"Well, it does make one 'nervy' as you might say." Angelee paused.

Pauley turned, leaning back against the door frame of the bandstand. Angelee turned also and leaned against the other side. She knew he was giving her time to think.

After a minute she said, "You know how a chick is safe inside its shell, developing and at the right time it suddenly has to face hatching out? Well, that's how I feel. I need to live the life God has planned for me. Even if I don't know exactly what that means. I need to bang my way out of my complacency and automatic compliance and take responsibility for myself.

"First whack against the shell— graduation no more hiding behind the safe routine of school. Another smack at the shell— turning eighteen; no longer a child who needs telling what to do, but I must make my own decisions. A fist rammed through the shell— Mrs. Parkham's 'command performance', —realizing that knowing what I don't want is just as important as what I do want. The shell pushed off of the top of my head—the library job disappointment—; discovering that sometimes a person has to endure the current situations and learn lessons even when she doesn't want to. And finally, Aunt Milly sharing her decision with the family—I have to step out of the egg because I need to learn to stand on my own two feet, rather than let others fight my battles."

Pauley silently nodded his head. "I know you need time to grow into the woman you feel God wants you to be. I'm sure those moments will always be significant to you. I have every confidence you will discover your calling."

"You have that much confidence in me?" Angelee marveled.

"Yes, I do. The Apostle Paul wrote, '... *being confident of this very thing, that he who began a good work in you will perfect it until the day of Jesus Christ.'* That's why I want to share something with you."

Angelee leaned forward to listen to him.

"On Friday, when Drew and I went to enlist in the National Guards it was a day of reckoning for me. It was clear that our government has determined I am a man—not an overgrown boy at college. It brought the time I've had at college into sharp focus.

"The first year I was busy—playing, studying, and socializing. For some reason, I found that I was popular with people. After a while, I'd find myself comparing every girl I met with you. She wasn't: sweet enough, or kind enough, or thoughtful enough, or not as pretty as you. And this one wasn't a funny as you. That one didn't love Jesus. The next one was only interested in herself. Then it hit me, Angelee, I love you."

"Of course you love me." Angelee smiled, affectionately. "We're friends, always have been. You love me because I'm familiar; I'm Drew's little sister. It only makes sense."

"Yes, Gee-Gee, I do love you as my friend. But by the end of my freshman year, I knew that I was also in love with you.

"I wanted to wait until I'd graduated from college before I said this to you. I wanted to court you, give you time to realize my feelings for you. But the war has changed things.

"Maybe I should take the option of finishing college—since I'm not required to sign up for the draft. But I needed to enlist so that I would respect myself. It could be that I might fail the physical and be rejected by the Guards. But I'm sure Drew and I will pass easily.

"I want to be a man who you will respect, as well as love. I do love you with the kind of love that a man feels when he wants to be a husband to a woman. I think I've always known that one day I would marry you."

"Oh, Pauley…" Angelee barely whispered.

Like a wave crashing on a broad beach, the intensity of Pauley's emotional confession washed over her. Incomprehensible emotion rose in Angelee's stunned mind and confused heart. Bursting into tears, she jumped up and ran toward home. Her sneakers pounded on the brick sidewalk as she sprinted home. She barely hesitated as she reached the front door, yanking the screen door open. Taking the stairs two at a time, she charged into her room, slammed the door behind her, and threw herself on the bed.

All she wanted was to be left alone, to cry, to pour out her heart to God. Now she understood the flirting, the 'knowing' grins, and the difference she had not been able to define. It was one more thing she wasn't ready to contend with.

Monday morning dawned. A night of crying and thoughts racing in cycles, prevented her from slipping into sleep, leaving Angelee with a migraine.

Fear, frustration, betrayal, and anger swirled amidst wonder, confusion, and hope. This overpowering mix made it impossible to come to terms with identifying which emotion was associated with situations she felt caught up in. And because so much had happened in the previous two-and-a-half weeks, Angelee felt numb with it all.

The grandfather clock's chiming at four o'clock in the morning was the last thing that she heard when exhaustion had overtaken her. She'd not even changed into her nightclothes.

When her alarm went off at six-thirty, her eyes felt gritty and every muscle from her shoulders up ached.   Smacking the alarm off, she rolled over, pulling the covers with her. Trying to doze was impossible. The tension in her neck tightened, and the headache grew worse. She needed a day off—from everything and everyone.

She looked across the room. Aimee's bed was unslept in. The vague memory of a sleepover with her best friend crept across her mind. No wonder she'd been undisturbed last night.

Feeling barely conscious, and aware that her wrinkled dress, uncombed hair, and bare feet bespoke her weariness, and probably hinted at her emotional turmoil, Angelee gingerly crept down the stairs and went to the dining room.

"I'm sorry," Angelee whispered. "But my head is pounding. Can someone please let Mrs. Parkham know that I'm not well?"

"I'll send Alistair over to Mrs. Parkham's with a note," Mommy said.

Angelee turned to go back upstairs.

Mommy called her back. "Gee-Gee, is there something you want to talk about?"

"Not right now, thank you." She turned again to go.

"Come back and have a cup of strong tea with sugar." Mommy insisted. "You need something in your system."

Angelee shuffled into the room. Bracing herself against the table, she lowered herself onto her chair. Mommy went to the kitchen to bring freshly brewed tea, along with a couple of pieces of buttered toast.

Feeling her pulse in her temples, she propped her head on her hand. She sipped the black, sweet liquid, feeling her stomach muscles relax. The toast tasted better than expected, the butter having melted into the crisped bread. Her mother had disappeared for a few minutes, returning with a glass of water.

"I've brought you some Bayer Aspirin. I suggest a hot bath as well."

"Thanks, Mommy." Angelee breathed out, then took the two white pills. "I'm sorry to be such a problem. But I just couldn't sleep last night."

Looking across the table at her sister, "I thought you were at Bonnie's?"

"Bonnie canceled at the last minute. It was pretty clear you needed some space—so I bunked in with Aunt Milly. Now that you're down here, I'm going to go get my clothes." She was swathed in one of Aunt Milly's nightgowns.

"Take your time. I'm not moving very fast today." Angelee said.

Aimee stopped by her sister's chair, wrapping her arms around her sibling, gently hugging and tenderly kissing the older girl's temple, and then whispered. "Get some rest."

Mommy brought out a boiled egg from the kitchen and placed it in front of Angelee. Indulging in a deep sigh, Angelee looked up, tears in her eyes. "I'm sorry Mommy."

"Sorry for what?" Mommy sat down next to her. She lifted her hand and wiped away the warm tears.

"To be such a bother..."

"Eat your egg, then go on up and get in the bathtub. I'll come up in a little while and wash your back."

The aspirin had upset her stomach, so she gratefully ate the egg. With a weariness that was more emotional than physical, Angelee shuffled into the kitchen with her dirty dishes before she retreated upstairs.

After the white porcelain tub was filled, Angelee slid into the water, which was as hot as she could stand it. The water soothed and relaxed her. Between the heat and the pain reliever, the headache dulled but didn't dissipate completely.

She was half-dozing when a knock on the door roused her. When her mother called her name, Angelee invited her in.

"I've brought some extra hot water." Mommy sat on the edge of the tub. Wetting and soaping a washcloth, Mommy's firm, strong hands began stroking Angelee's back, with slow, gentle, circular movements.

As Mommy's ministrations comforted, she reminisced. "You were a little girl the last time I did this." Picking up the enameled pitcher, she slowly poured the hot water over Angelee's back, rinsing away the soap, and aches in her muscles.

"Oh Mommy, that feels so good. But I am just so tired. My whole world has been turned upside down. I don't know what to think, or even how to act."

"You're overtired right now. Do you still have that headache?"

"Yes, but not as bad," Angelee admitted.

"Go back to bed. You'll feel better after sleeping. We'll talk then." Mommy walked to the door, turned, and said, "We love you, Angelee."

"I know."

After Mommy left the room, Angelee dried herself, then slipped on a sear-sucker nightgown and a cotton housecoat over it. Following her mother's advice, she went back to bed. With the headache sufficiently reduced, she quickly fell asleep.

Perspiration trickling down her neck awakened Angelee. The breeze lifted the curtains, and afternoon sunlight crept under the edge of the pulled-down window shade. Hunger rumbled in her stomach. She sat up, hanging her legs over the side of the bed. The last shadows of an unremarkable dream drifted from her mind.

After a trip to the bathroom, to wash the sleep from her eyes, she once again sat on the side of the bed. She was trying to decide whether to get dressed or go downstairs in her housecoat when the door creaked open and Mommy peered in.

"How's the head?"

"The headache's gone now," Angelee said. "But I'm still tired."

Mommy pushed the door open and brought in a lunch tray. "There's a roast beef sandwich here and some bread and butter pickles." She placed the food-laden tray on the desk. "Come and eat. It will help."

Angelee moved to the desk and sat down. The cold, sweet tea quenched her thirst and cooled her. The bread was still moist, the beef tender. Someone had spread on horseradish sauce and added leaf lettuce and sliced tomatoes. She couldn't help but think how blessed she was to have a family who cared for her, sharing their concern for her.

"Tell me what's going on." Mommy invited as she sat down at Aimee's desk.

"I'm feeling so much, I don't even know what I'm feeling. And I'm confused by my anger, my feelings of betrayal, guilt, and being aggravated. I am so frustrated it scares me."

Mommy inquired. "What has you feeling so confused and frustrated?"

"Even though it's been almost three weeks, I feel like Mrs. Parkham's *grand announcement* is haunting me. When I'm in town, people still stop and ask me about my plans for Wellesley. Inside I'm seething, but I have to be gracious while I explain that I am not going. Plus, I've overheard people laughing about how Mrs. Parkham became the 'Queen of the Evening' when the party was supposed to be for Olivia and me. I never thought Mrs. Parkham would be so presumptive towards me, imposing what she wanted on me.

"Not only that, but Mrs. Parkham keeps insisting that her nephew drive me everywhere."

"What's wrong with that?" Mommy asked mildly

"It's silly when it only takes ten minutes to walk into town. In the last few weeks, she's been sending me to Paragon, Gosport, and even Mooresville on errands. Mrs. Parkham says I have to go with Mr. Parkham to direct him since he doesn't know the area."

"Do you think it's a match-making scheme?" Mommy asked eyebrow raised.

"On her part, yes. But on his part, he seems to understand what she's up to and finds it amusing. I've tried to keep my distance. Yet, he is a genuinely nice man. It leaves me at odds with myself."

Mommy nodded understandingly.

"We've already discussed this before; Daddy and you disappointed me by believing Mrs. Parkham's desires for Massachusetts were mine. I was surprised that you didn't ask me to confirm it. Now Mrs. Parkham drops remarks about how happy it would make you both if I changed my mind and went to Wellesley."

"You must admit, Mrs. Parkham is highly trained at selling things and getting people involved with her causes." Mommy offered by way of mollifying Angelee. "You can't blame us for wanting you to have a taste of the world away from Martinsville."

"I just want you to support me, and let me make my own choices. Otherwise, I will never really grow up. When...and if...I get married, I can't depend on a husband to tell me everything to do. I need to know that I can make wise decisions, whether it's organizing my time, or how I spend money. I know Aunt Milly came to us because we were able to provide a home for her. But she lives her own life...going to church on her own, organizing prayer groups and fund-raising projects. She has her own friends. She doesn't have a husband to depend on."

Mommy had sat quietly, taking in all that was said. "Gee-Gee, your father and I have done our best, based on what we know, how we were brought up. You are a young woman who has more choices than I did. Regarding Mrs. Parkham's 'Wellesley Plan', we thought you would be thrilled to experience life away from us, to discover who you are without our constant watching over your shoulder."

Angelee took another drink of tea. "The problem is, I would be indebted to Mrs. Parkham, to give a constant account to her for all my social activities. I would be constrained by her expectations; to compare it against her plans to make me her full-time companion and secretary. I don't know why she decided that I would simply fall in with it."

"We should discuss this more when your father is here. What else are you feeling angry and frustrated about?" Mommy re-directed the conversation.

"I wouldn't say angry, but sad and a bit frightened. Aunt Milly is thinking of leaving us. I've gotten so used to her being here. Have we done something wrong? Why now? She's been with us so long that it feels like she's abandoning us. I suppose my head knows she needs to follow her heart. But my heart...well it feels like I'm losing a second mother. When Alistair was still a baby and needed your attention, it was so wonderful to have Aunt Milly to talk to. I feel so selfish about wanting her to stay. And then I feel guilty for being selfish..."

"Your Aunt Milly has been feeling restless for the last year," Mommy explained. "I think it all came to a head when war was declared. It will be hard for me too...like losing half of myself. Loving someone, to truly love someone, is to want them to fulfill their dreams. Milly has always been one for an adventure, and she needs a challenge now. God was gracious, in that we were there for her when she needed us—and she has been here when we needed her. But now it's time to love her enough to let her go.

"Angelee, your feelings are normal, natural. You will learn that emotions come and go, they churn, change, and adapt like a river when it rains.

"So, what do I do with the resentment in my heart towards Mrs. Parkham? How do I handle my broken heart regarding Aunt Milly?

"Sometimes emotions seem so big, so powerful, that we feel out of control. When that happens, we don't need to surrender to the flow but hold up our hearts and hands to God. He will send a life-line. A Bible verse might come into your head. Just the right person comes for a visit and shares something that seems insignificant to them—but is exactly what you need to hear. It might be while you're listening to a sermon. When you are caught off-guard while thinking about something else and suddenly you get the insight you need.

"The truth is, we grow into governing our lives by renewing our minds and trusting God's promises. We learn that faith is not logical, but neither is it emotional."

"Forgiveness is a key factor," Mommy said, reaching across to place her hand on Angelee's. "Forgive me and Daddy for not trying to see things from your perspective. Forgive Mrs. Parkham for being meddlesome; forgive Aunt Milly for letting you down. Don't let your feelings rule you—but rather you control them. Don't pretend you don't feel them. Admit how you feel, and find a productive way to let go of them.

"You came charging in last night, everyone was shocked by your behavior. What happened?" Mommy encouraged her.

"After we went to the White Star, the four of us walked over to the bandstand. Drew and Olivia kept walking, but Pauley and I sat down. I'd wanted to talk to him about Aunt Milly. And then there was the job at the library…"

"Wait a minute, did you say job at the library? And when were you going to tell your father and me about this?" Mommy asked sharply.

"I meant to last night, at supper. But then Aunt Milly told us about going back into missions, and it just didn't seem right. But it doesn't matter, Mommy. It came to nothing. The library wants someone with a college degree."

"I see." Mommy dropped her head for a second. "So, tell me about Pauley. What did he say that upset you so much?"

"But we didn't discuss any of that. I knew that Pauley had something on his mind. I had no inclination that he was going to open his heart to me. I just wasn't ready. He just bluntly told me about his feelings. I panicked. I ran. I didn't know what to say to him. Suddenly he was a different Pauley."

Mommy sat quietly; her hands folded in her lap. "You and Pauley have grown up together. What could he possibly say that you didn't already know?"

Angelee shared the short conversation, replaying the scene in her mind. The intensity in his eyes, the somberness of his voice, and the gentleness of his demeanor had amplified the power of his words. Had his feelings always been such?

"This is all so confusing because part of me thinks I should have seen it coming. I mean…" Angelee trailed off, not sure of what she meant.

Mommy now took her hands and smiled. "It's *because* you've known Pauley practically your whole life. You're friends with each other—not just associated because he is Drew's best friend."

"Exactly," Angelee affirmed. "I've been so caught up with finishing high school, dealing with 'The Boston Collective' and preoccupied with Aunt Milly's decision that I was astounded by what he said. I ran because I didn't want to hear any more. And I didn't know how I felt…well, I know I love him as a person. But being in love? Marriage, I'm just not ready for that."

Mommy squeezed her hands. "He's right about the world seeing him as a man. Your father and I both think of Drew as the ten-year-old who couldn't wait to grow up so he could grow a mustache! Look at him now—he is a man. Pauley has been around our house so much he is practically family. When he shared his heart with you, you became afraid of even more change. It isn't Pauley that scares you, it's the unknown."

"But I don't know what Pauley expects now. And I'm embarrassed by my behavior. It seems so childish now."

"The sooner you talk to him, the easier it will be. Come on, you know Pauley well enough to know he will give you the time you need to discover your feelings. But as he said, the war and enlisting have caused him to realize that he hasn't the same amount of time he did while a college student. War makes people re-evaluate life, the people they love, and how they are living. You owe it to Pauley to listen to the rest of what he wanted to say. He'll give you the time you need."

"I guess you're right," Angelee said, returning her mother's hand-squeeze. "Everything seems so incredible. And I'm still tired."

"In that case, go back to bed. It's the best thing you can do right now. Give yourself time to sort your emotions out. It isn't always easy."

Angelee shrugged her shoulders and twisted her head. "I think the headache is trying to come back."

"Take some more aspirin before you sleep."

Mommy stood up, pulling Angelee with her. "I love you, Daughter of Mine. I know I have to let you grow up, but no one says I have to like it." Mommy's eyes twinkled as she said it.

Angelee chuckled and hugged her mother. Mommy left with the tray. Finding the bottle of aspirin in the bathroom cabinet, she took two.

Reclining on her back, her eyelids slid down, almost of their own volition. In only minutes, her breathing became the natural rhythm of slumber.

Sunday night's sleep deficit was reclaimed by Angelee's dreamless slumbering on Monday. By Tuesday morning, the headache had disappeared and Angelee was ready to return to work. Mrs. Parkham showed genuine concern, instructing Angelee to take off extra time if the headache threatened to return.

After lunch, Cameron drove Mrs. Parkham over to Home Lawn for an appointment. This gave Angelee extra time, so after quickly eating her lunch, Angelee decided to go by the library. Skipping up the limestone steps and entering the building, she stopped by the 'new books' bookshelf and read the titles. None appealed to her, so she took a few minutes to browse the shelves before she found a couple of suitable choices.

Mrs. Johnstone, on duty at the checkout desk, smiled at Angelee. "I'm glad you came in today. Do you have a few minutes? I want to discuss something with you."

"I suppose I could spare a few minutes," Angelee said, as she placed her selections in her satchel.

Angelee, appreciating the sunlit and breeze-freshened office, followed the librarian into the organized room.

Mrs. Johnstone sat at her desk and indicated that Angelee should take the seat across from her.

"Yes, thank you." Angelee gave her an equally perfunctory reply. "What did you want to see me about?"

"I know how disappointed you were by not being able to apply for the new position here at the library." Mrs. Johnstone remarked.

"At least I still have the job with Mrs. Parkham."

"I'm sure that keeps you busy." Mrs. Johnstone replied. "However, I was wondering if you'd given any more thought to volunteer as a reader in our Saturday morning Reading Circle?"

"I apologize for not getting back to you sooner. I have some questions. I don't want to be in charge of a group of children without other adults around."

"I suppose that's understandable. I did mention that the parents sit in on the sessions as well."

"Well, what are the ages of the children? Will I have to pick all the books? Is it on every Saturday?"

"The youngest children will be around five and the oldest ones will be about ten years old. As for picking the books, the first couple of weeks you or I can make the selection. After that, we might ask the children or their mother's for suggestions." Mrs. Johnstone clarified. "I intend to run the Reading Circle every Saturday. But that depends on how many children come and how many volunteers I get. I don't know if it's realistic to ask for one person to commit to every Saturday. I might be surprised if someone was willing to."

"That information helps. But I'm still not sure. Would it be okay if I did it once or twice before I make a commitment?" Angelee offered.

"That's fair enough. Do you think you could try it this coming Saturday?" Mrs. Johnstone tilted her head to one side and smiled hopefully.

"Yes, I can do that. Do you have a book already chosen? That way I can practice reading it aloud a couple of times before." Angelee didn't expect the excitement that rose within her.

"Good thinking! I haven't had time to make any decisions. So if you have a favorite book, you can read that one."

"How about *The Tale of Squirrel Nutkin?* By Beatrix Potter. I loved reading that to Alistair when he was younger."

"Yes, that's a good choice. You can get through it in one session. Which is the objective." Mrs. Johnstone said.

The chimes from the courthouse clock carried through the open window.

"Oh wow, I've got to get back to Mrs. Parkham's," Angelee said, double-checking her wristwatch. "What time do you need me here on Saturday?" She asked, raising from the oak chair.

"Come at about nine o'clock, so you can help me set up the area downstairs." Mrs. Johnstone rose as well and walked around the desk to the door. "I'm looking forward to it."

"Me too." Angelee smiled broadly. "See you Saturday."

Angelee hurried out of the library and thought about Nutkin and Old Brown all the way back to Mrs. Parkham's abode.

Saturday, June 23rd, 1917
Reading Circle Launch

The courthouse clock struck nine o'clock as Angelee's patent leather shoes scraped on the limestone steps of the library Saturday morning. "Good morning, Mrs. Johnstone." Angelee cheerfully greeted the head librarian. "I came a bit early since I didn't know how long it would take to set up for the Reading Circle."

Mrs. Johnstone, a couple of steps ahead, unlocked the front door. "Glad to hear you've got lots of energy." She replied cheerfully.

The stairwell to the left led to the lower level of the library and a community room, usually used for social groups. It was also used by library staff to host story time. Before they could arrange the community room for the story-reading time, Mrs. Johnstone needed to open the rest of the library. Angelee followed her back upstairs.

"Any plans for later today?" Mrs. Johnstone asked as they walked past the card catalog and into the office. She stowed her handbag in a desk drawer before sitting down.

"Haven't given it much thought, to be honest. Olivia and I might go see a movie, "Angelee replied.

Sunlight fell through the rotunda's opaque dome lighting the room.

Carrying her satchel, which held a well-read copy of *The Tale of Squirrel Nutkins* by Beatrix Potter, Angelee returned downstairs.

Knowing that some mothers and children would be arriving early, Angelee worked quickly to arrange small chairs for the children and large chairs for their mothers. Deliberately, Angelee selected a child-sized chair to sit on for the reading, facing the other chairs. Reading out loud was hard work, especially if she wasn't familiar with the book. Thankfully, she'd read it so many times to Alistair she had memorized the story; which meant she did not have to read it upside down and backward. The illustrated book was large enough to hold up for the children to see.

As mothers and children arrived, Angelee directed them to a table. A writing pad and sharpened pencils ready, she invited mothers to write down the names of books their children might like.

"Listen, Mommy! Can we count the bell?" Forest Tucker's five-year-old voice burst. "Two, three…"

Without encouragement, the other children joined in, and the last chime from the courthouse clock was announced with a rousing "TEN".

Standing by the little seat in the corner, she clapped her hands to draw their attention. As she looked over the large group that took up half the basement, she noticed several mothers had knitting or crocheting with them.

"Good morning! My name is Miss Tilson. Today I'm reading *The Tale of Squirrel Nutkin* by Miss Beatrix Potter. Please be courteous and listen carefully—that means no interrupting or talking to each other while I'm reading. All right? Now, are we all ready?" She picked up the book opening it to the first page and began.

Angelee read with a flourish, changing her voice for the narrator, Nutkins, and his brother Twinkleberry. After reading each page, she lifted the book so the children in the back could see the pictures better. Throughout the reading, the younger children stared agog at Miss Potter's watercolor illustrations. Much to her surprise, even the older children sat politely, taking in the narrative of the wildlife yarn.

As she finished the last page, Angelee closed the book and made eye-contact with the children. Her heart lifted with joy and satisfaction.

"Now then, who can tell me what kind of squirrel is in the story?" Angelee asked the group.

Hands shot up and a little boy in a red jacket was waving his hand, wiggling his fingers so energetically she thought it best to call on him before he burst from excitement. "Yes, Jack?"

"Red squirrels, Miss Tilson! Red squirrels with big bushy tails."

"That's correct." She smiled at them. "Now, someone else tell me, who was the good squirrel?"

Jack harrumphed and scowled when Angelee didn't call on him again.

Scanning the group, she pointed toward a blond girl with blue eyes and freckles across her nose. "Samantha, I'm sure you know."

Samantha, who had been looking down at her shoes, looked up, surprised but happy. "That's Twinkleberry, Miss."

Nodding, Angelee continued. "Now then, everybody, was Nutkin a good squirrel or a naughty squirrel?"

A clamorous chorus of "NAUGHTY" rang from the group, anxious to answer questions.

"Very naughty!" Angelee laughed. "Now then who can tell me what he did that was naughty.

Once again hands and arms danced in the air, striving to be picked. Angelee looked toward the back. A curly-red-headed boy with porcelain skin and green eyes, named Hank, squirmed anxiously hoping to be picked.

"Okay, Hank, tell us about Naughty Nutkin."

"Nut-Nut-Nutkin didn't w-w-want to help…help pick up nuts. He…he…he would make up rid-rid-riddles for the bird. And…and…and the Owl didn't like it."

"Very good, Hank." For her next question, Angelee decided to pick one of the older children.

Bernice looked to be about ten years old. "Now then Bernice, tell me where the squirrels had to get the nuts."

Bernice was a round-faced girl, with rosy cheeks and brown eyes. "Well, Miss Tilson, they had to go to an island in the middle of the lake. And they had to take gifts to 'Old Brown' the owl."

"You listened very well, Bernice." Angelee praised.

"Who can tell about the gifts that Twinkleberry and his pals took for 'Old Brown'?"

"I can!" Blurted out Arthur. "They took mice, and a mole, and honey and BUGS!"

Laughter from mothers and children filled the room.

"Not my idea of a nice snack. Do you think so?" Angelee asked the group.

"Yuck! "No—I don't like bugs!" "Ooooooo." Came the cacophony of answers.

"Daniel, besides being rude, what else did Nutkin do to 'Old Brown' the owl?"

Daniel ran a hand through his closely cropped brown hair, thinking a moment, then said. "Well Miss Tilson, he up and jumped on the old bird's head."

"Who can tell me what happened next?" Angelee prompted. "Karl?"

Karl, a sturdy lad with sun-bleached hair, tanned cheeks, and brown eyes, raised on his knees to answer.

"That big ole' owl up and stuck Nutkin in his pocket. And just about the time 'Ole Brown' was gonna' skin that squirrel, Nutkin pulled so hard, he left half his tale behind."

"Absolutely correct...and did Nutkin tell riddles anymore?"

"No, Ma'am!" Karl replied. "He sure didn't."

"Give yourselves a round of applause—but make it softly. We don't want to bother the people upstairs!"

The children and mothers gently patted their applause for just a minute, and then Angelee raised her hand for silence. "Thank you all for paying attention so well. Now then, will a couple of you older boys help put the chairs away? And the rest of you can go find some books to check out."

Hank, Daniel, Karl, as well as a couple of the older girls, made quick work of re-stacking the chairs and placing them against the wall. Mothers guided their younger charges to the bookshelves, assisting them in making selections.

Just as Angelee was about to go upstairs, Mrs. Carmichael stopped Angelee.

"Miss Tilson, Janie and I were curious about this new activity. I can honestly say that Janie has enjoyed this very much. You kept everyone's attention with your little voices for each character. You are so natural with the children. Before I got married and had Janie, I was a school teacher. Watching you, it occurred to me that you'd make an excellent teacher." Mrs. Carmichael ignored Janie pulling at her hand to go.

"Oh my!" Hearing those words, Angelee's heart skipped a beat, and she placed her hand over her heart, trying to slow it down. "I can honestly say, Mrs. Carmichael that I'd never considered the idea. I've spent hours reading to my younger brother. So, I guess I did for the reading group what I've done for him. But thank you for the compliment."

"Just a minute, Janie!" Mrs. Carmichael reprimanded her impatient daughter. Turning to Angelee she smiled as she said; "Thank you for giving up so much pleasure this morning. And as for teaching, unless you're thinking of studying something else, or getting married soon, why don't you give teaching some consideration? I think you're a natural." Having made her point, Mrs. Carmichael gave into her child's insistent prodding to leave.

Angelee pondered Mrs. Carmichael's compliment and suggestion; the remark had felt like an arrow piercing her heart. It was one thing for family and friends to suggest teaching to her. But she'd never met Mrs. Carmichael before. She found it intriguing that a stranger would comment on her supposed aptitude for teaching. Angelee sensed that a significant moment had transpired. She couldn't offhandedly dismiss the thought, but she could relegate it to a back cupboard in her mind. Teaching was the last thing she wanted to consider.

Moving the chairs back into the storage room, she made sure the room was tidy before going upstairs to the office to collect her belongings before going home.

Mrs. Johnstone working at her desk. "How did it go? Did you enjoy it?" Mrs. Johnstone asked with a smile.

"It was fun and I did enjoy it. I'd love to commit to doing it. Do you have any other volunteers?"

"Not as yet. But if you can stick with me for a few weeks, I'll do my best to get a couple of other readers."

"That's fine, then. I'll stop by later this week to look over the list the mothers gave us. Now I need to get home. See you in a few days."

"Thanks, Angelee. I appreciate it."

Angelee was humming softly to herself as she left the limestone building.

Saturday, June 23rd, 1917
Mommy's Scheme

Walking home, taking deep breaths, effectively dispelled the last of the adrenaline from her system. Pleasantly tired when she arrived, she went to her room and changed into an old dress and she took off her shoes.

Angelee enjoyed the sensation of the smooth, cool, polished wood against her naked feet. Going to the kitchen, she poured herself a glass of tea from the icebox. She went out to sit on the porch swing.

Quietly rocking in the swing, drinking her tea, Angelee pondered life. Only a few minutes later Mommy came out onto the porch and joined her on the swing.

"What've you been doing today, Mommy?" Angelee asked.

"Hmmm...well, I grabbed the post before your father could—so that he didn't see something he shouldn't. Then, after convincing Alistair that he would appreciate the benefits of mowing Mrs. Smith's yard, I sent him down the street."

Angelee chuckled. "And what were the benefits? Staying up half-an-hour later tonight?"

"No, the knowledge that Mrs. Smith had offered to pay him if he did a good job."

"That would be difficult to resist. And it will give him a chance to ask her about the flowers he planted for her in the borders a few weeks ago."

"Yes, he is beginning to be very interested in planting and growing certain things. Anyway, after he left, I found Mee-Mee busy with sweeping and dusting. Talk about surprised. But then once I'd given it a look over, I decided to ask what she was after. Sure enough, she and two of her friends wanted to go see the movie this afternoon. Apparently, there is a new Mary Pickford movie showing."

"So, what was it that Daddy wasn't supposed to see?" Angelee said, feeling nosey.

"Confirmation of hotel reservations in Cincinnati; I've arranged a surprise for your father. I'm taking him away over the 4th of July." Mommy's eyes twinkled.

"It has been a while since you and Daddy went off by yourselves. Is this the last chance before Aunt Milly leaves us?"

"Angelee, please don't be so apprehensive about Aunt Milly. She isn't leaving in the next five days! Maybe not even the next five months. She isn't sure which of the doors will open. As for the 4th of July with Daddy, it's a belated 50th birthday celebration and anniversary present all wrapped up together."

"Do you think Daddy will enlist in the Army?" Angelee wondered.

"We've talked about it. As you know, Dr. Robinson has his National Guard office over at the Colonial sanitarium. Your dad went over and discussed it with him. It confirmed your father's conviction that he was too old, having turned fifty in January. Major Frank—Dr. Robinson—persuaded him that he had a responsibility to the town here. He's a doctor at Home Lawn and has a practice for town folk as well. Plus, he has us. I also think his duty is here at home."

"Have you seen Pauley since he expressed his feelings?" Mommy looked pointedly at Angelee. "It will be a week tomorrow."

Angelee looked down at the glass she held in hands, resting in her lap. "I haven't talked to him face-to-face. But I sent him a note apologizing for running away. I also asked him to understand that I feel so overwhelmed by things right now."

"I suppose you do. Not being able to find a different job. Mrs. Parkham persisting about Wellesley. Trying to figure out what you're supposed to be doing with this thing called life."

"I'm trying to discover who I am—just me. You know—not Dr. Tilson's daughter, or somebody's sister. I don't want to add, 'Somebody's Girlfriend' to the list." Angelee emphasized. "And to be honest, it scares me to think about my friendship with Pauley changing. Could we become friends again if the romance didn't work out?"

"Those are very valid concerns, Gee-Gee. I know you want to be seen for yourself. Just don't look so hard for what God wants you to do that you look past knowing God Himself. And don't withhold your heart because of fear."

Angelee gave her mother a puzzled look.

"What I mean is that you can trust Pauley's friendship, and don't avoid him. If he really does love you, then he will give you the time to need."

"I know you're right…but…with the war, and knowing he'll go…but not when he'll go. What are my real feelings? He is so familiar—but could I have deeper, romantic feelings?"

"Quit trying to get ahead of yourself, Gee-Gee. Until you meet up and discuss this with him, you're only confusing yourself more." Mommy chided.

"Okay, I'll walk down later and see him later." Angelee acquiesced.

"Now then, tell me about the library. How did things go today?" Mommy changed the subject.

Angelee shared everything about the morning. As she explained the response of the children, she laughed and waved her hands. "I was kind of looking forward to it. But I didn't expect to enjoy it so much. It felt so natural. And what truly surprised me was what Mrs. Carmichael said."

"What was that?" Mommy encouraged.

"She used to be a teacher before she got married and had children. She thought I would make a good teacher. You're always pestering me about being a teacher. But it is such a big responsibility."

"Gee-Gee, do you realize that we are just commenting on the gift we see in you? Even now you were so animated while telling me about the Reading Circle."

"I've never thought about that before," Angelee remarked. "I just see it as trying to help people, especially children."

"Every time you resist our suggestions to consider teaching, I don't understand your reaction. Why are you so quick to dismiss the idea?"

"I don't know. I suppose it's because I'm not good enough to take care of a room full of children."

"Did you ever think that maybe God isn't opening any doors because you aren't looking in the right direction?" Mommy suggested.

The swing rocked gently as they pushed it.

"What do you mean?" Angelee tilted her head.

"Well, let's say you secretly saw yourself as a librarian. Maybe seeing that job at the library was a hint. But you learned that you needed to have a college degree. Maybe you didn't get a job here in town because you need to go to college this fall."

"Not that Wellesley thing again?!" Angelee moaned.

"No, not Wellesley. As you pointed out, there is Indiana Central University, Butler College, Indiana University. If you don't fancy yourself as a secretary/companion, then you need to ask yourself what gives you joy. Would it be teaching? Would it be working as a librarian? Do you need extra qualifications? If so, what kind of training and where can you get it?"

Angelee dropped her defenses. "Oh, I see what you mean." Pondering quietly for a few minutes she replied. "I've never thought about what gives me joy. I don't have answers to any of those questions."

"Don't be so anxious. You are doing something useful now, for Mrs. Parkham. Daddy and I are already proud of who you are. We have talked about it, and want you to know we understand that working for Mrs. Parkham isn't what you want to do long term. However, we also know that deep down, you respect her—even love her. For some reason, the Lord needs you to serve Him by serving her. When the time is right, He will show you the next step for your life."

Mommy pulled Angelee close and she rested her head on Mommy's shoulder.

"I'm so glad I've got you to talk to. I'd be lost without you." Angelee confessed to her mother.

"I'd be lost without you and my other 'kidlings' too. I love being your mother—even though I don't always get things right."

"I hope, that someday when I'm a mother, I'm half as good of a mother as you are."

"I'm sure you will be," Mommy reassured her. "Now, let's go see if we can help get dinner on the table."

Nine o'clock in the morning, on Monday, 2nd July, knocking at the front door aroused the family's curiosity. Except for Mommy, who had insisted on answering it herself. To everyone's surprise, Grandy and Grandma Barnes walked in, with suitcases. They'd come to stay for the week. All three of them walked upstairs.

When they came back down, Mommy was carrying a different suitcase. This puzzled Daddy; until she told him they were leaving on the morning train and going to Cincinnati for a few days. He'd been speechless. After stuttering nonsensically for a couple of seconds, he'd found his tongue and blustered about his patients and Home Lawn. His concerns were dispatched quickly enough. Mommy had made arrangements with some of the other doctors in town. Drew drove them to the train station that beautiful July day.

******

"According to last night's paper," Aimee said. "The Feast of Lanterns is going to be right outside our front door." Hammers banging on wood, and voices shouting instructions, came through the open windows.

The family sat eating breakfast.

"What is this Feast of Lanterns?" Grandy asked, sipping piping hot coffee.

"Since it's the 4th of July, the Tri Kappa ladies decided to have a Red Cross Benefit. They're closing off our block and setting up games and programs. The Boy Scouts perform at seven o'clock this evening." Aimee explained. "There's also going to be entertainment under a tent."

"I think I should become a Boy Scout!" Alistair announced.

"That is a fine idea, my boy." Grandy Barnes encouraged.

"Did you say entertainment? What kind?" Grandma Barnes asked.

"I understand that a French aviator, who is also an opera singer, will be performing. Besides that, there will be short plays, and maybe some skits. Mr. Grubbs says a tent is being set up for the shows. And Mrs. Parkham's friend, Mrs. Rheinaear, is scheduled to do some dramatic readings. They met at Home Lawn." Angelee said.

"What a wonderful thing to do. We can sit on the porch and watch it all." Grandma Barnes said.

"Especially the Wheel of Fortune—which is going up in front of our house! For a dime, you get a prize." Drew chuckled. "I bet that will bring a lot of attention."

"Since it doesn't start until four-thirty this afternoon, Olivia and I made arrangements with Mr. Cameron Boyer-Parkham to go for a drive this morning," Angelee informed.

"Who is he?" Grandma Barnes piped up.

"He is Mrs. Parkham's nephew. He invited us on Sunday. Daddy and Mommy know him."

"I see no problem then..." Grandy Barnes began.

"Provided you bring him in and introduce him to us." Grandma Barnes interjected.

"Exactly," Grandy added, raising an eyebrow at Grandma. "Did you say he is Mrs. Parkham's nephew? Isn't she the one who commandeered your party?"

"That's a very good description of what happened." Aunt Milly concurred.

"Are you sure that you want to spend time with that young man?" Grandma asked, suspicion in her voice.

"To be fair, Mr. Boyer-Parkham is quite congenial." Angelee countered. "He dotes on Mrs. Parkham but is quite independent. Mrs. Parkham's birthday is on Saturday, and he asked me and Olivia to assist him in finding a gift for his aunt."

"Don't worry, Papa." Aunt Milly affirmed. "Mr. Boyer-Parkham has never shown any inclination of having designs on Angelee or Oliva. I can vouch for his affability."

"Can I go too?" Alistair suddenly asked.

Angelee hesitated. She was planning on a driving lesson. Would Alistair keep a secret? "You're going to have to wait until Mr. Boyer-Parkham gets here. We have to ask him if he minds." Angelee deferred, hoping her grandparents would say no.
****

The grandfather clock was chiming ten o'clock when Angelee heard Alistair yell up the stairs.

"He's here Angelee! Hurry up!"

Angelee marked her place in Dorothy Canfield Fisher's latest book, '*Understood Betsy*'-- her next book selection for the Reading Circle. Placing the book on the desk, she left her room.

"Gee Whiz Alistair. You need to learn to be patient." Angelee ruffled her young sibling's hair as she took the last step.

She met Cameron at the door before he had a chance to knock. "Please come in." She pushed the screen door open. "My grandparents are in the family room. They're looking forward to meeting you."

Alistair, barely a half step behind them, followed. "Mr. Parkham, can I..."

Angelee glared at him. Sulking, Alistair fell silent.

Inviting Cameron to sit, Angelee made the introductions. He held his hat in his lap, which he'd immediately removed upon entering the house.

"Grandy, Grandma, if Mr. Parkham doesn't mind, would it be okay if Alistair came with us?" Angelee looked at the three.

A series of glances passed among them.

"Mr. Boyer-Parkham..." Grandy began.

"Please, call me Cameron."

"Cameron, are you inclined to let this scamp tag along on your outing?"

Cameron chuckled and looked over at Alistair. Angelee followed his glance and had to giggle at the boy with his eyes wide, pleading and his hand tightly clasped together as if praying.

"With such earnest hope written all over him, how can I say no?"

Alistair let out a whoop and jumped up and down.

"Calm down!" Grandma commanded. "And don't pester Mr. B...Cameron while he's driving."

Angelee heard the three knocks resounding from the front door before it was opened and closed.

"Hello? I'm here!" Olivia called.

Cameron stood, shook hands with Mr. and Mrs. Barnes before he ruffled Alistair's hair.

"What is it with everybody messing up my hair today?" Alistair complained, smoothing his hair back down.

As the foursome left the house, they walked by volunteers unloading trucks to construct booths for ice cream, lemonade, and games. Ladders leaned next to lamp poles, where red, white, and blue pennants were being tied up.

"This way; I parked on Morgan street." Cameron directed them to the blue 1916 Cadillac Type 53.

Olivia and Angelee sat in the back, so Alistair could watch Cameron's movements to maneuver the car.

After cranking the engine to life, Cameron climbed into the driver's seat. "I thought we'd head toward Brooklyn."

Rolling past the businesses on the town square, Cameron turned north onto Main street. Alistair mimicked Cameron's actions with the peddles, gear stick, and steering wheel. Angelee and Olivia laughed.

"We ought to be doing the same if we're serious about learning to drive," Angelee said to Olivia.

"I suppose you're right. But I'm sure the controls feel very different when we actually have our hands and feet on them." Olivia countered. "But does Alistair know we're having a driving lesson today?"

"No, but when we stop, I'll make him promise to keep our secret. I need to be the one who tells Mommy and Daddy."

"Well, you'd better tell them as soon as they get home this weekend." Olivia admonished.

Cameron stopped the Cadillac next to farm tracks, about five miles from Brooklyn. They all dismounted from the car.

"What are we stopping for?" Alistair asked.

"I need to talk to you, Alistair." Angelee took his hand, pulling him out of the front seat.

Olivia followed Cameron to the front of the car.

"Alistair, the real purpose of this trip is for Mr. Parkham to give Olivia and me driving lessons. But I've not told Mommy and Daddy. You can't say anything to anybody about this; not until I tell them first. Before you ask, no, you cannot have a driving lesson too."

Alistair dropped his head in disgust. "I don't see why you can and I can't."

"Because I'm eighteen now, and I can make my own decisions about things. But you're too young to do things without Mommy and Daddy agreeing to it."

"But that's not fair!" Alistair complained.

The car fired to life, as Olivia came to terms with the crank.

"I know it isn't!" Angelee commiserated. "But many things in life are not fair. And you've got to promise me that you won't tell anyone about our lessons."

"Okay. I promise not to tell anyone." Alistair sighed, shrugging his shoulders.

"You can sit in front on the way home." Angelee offered him appeasement.

"Thanks." Alistair rolled his eyes.

"Come on Angelee, it's your turn," Cameron called to them. "Olivia's mastered the crank start."

Angelee stood in front of the car, suddenly seeing the powerful machine in a different light. Her heart raced, and apprehension rose from within her. She'd always enjoyed riding in the vehicle, but never considered the strength and concentration required to control and direct the massive monster on wheels. Determined, she paid careful attention, followed Cameron's instructions, while facing newly recognized fear.

Alistair acted as though he also was having a lesson, even though he'd been denied permission for this session. That was Alistair. If he was interested in something, he focused totally on it.

Over the next hour-and-a-half, Olivia and Angelee wore themselves out learning how the engine worked, shifting gears, and turning the steering wheel. Dust rose from the hardened dirt roads they accessed. Arriving in Brooklyn, Cameron decided they had started well, and finished the lesson for the day.

"Please, Mr. Parkham, can I have a turn too?!" Alistair pleaded.

"NO!" Angelee swiftly and adamantly interjected. "We've already discussed this. I will talk to Mommy and Daddy when they get home. One more word and I will make sure Mr. Parkham doesn't bring you again...EVER." Angelee stood rigid, hands on her hips.

"Sorry, Alistair. Big sister has spoken." Cameron looked down, smiling compassionately.

Alistair turned his back to them, and Angelee knew he was going to cry.

Turning her younger brother towards herself, she apologized. "I'm sorry I snapped at you. Alistair, we have to ask Mommy and Daddy. Right now, we need to get home for lunch. Tell you what, when we get back, I'll try to make sure you get to meet that French Aviator, Mr. Carnes. We'll get his autograph and you can ask him about flying planes."

Alistair blinked hard and crossed his arms. "I'm not crying, you know."

"Of course you weren't. Why would I ever think that you were?" Angelee refrained from hugging him. Alistair was ten now—trying hard to be a man.

"And I get to ride in the front?" Alistair reiterated his claim.

"Fine by me!" quipped Cameron.

As Alistair ran to the car, Cameron smiled at Angelee. "You certainly have a way with him."

"Well, he is my baby brother," Angelee replied. "He's a good kid, just overly curious and fearless."

"I could think of a lot of worse things than having you as a big sister. So, how are you going to find Mr. Carnes?" Cameron said.

"I'm not sure. But he's been reading stories in the newspapers about pilots. I wanted to find a way to make it up to him"

"It's a good thing you don't have any planes here," Olivia added. "He'd probably be pestering you all the time."

"Let me help you with arranging the meeting with Rene Carnes. I met him while I was in Europe."

"Wow! I hadn't expected that! But it is an answer to prayer!" Angelee said.

Olivia checked her wristwatch. "We need to get a move on. Mommy hates it when I'm late for things—like lunch."

Cameron gave a mock salute, and turning on his heel, made a performance of opening the back door, so the girls could ascend into the back seat. Cameron cranked the engine over, took his place behind the driver's wheel, and steered the car in the direction of Martinsville.

Lunch was informal, cold-cut sandwiches, garden salad, and fruit. Angelee insisted that Aunt Milly and Grandma Barnes rest afterward and volunteered to clean the kitchen. As she wrapped leftovers and put them in the icebox, she wondered how to proceed with the afternoon.

No formal arrangements had been made by Cameron regarding Monsieur Carnes.

Angelee originally thought of taking Alistair to watch the French performer's arrival in a field, southwest of town. Upon arriving home, she'd learned that his arrival transpired while they were out for the driving lesson.

Angelee found Alistair sitting on the top step of the front porch, watching the workers adjust the wheel-of-fortune. Legs pushing up and down, arms outstretched and turning clockwise, then counter-clockwise, he brought a smile to Angelee's face.

"Whatcha doing?" Angelee asked, sitting down next to him.

"Practicing my driving."

"I can see. You aren't speeding, are you?"

"No. Just waiting for Bart. We're going to talk to the Boy Scouts and see what you have to do to join." Alistair craned his head to look up at her.

"When do you expect him?" Angelee said, watching pennants flutter in a subtle breeze.

"Not sure! But before it gets too late. You know babies can't stay out too late." He said knowingly.

"You're right. How about a game of backgammon?" Angelee offered.

"Sure!" He jumped up off and ran into the house.

By the time Angelee stood up and walked over to the metal garden chairs and table, Alistair had returned with the board game. "Dibs on red!"

Angelee and Alistair entered their own little world, strategy, trying to anticipate each other's next move.

"Ah, the battle of backgammon." An accented voice broke through their concentration. Angelee's hands clutched her chest, while Alistair nearly flew out of his chair.

"Apologies, Mademoiselle." The foreign man said, offering a short bow.

Chuckling, Cameron made the introduction. "Miss Angelee Tilson, Master Alistair Tilson, it is my pleasure to introduce to you, Captain Viktor Carnes."

Captain Carnes's light blue tunic boasted shining, polished, buttons from the stand-up collar, down the front, and on breast pockets. Draped over his right shoulder and down to his waist a leather belt attached to a wider leather waist belt. Gold braid formed a triple-striped chevron on each sleeve. His breeches sported red stripes down each leg. Brown leather knee-high boots complemented the striking outfit.

Captain Carnes stepped forward, took Angelee's offered hand, and leaned forward.

Angelee widened her eyes when the pilot leaned forward, placing a kiss on her right cheek, then her left cheek, and then her right cheek again.

As Captain Carnes stepped back, Cameron stepped forward and also took Angelee's hand. "A great opportunity to practice my French culture!" Cameron kissed each cheek, following the example of Captain Carnes.

Whistling announced the arrival of another guest.

"Now that I'm here, I might as well follow suit!" Pauley said. He casually took both Angelee's hands, leaned forward to kiss her right cheek, left cheek, and right cheek. His mischievous grin reflected how pleased he was with himself.

"Pauley Bannister, you certainly have some nerve!" Angelee chided in a lowered tone, meant for only him.

Pauley leaned back on his heels and brought out his trademark peace offering. "Do I now?" He raised his eyebrows.

"Yes, pretending interest in French culture when you never have before!" She hissed, taking the black-eyed Susans from him.

"Les feux d'artifice racontent tout..." Captain Carnes quipped.

"What did he say?" Alistair asked, looking up at Cameron.

"It translates, 'The fireworks tell it all.'; Angelee's lively reaction to Pauley's cheek-kissing reveals her hidden passion." Cameron interpreted, winking at Alistair.

Feeling like a mouse being toyed with by a group of cats, Angelee swallowed her frustration and found a reason to extricate herself from the group. "These need to be put into water."

She turned and smiled at the guest. "Alistair has been so excited about the thought of meeting a real-life French pilot. Do sit down, and I'll organize some drinks."

As she maneuvered around the table the grinning young men stepped to the side. Angelee let the front door slam as she went into the house.

Wednesday, July 4th, 1917
Feast of Light Dance

After delivering a tray of glasses and a pitcher of lemonade to the porch for the young men, Angelee had excused herself and retreated into the house. Wanting to make herself inaccessible to them, she decided it was a good time to take a bath.

As she sat in the tub, splashing and scrubbing herself, she fumed. The French salutation with kissing had been totally unexpected. She felt no ill-will toward Captain Carnes, as he was doing what was natural for him. But Cameron had never shown any inclination to practice the cheek-kissing greeting until he'd introduced the singer/aviator. She'd been taken aback; left speechless. Pauley had added to her embarrassment by joining the demonstrative greeting. She regretted blurting out her consternation at his impromptu kisses.

Already blushing from Pauley's opportunistic flirting, Monsieur Carnes's misinterpretation of her heated response felt humiliating. The truth was, she wanted to take Cameron to task as well—for not explaining the French custom previously. Maybe she should have stayed and confronted him when she delivered the drinks. She suspected Captain Carnes would not be convinced of her protestations; Cameron and Pauley would simply laugh at her. It would have been too late by then. That being so, Angelee excused herself and avoided any further interaction.

She and Olivia were meeting up for the evening and Angelee was glad of moral support. To attend the dance this evening at Home Lawn's new lobby meant an encounter with Cameron and Pauley. And of course, there was the concert in the big tent, featuring Monsieur Carnes.

Tri Kappa's *"Feast of Lanterns'"* officially started at four-thirty in the afternoon. Few guests wandered through the stalls and games in the afternoon. It wasn't until after the supper hour that several hundred of Martinsville's citizens made their way to the food, games, and entertainment held on the five-hundred block of Washington street.

Because the Wheel of Fortune was situated right outside of the house, Olivia and Angelee stopped and took a turn. The small packages they won brought laughter when opened. A Brownie troop, right next to the game of chance, were selling boutonnieres. Though meant for the gentlemen, Angelee and Olivia each purchased one for the front of their short-sleeved, summer frocks.

Pushing by the growing crowds, the girls hurried towards the vaudeville show under the big tent on the corner of Lincoln Street and Washington Street. They wanted to see the earliest program if there was room. Although Angelee felt a trickle of apprehension of being seen by Captain Carnes, he would be leaving town early tomorrow morning; who cared what he thought?

Captain Carnes performed several solos from operas in which he had previously participated. Following his singing, an orchestra played patriotic music and popular songs. The show ended with comedy skits given by a group of girls.

A tent flap near the front of the stage was opened to allow the audience to leave easily while the incoming crowd waited outside the front of the tent. Angelee and Olivia made their way around to the lawn where a small café-like seating arrangement of small tables provided seats to eat cake and ice cream. Aimee was busy serving tables and came quickly to take their order. Wearing the Red Cross uniform with an elfin sweetness, Aimee seemed to be thriving with the challenge of handing over dessert and taking the money.

Friends from school came over to share their table. It was difficult to say which was more popular, the seats for a short rest or the delicious, tempting sweets.

As Olivia and Angelee sauntered around the booths, they met Drew, Alistair, and Pauley. Drew had already been to the animal show under a tent on Home Lawn's front yard. He'd made a point of finding the youngest Tilson in order to take him to see the double-headed calf, two dogs, a pen of Guinea Pigs, and an alligator.

"I'm sorry about this afternoon," Pauley said. "It seemed a good idea at the time."

"I can see where it would have been a good opportunity." Angelee acknowledged. "I'm sorry I snapped at you in front of the others."

Pauley smiled. "Are you attending the dance later?"

"That's where we're going next," Angelee replied.

"Great. Will you save a dance for me?" Pauley asked, his head tilted to the side.

"Maybe…probably…but just one." Angelee looked up from underneath her lashes.

"I look forward to it," Pauley said.

Pauley smiled and then turned to join Drew and Alistair as they walked toward the menagerie.

"What was that all about?" Olivia asked as they meandered along.

Angelee recounted the unexpected French greeting and her reaction to the situation.

"Wow!" Olivia quipped. "Maybe it would have been better if Cameron hadn't interpreted the singer's remark."

"I agree. But I just tried to escape as quickly as possible. I could only see things getting worse if I stayed."

"I'm so thirsty. Let's go home and get some iced tea. I don't want any lemonade after that cake."

Angelee agreed with a chuckle. "Our house is closest. It's time for the Boy Scout Exhibition drill. Let's go watch it up on our balcony."

They crossed the street to the Tilson home. Getting their drinks, they climbed the stairs to sit on the upstairs porch. As they drank the dark, cold liquid they could perfectly see the boys, clad in green uniforms, perform their parade routine. The Boy Scouts' hard work was rewarded loudly and enthusiastically as the crowd shared their approval and delight with yells, clapping, and even stomping on the street and sidewalks.

The girls waited until the crowd had drifted away in several directions before they left their perch. They returned the glasses to the kitchen and left the house again to cross Washington Street.

"The paper advertised the evening as a Honky-Tonk. I wonder what that means." Olivia said.

"We're about to learn! I suppose it means there are no waltzes." Angelee giggled and put her arm through Olivia's.

Drumming and rhythmic piano playing, accompanied by banjo, mandolin, and guitar filled the lobby of Home Lawn. Angelee wasn't sure what to make of the high-energy, jazzy sounds provided by the musicians.

Angelee pointed to a couch where they could sit. As they settled onto the new furniture, Olivia seemed perplexed by the raucous music in the air.

"Well, it's certainly upbeat!" Angelee said.

"Do you think we should stay?" Olivia asked, somewhat hesitantly.

"It's just different," Angelee observed. "Maybe the music isn't so bad…just has a bad reputation because it's played mostly in bars."

"I think it's growing on me." Olivia acknowledged, keeping time by patting the couch arm with her hand.

"Good evening, ladies." Cameron greeted them. "I'm glad you decided to join the party here. Can I get either of you some punch?"

"No thanks. We just had some iced tea at home, watching the Boy Scouts up on the balcony." Olivia answered.

"As you can see, this is great music to dance to. Angelee, would you do me the pleasure and dance with me."

"I'm afraid I'm more comfortable with waltzing. This music is too fast for that."

"Let me teach you to fox-trot. It's simple." Cameron entreated.

"Well, I do want to talk to you about this afternoon." Angelee stood and walked toward the dance floor.

"You mean Captain Carnes's visit with Alistair?"

"No, I mean your sudden embracing of French customs!" Angelee retorted.

Cameron's brow furrowed, as he took Angelee's hand and guided her around the floor. "I think we need to step outside to talk about this." With that, he led her out onto the side yard.

"Now, tell me, did I do something wrong?" Cameron asked.

Putting her hands on her hips, Angelee gave him a level look. "I am used to your British idioms, and tales of life in England. Yes, the British are all reserved, polite, proper. Then you show up at my home, and suddenly you're greeting me "French style" because you're with your friend, Monsieur Carnes. You and Pauley presumed that I would not mind because it was novel. Well, I was totally flabbergasted—and embarrassed. Your enjoyment was at my expense. And I resent that."

Cameron's grey eyes turned dark. "Listen, don't you think you're overreacting? It was simply three pecks on the cheek. You're behaving like a naïve girl!"

"That's because I AM a naïve girl! It's easy for you to be condescending—you're older, you've lived abroad and you're experienced with women. At least I'm not walking around behaving one way on Monday and differently on Tuesday!"

"What exactly is it you want from me, Angelee? I try to be a friend and help you keep a promise to your little brother. Instead of appreciating my effort, you find a pretext to be offended. It was rude of you to leave the drinks and disappear. You should have called me aside right then and told me how you felt. You certainly didn't care about Bannister's feelings."

"My world is changing so fast; I don't know how to make sense of it. I'm not worldly or sophisticated. The Captain was so exuberant. I didn't know what to think of your sudden 'French-ness.' And Pauley is always teasing me. I felt so gauche, I just wanted to hide."

Cameron turned his head away. "Well, I see."

"Context is everything." Cameron turned to gaze at her. "The Captain was just following his customs. Pauley was teasing you. But for me, well, you don't know where I stand." Cameron ran his hand over his russet locks. "Okay, I concede that my intentions might seem a mystery. But I just want you to know, I like you. I find you refreshing, interesting, and enjoy watching you learn. So, forgive me for my audacity earlier today."

"Thank you for your apology." Angelee dropped her arms, sighing. "But now I feel ashamed of myself."

"Please don't. I understand you better now." Cameron offered a reconciliatory smile. "Shall we finish our dance lesson?"

"Sure, why not?" Angelee followed him back into Home Lawn's lobby.

The close air in the room grew stuffier as people drifted in. Cameron's words niggled at the back of her mind; he found her interesting. What did he mean by "refreshing"? The heat of the room, the clamorous music, and Cameron's distracting comments prevented her from focusing on the dance steps. After the song ended, Angelee thanked Cameron and suggested he find another partner.

With hand signals, she motioned to Pauley she was ready for their dance. Accustomed to afternoon tea dances, she followed Pauley's lead. As they whirled around the room, Angelee realized the preciousness of these moments; Pauley, Andrew, and many other young men would soon be leaving for National Guards' training camp. She couldn't wait for the dance to be over. Carrying stress in her shoulders and neck, she could feel a headache beginning to build.

"Enough!" she thought to herself. "Enough of this boisterous music! Enough of these men stirring up new and confusing emotions! Enough of this socializing for the night! Time to go."

"Pauley, I'm done for this evening. I'm going home." She dropped his hand and went to find Olivia.

She found Olivia standing next to the punch bowl, with a cup of punch. Encouraging Olivia to stay as long as she wanted, she bid farewell and weaved her way out of the lobby. Outside the summer night was a cool, though balmy.

"Mommy, I will be so glad when you and Daddy get back from Cincinnati," Angelee said out loud, absent-mindedly.

"When are they back?" Pauley asked.

Annoyed, Angelee snapped. "What are you doing? I live just across the street."

"Oh, I'm in it, again am I? Sorry, but you seemed upset. I wanted to make sure you're okay."

"You're missing the dance. Mommy and Daddy are back Sunday night. And I just need some time to think. A headache isn't going to kill me." She hoped her curt answers would send him away.

"I'm not missing much in terms of the dance." Pauley quipped. "But, just so you know, I am not walking you home."

"What are you doing?" Angelee said, stopping to give him a suspicious glare.

"I have a clandestine date with Aunt Milly," Pauley said, winking at her.

Despite herself, Angelee smirked. "Snickerdoodles..."

With a wide smile and nod, Pauley replied. "Enough said!"

They crossed the street laughing.

Making Peace

Finishing her work duties early, Angelee had returned home for the day. Enjoying the breeze, Angelee settled on the porch swing with a glass of iced tea and picked up a book.

A familiar whistle pervaded the air and distracted her. Looking up she had to smile.

"Hello, You!" She greeted him. "No Black-eyed Susan's today?"

Shaking his head, Pauley mounted the steps. "Figured the ones I brought yesterday were still in good shape. Whatcha reading?"

"'*Aurora the Magnificent*' by Gertrude Hall Brownell. Haven't gotten too far yet."

Pauley eased himself down onto the swing next to her. "So, am I forgiven for my impudence yesterday?"

Angelee marked her place with a bookmark and set it on a side table.

"Of course. Just so you know, I was put out with Cameron as well. I let him know about it last night."

"Really?" Pauley raised an eyebrow. "I thought you were accustomed to his European manners."

"His British-isms, yes. But he has never greeted me with that French-cheek-kissing business before. I was so surprised and embarrassed by it all. I felt like you both took advantage of me."

"I confess, it was such an obvious opportunity to tease you. So, what did *Mr. Cameron Addison Boyer-Parkham* have to say for himself?"

"He said that I was being silly, naïve. Besides, I wasn't sure of his motive. Was he teasing? Was it doing it to make Monsieur Carnes feel comfortable? Was he showing off?"

"Did you ask him?" Pauley started the swing moving.

"I explained that I had no idea how to interpret his actions. That's when he admitted he hadn't meant to disconcert or distress me. He said he liked me. He thinks I'm "refreshing" and that he enjoys watching me learn things."

"It sounds like I may have some competition for your affections," Pauley said softly, and the swing stopped.

Angelee turned to gaze at his face; a face she was so familiar with, a boy she'd grown up with. But his confession of love had made her realize that he was no longer the boy from down the street. He was a man.

"Pauley, all my life I've known that one day I would fall in love with someone I respect enough to marry. I've never thought about who that might be, or how it would happen. To me, getting married means having children.

"But when I was a young girl, a toddler in my care got hurt. Since then I've been afraid to be alone with children— especially babies and toddlers. They would always be at risk with me. Maybe I shouldn't be a mother."

"You're being too hard on yourself. You were a kid yourself." Pauley countered.

Angelee pushed with her foot, setting the glider back and forth. She considered Pauley's input.

After a few minutes, Pauley added. "Angelee, you love your little brother to distraction. I know for a certainty that you would never truly put Alistair in a threatening situation. You would protect him with your life. If no one else were around, you'd do the same for any other youngster."

"Pauley, I know I hear the truth when it is spoken. Thanks for the perspective."

"That's what friends are for." Pauley draped one long leg over the other.

"You have always been a good friend," Angelee said softly. "I just need to know if you're willing to wait until I can figure out what I'm supposed to be about."

"You may be the one who has to wait for things since I've enlisted. But, explain what you mean when you say, 'what I'm supposed to be about.'"

"You remember the story about Jesus; when he was about twelve years old? His parents had started home. After a day they turned back to Jerusalem because they couldn't find him. When they discovered him in the temple, they asked him why he'd remained behind. And Jesus said; 'Didn't you realize I must be about My Father's business?'

"My biggest question to God right now is; 'Father, what business do you have for me?' I've never known what *that* purpose is—that 'gift' that needs my attention, my passion. Every time Olivia talks about becoming a nurse, and Amy talks about art, I feel left out. I know there should be some way I can help people that comes naturally. I seem to be oblivious to it."

"We all go through times of uncertainty, with more questions than answers. It is the things that I'm sure of that keep me moving in a direction." Pauley said. "For example, when I'm practicing for Latin class, I wonder why I'm taking it. But it will serve me if I want to go to law school, or if I want to study other foreign languages. What I do today will prepare me for tomorrow."

Angelee nodded. "The other night you seemed so sure of yourself, telling me that you are in love with me. I'm sorry I ran away. A person could say that we've known each other all our lives. So maybe it feels crystal clear to you that we belong together. But for me, it was just an added pressure from people who were trying to pull me in directions they thought best for me."

"I know I should have waited. The graduation/birthday party was quite a fiasco." Pauley admitted.

"Mrs. Parkham is a sophisticated, shrewd, and strong-willed woman. I felt privileged because she had chosen me to help her— even though I had no experience. I felt flattered that she wanted to take me under her wing and invest so much in me. But at the party, it suddenly felt like she had called in debt I didn't know I owed."

"Have you been able to see it from her point of view? She has a strong affection for you and wanted to do something of great value for you." Pauley countered.

"It seems there are a bunch of people going around trying to do the right thing but doing it the wrong way. If Mrs. Parkham and my parents had sat down with me and told me about the plan, then I could have been honest with them."

"So why don't you want to go to Wellesley?" Pauley prodded.

"Not YOU TOO!" Angelee moaned.

"No, not me too! I just want you to explain to me why you don't want to go."

"Wellesley is a college for women who want to acquire social graces and professional polish, to be movers and shakers. I have no great aspirations toward politics or social reform. The very fact that Wellesley is a college, in and of itself, creates a problem for me. What would I study?"

"You'd have a couple of years to figure it out. All institutions of higher learning require you to take general courses before declaring an area of major study. And education is never a waste."

"See, you are on their side." Angelee protested.

"No, I am not on their side. I'm not on anybody's side. I'm just letting you know how the system works."

"All the same, I don't feel ready for college. I would rather take some time, maybe work for a while and find something that truly interests me. I know studying isn't a waste of time...but I also know that I don't want to be so far away from home and my family."

"That is a good point. So, could it be, that you're saying you might be interested in going to college at some point if you discover 'the Father's purpose' for you?" Pauley asked.

"Yes...I suppose so...and that purpose required a college degree." Angelee consented.

"It's more that you'd want to be in Indiana, to study close to home?" Pauley clarified.

"Yes, exactly."

"What do your parents say about that?" Pauley stretched his legs out straight in front of him.

"I think Mommy is accepting it better than Daddy is. He still wants me to go to Wellesley. But until I have some clear direction, I think it's better if I just keep working."

"Angelee, all I can say is, take each day as it comes. Remember, Jesus said, *'Be not therefore anxious for the morrow: for the morrow will be anxious for itself. Sufficient unto the day is the evil thereof.'* In other words, don't worry."

"Thanks Pauley. I know you're right." Angelee replied, thoughtfully.

"Come on, let's go for a walk." Pauley stood and held out his hand.

"That sounds like a good idea."

Angelee took her empty glass and library book into the house and re-joined Pauley on the porch.

Clear skies allowed the sun's heat to bathe the earth, and summer gardens flourished. Returning from the Saturday morning reading group, Angelee pondered how to bring up the driving lessons to her parents. She didn't want way-lay them the moment they arrived. They would be weary after spending so much time on the trains.

However, she couldn't leave it too long, because Alistair had already pestered her twice that morning. Being young, he had not learned the value of picking one's moments for certain conversations. Nor had he learned the importance of waiting quietly.

As she reached the steps to her home, Drew maneuvered his 1912 Chevrolet to the side of the house and parked. Hurrying over to the car, she discovered that her hunch was correct; Mommy and Daddy were home. Opening the door, Angelee helped her mother alight from the car, embracing her tightly.

"Did you have a good time?" She asked, leaning back to see her mother's face, hidden under a wide-brimmed hat.

"Joyous!" Mommy sighed delightedly. "Just what you father and I needed."

"How long did it take him to get over the shock?" Angelee asked, looking toward her father, who had also exited from the car.

"By the time we changed trains in Indianapolis, your father was sliding full-force into vacation mode. He didn't mind the idea of shopping, as long as I was willing to sit through a Red's baseball game. How could I say no? And we took a day to walk the grounds of the Time Hill, where the Gruen Watchmakers Company has constructed new buildings. Other days we rested and just enjoyed each other's company." Mommy said, putting her arm through Angelee's as they went into the house.

"Did Daddy make good use of his camera?"

"Yes, and I am sure you'll enjoy seeing the photos once they're developed."

Aunt Milly came out of the kitchen. "I thought I heard my dearest twin in the house!"

Hugging her sister, Mommy said, "Thanks for helping to hold the fort while we were gone. Where are Grandma and Grandy?"

"They took a stroll into town. They're due back anytime. I've just finished getting lunch ready. You couldn't have timed it any better."

Within half-an-hour the family had assembled around the dining room table, eating tuna salad sandwiches, with sliced vegetables, chattering away.

"Guess what?!" Alistair exclaimed.

Angelee's heart skipped a beat, and her stomach sank. Before she could open her mouth, Alistair continued.

"Angelee is taking driving lessons! And she took me with her!"

Every head turned; every eye focused on her.

"Is that what you were actually doing on the 4th of July?" Grandy's eyes narrowed and hardened.

"How long has this been going on?" Daddy's voice lowered and clenched his jaw.

"Oh, An-ge-lee!" Grandma's hands flew to her chest, startled by the announcement.

Angelee looked at her aunt. There she found an ally. Aunt Milly's eye's twinkled and she tried to suppress a smile.

Mommy's questioning eyes, accentuated by the tilt of her head, expressed her apprehension.

Angelee opened her mouth, closed it, struggling to find a way to explain.

"Who's teaching you to drive? Pauley?" Drew threw out his question.

"Mr. Parkham is teaching me...and Olivia..." Angelee blurted. "But that was our first outing."

Angelee looked over at Aimee, who was taking everything in with wide-eyed wonder. Unusually, she was silent.

"Cameron Parkham?" Drew asked. "Why him?"

"That's the question I should be asking—am asking." Daddy interjected.

"Mr. Parkham has been chauffeuring me around town on errands—at Mrs. Parkham's insistence. He suggested that I should consider learning how to drive. And he kept pestering me about it."

"So, you didn't ask him to teach you?" Mommy wanted to clarify.

"No, I hadn't even considered it. But the more he talked about the women ambulance drivers in England, it seemed like a good skill to have."

"Why didn't you talk to us about it first?" Mommy wanted to know.

Angelee sighed. "I don't know. I guess I thought you'd try to talk me out of it. It just felt like if I talked to you, I was asking your permission. I wanted to make the decision myself."

"We," Daddy nodded toward Mommy, "can appreciate that. And in the end, it is your decision, if you truly want to learn to drive. But what concerns me is that you took Alistair with you."

"I did ask Grandy if it was okay for Alistair to go. Mr. Parkham did come in to meet Grandy and Grandma. I know I should have told them that Olivia and I were planning to have a lesson. Maybe they would have said no to Alistair joining us. But Alistair was so adamant that he wanted to go." Angelee looked over at Alistair, who was staring at his navel.

"Alistair, did I let you drive?" Angelee enticed an answer from him.

"No!" Alistair sulked.

"And didn't I ask you to wait for me to speak to Mommy and Daddy?" Angelee softly reminded him.

"Yes." Alistair's lower lip quivered.

Angelee looked back at her parents. "We did have a bit of disagreement while we were out with Mr. Parkham. Alistair didn't think it was fair that I could decide for myself, while he couldn't. But I was determined that we were going to discuss it with you first. He wasn't happy at the time."

"Mommy, Daddy," Angelee continued. "When Olivia was having her turn, I stayed out of the car, sitting with Alistair. And when I had my turn, Olivia entertained Alistair. I thought it was safer that way—in case one of us wrecked the car. And Mr. Parkham was in the car with Olivia or me giving us instruction. We weren't on our own trying to drive. We were trying to be wise."

"Now that you've explained, it isn't as dramatic as I envisioned." Daddy said. "When were you planning to fill us in on this escapade?"

Mommy couldn't help but grin at Daddy's use of the word, "escapade."

"This evening, after supper. I wanted you to get settled before I approached you both. But I didn't get the chance." Angelee remarked, throwing an accusatory look at Alistair.

"Sorry, Angelee," Alistair mumbled.

"Angelee, it's true that you may have gotten ahead of yourself in this situation. But it does sound like you've done your best to handle it wisely." Daddy said, leaning back in his chair.

"Alistair, please look at me." Daddy instructed. Alistair looked his father full in the face.

"I know it's rough being the youngest." Daddy spoke gently but firmly. "You see your brother and sisters getting to do things you can't. But they had to wait to be old enough, or big enough, to do challenging things. As for driving, you need to be taller and stronger. When you can reach the peddles in the car without sitting on the edge of the seat, or needing a pillow behind you, then you can learn to drive. But I don't mind if you accompany Angelee and Mr. Parkham—if they are agreeable. But, if I hear that you've been trying to drive on your own, there will be no more jaunts out with your sister. Do we understand each other?"

Alistair, his eyes wide, and brimming with tears, nodded. "Yes, sir."

"Good. Now then, let's have some dessert!" Daddy smiled at his family.

The freshly baked chocolate cake was cut and served, while Mommy and Daddy shared incidents from their vacation in Cincinnati.

Driving lessons for Olivia and Angelee integrated into the daily routines of work, church attendance, and the occasional social activity. Daddy started taking them out on Saturday afternoons, in the family car for practice. They often came home tired but pleased.

Mrs. Johnstone had been unable to find any more volunteers to lead the reading group. Angelee had begun anticipating the Saturday morning sessions, finding joy in interacting with the inquisitive and amusing children that came each week. In the back of her mind, Mrs. Carmichael's words niggled. Could she be a teacher? But she feared being solely responsible for one child, let alone a group of them. It only took one child to have an accident to set the others off in a panic. She didn't want that commitment.

Angelee had only shared Mrs. Carmichael's suggestion with her mother. It didn't occur to her that the palpitating heart and excitement she'd felt was related to discerning guidance for the future. So, although the idea kept popping into her mind, she kept brushing the idea to the back of her mind.

Summer heat and humidity rose during July and August. Kitchen gardens provided tomatoes, cucumbers, onions, beets, and green beans in lavish amounts. Like most Indiana kitchens during late summer and fall, the Tilson kitchen became a food preservation factory, prolifically producing canned and pickled fruit and vegetables. The majority of that workload fell to Mommy and Aunt Milly, although Aimee and Angelee contributed to watching the boiling pots, which required three hours of heating.

Over the days following her parent's trip to Cincinnati, Angelee noticed subtle changes in her mother. She tired easily and complained of nausea, and would have to eat a few saltine crackers with a cup of hot tea. Headaches became almost a daily occurrence. When Angelee mentioned her observations to her mother, Mommy had dismissed it as the heat. It was puzzling, because Aunt Milly wasn't suffering from the heat, and they were twins. But Angelee left it.

On Sundays, the industry of preserving food was not practiced. It was a day of rest; a day to spend together as a family. In that year of 1917, the first Sunday in August, the fifth, was designated a family-only day.

It was a rare occurrence. Normally their Sunday dinner table practiced Hoosier Hospitality in full measure. Alistair's birthday would usually mean inviting his best friend, Bart, to dinner. Maybe the whole Hanson family. Equally, Drew having enlisted, thought he would be leaving in September. It seemed peculiar, however, for that particular day, parental insistence dictated it was to be family only. Mommy and Daddy reasoned it might be the last time that every member of the Tilson clan would be together for quite some time. It was going to be a bittersweet birthday for Alistair. Yet, for some reason, Angelee suspected there might be another reason for the 'family only' stipulation.

Each summer they set up a semi-permanent table in the side yard. To protect from the sun and rain, they erected a shade-producing, canvas canopy to enjoy the good weather. They enjoyed the fresh air, especially since it was cooler outside than in the house.

Alistair had requested fried chicken as his birthday meal. The chicken, cooked the night before, was flanked by a garden salad, pickles, potato salad, and coleslaw.

"Okay, who is taking the first turn on the ice cream churn?" Daddy asked. If you don't take a turn, then you don't get any."

"Does that mean if I turn the crank longer than the others, I get more ice cream?!" Drew joked.

"I suppose in theory it would work that way. But I figure that each of us can do about ten to fifteen minutes each until we get a good result."

"Let me go first!" Aimee said. "It's easier when the milk is not too thick!"

"I'm second!!" Angelee jumped in.

"I shouldn't have to, because it's my birthday!" Alistair announced.

"All right, all right, it's good to know *everyone* is so enthusiastic." Daddy chuckled. "So, are we adding cherries, strawberries, or blackberries?"

"Do we have to add anything?" Alistair grumped. "Can't you just put what you want on top? I mean, we're having cake too."

"Who feels the same as Alistair?" Daddy asked.

"Doesn't make any difference to me," Drew said. "I'll eat it however it comes."

"I'm in agreement with that." Aunt Milly said. "As long as we all have some, that's all that matters to me."

Angelee thought for a moment then said. "I'd like to add all three to the ice cream. But that just complicates the issue."

"I think it's fairer if leave out the fruit and then each of us can add what we want," Aimee said.

"Looks like Mommy has to make the decision." Daddy summarized.

"This is silly!" Mommy said. "A family dilemma over ice cream! Well, since two of you want no fruit, and two of you don't care, it will have to be no fruit added. Nice try, Darling. You didn't get your way this time."

"That's okay." Daddy said, laughing. "I just wanted to watch the reaction."

"Shall I start clearing the table?" Aunt Milly asked.

"Not just yet." Daddy said. "Since we are all here, there is something you should all know."

Aunt Milly sat back down.

The conversation stopped and everyone looked at him.

"Does this have to do with Drew leaving soon?" Alistair asked. "Because I don't want to think about it."

Mommy and Daddy exchanged a look, and Daddy nodded.

"No, it has nothing to do with Drew," Mommy answered.

"Well, is it a birthday present?" Alistair persevered.

Laughter filled the air.

"Well, it is kind of birthday related. But not yours." Mommy said vaguely. "As you know, I've not been feeling well lately—headaches, getting tired out easily, nausea. At first, I thought it was hay fever or the heat. However, I decided that I would go to see Dr. Jackson. His diagnosis is that it will be in late March or early April before I get over my condition."

Angelee watched as her aunt touched the top of her fingers. Angelee counted along with her, seven. Seven months? Why would Mommy be unwell so long? Then she remembered that Mommy had been shown the same kind of symptoms when she was pregnant with Alistair. Was Mommy really telling them there was to be another baby? She found herself holding her breath, and refusing to be the one who asked bluntly for a confirmation.

She looked over at Aimee, who also sat with wide eyes, uncertainty mirrored there.

"Mom, what are you saying?" Drew's eyes were furrowed. "You're going to have another baby?"

"Yes, Drew, that is what I'm saying. Come next spring, there will be a fifth Tilson child—Lord willing."

Angelee looked around the table. Daddy's joy and pride twinkled in his eyes. Alistair had dropped his head. Clearly, the baby announcement had stolen the thunder of his birthday celebration. Drew sat, his mouth gaping open. Aimee's hands covered her mouth—amazement spilling from her eyes. Aunt Milly had tears running down her cheeks. She was the first to move, leaving her seat to walk around to Mommy. She wrapped her arms around her sister and kissed her cheek.

"I'm sorry, Millicent. I know this is hard for you." Mommy said softly to her sister.

"Why is it hard for Aunt Milly? She isn't the one who just had her birthday spoiled." Alistair complained.

Angelee, who was sitting next to Alistair, hit his leg. "I'll explain it later. But right now, be nice to Mommy."

"I was quite shocked when Dr. Jackson told me," Mommy said. "So was Daddy. We thought I was getting too old."

"You shouldn't be mad, Alistair," Aimee said. "Finding out about a baby is a great birthday present." She had gotten up and hugged her mother as well. "And I'm sure we can all help with things."

"I'm not a girl! And who wants a crying baby around?" Alistair pouted.

"But you're going to be a big brother!" Aimee explained.

"I don't *want* to be a big brother. That's Drew's job. He does it just fine." Alistair protested.

"Alistair Jackson Tilson, you're being a brat!" Angelee reprimanded. "We're all just as shocked as you are, so stop being rude."

Mommy opened her arms to Alistair and motioned him to come.

Expecting Alistair to run into the house, Angelee was surprised that Alistair scurried over to his mother.

Mommy embraced him, and he started to cry. "It's okay, Alistair." Mommy soothed him, patting his back. "All of us are going to have to adjust to this new little life. I know it isn't the gift you were hoping for on your birthday. But he—or—she, is indeed a gift—a present from God. Just like you were a present from God. Daddy and I won't love you any less. And you will have another person who will grow up loving you."

Drew came around the table to stand beside his mother and brother. Gently placing a hand on Alistair's shoulders, and turning the boy around, the eldest picked up the youngest, who wrapped his arms and legs around him.

"Listen, Little Brother, you are a great little brother. But you know, it's also great to be a big brother...take it from me. I will probably be away when the baby is born. But since I can't be here, you've got to hold the fort for me—till I can come home for good. Okay?"

All Angelee could see was Alistair nod his head. She now felt guilty and walked over to the boys.

"Alistair, I'm sorry I called you a brat. And you know what? Aimee was upset when Mommy told us that she was going to have a baby—and you were that baby."

"Gee thanks for being a tattle-tale!" Aimee sighed, rolling her eyes.

"But it's true!" Angelee said. "To be totally honest, Alistair, I also cried and had a tantrum when Mommy told me I was going to be a big sister. But then Aimee was born and everything changed. I was glad she was born. And I was glad when you came along too."

Alistair, still in Drew's arms, looked down at his sisters. "Really?"

His sisters nodded their assent.

Daddy walked over to the group and took Alistair from Drew. "Now then, young man, don't think that because we have this big news that we've forgotten that it is YOUR birthday. Let's go get the ice cream churn ready." Setting the youngster down, they walked hand-in-hand toward the garage to find the wooden bucket and metal canister that fit inside.

Angelee and Aimee cleared the table while Mommy and Aunt Milly went into the house to mix up cream, milk, eggs, sugar, and vanilla to be churned in the ice cream maker.

Drew had filled the kitchen sink with lye soap and hot water to wash up the dishes while his sisters finished clearing up and then got the dishes ready for cake and ice cream.

The kitchen put into proper order, they collected Alistair's presents to be opened desert.

Gathered by the side of the house, the family made a game of the hard work of churning ice cream. They chanted rhymes, sang silly songs, and competed to see who could crank the handle the greatest number of times in a minute. By the time seven of them had turned for ten minutes each, the ice cream was ready.

The buttermilk chocolate cake was carried out, flames dancing on nine candles, and presented to Alistair, complete with a rousing rendition of "Happy Birthday to You."

After enthusiastically opening his gaily wrapped parcels, the boys had a second of helping of cake and ice cream.

When Alistair went off to enjoy his new treasures, Daddy and Drew heading to the kitchen to wash the dessert dishes.

Angelee invited Mommy to sit on the front porch.

"I should help with the dishes," Mommy said.

"You've done enough for now. Just sit for a while." Angelee encouraged.

Within minutes Aunt Milly and Aimee joined them on the front porch. "We've been dismissed." Aunt Milly said. "You have a rare treasure in your husband!"

"I'm going to wait a bit longer to apply for a missionary position." Aunt Milly said. "I want to stay here and help you during this time. You know to help with the baby."

"I know it is a temptation for you," Mommy said. "But you can't keep putting your life on hold for me—or my family. You still have a chance to marry again and have a family."

Aunt Milly turned her head, but Angelee saw her blink away tears.

"Aunt Milly, you know that God has the best plans for you," Angelee said. "Don't you think you should pray about it before you make a final decision?"

"You are right, I know. But I love you all so much. And I do want to meet this baby." Aunt Milly agreed.

"Don't worry, God knows your heart. If the doors are open right now, you need to see what is beyond it. But if the door closes, then you know you belong here." Emileah encouraged her sister.

"Mommy, when can we start telling people about the baby?" Angelee asked. "I don't want to announce it to the whole town. But it would be good if I could tell Olivia."

"I don't mind if you tell people—but only if the opportunity is right. It will eventually be obvious anyway." Mommy grinned.

"What do you think we should name the baby?"

"All I know is that it should start with an "A"—since the rest of you do. But I've not had time to think about it beyond that."

"Come with me, Darling Sister. I need a walk." Mommy said. "And you two girls, go find some way to amuse yourselves. This time of day is just too nice to waste sitting around."

While Mommy and Aunt Milly went walking. Aimee decided to go see her best friend, Lucy. Left on her own, Angelee wished she had a car of her own. The pristine weather would have made for a lovely drive in the country. As it was, she decided to see if Olivia was available for a walk to the high school and share her news.

The September sun hung in a cloudless sky, warming the skin. Angelee stood on the bottom step of the First Christian Church, preparing to walk home after the service.

"I've heard there's speculation that Company K will be leaving Martinsville for Fort Harrison on Friday. Has Drew said anything to you or your family?" Rev. Matthias asked.

"Drew leaves early every day to go to the Armory. He doesn't come back until late, so we don't have much time to talk. Although, Thursday evening Drew came home earlier, and Pauley stopped in to say hello."

As if on cue, Pauley came around the corner, his seven-year-old, twin sisters hanging from each arm. Their escort of Pauley looked like a game of push-and-pull.

"Speaking of Pauley, it looks like you have two shadows!" Rev. Matthias remarked.

"My only reprieve is when I'm at work." Pauley grinned good-naturedly.

One of the girls punched his arm, playfully.

"Lucy, there will be consequences if you do that again," Pauley warned.

Lucy giggled, mischief twinkling in her eyes. It was obvious she was toying with the temptation to test her brother's threat.

"How do you tell them apart?" Rev. Matthias was in a quandary, looking at the identical girls.

"Like most twins, once you've been around them for a while, you notice the differences. Lucy has a small gap between her bottom, two front teeth. And Lori has a freckle on her left ear. But, since I've known them all their lives, I have my own ways of telling. For instance, Lucy is the 'mean' one. And Lori is the soft-hearted one." Surely meant to provoke, this comparison earned him another punch on the arm from Lucy.

"I warned you, Lucy!" Pauley leaned over, picked up his sister around the waist, and proceeded to tickle her. She squealed, delighted, flaying her legs trying to work her way free.

Family, friends, and other church acquaintances nearby joined in the laughter.

"Not fair!" Lucy shrilled. "Not fair!"

"I know it...but if you can't be nice, then you have to pay." Pauley reminded his younger sibling.

"You deserved it!" Lucy taunted. "You never do this to Lori!" She complained, laughing despite herself.

"Lori never punches me," Pauley replied nonchalantly.

"But she teases you!" Lucy protested.

"And you know I tease her back. Say 'enough' and I'll put you down." Pauley offered.

"No!" Lucy rebelled.

Uninvited, the thought crossed through Angelee's mind that Pauley would be a good father someday. She brushed the thought away, wanting to distance such thoughts from her mind. Purposely told herself that Drew would be a good father as well. He'd always been a good brother.

Pauley shifted Lucy so she was more secure, then tickled her even more. "That can only mean you want more of this."

"No!" Lucy repeated.

Pauley repeated the instructions to say 'enough'. Lucy resisted again. More tickling. Finally, Lucy declared. "Enough already! Enough!"

Pauley tossed her up, caught her again, and then gave her hugs and kisses. "Nice to know I'm still the boss!" He said, setting Lucy on her feet.

Lucy made a show of straightening her dress, pulling down the sleeves, and shaking out her skirt. "You just think you are." She gibed.

Pauley laughed. "Lucy, Girl, you certainly are a live-wire. But since you *think* you're the boss, is it okay if I ask Drew to come over to play checkers tonight?"

Lucy crossed her arms, looked at her sister. "What do you think? Should we let Drew come over?"

Lori picked up her left braid and began to fiddle with it. "Hmmm..." Lori tilted her head in 'thinking mode.' After a few seconds, she replied. "Only if he brings Angelee. I want to show her the latest doll's dress I've made."

"Books and Dolls! That's all you ever think about!" Lucy complained. "But having Angelee come over is a good idea."

Both girls looked up expectantly at Pauley. "Well, are you going to ask Angelee as well?" Lucy exacted.

Angelee loved the twins and thought it was cute to see them maneuver Pauley around to what they wanted. She looked at Pauley, who was also looking at her.

"Are you going to let them get away with that? Because, you know, if you give in to their demands, then you truly are no longer the boss." Angelee playfully challenged him.

Pauley crossed his arms and rolled his eyes up toward heaven. "Not at all, not at all. See, they know that if they ask me for something I already want, then we all win. But it's your choice."

"My choice to what?" Angelee bantered back. "My choice to ask you something? My choice to decide something? Nothing is clear right now."

"Oh, please excuse me for presuming that I could follow on from the girls' obviously stated request of you," Pauley remarked, the grin widening on his face.

"But you see, it was a conversation about me, not a conversation including me. You seem to be implying that I don't need to be asked directly."

"Well, please forgive my oversight!" Pauley followed along with the game.

"Just get on and ask her already." Demanded the impatient Lucy.

"Gee whiz, this child." Pauley griped. "Miss Angelee Tilson, my sisters would like to invite you to enjoy their company later today. Would you be so kind as to oblige their heart's desire and accompany your brother over to our abode?"

Angelee was so amused by the overplayed request she felt inclined to drop a curtsy. When she did, Lucy and Lori giggled. Pauley laughed out loud.

"My Goodness! Such a polite, downright chivalrous invitation. How could one possibly resist?" Angelee replied.

Pauley turned to his sisters. "Satisfied My Darling Sisters?" The girls clapped their hands. "YES!"

"Do you have any new pocket dolls?" Lori asked of Angelee.

"As a matter of fact, I ordered some a few weeks ago. Shall I bring them along?"

"Oh, yes please."

"What time shall Drew and I come?" Angelee asked.

"Oh, any time after three," Pauley said. "Come on, Lucy, Lori. I see Mom waving for us to come."

Once again, the girls latched onto his hands and the three walked off.

"It's been a while since I've witnessed such an amusing repartee." Rev. Matthias. "You know, Angelee, you and Pauley sound like an old married couple."

"Hardly! It's just that Pauley's spent so much time with us." Angelee shrugged, nonchalantly. "He's like another brother. You know, to see Drew is to see Pauley."

Rev. Matthias laughed and grinned knowingly. "You can deny it if you want to. But I can tell there is a difference between the way you feel about Drew and the way you feel about Pauley."

Angelee shifted from one foot to the other, uncomfortable discussing a topic she wanted to avoid. "All I will say is, we are good friends. Both of our families are."

"I think that's evidenced by Lucy and Lori wanting you to come over." Rev. Matthias observed. "I'm sure you will all support each other when the boys go away."

"I cannot begin to imagine what that will be like," Angelee remarked.

"At least you've got the experience of them being at college." Rev. Matthias sympathized.

"But knowing they are going to be at war—even just training for the war is so different. I never thought about them being in danger's way at college."

"There are different kinds of danger. Sometimes it is clear and apparent to us—like physical risks. Other times it isn't—like intellectual or emotional vulnerability. There is the danger of complacency, of taking things for granted. There is the danger of being exposed to ideas that rob of us our faith, our hope, and our relationships. College can be a place of losing one's way as well as finding one's way." Rev. Matthias explained.

"I'd never thought about that," Angelee admitted. "So maybe it's a good thing I haven't decided about going to college... or where to go to college if I realize that I need to."

"My concern for Drew, Pauley, and all the young men who are leaving home soon is that they will be exposed to hardness, cruelty, and violence that will change them into bitter, cynical and unforgiving men. I can only pray that they will cling to the promises of God and practice the teachings of Jesus."

"It seems like we are fighting two different wars on two different levels." Angelee pondered out loud.

"Truly it does. Every day, each one of us must contend for our belief in God's love. It doesn't matter where we are, or what we are doing. Some days the fight is easier than others. That is why we need each other. And I am praying that the church and the greater community will continue to work together to support not only the soldiers going off to fight, but their families as well."

Suddenly Angelee chuckled. "I'm sorry, Rev. Matthias. I just feel like I've been given the addendum to your sermon."

Rev Matthias joined in her amusement. "Do you think I should have brought the pulpit out with me? Maybe attracted a bigger audience?"

"That would have been too much work for too little result, I think. Maybe I was meant to hear that private sermon." Angelee offered for consideration.

"Experience tells me that the Lord does orchestrate these situations. So, I won't consider any of it lost. Jesus met the woman at the well with a message uniquely for her, after he preached to the multitude. I guess it's all in a day's work." Rev. Matthias removed his glasses and rubbed them on his robe. "Now it is high time I make sure everyone is out of the church so I can lock up. Then, I can go see about my Sunday dinner."

"Who are you joining this week?" Angelee inquired.

"The Jones family. If I leave now, I shall arrive there in plenty of time."

"Thanks for the chat," Angelee said, proffering her hand to him, which he took.

"You're very welcome. I'll see you soon."

By the end of August, draft boards had screened thousands of men for selection. In early August the Indiana National Guard began assembling troops for federal service. Men already trained and on active duty would be joined by units from Kentucky and West Virginia after reporting to Camp Shelby, Mississippi. These three units would form the 38th Infantry Division.

On Tuesday, 4th September, the *Daily Reporter* reported the first contingent of Morgan County men would be leaving by the end of that week.

Alarm clocks in the Tilson home started jangling at five-thirty, Friday, morning September 7th. Heavy, humid air prevented any breezes coming through the windows. Odd moments of sunlight broke through the blue-bottomed clouds threatening rain.

The family gathered to spend precious time with Drew. A spread of his breakfast favorites appeared on the dining room buffet.

"The recruiter told me that we might get to come home for the weekend after we complete basic training," Drew remarked, spooning sausage gravy over fluffy biscuits, and yellow scrambled eggs. "I hope that's true."

"We all do." Daddy spoke for everyone. "But better enjoy this breakfast. It will probably be your last home-cooked meal for a while."

"I've heard rumors that that is true," Drew replied with a chuckle. He added more bacon and sliced tomatoes to his plate.

"I hope the weather is good. I'd hate being too hot, running around, and doing whatever else you'll have to do." Angelee said.

"Will you learn how to shoot a gun?" Alistair wanted to know.

"I'm sure we will. Although, I'm not sure ambulance drivers will be shooting while taking soldiers to the hospitals."

"I'd like to learn how to use a gun," Alistair remarked. "I'd be ready for anything then."

"Don't be in a big hurry to grow up." Mommy admonished. "Taking a life—whether it's an animal to eat or a person who is your enemy—is not as easy as you think."

"How do you know?" Asked Aimee, forking open a biscuit to butter.

"I have had to kill a chicken or two in my younger days," Mommy informed her. "They were silly birds, but it still wasn't easy to execute them."

"If only war were illegal—so no one could kill another person." Aunt Milly commented. "It just seems so senseless, shooting people you don't know, cutting their lives off because they are a different nationality."

"Murder would still happen," Drew stated.

"Yes, but most times, it is one person killing another person one-on-one. There wouldn't be the wholesale slaughter of towns—civilians—innocent by-standers." Aunt Milly pointed out.

"I suppose you're right. But no one has ever managed to find a way to eradicate the evil in the hearts of mankind. And as long as people are self-centered, there will always be wars. Jesus even said so." Daddy philosophized.

"That is true." Aunt Milly conceded. "But it doesn't make war any less horrible."

"Goodness, this conversation is a bit heavy and depressing for this early in the morning," Mommy said.

"What are you going to do with your car, Drew?" Alistair suddenly asked, changing the subject.

"Now that *is* a good question." Drew smiled at his younger brother. "I wish I had someplace I could store it out of the weather. But renting a space is more than I can afford."

"Daddy, what do you think of building a small lean-to next to the garage?" Angelee said.

"Hmmm, that is a thought. But I might have to get planning permission from the town board. If I can get permission, then Drew will have to pay for the materials."

"That might work out just fine, Dad. That's a good idea, Angelee. How'd you think of that?"

"Last Saturday I overheard a man who'd come into the library wanting books of building designs. Mrs. Johnstone showed him how to look for books in the card catalog."

"The town board meets only once a month. I'll have to write and let you know what I find out." Daddy said. He pulled his watch from his vest pocket and checked the time.

"Is Pauley meeting you at the Armory?" Mommy wanted to know. "I have a feeling the train station is going to be surrounded by families seeing their boys off."

Angelee's heart skipped a beat at the mention of Pauley's name. It just didn't seem real that her brother and his best friend were going off to the Medical National Guard. She told herself that they were just going away for a short while to learn more skills—not to war.

"Yes, Captain Waters told us to report to Pike Street at nine o'clock, sharp. The whole company is going to march to Pennsylvania station. Gee-Gee, would you like to use my car while I'm away?" Drew offered.

Angelee pulled her mind out of the clouds and stared at her brother for a moment. "Are you sure you trust me with it?"

Drew gave a cock-eyed smile. "Yeeuup! I'm sure Daddy can help you with the adjustments if you need help."

Drew stood up. "Excuse me, I've got a few last-minute things to put in my case. I don't want to start my military career off on the wrong foot!"

Angelee collected plates and cutlery from the table and headed toward the kitchen. The ache in her heart swelled, and she chided herself for nearly giving into the temptation to cry. She promised herself she would cry later in the afternoon—after they were back from seeing the young men off.

Aunt Milly walked into the kitchen with empty serving bowls. "I love it when there are no leftovers! It makes clean up easier."

Angelee, lost in thought, gave an absent-minded, "uh-hmmm."

"So, you're going to write to him, aren't you?" Aunt Milly queried, raising her voice.

"Oh...what? Oh yes, of course, I'll write to him. He is my brother, so it would be really strange if I didn't."

"I wasn't talking about your brother." Aunt Milly gibed. "I was talking about *Pauley Alexander Bannister*."

"Aunt Milly, you are *not* very subtle." Angelee huffed. "He *is* my friend. I know how he feels about me. And Pauley knows how I feel about him. So, I will absolutely correspond with him. And...before you ask...I will, assuredly, miss him."

Aunt Milly crossed to the sink, where Angelee was busy washing up, and gave her a one-armed hug.

"I'm going to tell you something, my Dearest Niece." Aunt Milly said softly. "I tease you and push you because I think you know deep in your heart what you want. I never talk about your Uncle Edwin, "Neddie", these days. But there is never a day that I don't miss him. He was my closest friend—and now I regret that I dithered so much about whether or not to let him into my heart. Had I known that I was going to have such a short time with "Neddie", I would not have wasted so much time. I don't want you to make the same mistake."

Angelee removed her hands from the water, dried her hands on a dishtowel, and embraced her aunt.

"I hear what you're saying, Aunt Milly. But I don't want to mistake appreciation and affection for the deeper, respectful love that comes with being in love. You must miss Uncle Ned a lot."

"In the last few months, I began to realize that being comfortable here with all of you would have been disappointing to Ned. He would have told me that I was playing "Jonah", hanging out here." Aunt Milly released her and held her at arm's length.

"I understand your desire to discover your calling. Well, you aren't the only one going through that. Sometimes you think you only have to discover your purpose once, and then you're set for life. But circumstances transpire and you have to re-evaluate what God seems to be saying. I've been in touch with the Missionary Baptist Church in Indianapolis, as well as the Methodist Missions board and the Christian and Missionary Alliance church. I'm still praying about each opportunity, trying to discern where my heart is. And that's why I'm going to visit some missionaries who are home on Sabbatical. It might make things clearer."

"All I know is, there is a lot of change going on in this family," Angelee said.

"Hey, you two! We're getting ready to take Drew to the station. Get a move on!" Aimee commanded.

Angelee turned, pulled the plug from the kitchen sink, and removed the apron. Aunt Milly also removed her "uniform" a pinafore apron and hung it up on the hook by the doorway. It only took a minute to join the others in the car.

****

Angelee almost wished they had gone to the armory with Drew; perhaps they would have had a greater chance of seeing him arrive at the station. A throng, block deep, surrounded the

Pennsylvania train station. As the company marched into sight, the crowd erupted in cheers and whistles.

This company was not the first to leave for Indianapolis, and eventually France. In this great number of people were many who already seen family and friends leave with the sanitary detachment, under the leadership of Major F. C. Robinson. The multitude created such a spectacle that business on the square came to a standstill. Some store owners even closed in order to see the soldiers off.

When it was evident that the train was going to be late, Captain Waters permitted for his company to visit with their family and friends. Angelee wasn't sure how Drew would ever find them in the press. But people understood and helped each other connect with their enlisted men.

While they were waiting, Q. A. Blankenship, a Paragon resident, used the opportunity to give 'The boys' a pep talk.

"You are going forth to participate in the greatest cause know to mortal men—the making of the world safe for all peoples. You are going forth not to establish liberty for that has been established, but to maintain that liberty, and to uphold the honor of the stars and stripes, the glorious banner of our country… Boys, we love you and will think of you always. God bless you. Come back, and we'll take care of you." [1]

Mr. Blankenship finished his address, encouraging the crowd to make sure every young man departing had someone that would correspond with him. Perhaps even sending the soldier a gift from time to time.

Cheers expressed the crowd's favorable support of Mr. Blankenship's words. Too soon the train's whistle sounded from down the track signaling its imminent arrival. Captain Waters recalled the company into formation. As they boarded the train and found seats, they opened windows and stuck out heads to call back to their loved ones. Mothers, wives, and girlfriends did their best to find them, reaching out to touch hands one last time before the train departed.

Another blast from the train whistle announced the inevitable parting. The crowd cheered, some weeping, some singing hymns while others yelled words of encouragement. The majority of the group stood watching until the caboose disappeared.

Daddy put his arm around Mommy, who now giving into tears. He guided her to the car, and Angelee walked with them. Once in the car, they waited for the rest of the family to arrive. Tears of pride, sorrow, and love mixed, sliding silently down her father's face.

Angelee's heart was breaking; she didn't know if her feelings for Pauley were deeper than friendship. Was he just like an extra older brother? She wasn't sure. But she did know that she missed Drew and Pauley already.

Aimee sat on the chair next to her desk while Angelee's fingers entwined in her sister's dark blond tresses, pulling and wrapping them into an elaborate braid to encircle her sister's head.

"How is that feeling?" Angelee asked.

"Pretty tight. But my eyes aren't watering yet." Aimee said. "I can't wait to see what it looks like finished."

"Me neither," Angelee replied flippantly. "I just hope it will last for a couple of days—all the hard work I'm putting in."

"I do appreciate it," Aimee said. "Ouch!"

"Sorry, I didn't mean to pull that hard."

"You didn't; it was just one hair that you got," Aimee explained. "Are you sure you don't want me to do your hair?"

"So you can exact revenge? No way." Angelee teased. "You still need to iron your dress, remember? You don't want to rush doing that."

"You're right. I've been waiting for this for weeks." Aimee said.

****

Angelee grew silent, concentrating on her handiwork. But her mind slipped back to the day that Aimee had come running into the house, breathless, her eyes shining.

"Guess--what?!" Aimee gushed. "Mommy! ... Angelee! ... Aunt Milly! ... Guess--what?" Her words spouted between puffs. She burst into the kitchen, where they were preparing dinner. "The most fabulous thing has happened."

"Slow down, calm down, and sit down." Mommy had instructed her youngest daughter.

Aimee gratefully plopped onto a kitchen chair and took the glass of water her mother handed to her, which she gulped at great speed. Angelee was a little concerned that her sister might choke. Finishing the drink, and catching her breath, Aimee launched into her announcement.

"Today Monsieur Torrington got a letter from a friend. And you know who that friend is? None other than Signor Guido Ciccolini. You know the famous opera singer. Signor Ciccolini is touring America and he's coming to Martinsville." Words gushed from the Aimee like waters over the rapids. "And Signor invited M. Torrington to come to hear him! And M. Torrington invited me to join him." The girl bounced on the chair. "May I Mommy? Can I go?" Aimee's anticipation and hope shone from her eyes.

"When is it?" Mommy asked.

"On a Friday night, and it's at the high school auditorium," Aimee said.

"Which Friday night?" Mommy probed.

Aimee reached into the pocket of her dress and pulled out a piece of paper. "The invitation is for October fifth."

"You know you can't go without a chaperon." Mommy reminded.

"Is there anyone else going besides Mr. Torrington? Aunt Milly inquired.

"I never thought about that." Aimee's shoulders sagged and her smiled faded. "If M. Torrington can get tickets, will you go with us, Angelee? I'm sure he'll understand."

"I don't have anything else on, so sure." Angelee shrugged. She didn't know much about opera, but with Drew, Pauley, and Olivia away, she occasionally found herself feeling bored and lonely.

The recital was by a card of introduction. Signor Ciccolini had sent only two tickets, sure that M. Torrington would want to bring a friend. However, M. Torrington had then been swift to acquire the secondary complimentary ticket from the Staley Piano House.

****

Angelee wrapped the end of the braid, before weaving it out of sight and placed the last hairpin. "There it is. Let me get the mirror."

Aimee rose from her chair and standing in front of the wardrobe with the full-length mirrored glass, checked the intricate style she'd been given

"Wow, that's amazing. I like it." Aimee turned; hugging her sister fiercely. "I hope Steffken—M. Torrington—notices it." The younger sister half giggled and looked down at the floor. "He has seen so many beautiful women."

Holding her sibling away from herself, Angelee searched her face. "Oh, Aimee...please be careful. M. Torrington is so much older than you are. You still need to finish high school. And being an artist isn't an easy life."

"What do you mean?" Aimee averted her eyes.

"I'm not sure about my own life right now, so I should keep my mouth shut." Angelee prefaced her remarks. "I see how your eyes shine when you're around him. It isn't too difficult to figure out that you have some pretty strong feelings for him."

Aimee looked up, straight into Angelee's face. "Are you feeling sorry for me?"

"No, not at all. We can't help what we feel—or don't feel." Angelee said. "But I wouldn't be a good big sister if I wasn't concerned. I don't want you to get hurt."

"I haven't told anyone else how I feel. But if you can tell, I'm sure others can." Aimee's voice trembled, full of anxiety. "I don't think he even notices how I feel. He doesn't flirt with me. He doesn't belittle me in any way. But I can't help finding him interesting. He's been so many places, met so many interesting people. Most of all, he knows so much about art. He is very strict with me when we have lessons."

Aimee's ramblings testified that she did not expect her attraction to be reciprocated. Angelee pulled her sister back into a comforting embrace.

"Oh Mee-Mee, please don't' worry. It's just because we're so close that I noticed it. I won't say anything else about it. M. Torrington invited you because he likes you and knew you'd find pleasure in it. This concert must be a special evening to remember. We are about to become introduced to opera. So, let's make a promise to each other that we will make the most of the evening."

"Thanks, Angelee."

Aimee went off to iron her dress and Angelee attended to her own hair and preparations.

M. Torrington called for the sisters about five-thirty that evening.

M. Torrington drove over to the Martinsville Sanatorium on West Harrison Street, where they enjoyed a meal at its in-house restaurant. They joked and laughed about going to a fancy concert in his blue model T Ford truck. The early meal gave them plenty of time to drive over to the new high school building on South Main Street, which had been officially opened for classes in 1915. At two years old, it still looked new.

Seating themselves in the main floor seats they observed the people around them. It was impossible to not hear conversations around them.

"Wasn't that a rousing send-off for the boys this morning?" A lady behind them commented, referring to the second contingent of National Guardsmen who had seen off to Fort Harrison and who would later transfer to Camp Taylor in Kentucky.

"Those young men deserve it. They need to know that all of Morgan County supports our men in uniform." A gentleman replied.

"It was so moving to see all those veterans marching along to the drum corps. Some of them looked like they would have been proud to join up again." The first lady said.

"They looked so regal, parading from the National Bank over to Vandalia Station to catch the 9:28 train." Another lady said. "It said in the paper that they'd have dinner in Indianapolis before leaving for Camp Taylor. There's a special train—taking men from all over Indiana."

Aimee leaned over to whisper to Angelee. "I don't know if I should bust from pride for my brother, or cry because I miss him so much."

"I know what you mean. It's almost a month since they left." Angelee commiserated. "I was hoping this concert would provide a distraction from thinking about them...just for a little while."

"Good Evening my dear friends!" a familiar voice drew their attention. "Thank you, Steffken, for saving a seat for me," Cameron said, sitting down next to Angelee.

"Deer? I don't see any deer? When did they let those lovely creatures in?" Aimee joked, her self-defense when caught off-guard.

Steffken and Cameron chuckled, appreciating the pun. Angelee gave her sister a sideways glance, rolling her eyes.

"I could have said, 'beloved' friends, but I thought it might prove to embarrass one or all of us." Cameron chortled.

Angelee felt the heat rise in her face as the conversation became too flirty for her comfort.

"When did you decide to come to the concert?" she asked.

"As soon as I knew about it."

"Have you heard Signor Ciccolini sing before?" Aimee asked. "I mean you're from Boston, and they have lots of classical music programs there."

"On occasion, I've escorted Aunt Marchaline to performances. But I've not heard Signor Ciccolini perform."

Angelee removed her arm from the armrest and rested her hands in her lap.

"I am not being the best host to you Mademoiselles." M. Torrington interjected. "I should be filling your minds with silly tales regarding my brief acquaintance of Signor Ciccolini."

He had no chance to do so. The lights went down and Mr. Staley from the music store came on stage.

"Ladies and Gentlemen, this evening we have the most extraordinary opportunity to hear the amazing talent of Signor Guido Ciccolini. This young man, originally from Italy, found a home on stage, performing in Paris, Milan, Petrograd, and London. Even if you are not familiar with the art form of opera, you will grow to appreciate his pure, lyric tenor voice. Not only will you find his presentation amazing, but you will also find he has the most gracious of dispositions.

"Signor Ciccolini will be assisted by a special representative of Mr. Thomas A. Edison, violinist Elias Breeskin. This evening of exceptional entertainment is not only to delight you with a live presentation of beautiful singing, but you will witness Mr. Edison's new Art Sound Re-creation. "

Mr. Staley removed the cloth which had covered the large wooden instrument.

"And now, with no further delay, here is Signor Ciccolini."

The audience clapped, full of anticipation.

There was no printed program. As the evening progressed, Angelee was glad she had not known what to expect. Had she presumed that the evening would have three acts and costumes, she might have been disappointed. As it was, the evening provided the audience opportunity to compare the live tenor voice to recordings he had made for the New Edison.

Angelee was fascinated as Signor Ciccolini would begin to sing a song, only to stop singing throughout intervals, allowing the recording to continue the piece without the singer. The audience burst into thunderous applause—for the performer and the machine.

Throughout the evening, Angelee was aware of Cameron in the seat beside her. He tapped his fingers to the rhythm of the songs, or kept time bouncing his foot, as he rested his ankle on his opposite knee. He'd applied a scent, something blended with bay-rum. During moments of audience applause, she'd catch him smiling as he observed her.

Why did she have to be drawn to him? Life was confusing enough, knowing that Pauley was in love with her. And Cameron had admitted her found her interesting, that he "liked her". Part of her wanted to ask him what "liking her" meant. But she didn't honestly want to know. It would be one more thing she would have to deal with. Apart from politely responding to him, she chose to ignore him and tried to focus on the concert.

When the program ended, it suddenly occurred to Angelee that several Martinsville citizens would be parting with their hard-earned money to procure the latest invention for the family home. And the Edison Company was providing payment schemes to help potential customers to acquire the phonograph player.

"I must say, his voice truly takes you along with him," Aimee said.

"I think I would have liked it more if I'd known what the songs were about—at least the pieces from *Tosca* and *La Traviata,*" Angelee remarked.

"Do you think Daddy could be convinced to buy one?" Aimee asked.

The audience was making a slow exit. Cameron rose from his seat. "Thanks again, Steffken, for saving me a seat. I hope you'll excuse me, as I need to take my leave. An early trip into Indy tomorrow. Lots to organize and prepare. See you all later. Good night."

M. Torrington invited Angelee and Aimee to wait while the hubbub dissipated before rising from their seats.

"Now, Mes Cheris, though the hour, it grows late, let us go find my friend and I will introduce you."

Because they had waited, they were at the bottom of the stage steps when Mr. Staley and Signor Ciccolini came down them.

"Buona Sereta, Mio Amico!" M. Torrington greeted the Italian singer. "Thank you for providing me with the tickets."

"It's my pleasure. And who are your lovely companions?" The black-haired man asked, his brown eyes sparkling.

"It is my pleasure to introduce you to Signorina Aimee and her sister, Signorina Angelee Tilson."

"And which of these *Belle Signorine* is your protégé?" The singer inquired softly.

Angelee felt the heat rise in her own neck and face, watching Aimee's blush turn from pink to rose as she turned her head away. Angelee knew her sister feared that her secret would be revealed. Angelee didn't give M. Torrington time to reply but immediately came to her sister's rescue.

"Signor Ciccolini—did I pronounce that correctly?" She hesitated until he nodded. "M. Torrington is a friend of our family. He's often at our home. Because he thought it was a great pleasure to receive the tickets to hear you sing, he first offered them to my parents."

Angelee hazarded a look at M. Torrington to see if he were going to contradict. However, M. Torrington seemed relieved that she had undertaken to explain their association.

"But my parents thought it would be profitable for Aimee and me to experience the rare event of hearing a world-renowned performer. So, M. Torrington was kindly persuaded to bring us in their stead."

"This family has been most hospitable to me since I arrived in this community." M. Torrington chimed in. "Besides these two lovely ladies, Dr. and Mrs. Tilson have two sons. The oldest one has been selected to serve in the Army and is now at Camp Taylor. The youngest son is still a boy—a very clever one. Having experienced for this myself, the transporting effect of your marvelous voice, I thought they should taste of such a delightful distraction." M. Torrington nodded toward the girls.

A wide grin grew across the tenor's face. "Ahhh…Famiglia. It is most important to share the good with the bad. Are you sure, Mio Amico, that is wise to miss such an opportunity to become part of such a beautiful Famiglia?"

"Well, now I've seen it with my own eyes!" Aimee suddenly found her courage. "They say all Latin-based languages are romantic. Well, we have an Italian and a Belgium together and suddenly it is all about love and family!"

Signor Ciccolini burst out laughing, as did Mr. Staley. After the initial shock of Aimee's words passed, M. Torrington joined in the cheerful chorus. The laughter became contagious, drawing Aimee and Angelee in as well.

Mr. Staley was the first to collect himself. "Signor Ciccolini, it is getting late. You need to get up early to catch the train back to Indianapolis. I'd better get you back to the hotel."

"Thank you so much for an amazing performance, Mr. Ciccolini," Aimee said, offering her hand.

Signor Ciccolini took her hand and kissed the back of it. He repeated the gesture with Angelee. He took M. Torrington's hand, then kissed him on both cheeks, as was the French custom.

"Grazi, Buon Amico. It has been good to make your re-acquaintance. I shall come up to Indianapolis to see you again. We will have lunch or dinner together. Si?" M. Torrington promised.

"Si! We will dine together. But I must go now."

Mr. Staley helped Signor Ciccolini into his overcoat and they walked out of the auditorium, down the steps and out the doors.

"So, Mes Cheris, have you developed a taste for the opera?" M. Torrington asked, assisting the girls with their coats.

"I'd have to learn Italian first," Aimee replied. "But that wouldn't be bad, because there are so many famous Italian artists.

"I'm going to do some homework," Angelee answered. "I'm going to research Tosca and the stories of other famous operas. If I like the stories, then maybe I'll try it again. But for now, I'm ready to get home. I've got work tomorrow."

As they climbed into M. Torrington's blue truck, Angelee asked. "What was your favorite piece, Aimee?"

"The piece of my mind that kept wondering if we would convince Daddy to buy one of those Edison's!" Aimee answered with aplomb.

Angelee's laughter burst out, triggering the other two. A critique and complement session of the evening's entertainment filled the car on the short drive home. Angelee looked forward to recounting the evening to Drew and Pauley in a letter.

After leaving Martinsville, Drew and Pauley had arrived at Fort Harrison for training. They had been assigned to serve with the Fifteenth Ambulance Company as a part of the Fifteenth Field Hospital Company.

Letters contained limited information about their training, the new friends they had made, and tit-bits of their daily life. Angelee was accustomed to getting a couple of letters a week. That changed in November, as no letters arrived for her or Mommy.

Mrs. Parkham had kept Angelee busy that Tuesday, dictating personal and business letters. After typing the correspondence, Angelee left the office to complete her list of tasks. Angelee stopped first at the post office to mail the letters. The library was the next destination; besides returning read books, Mrs. Parkham had wanted Angelee to check the Indianapolis paper for a report of the New York stock exchange.

Casually flipping the pages, in search of the report, her eye caught a headline. On page 15 the article provided her with a clue as to what may have happened to the boys.

"MEDICS WILL GO TO DIXIE CAMP—Doctors Officers All to Be Away from Fort Harrison by First of Week. By the first of next week the medical officers' training camp at Fort Harrison will have been removed to Fort Oglethorpe, Georgia. Col. Percy Ashburn, commander of the medics' training camp, will by that time have departed for the Georgia station and with him will have gone 550 medical officers, who will continue their training in the South.

Meanwhile field hospitals and ambulance companies, which have been in training at Fort Harrison, will have departed for Fort Oglethorpe overland. It is understood that all of the motor equipment to be sent from this post to Fort Oglethorpe will go overland under its own power while the mule-drawn ambulance and other equipment of the field hospital units will be sent by train.

Both the motor units and mule-drawn outfits will carry with them a large number of men. What is to be done with enlisted me of the training camp who are not members of any organization is not known.

Medical officers whose training has been finished are leaving the post daily in groups and singly for stations throughout the United States and even for France. Instructors in the camp have for the most part received assignments and are preparing to leave. Some of them will accompany Col. Ashburn to the Southern school, while others are being given assignments which indicate they will see early service in France." [2]

Angelee sighed as she digested this snippet of information. Would she begin a letter to each of them, adding to it until she knew for certain they had shipped south? Or should she write in care of Camp Harrison, believing that the letters would be forwarded?

Well, tonight she would write to Oliva. Although Angelee knew lots of people, none of them replaced her best friend. Since beginning her college career at Butler in September, Olivia had found short chunks of time to write. From these letters, she learned that Olivia had to be up before six o'clock each morning, and ready for "Prayers". Mornings were filled with lectures, and afternoons were spent in study.

In a previous letter, Angelee shared the interesting evening of opera at the high school. While she'd included a description of the Edison machine and how the evening progressed, she'd purposely omitted any information about Aimee's feelings regarding M. Torrington. She was equally silent about her discomfort around Cameron Parkham. She wasn't going to start a conversation about a topic she had no desire to think about herself.

Angelee turned the page, finding the stock exchange report on the Commerce, Markets, and Finance page. She closed the paper and hung it on the holding stand. As she was about to leave, she heard someone addressed her.

"Afternoon, Miss Tilson." Jimmy Foster stood next to her. Jimmy was three feet tall, blond-haired, blue-eyed, and six years old. "Could you help me find a book?"

Mrs. Foster, his grandmother, held his hand and was smiling down at him. "He's been after me all day to bring him here. He wanted to ask you himself. I told him that you might not be here."

"Well, see, sometimes things are just meant to be!" Angelee smiled at the small boy and the older lady.

Angelee knelt by the lad. "What kind of book are you looking for? Is it for learning to read? Is it a book about an animal? Is it a book about stars?"

"I liked that one about the twins," Jimmy said.

"Do you mean the Bobbsey Twins?" Angelee asked.

"Yes, please," Jimmy confirmed.

"The Bobbsey Twins are fun. And, maybe, we can find a couple of books for Grandmother to read to you."

Leading the older woman and the young boy to the children's section, she found a small chair and sat down. "This is how we find the books we want. First, we look for the author's name."

"What's that?" Jimmy asked.

"An author? That is a person who writes a book." Angelee explained.

"Oh, I see." Jimmy was all ears. "So, what name do we look for?"

"Since I've read so many of these, so many times, I know the name we want is Laura Lee Hope. We always look for the last name. Can you tell me what letter 'Hope" starts with?"

"I think it starts with 'H'," Jimmy stated.

"Then you are right." Angelee smiled encouragingly at him.

Using her right index finger as a pointer, she moved her hand across the shelves, looking for the correct book. She found it and pulled it out. This is the one *The Bobbsey Twins in the Country."* Angelee looked to Mrs. Foster. "Do you want to take more than one?"

"No, I read a chapter per night to him, before he goes to sleep. Or his father does." Mrs. Foster said.

"There are several more here. Let's take this up to the desk and we'll get it checked out for you. Would you like me to make a list of the books, in order? That way if I'm not here, you can ask Mrs. Johnstone to find them for you."

"That is so kind of you." Mrs. Foster said. "Do you have time to do that?"

"Of course, I always have time to help people find what they need," Angelee reassured her.

She walked to the card catalog, with a pencil and a small notebook. Looking up the information, she quickly wrote it down. She went back to the desk and handed the paper to Mrs. Foster.

"Angelee, I was talking to Rev. Matthias a couple of days ago." Mrs. Foster said.

"He is such a lovely man." Angelee couldn't help but smile.

"That's true. I was telling him I needed to find a new Sunday school teacher. He said that several of the ladies from church bring their children over to the Saturday morning reading sessions that you lead. These mothers seem to think you have a way with the children."

"So I keep getting told." Angelee chuckled and shook her head. "We do have a good time."

"Well, Rev. Matthias suggested that I ask you if you would take the first and second grade Sunday school class—even if it is just for a couple of months. Will you think about it? Sunday will be fine to give me an answer. And I'll understand if you say no."

"Wow! I wasn't expecting that? Yes, I will give it some thought. But you'll have to tell me what to do and how to do it."

"I'll pair you up with someone who is experienced." Mrs. Foster encouraged.

"That makes it less scary." Angelee quipped.

"I must get going. James likes it when I have dinner ready when he gets home. That way he can bathe Jimmy and get him ready for bed."

"I bet your son is very thankful to have your help."

"We help each other." Mrs. Foster said, patting Jimmy's head. "I'll have James bring Jimmy over Saturday morning. That way I will get some time to myself to do all those little things you don't get a chance to do when others are around."

"Great. Bye-bye Jimmy. Hope to see you Saturday." Angelee ruffled Jimmy's hair.

The boy ran his hand over his head, smoothing his hair back down. "See ya!"

Mrs. Foster took his hand, and carrying the book, led him out of the library.

Mrs. Johnstone walked over just as Mrs. Foster exited through the foyer door. "She is a woman of admirable courage. It's been hard on them since her daughter-in-law passed away."

"When many women would say. 'I've done my part; my children are raised. It's his problem', she took her son and grandson back in and is making a home for them." Angelee observed.

"At church a few weeks ago, I overheard her say that since she's a widow, she had been thinking of selling her big house." Mrs. Johnstone remarked. "She didn't know if she wanted a smaller house or wanted to rent an apartment someplace. Someone had suggested that she take in a lodger. But when Harriet fell ill and died, she realized that it just made sense to have James and Jimmy move in. I know it makes her tired, but she feels wanted and needed."

"She also has a lot of love to give," Angelee observed. "Did you hear her ask me to take a Sunday school class?"

"Really? You're so good with the children. I think you have a gift there. It would be a bit like the reading group on Saturday. I think you should do it."

"She gave me until Sunday to think about it," Angelee said. "Right now, I need to get back to Mrs. Parkham."

"Okay, see you Saturday." Mrs. Johnstone said.

Angelee shrugged into her coat, wrapped a scarf around her neck, and carried out her briefcase into the afternoon.

Thursday, November 29th, 1917
Thanksgiving

"Mommy, what are you doing? Let me take that!" Angelee chided her mother. "This Thanksgiving you're going to have to trust the rest of us to do everything. You know you're not supposed to be lifting heavy furniture." She took the dining room chair out of her mother's hands, moving it to the place her mother wanted it.

"Would you stop fussing? I'm having a baby; that doesn't make me an invalid." Mommy protested, rubbing the roundness of her stomach.

"You had trouble when you were pregnant with Alistair. You don't want complications with this one too." Aimee supported Angelee's reprimand.

"Listen to your wise daughters." Aunt Milly remarked, gently moving her sister.

"Go sit down, Mommy. We can handle this." Aimee instructed her mother as they added two leaves to the table.

"If all of you are going to bully me, then I have no recourse but to leave." Mommy crossed her arms, harrumphed, and went into the parlor.

"How many are we expecting?" Aunt Milly asked.

Angelee counted off on her fingers. "Mrs. Parkham, her nephew—Cameron—, M. Torrington..." She walked over to the doorway and looked toward her mother. "Have you heard from Nori Hanson?"

Mommy raised her voice to be heard. "Yes, the family is coming. They'll be here about eleven-thirty this morning."

"That makes fourteen if you count the baby." Angelee summed up.

"That baby won't eat much." Aunt Milly laughed.

Ever since Angelee could remember, the Tilsons had invited extra people to their holiday meals. The tradition has grown out of the days when Daddy and Mommy were newlyweds. Newly settled in the town, and hard-pressed financially, holiday celebrations would have been sparse.

A mature couple from the Christian church took Daddy and Mommy under-wing, sharing their wisdom and friendship, especially during the holidays. Now the Tilson family often befriended those in unfortunate circumstances, as was the case with Mrs. Hanson.

Jasper had been one of the first selected for the draft, even though he had dependents. An exemption had not been made, as Nori technically had parents who could support her if they chose to do so. So, Jasper had made the trip to Fort Harrison along with Drew and Pauley.

Nori found out that her step-father had taken to beating Bart. Motivated by love for Bart and anger at the abuse, Nori had demanded that her mother relinquish legal custody of her younger brother. Bart was happy to be rescued and live with Nori; he wasn't too excited about attending church. At least to begin with. Once Alistair initiated a friendship, Bart decided that it was okay. Now he was friends with several boys.

On a Sunday in October, Angelee had found Nori huddled in a corner of the church's ladies' room. Face covered with hands, the baby sat by her feet, Nori was crying. Angelee's first thought was to leave Nori in peace, rather than embarrass her. But overwhelming compassion compelled her to quietly approach Nori and put an arm around her.

"Mrs. Hanson, what's wrong? How can I help?"

Nori scrubbed the tears from her eyes, took a deep breath. "So sorry, just couldn't hold it in anymore. The baby just kicked, and I felt so all alone."

"I didn't hear Louis fussing. How did he kick you?" Angelee asked softly.

"It wasn't Louis—I'm pregnant again. I just found out yesterday."

"Oh my goodness—you already have your hands full," Angelee observed.

"I know. It wouldn't be so bad, except that I don't have anyone to help me."

"What kind of help do you need?" Angelee asked.

"Someone to watch the baby so I can get some sleep. See, I put Louis to bed, then I leave Bart in charge. I know he's only nine, but I've got to go to work. I've been washing dishes in at the Martinsville Sanitarium kitchen in the evenings. Every night I worry about them. Jasper paid up the rent for a few months. But I still need money for food, and other expenses. I'm just so tired."

After church, Angelee commandeered the young family to the Tilson home. During the afternoon, Nori had been allowed a long sleep while Angelee and Aimee cared for the children. After much discussion, the Tilson women had organized a solution for Nori, including caring for the little ones during her shifts. It was only natural the Hanson family would be coming to feast with them.

Mommy got up from the couch, walked into the dining room. "I may not be allowed in here. So, I'm going to the kitchen. I can peel potatoes and carrots sitting down. And I can tear up bread for dressing, also sitting down. Does anyone object?"

Angelee looked around the room, and after a party of shaking heads, Mommy went into the kitchen.

"I'm hungry!" Alistair said, coming into the dining room.

"But it's only ten o'clock—lunch isn't for another two hours!" Aimee gave her brother an astonished look.

"I can't help it!"

"I think Alistair is going through a growth spurt." Aunt Milly said. "Now then, if you do me a favor, I'll see about finding you a snack."

"What kind of favor?" Alistair crossed his arms across his chest and leaned back.

"Go up into the attic and get down the high chair. Little Louis is going to need it this evening when we have dinner." Aunt Milly replied.

"The high chair? I think I'll need help." Alistair complained.

"Aimee, can you help your brother?" Aunt Milly asked.

"Come on...we've got lots to do. Aunt Milly wants to get back to the kitchen. Mommy's trusting us to get the table all sorted." Aimee turned and started toward the stairs.

While the youngsters went on the errand, Angelee and Aunt Milly took plates from the storage section of the sideboard and stacked them on top.

"Right, back to the kitchen to baste that turkey. I'll leave the table with you."

"So, what about Alistair's snack?" Angelee smiled at her aunt.

"Oh, that...I'll tell him to help himself to cheese and crackers. There's peanut butter sandwiches or egg salad for lunch." Aunt Milly explained before walking into the kitchen.

By the time Aimee and Alistair came clunking down the stairs with the high chair, Angelee had put on the table cloth, folded the napkins, and begun placing the cutlery around the twelve place settings.

"Making good progress Gee-Gee." Aimee encouraged. "Where should we put this?"

Angelee indicated the corner next to the windows.

"Alistair, can you get me the furniture wax and a cloth from the cupboard?" Angelee requested.

"I want to go get my snack. I'm hungry." He complained.

"Get the stuff for me first, then you can go." Angelee insisted.

He went to get the tin of polish and remains of an old diaper.

Alistair shuffled back into the dining room. "Here it is, Miss Bossy-Pants."

"Thank you, Mr. Surly Sir. Now, go get your snack." Angelee retorted.

She sat to work removing the dust from the high chair, and applying a coat of wax for polishing.

"Who would have thought we'd need that high chair again in our family?" Aimee mused out loud.

"I know, Alistair was supposed to be the last—or so we thought!"

The doorbell rang, announcing the arrival of Nori with her little family. She had insisted on everyone calling her Nori because she was younger than Angelee. Nori, who was the same height as Angelee, was willowy. And like a willow, she was stronger than she appeared. She joined in the preparations, while Aimee took over babysitting.

Alistair was elated when Louis arrived. Although temperatures hovered near freezing, and the grey skies threatened rain, the boys had gone outside to play ball, hide-and-seek, and run races. Once the rain started, they repaired to Alistair's room to play checkers, backgammon, and building with an Erector set.

The sun had set by four-thirty that afternoon. Grey-black rain clouds, scudded gustily across the evening sky, pulled dusk's dark veil across the horizon earlier than usual. In windows around town, lights burned bright yellow, blinking as shades were pulled against the black night. Laughter, tears, prayers, and feasts were all hidden from those passing by on the streets.

Precisely at five o'clock M. Torrington, Mrs. Parkham, and Cameron arrived to join the family's Thanksgiving observance.

"The table looks beautiful." Remarked Daddy, as he sat down. The grandfather clock struck five-thirty as guests and family settled around the table.

"All of us have people we wish were with us at this feast. Although we miss them, we must remember that this is a holiday with a specific purpose—to give thanks to God for His many blessings." Daddy began the evening. "So, we will take a few minutes to go around this table, each one sharing one thing for which we are thankful. Then we will sing the benediction before we eat."

"May I go first?" Nori asked shyly.

Daddy smiled. "Of course."

"I'm thankful for the day Angelee found me crying in the ladies' room at church. I didn't think so at the time. If she hadn't, I would still be struggling alone. But you all have been so kind. I appreciate it so much."

"Me too!" Bart chirruped. "I'm glad I get to eat turkey!"

This brought a round of laughter. "I think that is a very good thing to be thankful for." Daddy affirmed.

"I should also like to say, 'Merci Beaucoup' to my dear friends at this table." M. Torrington started his contribution. "Just as America is proving to be a faithful ally to France, Belgium, and England, the Tilson family has proven to be true friends to me. For this I give thanks."

"I am thankful for my children—because each one has proven to be a gift from God," Mommy said, her eyes shining. "I miss Andrew junior, very much. Yet I am proud that he is showing his loyalty and service to our country at this time."

"Beautifully spoken, Mommy," Daddy added, tears shining in his eyes.

Listening attentively, Angelee debated which of the many blessings she wanted to voice. She was surprised by the next person's confession.

"Perhaps I am most gratified that I have learned that I am never too old to learn a new lesson." Mrs. Parkham spoke up, firmly, and graciously. "I know that I am reputed to be iron-willed and resolute—which I hope is true because I have worked hard to be that way."

Her words brought smiles from everyone, plus a few nods.

"But this past year I have learned that it takes courage to admit when one is wrong; that forgiveness is the most important gift to give and to receive. So I say, "Thank You": first to the Lord for teaching me this lesson; secondly to Angelee for having to courage to be the instrument in His hand."

Angelee kissed the tips of her fingers and blew a kiss across the table to Mrs. Parkham.

"I'll go next," Cameron said. "I am glad of two things. One is that I have survived my time of service in the Army Air Corp and can contribute to the war effort in other ways. The other is the new friends I have made here in Martinsville. Thank you."

M. Torrington patted Cameron on the shoulder, conveying everyone's appreciation of his service."

"My turn!" Alistair spoke up. "I'm glad I helped with the food collection at the church this year. We always have enough food here at home. I'd hate it if I was hungry all the time. So, thanks, Mommy, for letting me help give food to poor people."

Aunt Milly spoke next. "This year we've all faced challenges. It might sound a bit crazy, but I've decided to count it all joy when I'm in the middle of a dilemma. I'm thankful that the Good Lord gives us the courage to take on conundrums, to reach for new goals. I'm thankful for the wisdom and guidance provided through family and friends." All was quiet for a moment, while each person considered the different trials and challenges being faced.

Aimee shrugged her shoulders in a self-hug. "For me, I rejoice that God has provided beauty in the world. There are so many ugly things—like this mean war, and people without enough coal to heat their homes. Yet, every morning there's the colors of the sun turning the sky all red, and orange and yellow. There are flowers, like the chrysanthemums in bloom right now. There are so many amazing things that bring joy to people—like hugs, and presents and good food." She shrugged again. "That's me."

"Angelee, what about you?" Daddy asked.

Angelee looked around. "I'm thankful to be a part of this family—especially that Daddy and Mommy have taught me to love Jesus, by their example. I am also thankful that we have friends that have become family—who we can share this time together. And I am so blessed that we have a warm house, nice clothes, and food to eat." Angelee shared. "While I am glad there is food in the house, I'm even more glad that Mommy and Aunt Milly are amazing cooks."

There were a few 'amen' for the last remark.

"Well, there's certainly a lot to meditate on." Daddy said. "Serving people, helping them find good health and even faith in God fills my heart with awe every day. I'm grateful I get to share my life with friends and family. Now, let's sing the doxology together and tuck into this bountiful feast."

The gas light chandelier dispelled the darkness from the room, casting a warm glow over the room.

"This is my first Thanksgiving eating with a family." M. Torrington informed them. "Usually I have been to a restaurant or the dining room of a hotel. So, it is another thing for which I give thanks."

"Do they celebrate Thanksgiving in Belgium?" Bart asked.

"Thanksgiving is indeed a good tradition to observe. But I think it is true to say that Thanksgiving, as celebrated in this way, is mostly an American holiday. In England, the Church of England has harvest celebrations in September or October." M. Torrington explained.

"What do they eat in Belgium?" Alistair asked. "I've wanted to know for a long time, but never get the chance to ask you."

"We love our mussels, Stoofvlees—beef cooked slowly in beer, and rabbit cooked in prunes. We also like to drink wine."

"But Christians aren't supposed to drink beer or wine, in case they get drunk." Bart blurted out.

"But they are supposed to eat their vegetables. So eat some sweet potatoes!" Nori instructed her younger brother. She spooned mashed sweet potato into the thirteen-month old Louis's mouth.

"What kind of vegetables?" Alistair asked, before shoving a well-buttered roll into his mouth.

"In Belgium, we eat our vegetables, of course; potatoes, asparagus, cabbage." Spearing the food on his plate he lifted it. "These green beans must have justice done to them, so I do that now."

Chatter filled the air, and plates emptied as the feast was consumed. Even with second helpings of turkey, dressing, mashed potato, homemade noodles, and gravy, everyone was determined to have pie.

Daddy tapped a spoon on the side of his water glass. When all eyes were on him, he said. "Ladies and gentlemen, every home has its own protocols."

"What's pro-col?" Bart asked.

Daddy chuckled. "That is a fancy word for 'how things are done.' Here in our home, after someone has been here more than once, we like to consider them family. As such, Mommy and I decided years ago that if the women did all the cooking, then the menfolk had to earn dessert. So, after the feast, the women go off to entertain themselves in the parlor and the men clear the table and wash up the dishes."

"Wow, Alistair, we are boys! So, we don't have to wash dishes—just the men."

Alistair looked at his friend. Regretfully shaking his head, he reported, "Hate to tell you this, but we gotta help too."

"But he said MEN!" Bart complained.

"That's enough, Bart. If Mr. Tilson says you are helping, then you will help." Nori insisted.

"Don't look so glum, Bart." Mr. Tilson grinned encouragement. "I'll make sure you get a second helping of dessert as a reward for hard work. Now then, Bart, you will be on my team with Alistair. Our job is to clear the table, the sideboard and put away all the leftovers. Steffken, Cameron, I'm leaving it up to the two of you to decide who washes and who dries. I'll be on hand to put away. So, let's get to it."

Nori took her three children up to the bathroom to wash food-covered hands and faces before joining Mommy, Aunt Milly, Mrs. Parkham in the parlor. Angelee and Aimee went upstairs; Angelee to get her sewing basket. She'd been embroidering a set of pillowcases and wanted to work on them. Aimee collected a set of drawing pencils and a sketchbook. The girls joined the older women enjoying the gas fire.

"How did you ever get Mr. Tilson trained to wash dishes?" Mrs. Parkham asked. "My husband felt that was woman's work, and far below him. He'd be horrified if *I* had been found in the kitchen. Our status in town meant servants."

"To answer your question, Mrs. Parkham, it was nothing to do with me. We were spending our first Christmas away from home. I'd invited an older couple to join us for the meal. By the time we'd eaten our Christmas ham and fixings, I was totally worn out. The kitchen was a complete mess, and I still had the baby to bathe, feed, and get to sleep. Mrs. Goodrich took Drew from me and bathed him. Mr. Goodrich collared Andrew and took him off to the kitchen and gave him some advice about a good marriage. They cleared and cleaned, making sure I got to sit quietly. I must have dozed off because Mrs. Goodrich had to wake me so I could nurse Drew. He was only about two weeks old. Since then, it's become a custom."

"It sure does seem strange with Drew and Pauley being gone," Aimee said. "I hope they get a nice meal at Camp Shelby."

Angelee reached across to take Nori's hand. Silent tears rolled down Nori's rosy cheeks. Louis, snuggled into Nori's shoulder, fighting sleep as Jillie, climbed up on the settee, trying to get onto Nori's lap as well. Louis fussed, using his feet and hands to push away his sister. In an attempt to accommodate them both, Nori pulled Jillie down next to her side, and draped an arm around her, while insisting that Louis sit across her lap, embracing his waist. Futilely rubbing his eyes, Louis succumbed to sleep. Jillie quickly followed suit.

Angelee sat down on the floor to play with four-year-old, Bobby realizing that he was too young to join Bart and Alistair. After fifteen minutes, Bobby settled into Angelee's lap and also fell asleep. Slumbering deeply, the children gave no resistance as they were moved onto a pallet, lying in front of the fireplace.

"You'll forgive an old woman for being nosey, but how did you and Jasper meet, Eleanor?" Mrs. Parkham asked.

"It was through Bart, to be honest. Bart likes playing baseball. My parents were pretty mean most of the time. But Bart has a real baseball talent, and Pappy liked his baseball. So Pappy let Bart go and play with 'Doc' Merritt's team.

"Jasper, he loves that stupid game as well. He helped coach the team or would umpire. After the games, Jasper used to drive the boys on the team home. And one afternoon I happen to be in the yard when Jasper pulled in to drop Bart home. We kinda hit it off, ya know? I heard someplace that when you meet the right one for you, you just know it. I wasn't sure believed it. I mean I was barely sixteen. But there was just somethin' about him that made me feel safe, and loved."

Angelee had heard someone say that when the right man came along, you just knew it. But how? What were the signs? And why did Aunt Milly keep trying to convince her that she was already in love with Pauley?

"If felt the same way about Andrew when I met him," Mommy said.

"How do you mean, Mommy?" Aimee asked.

Sitting in her rocking chair, Mommy rocked gently, rubbed her rounded stomach. "Like Nori, I was sixteen, nearly seventeen, when I became aware of Andrew. He started coming to the same church as my family. He was a successful, young, and handsome doctor. The single girls and ladies were always hovering around him, inviting him for dinner. He could have had his pick. Well, thinking I was invisible to him, I didn't even try to get near him. One weekend, there was a cake auction at our church to raise money for missions. The guys had to bid for the cake. When a young man won, he got to sit and eat the cake with the girl who made it. Since it was for a good cause, both Milly and I baked cakes."

"That's right." Aunt Milly joined in. "You made that special chocolate cake. I made my favorite applesauce and spice cake. And we both met our future husbands that afternoon."

"Was there a bidding war?" Angelee wanted to know.

Mommy and Aunt Milly were laughing. "Not in the way you think." Aunt Milly said.

"Edwin O'Neil bid for the chocolate cake, thinking it was mine. It wasn't until the bidding got up to two dollars that I slipped him a note that said mine was the applesauce cake. Then Andrew stood a chance."

"Andrew, on the other hand, was in a real pickle. Every girl was trying to convince him that her cake was the best, and get him to bid for it. He told me later that he had considered giving the first bid on lots of cakes—like a token bid. But then he realized that he might get stuck with the wrong cake, and therefore the wrong girl. He made sure that it was my cake he bid for. I think my sister had something to do with that."

"He did come and ask me which one was yours!" Aunt Milly half confessed.

"So we all four sat and ate cake together. The way your father looked at me, well, I just knew we belonged together. It was the first time we'd had a real conversation...sitting on the church lawn, drinking tea, and eating cake. I just felt like I'd met my best friend; like I wanted to tell him everything and hear everything he had to say."

"What about you, Aunt Milly?" Angelee asked.

"Edwin and I were in the same Sunday school class. One month our Sunday school teacher had a missionary who was home on furlough with his family, come in to talk to our class. That family needed to build a hospital in China. Our teacher challenged us to raise all the funds. So, Edwin and I joined a couple of others and worked hard to earn that money. We washed windows, baby-sat for children, ran errands for older folk, painted porches, and had a baked goods sale...anything and everything we could think of. And it was in the course of meeting that challenge that Edwin and I both discovered that we wanted to be missionaries. The rest just kind of followed."

"What about you, Mrs. Parkham?" Angelee asked. "Did you just know that you wanted to marry your husband when you met him?"

"That is a bit of a story!" Mrs. Parkham said.

Mrs. Parkham leaned back in her chair, the image of regal authority, from years of perfect posture and subdued emotions. "You wouldn't have cause to know this, but in all my adult years none of my associates have ever asked me about my personal life—let alone my marriage. You must give me a few minutes to ponder how to answer this question."

"Madam and Mademoiselles, would it suit you to have dessert now?" M. Torrington's voice intruded upon their womanly talk.

"I'm ready!" Angelee said. "Should I come and help?"

"Oh contraire, you must remain at ease, while the men become your servants this evening. The dessert menu is pecan pie, pumpkin pie, persimmon pudding, and applesauce spice cake. We have whipped cream to go with your choice. Who will have which...or all?"

Alistair and Bart carried small plates to the ladies and Cameron delivered coffee on a silver serving tray.

"Don't worry, we'll do the washing up for this lot as well," Cameron reassured them. "A little competition goes a long way in getting the job done."

"Who's been competing?" Aimee asked.

"See, Mr. Parkham, he was washing. M. Torrington and Me were drying." Bart said.

"That is M. Torrington and 'I', not 'me', Bart." Angelee corrected.

"Okay...anyway we were drying. And we were trying to keep ahead of Mr. Tilson and Alistair putting the dishes away. They had to, 'cause they know where things go." Bart explained.

"But we kept up with them!" Alistair boasted. "We caught up pretty fast."

"When you boys finish your dessert, you can go upstairs and play." Daddy said. "You've earned it. We 'older boys' will finish up with the second round of clean up."

Bart and Alistair ate the pie in 'double-time' and scurried upstairs.

Daddy and the other two men headed back to the kitchen. They would probably sit at the kitchen table and discuss politics, the war, and the world in general.

"Well, Mrs. Parkham, have you had enough time to consider your answer?" Angelee asked.

Mrs. Parkham sat down her empty coffee cup and saucer. "Yes, I have. After the Civil War, Boston was a place of great opportunity and dire misfortune. With its harbor, it provided many jobs, a place of adventure. Manufacturing thrived in Boston—shoes, paint, locks, ice harvesting, iron—just to name a few. People came up from the south, with high hopes, looking for work, for fresh starts. Especially the former slaves. There were war widows, orphans, and ruined families, needing help in many ways. Many of them took lodgings in hotels at a weekly rate. Others found rooms in boarding houses.

"Now you need to know that the Parkham family was one of the families in Boston known as the Boston Brahmans—very upper class. They had made their fortunes by investing and managing properties. They were proud of their social standing.

"Now the Parkham Family was a large family, with several sons working in their father's employ. These sons managed different properties; some collected the rent in person. Others hired men to do the collecting for them. This was not always an easy job, as there were all sorts of people living in those buildings; there was such a high turnover of people in these hotels and boarding houses, it was difficult to keep up with the maintenance.

"Some of these houses and hotels began to fall into disrepair. Some landlords simply didn't care. Others were often so busy with other business they had no idea the status of the buildings they owned."

Angelee finished her coffee, giving her full attention to Mrs. Parkham.

"My parents, on the other hand, owned and managed a general mercantile store. We worked hard as a family, and though we never wanted for anything, we were not rich by any standard.

"My father had brought my siblings and me up to be good citizens; to fight for the poor and unfortunate."

"Sorry to interrupt, Mrs. Parkham, but how many brothers and sisters do you have?" Mommy asked, gently rubbing her stomach.

"I had a sister who died while she was still a child. And my brother, Lowell, who is Cameron's father."

"Please do continue with your story." Aunt Milly encouraged.

"Well, Papa supported the liberation of slavery, feeling that one human being had no right to own another person." Mrs. Parkham continued. "The church we were involved with was full of like-minded people. Each week members from the church visited the slums and boarding houses. We took food, clothing, and provided medical care when we could. Some of us would read to the sick and poor residents. That turned into a Sunday school for the children."

"Now it came to my attention that one of the buildings was actually owned by the Parkham family. It was in such a shabby condition, it was dangerous. I asked the residents when the landlord came to collect rents. They told me he came on a Friday night—as that was when workers got paid."

"One week I was so angry about a small child falling through a stair banister, and being nearly killed, that I determined I was going to do whatever it took to make the Parkhams take responsibility for their property. I collected the rents from each tenant, explaining to them the agent would only receive the money once I had spoken with Mr. Parkham."

"Wow! That was bold!" Aimee said. "Were you scared?"

"I was too frustrated and angry to be scared." Mrs. Parkham tilted her head. "Looking back, I suppose I was also a bit self-righteous. But it kept the fear at bay. I wanted to get these people justice. It didn't matter that some were black, or Irish, or Southerners. They were human beings without the resources to fix things themselves.

"Later that evening, the agent came to collect rents. When he knocked on the door, I was waiting." Mrs. Parkham made a sweep with her hand. "He stood six-feet-two-inches tall. It didn't matter to me that I was only five-foot-tall. With as much dignity I could summon, while I stood on a chair, I looked him in the eye. With steely determination, I made sure he knew that I was determined to talk to Mr. Parkham."

"That must have been an amazing sight," Angelee said, grinning as she imagined a young, feisty girl standing up to a man twice her size.

"We had loud words, some not repeatable! I told him that I had put the money aside, in a safe place. Of course, I had back-up and I pointed out the tenant, who was every bit as tall as the agent, but broader. I informed the agent that I would only hand the money over to Mr. Parkham. The agent was going to have to deliver a note to the Parkham family. I'd stipulated in the note that either I be given an appointment to meet at the Parkham office, or that Mr. Parkham had to meet me at the tenement house and then he would receive his money."

"So, how did you get the agent to cooperate?" Angelee asked.

"Shame is a grand motivator! I told him that he'd be ferocious as a she-bear bereft of her cubs if his own mother had to live in such a place. His mother must have been a fine woman, to bring up a strapping man like himself. Then I asked him how he'd feel if she had to live in such an unsafe place. He hung his head. Then I bribed him, offering to pay for his bottle of whiskey if he delivered the note. That sold him."

"So, did he return with a note later?" Aimee asked.

Mrs. Parkham laughed. "No, young lady, he did not. I'd included my home address in my note—so he could reply. But at six o'clock the next morning there was a thundering pounding on our front door. When my father answered it, there stood Horacio Parkham, himself. He wanted to see me.

"What could my father do? He invited Mr. Parkham in, offered him coffee, and then came to wake me up. Getting dressed in a hurry isn't easy when a person is still half-asleep and suddenly terrified. I got caught with my guard down, you see."

"I rushed downstairs and suddenly I was absolutely awake. He was a grand man, impeccably dressed, complete with a walking stick. So, I summoned all the bluster I could, on an empty stomach, and informed him that I wasn't handing the money over until he'd gone on a tour of the former hotel, now tenement building. Not only that, but I insisted on accompanying him."

"What did he do?" Aimee asked.

"What did he say?" Nori added.

"I just stood there, hands-on-hips, looking him in the eye. He didn't know my knees were knocking. The effect on him was priceless." Mrs. Parkham smirked. "Mr. Parkham clenched his jaws, his face turned red, and his eyes burned into me. It was like having electricity flashing from his eyes."

"He turned to my father and said, 'Has she always been such an impertinent, meddlesome, demanding brat?' And my father calmly looked at him and replied; 'My daughter is a young woman of strong convictions—but I've never seen her behave in this manner before.'

"Well, Mr. Parkham didn't want to believe that. Yet, my father reassured him that I could be reasonable, and be reasoned with. He asked Mr. Parkham to wait until Lowell could be gotten up and breakfast was eaten. I could tell Mr. Parkham wasn't happy about it. But for some reason, he obliged.

"Did he have breakfast with you?" Angelee asked.

"No, just drank more coffee. It was the quietest meal we'd ever had in our home. Directly afterward I got my coat. Lowell and I sat across from Mr. Parkham's carriage as we rode to the boarding house.

"Upon our arrival, I looked him in the eye. I thanked him for indulging me and told him that I had been very angry when I wrote the note. The previous day a toddler had fallen through the stairwell banister because the bars had been knocked out. I told him that I could have written a list of things wrong with the place, but he needed to see it. With that, we walked in. He was shocked at the splintered floorboard, missing steps on the staircase, doors with broken hinges, doors not properly hung, rooms where the stoves couldn't be used because the flews were blocked, exposed ceilings from where the plaster had fallen, gaps where mice and rats could get in, etc.

"That tour was a real eye-opener for him. I handed over the purse with the money in it.

"That's how I met my husband. It was true, he was quite a bit older than I am. We talked about it later. He'd been confounded that a woman could tame one of his agents into submission. However, to actually see me the next day, looking more like a child than an eighteen-year-old woman—well that astonished him. But when I directly confronted him, even defied him before being properly introduced, well that confounded him. He'd never encountered so much passion in such a small person before."

"But when did you know he was the right man for you?" Angelee asked the question again.

Mrs. Parkham opened her mouth, then closed it. She pursed her lips, and her eyes narrowed as if focusing on a distant memory. "It was that same morning that I knew I'd met a man who could match me in temperament. Just imagine, a man who is accustomed to being deferred to, a man given to issuing orders and not being questioned by those who worked for him suddenly being affronted by this diminutive woman.

"My father used to say to people that what I lacked in physical stature, I made up for with a powerful personality. Besides being young, I was idealistic, determined to make a difference in the world. Serving the poor, fighting for those who had experienced injustice, and caring for the orphans and widows were part of being socially responsible, a Christian duty.

"Most of the men in my neighborhood were good men, businessmen who worked hard. A good number of them came knocking on our front door, asking my father for permission to call on me. But I often felt that they were patronizing. They seemed to think that if they offered me marriage, I'd give up my charity work and be content to clean house and have children. None of them cared about the things that I wanted to accomplish.

"Yet, in those moments of staring down Mr. Parkham, I saw a man who had the same forceful disposition. It was a very quiet ride to the boarding house. While I was aware of this friction between us, I was determined to be effective in making that building safe and habitable for the people living there."

"I would have loved to be a mouse in the corner of that buggy!" Angelee said.

"We glared at each other the whole ride." Mrs. Parkham continued. "Once we arrived, I climbed down and walked into the front door, without waiting for him. He was almost directly behind me, which I was hoping for. I made a point of taking him down to the basement, to show him how rats and other pests got in. We stopped and visited families on each floor.

"Now it surprised me to see Mr. Parkham take out a small notebook and a pencil and start making notes. He listed every missing shutter, every door that was missing hinges, steps that needed replacing on the stairs, broken banisters, dangerous chimneys, and stovepipes, etc.

"When we finished the inspection, I gave him the money. I thanked him for his time. He, in turn, asked me to have coffee at a local tea room. This was unexpected, but I accepted the invitation. On that first morning of our acquaintance did I know I would marry him? I thought it an impossibility. The age difference, the diversity in our social status seemed like a problem, and of course the contrast in our financial standings.

"But as we sat there talking, it became clear that our views were common. We both wanted to live purposefully, making a difference. Something happened inside of me, which I could only describe later as falling in love. Hardly did it seem a feasible match."

"So, how did it happen?" Aimee wanted to know.

"Now what happened next is very interesting. Horacio sent me a note, requesting that I come to his office. So, I went—not in a hurry, but the next day. His secretary brought in tea for us. Then he told me that he'd counted the money, three times. He said that there was more money than required, about ten percent over what should be there. He asked me how much I had asked for. Because I didn't know how much the rent was supposed to be, I had asked each family to pay what they normally paid.   So, looking into it, he discovered that the agent had been overcharging the tenants and skimming that amount off. Mr. Parkham had the man arrested for fraud."

"My teacup needs a refill." Mrs. Parkham stopped in the middle of her story.

Angelee rose to go to the kitchen. As she started to leave, Mommy stopped her.

"Ask Daddy to make us a fresh round of tea. He's on duty this afternoon."

Angelee returned from her errand and asked if the others wanted anything else besides coffee or tea.

Mommy stood up and headed toward the stairs. "While we wait, I'm going to check on the boys." She slowly mounted them.

"I think that's just an excuse to move a bit." Aunt Milly said. "Emileah has always been an active person. And I think the baby is making itself known."

"Did the agent spend long in jail?" Aimee asked.

"A couple of years." Mrs. Parkham said.

"Tea and coffee are on the table, ladies," Cameron called from the dining room.

"Come on, Aimee, let's pour for the others," Angelee said.

Angelee filled the cups with hot liquid and Aimee passed around the food. There was casual chatter as the ladies enjoyed the repast. When done, Angelee and Aimee collected empty plates, cups, and saucers and left them on the dining room table.

"We left off with the agent in jail—but no closer to knowing how you and Mr. Parkham got married." Nori summarized.

"Yes, Dear Girl." Mrs. Parkham removed her glasses and polished them on her handkerchief.

"Unexpectedly, Mr. Parkham offered me a job. Not to collect rent, but to help him keep track of the condition of the many buildings he owned. Each Monday he would send a driver for me. Stanley would drive me to different properties and I'd do a walk-through. Sometimes I'd wear Lowell's clothes—making me look like a boy. I'd talk to the renters and see if there were any complaints. I'd ask them if they thought the rent was appropriate. I learned not to ask if they thought it was fair—because some thought the only fair price was free!"

The room filled with feminine laughter.

"I don't know if Horacio truly needed the information, or if he was just looking for a way to spend time with me. He never wanted a written report, it was always a meeting in his office."

"What about repairs? How did he do those if you didn't write it down?"

"That was the only thing I could do with a pencil and paper—a list of practical problems that needed addressing. It was the attitude of his clients, the type of people who rented from him that he wanted me to tell him about. And he wanted to know about the neighborhoods—did they need a doctor in the area? Were the children in want of schools?

"I'd been doing the job about two months when he asked me for a favor. Would I make friends with Mrs. Seelye, a friend of his? I was a bit puzzled but agreed. This was in response to an exception I'd voiced one day about my lack of the kind of social graces that people in his social circle employed. He had remarked that behaviors could be learned, but that character was more important.

"Horacio hosted lunch at his home one day, and the Seelyes were also invited. He let us decide for ourselves if we liked each other. We did, thankfully. Mrs. Seelye became my mentor—helping me learn proper etiquette for any-and-all social occasions.

"What I did not know was that Mr. Horacio Parkham had intentions toward me—and he was implementing the plan to remove the obstacles—my objections, his family's doubts, and society's disdain. By befriending me, Mrs. Seelye lead me into her social circles as I grew in confidence. This disarmed and dispelled the nay-sayers, and enabled me to finally marry Horacio Parkham."

Baby Louis began to cry. Nori picked the baby up off the floor. "I'll take him upstairs. After he's changed, I'll need to go home. Bart has school tomorrow, and both the boys will need a bath."

Nori lifted the blanket from the floor and draped it over the fussing baby, disappearing from the room and up the stairs.

"That's one thing I never had the pleasure of experiencing. Neither Horacio nor I ever knew why we weren't blessed with children of our own. He was thirty-seven when we married, and I was twenty. We didn't think we were too old. But it just didn't happen. It was a sadness for us. My brother, Lowell, and his wife had six children. They hit a rough patch when Cameron fell ill. Being used to helping people, Horacio, and I thought nothing of taking care of Cameron. He was only five years old at the time. We got so attached that we wanted to adopt him. Lowell thought it wouldn't be fair to the other children—who missed him. We could see that, so when he was strong enough, he went home. However, we made a point of having all the children come to see us over their summer vacations. When it was time for Cameron to go to college, he came to live with us and attend Boston University."

"Did I hear my name?" Cameron walked into the room.

"I was just telling them what a naughty child you were." Mrs. Parkham winked at the other ladies.

The grandfather clock chimes struck the hour.

"Me? Truly, I was not." Cameron laughingly denied. "Well, maybe I did see how close I could get to the line in the ground. But, Dear Aunt, those chimes confirm it is nine-o'clock and we should consider that it is time to go home."

"In that case, we need to properly thank the Tilson family for such an enjoyable afternoon and evening."

Mrs. Parkham stood to her feet and slowly straightened. "Emileah, thank you for asking about my late husband. Though I think of him often, I rarely talk of him; it was a pleasure. And of course, I truly thank you for that beautiful meal. Now, if you'll help me with finding my wrap, I will let this boy take me home." She patted Cameron's arm.

A hot water bottle was procured and filled for Mrs. Parkham, for her to keep warm on the way home in Cameron's car.

Angelee offered to drive Nori and the children home. However, M. Torrington insisted on taking them, having driven his Model A truck over.

It was later when everyone had settled into the comfort of warm beds that Angelee let her mind ruminate upon Mrs. Parkham's love story. She was surprised by the woman's openness.

Mommy's story about meeting Daddy, Aunt Milly's tale of romance with Uncle Neddy, and Mrs. Parkham's narrative all held the same theme; PURPOSE, along with sharing that purpose, and working toward the same calling. Love seemed to be more than a racing heart and changeable emotions. Beyond attraction, there had to be respect, communication, and friendship. A foundation of faith must be laid—in God and each other.

Perhaps this understanding would be like the chemistry used by a photographer, who let the developer and fixer swish over the image on the paper. Just the right amount of time in the liquid and the picture became clear.

Angelee fell asleep, feeling that she'd been given a key insight to help her discover her own heart.

Thanksgiving past, Christmas preparations became the central focus for everyone. Angelee sat at her office desk; scrunching her shoulders together, turning her head side-to-side, trying to ease the tension building from copious card writing. On the right side of the desk sat a stack of unaddressed envelopes and Christmas cards. On the left sat stacks of completed ones. The list of Mrs. Parkham's business associates, tenants, and friends in Boston seemed endless and she insisted each card be hand addressed. A typed envelope seemed impersonal. Christmas must be as personal as possible, even when nearly one-thousand miles in between.

As she sat, she closed her eyes to rest them, allowing her mind to wonder. What were Drew and Pauley doing now? Did Pauley have time to think of her? As much as she tried to think about what his life must be like, she couldn't truly visualize what the daily routine was like.

After settling in Ft. Oglethorpe, Georgia, their correspondence had resumed. According to the letters that Drew and Pauley wrote the food was substantial. Although some of the officers, from well-moneyed families, thought it intolerable. But the thousands of farm boys who had known hardship had a great appreciation of the simple food. The lads were also encouraged to engage in sports, basketball, baseball, boxing, soccer, and track, and field athletics. This was part of their entertainment as well as contributing to their physical training.

Footsteps on the stairs interrupted her reverie. "Come play hooky with me!" Olivia's teasing invitation rang out.

Jumping up, Angelee raced across the room, to greet her unexpected friend. "What are you doing here? It's a Wednesday afternoon!"

"I know! Gladys Drinkman had to come home, so I caught a ride with her. I'm taking the interurban back after dinner. But I just had to stop by and see you."

"Look at us! Still standing here, and you with your coat on." Angelee laughed. "Come on down to the kitchen. I need a break. I'll have Frances make us a pot of coffee! The smell of ginger has been driving me crazy! I think she's making gingerbread men!"

Olivia slid her coat off and draped it over her arm. The girls negotiated the stairs, swapping news.

"Do you think Frances would be persuaded to make hot chocolate instead?" Olivia asked. "That was a cold ride down. The Drinkman car is drafty. That canvas top isn't snug."

"Let's ask her! Did you just come for a visit? Or are you on a mission of some sort?"

"I was just missing everybody. Plus, my roommate has a nasty cold. When Gladys asked me to join her, I took advantage of it. While I'm home, I'm going to ask Mommy if she'll make some almond spritz cookies and maybe some lebkuchen."

"Why not stollen?" Angelee suggested.

"I can share the cookies easier than a stollen."

Arriving in the kitchen, Olivia draped her coat over the back of a chair.

"I hope we're not interrupting you, Frances," Angelee said.

"Hello, Girls!" Frances smiled, moving gingerbread men from a baking tray onto newspaper to cool. I take it you're taking a well-earned break!"

"Me or Olivia?" Angelee asked.

"Both!" Frances laughed. "Want one?" She pointed to some iced ones on the counter-top.

"Who would say no to that?" Olivia quipped.

Angelee looked around, noticing the coffee pot already on the stove. "How old is the coffee?"

"Ugh! Pour that out! It's been sitting there since breakfast this morning. I'll make more!"

"Could I beg you for some hot cocoa instead?" Olivia titled her head like a small child and widened her blue eyes.

"How can I deny that face?" Frances chirruped, rolling her eyes. Pulling an envelope from her apron pocket, she passed it to Angelee. "Did your mother get one of these? I have a feeling several women in town must have gotten letters like this."

Angelee held the letter up and read it aloud:

"Dear Madam,

"Your boy has probably told you what a good time the ordnance detachment had on Thanksgiving Day. Now the officers ask you to join us in a surprise for him and beg you not to disclose the secret. We are promised a fine big Christmas tree and in order to carry out the idea of Santa Claus, would you care to send the

presents for your boy addressed to me on the outside wrapper and put his name on the inside wrapper. These will all be stored and not be distributed until Christmas morning when we will all get around the tree and have Santa Claus do his part. Some of the men have more friends than others, so if you can spare a present or two for the less fortunate and address the package to me, personally, we will see that it is well placed. Let us urge you to 'do your Christmas shipping early' for the post office at the camp is going to be sadly congested around December 25.

"We would suggest that packages be not too bulky. Being acquainted with the life here, we might offer the following ideas..."

Angelee looked up. "This is quite a list...but you can read it later." She continued reading.

"Our Christmas meal promises to be even better than on Thanksgiving Day, so cakes and 'eats' are unnecessary. Sometimes the boys have to go to the hospital too. The government supplies slippers and bath robes, but a few of these for our exclusive use would be acceptable.

"If this Santa Clause idea meets with your favor, will you please keep it a secret and address the packages as follows: Capt. Louis Waefelaer, Camp Ordinance Officer...

"We have the pick of the division in the ordinance detachment. They are all clean-cut, intelligent men, who feel that they are in this war to protect you, their sisters, their sweethearts and our liberties and to save us from the atrocities that Belgium has been subject to. They are determined men, but they are going about their work with a smile and under those conditions I believe they are irresistible.

"If there is any possibility of your being with us at Christmas time, we would like very much to have you here. We will take good care of you and you can see for yourself that your boy is being as well cared for as is possible under the circumstances.

Very truly yours, Louis Waefelaer."[3]

"Wouldn't that be great, to go visit the boys?" Frances said, pouring the steaming chocolate milk into cups, passing them around. "We must do our best to find some really special things."

"This letter must be for the boys in Mississippi," Angelee said. "Drew, Pauley, and Jasper are in Georgia."

"My baby brother, Roger, is in Fort Shelby," Francis said. "But I'm sure you can send presents to Georgia, through the Red Cross."

Olivia picked up her handbag and pulled out a small notebook and a pencil. "I'm just going to copy this down—you know the list. I'm sure Mommy will want to send some parcels. And I'll send something to Drew and Pauley from Indianapolis."

Angelee began laughing. "Drew sent us his wish-list the first week of November.

"What do you think of this? Olivia's eyes twinkled. "Just as a joke, we send him a small box of twigs—with a card that reads 'mini-switches'. Of course, we'd mark that box number one."

"You have a truly ornery mind, my friend." Angelee quipped. "I think it'd be great fun if he were here and we could see the look on his face. But Drew can be so clueless, he'd miss the joke without us around."

"I know you're right," Olivia said, before taking a long drink of the hot liquid.

"Well of course I am NOT going to send Drew any sticks. He'd never live it down in the camp." Angelee said. "But sometimes we can't help getting a mischievous idea—when we're together." Angelee nodded toward Oliva.

"Unfortunately, our time together is over for today," Olivia said, drinking the last of her cocoa. The notebook and pen went back into her handbag. "I've got to get home and help get dinner done. I can't afford to miss the interurban tonight." Olivia took her cup to the sink, collected her coat, and put it on.

Angelee walked her to the front door. Thanks for making an effort to see me. I really miss you." The two hugged tightly before Olivia walked out the front door.

Angelee sighed and squared her shoulders. "Now then, back to addressing Christmas cards."

****

December twilight, dusky skies met Angelee's view as she left Mrs. Parkham's home office. Sunset was at four-thirty. The sun's retreating golden light gave way to the lavender and pink colored clouds and approaching deep blue. By the time she had stopped at the post office to deliver the bundled cards, all that remained was the indigo sky. Taking a deep breath, the crisp air stinging her nostrils, she reveled in the stimulating evening; hurrying home, wanting to share her ideas for making Christmas special for "her" soldiers.

Once home, Angelee changed her dress then joined Mommy and Aunt Milly busy with preparing the evening meal. In the kitchen, familiar routines and rhythms created harmony and a contented atmosphere.

As Angelee washed up dishes from preparing the food, she was distracted with thoughts of what to send Drew, Pauley, and Jasper.

"Hey, Dreamy! Are you going to condescend to come back to the land of the living?" Mommy teased.

"Sorry, I was just making a mental shopping list for Christmas presents." She grinned.

"Well, I suggest that we have a pow-wow with Aimee included. We can compare ideas and decide what each of us is going to send. Drew won't need four sets of playing cards." Mommy said.

"You're right. Especially since we need to send things as soon as possible." Aunt Milly made a suggestion. "Let's ask Nori over for tomorrow evening—we can ask about things Jasper would like."

"Oh, good idea. I just hope she doesn't feel like we are pitying her and the children." Mommy replied.

"She knows we consider her family. Let's ask her to bring her special rhubarb cake for dessert. If Bart and Alistair are involved it will be a big family project." Aunt Milly advised.

"Does she work tomorrow? If so, then she may be too tired to come." Angelee said.

The back door opened, admitting Aimee and a blast of cold wind into the kitchen. Quick closure stopped the frigid intrusion, and Aimee scurried to thaw out by the stove.

"Aimee, I have an errand for you," Mommy said. "I need you to go over to Nori's and ask her if she can come over tomorrow evening for dinner. We need to plan Christmas."

"Urrrgh! But it's freezing out there." Aimee complained. "And can't Alistair do it?"

"He will be home in a few minutes, so take him with you." Mommy insisted.

"But can't Angelee go in the car?" Aimee whined.

"Angelee is busy helping with dinner. Stop arguing and have a glass of milk with a couple of cookies. Dinner is still over an hour away. And you'll need the energy to keep warm."

Aimee took off her coat, raided the cookie tin, and filled a glass with milk, preparing the same for Alistair. "I want to make sure that Alistair and I can do our errand as soon as possible. It's already dark and miserable out there."

"Oh, cheer up! Think Christmas! Think presents!" Aunt Milly interjected. "Sing Christmas carols on the way to Nori's. It will make you feel better."

"Oh yeah!" Aimee rolled her eyes, and shook her head." "That will *really* work...just like trying to use a knitting needle to sew in a hem." Aimee quipped.

Alistair, who had used the front door, came into the kitchen. He was rushed through his after-school goodies.

"Off you go!" Mommy said. "And don't dawdle."

As the messengers trooped through the back door, Angelee—who had been softly humming Christmas carols since Aunt Milly's suggestion—heard Alistair challenge Aimee to a race. That would keep them warm!

For now, all she could think of was how this Christmas was going to be different than any she'd experienced before.

Two-and-a-half weeks passed, proving that truly unlike previous years, the time leading up to Christmas was indeed different; mainly, not having to worry about taking school exams before Christmas break. For this, she was truly thankful.

However, Mrs. Parkham had kept her busy; proof-reading end-of-year reports; shopping trips to Indianapolis, and even a Christmas party for the Sunday School class.

Angelee didn't remember the exact moment she got wrapped up in assisting with the Nativity play at church. Mrs. Michaels, the Sunday School superintendent, thought it a foregone conclusion that she would naturally help coach the children, and assist the regular Sunday school teachers. After all, she mused, it was well known that she spent every Saturday morning at the library, presenting Story Time to many of these same children.

Christmas Eve, an hour before the Nativity performance, Angelee entered the basement of the First Christian Church, carrying the box with the carefully ironed costumes.

"This rain doesn't seem very Christmas like, does it?" Mrs. Smith said.

 "At least it isn't like the blizzard earlier this month, and all those below-freezing days." She set the box down and shrugged out of her water-proofed coat.

"That is a point. If we had deep snow, the Nativity play would have been canceled." She half grinned and observed while holding up a robe. "I know some of the boys would not have been too disappointed by that."

"You're probably right. But others been working very hard and can't wait to perform." She reminded the Sunday school teacher, with a nod to acknowledge Mrs. Smith's perspective.

Across the room, the fifth and sixth-grade children were practicing their numbers for the program. The first and second graders that Angelee taught were arriving with their parents. Out of the box came robes, some striped, some solid blues, reds, and greens. When each child arrived, Angelee asked mothers to make sure they had been to the toilet before a robe was dropped over their heads and wide sashes were tied into place.

"I ain't wearing no scarf on my head!" Willy Hammond declared. "That's for sissies!"

"Well, it's a good thing you're a shepherd and not a wise man," Angelee reassured him. "Sissies can't be shepherds either."

"But I like sheep!" Annabelle Tucker lamented, tears suddenly appearing on her cheeks.

Angelee wrapped her arms around the seven-year-old. "Annabelle, a girl can be a shepherd. But when I said 'Sissies' I meant people who don't like animals. Now see, you're a brave girl, just like Willy is a brave boy because you both like sheep."

Angelee turned toward the defiant boy. "Willy, some shepherds do like to wear handkerchiefs on their heads. It keeps their head safe from the sun and wind and rain. But I suppose some of them don't."

"Good, 'cause I ain't wearing it!" He repeated his adamant refusal.

"Willy, you need to say you are not wearing it—don't use the word ain't." Angelee felt it was important to address the incorrect grammar this time.

"That's what I said...I ain't wearing it." Willy crossed his arms.

"Willy, repeat after me: I am not wearing it." Angelee persisted.

"Why can't I say ain't? How come I have to say, 'I am not wearing it.'?" Willy complained.

"Because you are a clever boy, and you want everyone to see how smart you are to use the correct word. If you want to look like a sissy, then say 'ain't'. Only Sissies say ain't"

Will looked hard at Angelee, trying to determine if Angelee was making fun of him.

Looking up at Mrs. Smith, who was helping another child put on his costume, Angelee said. "Isn't that right Mrs. Smith? Only sissies use the word 'ain't'?"

"That's true Willy." Mrs. Smith confirmed.

"I'm not weary a stupid hanky on my head either!" Myron protested. "If Willy isn't, then I'm not either."

"See what you've started?" Angelee looked at Willy. Willy just shrugged, looking as though he was still contemplating the use of the word 'ain't'.

"Myron, you do surprise me. Besides the shape of the headpiece, what's the difference between the handkerchief and a hat? You always have a hat on."

"Not always...Mommy makes me take it off in the house. And you make me take it off in Sunday school. And that towel don't look like a hat."

"How about this? How about we let you wear your hat for the pageant? Only during your performance though." Angelee suggested. All she wanted was for the children to cooperate, even if it meant compromises.

"Well, I could do that." Myron capitulated. "AND I don't say 'ain't'." He bragged.

"What makes you so sure, Miss Tilson? Are you a teacher, or something?" Willy gibed.

Angelee was taken aback by Willy's words; that odd sensation of truth resonating in her heart sent chills up her spine.

"Miss Tilson also works at the library, so she knows about using the right words." Mrs. Smith said.

Willy's question *'Are you a teacher?'* pulsed through her being while she carried on dressing the little actors. She made a conscious effort to put that thought to the back of her mind and began organizing the children to go upstairs to the sanctuary.

This was Angelee's first year to be orchestrating the Christmas pageant. Last year she had been one of the young students performing. It indeed was turning into a very different kind of Christmas. She was missing those minutes of preparing for the time before the congregation when she either sang with the others in her Sunday school class or the recitations she was to present. This year her focus was not on the meaning of Christmas, but on the other teachers who were depending on her help with getting anxious, distracted, and excited children into the proper wraps, leading them to the sanctuary and getting them to hit their cues.

Angelee was glad that they had chosen a nine-year-old from the fourth-grade class to be Mary, and a ten-year-old to be Joseph. It was challenging enough to keep the small ones quiet, and moving at the same time.

"Miss Tilson, I need the toilet!" Annabelle pulled Angelee's sleeve.

"I thought you went before we put your gown on," Angelee asked softly.

"I did! But I need to go again." Annabelle whined.

"Mrs. Smith, can you handle them? We're on in three minutes." Angelee looked at her fellow teacher.

"Yes, go on. And take Donna with you." Mrs. Smith passed the child's hand over to Angelee.

Quickly guiding the girls to the ladies' room, she helped them manage their costumes. It was a relief that both of them managed the task without mishap. They hurried up, holding skirts and costumes up so they wouldn't trip. The girls joined the group just as they were taking their places in front of the platform.

Mrs. Smith sat down, in a chair next to the piano, while the pianist played the introductory chords. Angelee, seated on the front row, raised her hands, making sure all the children were watching her.

"Away in a manger..." The children's voices rose in the sanctuary.

With the first word, Myron reached up and pulled off his hat, holding it in front of himself with both hands. This elicited soft laughter from the congregation. From inside her robe, Rosie Carroll pulled a tiny lamb and cradled it in her arms. There were a few "ah's" from several people near the front. Little Charlie Edwards got caught up with the music and began waving his arms, looking for all the world like a miniature conductor.

For their second song, the choir director had written a set of Christmas lyrics to go to the tune of "Baa-Baa Black Sheep." Mrs. Smith had added actions for the song and the children sang with great gusto and exaggerated gestures. The number was repeated a second time, as there was a rousing response to the children's performance.

The children bowed. Myron replaced his hat, determinedly pulling it down. Angelee made the class members hold hands to lead them back out the way they had come in. Willy folded his arms again, refusing to take Annabelle's hand. Since he was the last in the line, Angelee let it pass, knowing Willy would still bring up the rear. Angelee led them downstairs, where she and Mrs. Smith helped them out of their costumes. Once the task was done, Angelee quietly led the class back up to the sanctuary to a pew near the door.

During Rev. Matthias's short Christmas message, a couple of the children fell asleep and Angelee couldn't help but smile. She was proud of her charges, her heart and mind filled with not only tenderness, but of fulfillment. Although she should feel guilty for not paying strict attention to Rev. Matthias's words, she reflected on the innocence of the children. Her thoughts drifted to the war in Belgium, France and Germany. How many of those children would be cold, hungry, some ill, and all of them unaware of Christmas? How many of them had lost parents, brothers, sisters— all their family? A large lump grew in her throat, tears trickled down her cheeks and Angelee prayed for the orphans and widows made so by the war. "Lord, my heart aches for them. Show me if there is anything I can do for them...to bring them hope and comfort."

Rev. Matthias's voice brought Angelee back to the service. "Do you think Mary genuinely understood what her obedience meant to mankind? I don't think she did. All she knew was that God has sent her an angel." "Luke writes in chapter one, verse 28:

"Hail, thou that art highly favored, the Lord is with thee. But she was greatly troubled at the saying, and cast in her mind what manner of salutation this might be. And the angel said unto her, Fear not, Mary: for thou hast found favor with God."

"May I suggest to you, that God is saying to us, today, that we are highly favored? Does this leave us troubled? By *what* are we troubled? That His favor will require something of us? But the message to us tonight, on Christmas Eve, is that we are to fear not. Gabriel gave Mary specific instructions and spoke of the Heavenly Father's purposes to be accomplished.

"God has holy intentions and plans for each of us. He will send us a messenger. Granted, our Angels may not be seven feet tall, with shining light all around. But for each of us, there will be an encounter, with a specific message that gives us direction, that gives us hope, and that even creates a holy fear. But imbedded in the message are the instructions, 'Fear Not'.

"Sometimes those encounters are 'Ah-Ha' moments, when several ideas will come together in a way that makes sense, providing a picture we couldn't previously see clearly. Angels can appear as human beings with a familiar face—like a friend, a child, even a favorite pet. With these God-breathed moments, we feel truth resonating through our emotions, our minds, and produces within us a desire to obey.

And this is what Luke records in verse 38:

"And Mary said, Behold, the handmaid of the Lord; be it unto me according to thy word. "

"Dear Friends, we live in a world full of fear, anger, and pain. But for us, Christmas should not be one night, or one specific date on the calendar. Christmas should be every day. Each morning we can wake up and remind ourselves not to fear. We may not understand why our journey takes us through times of darkness, times of sorrow. But Jesus Christ embraced human-kind by entering our world as every other human being has since Adam and Eve. When we respond, like Mary, simply saying, 'Be it unto me according to thy word', God's favor will empower us to do that which will affect our world for His kingdom. Maybe we will never see the impact we are making this side of heaven. But let's keep our hearts and minds full of expectation; Angels arrive when we need them. And God's favor is His Christmas gift to us today, tomorrow, and every day beyond. Amen."

Rev. Matthias motioned for the choir to stand and the organist moved onto the bench. The pianist and organist played the introduction to *Joy to the World*, signaling the finale for the service.

Angelee stood, automatically singing the memorized words, but thinking that perhaps Willy was an angel. His words had created a reaction she'd not anticipated. And she remembered the encounter at the library when a mother had expressed the opinion that she would make a good teacher. Was it quite possible she was finding God's purpose for her life?

Tuesday, December 25th, 1917
Christmas Day

Sunrise on Christmas day provided only two minutes more daylight than the 21st of December, the Northern Hemisphere's winter solstice. Like most years, those minuscule moments were unnoticed that year; the first Christmas observed during America's official, military involvement with World War One. It would be another year before Americans recorded that 1917 was the only Christmas celebrated during the United States official participation in The Great War.

****

"Come ON, already!" Alistair's insisted, looking around the bedroom door. "It's seven o'clock. I want to open presents."

"Merry Christmas to you too, Alistair. Gee-Gee, why can't he be excited when we try to get him up for school?" Aimee groaned.

Angelee stretched and yawned. Letting out a deep sigh, she replied. "I don't know. But it is Christmas. Curiosity is eating away at that boy. I bet he didn't sleep much."

Aimee rolled out of her bed and pulled on her housecoat.

"Will you hand me my hairbrush, please? By the way, if you get a new housecoat for Christmas, will you be able to finally let that one go?" Angelee grinned teasingly at her sister.

Aimee ran her hand over the arm of her chenille housecoat. "I don't know. It will be hard. It's so soft...and comfortable."

"And threadbare, and mended, and sporting another hole in the back."

"What about you? You keep wearing that old flannel nightgown when you have two new ones in your drawer." Aimee protested.

While the banter continued, Angelee slid the brush through the curly tresses, removing the tangles and smoothing them into obedient tendrils. Aimee searched under her bed for her slippers.

"I never thought I'd miss Drew coming in and shocking us awake on Christmas morning." Angelee felt her throat tighten with tears.

"I know what you mean. Alistair just shouted around the door. It just isn't the same as Drew creeping into the room, leaning right next to our ears and yelling Merry Christmas." Aimee concurred, taking up her own hairbrush.

"Do you think we should get dressed?" Angelee asked. "Or should we do it after presents?"

Looking over at Aimee, Angelee saw she was busy pulling on stockings.

"You haven't answered my question. Although, it looks like you're all for getting dressed."

"Just habit I suppose."

Someone thumped on the door. Aimee, with one sock now on, stood and answered the door.

"That mother of yours!" Aunt Milly came in with a tray. "She's supposed to be taking things easy. But she's been up for an hour already—said the baby was restless. She's not even due till April! Anyway, here's hot cocoa girls!"

Placing the tray on a desk and Aunt Milly handed Angelee a cup. Angelee took the cup and ventured to take a sip. "Mommy put peppermint into it!"

"HEY IN THERE!" Pounding shook the door. "Will you hur-ry?! I can't wait much longer!" Alistair called through the door.

Startled, Angelee, jerked, nearly spilling the drink, the sloshing caught by the saucer.

"Give us five minutes, will you?!" Aimee demanded back.

"Okay! But not more than five."

"At least get your other stocking on, Aimee. We don't have time to dress." Angelee sighed.

Aimee, frustrated by Alistair's impatience, swallowed her hot cocoa in two big gulps. "OHHH...that's HOT all-the-way down!"

"Guess Alistair made that decision for you!" Collecting the empty cups onto the tray, Aunt Milly smirked as she walked out the door.

By the time the sisters arrived, the rest of the family were settled in the salon.

"Now then, before we pass out any presents, or open any of them, we are going to do something different this year." Daddy began. "We are all missing Drew, Pauley, Jasper, and the others from our community who are away. Since they are not here, I thought the best thing would be to pray for them. It's the best gift we can send them. Mommy, will you start us off? I'll bring us to a close." He concluded his direction.

Everyone bowed their heads, and peace settled in the room. Mommy prayed, as though speaking to a friend. Aunt Milly followed next. The circle of prayer included everyone; prayers for protection, strength, and wisdom. Daddy ended the final prayer, and lead them in the doxology. Tears were shed. Peace filled the room, bringing smiles to the family's faces.

"Now then, Alistair, you will be our parcel passer this year." Daddy said.

Alistair jumped up from his chair and knelt next to the tree. As he pulled a box from underneath the decorated branches, the doorbell rang.

"I'll go!" Aimee said.

A squeal came from the hallway. "I can't believe it!" Aimee shrieked.

Seconds later Drew walked into the room. Alistair dropped the package, ran, and jumped into his brother's arms. Mommy rocked on the settee, trying to rise. Daddy immediately took her arm and helped her. While Aimee jumped up and down, Aunt Milly clapped her hands. Angelee crept behind Drew, slipping her arms around his waist. Encircled, Drew was mauled with hugs, kisses, and slaps on the back in the cacophony of laughing, crying, and talking over each other; yet no one was listening.

"TWEEEEEEEEETTT" Daddy's shrill whistle burst out and silence prevailed before laughter once again rippled through the room.

"We all want to know the same thing; how did you get home?"

"On Wednesday we—Pauley, Jasper and I—were told by our first sergeants that we could apply for Christmas or New Year furlough. We just got approved on Friday. We rented a car and drove up. We only have a week. But we were determined to get home for Christmas."

"But all your presents have been sent to Fort Oglethorpe." Mommy lamented. "And we are just about to open our gifts."

"Come help me Little Brother!" Drew commandeered Alistair by throwing his arm around his shoulders and leading him out to the car.

"In that case, I'll go make a pot of coffee! You must be tired, hungry, and cold." Aunt Milly said rushing to the kitchen. Angelee refilled the coffee pot and set to boil on the stove then pulled a serving platter out and piled it up with Christmas cookies and gingerbread men.

Upon their return to the parlor, Angelee and Aunt Milly saw that Drew had returned from the car with a canvas duffle bag. "We were able to collect our mail from the Camp post office, including our presents."

Drew sat on the floor in front of the fire. "Gee-Gee, Pauley told me to tell you that he'll be over tomorrow."

Angelee's heart raced. What she feared would be a difficult Christmas, had just turned on its head. Her brother, her good friend, and Nori's husband had been granted leave. This was a wonderful Christmas, almost miraculous. Thanksgiving, praise, joy, and love-filled her heart.

"I don't care if there are no other presents for me!" Mommy said, tears trickling down her face. "All my children are home for Christmas."

"Amen!" Daddy avowed.

"Well, I'm opening my presents even if no one else is!" Alistair asserted.

The room momentarily fell silent. Drew's laughter spilled out and was contagious. "Get busy Little Man! Gotta keep us on track!"

"Go on then!" Daddy waved Alistair on toward the tree.

Alistair picked up the first box again, then set it down. He ran to Drew and threw his arms around his neck. "I'm glad you're home, Drew."

"Glad to be home!" Drew returned the hug quickly, then lifted Alistair, and pushed him back towards the evergreen. "Now, pass those parcels around!"

For a while, the family forgot about the war, the weather, and the world outside.

Drew's unexpected arrival produced a light-hearted atmosphere in the Tilson household. Once the presents had been distributed, the tradition of round-robin opening began.

"Drew, you're next," Angelee said. "But see that little one, marked number one? You need to open that one first." She instructed.

Drew dutifully obliged her instructions. "Hey! What's this meant to be?" he protested, holding the cardboard box filled with tiny sticks for all to see.

Angelee and Aimee burst into laughter, glad to be witnessing first-hand Drew's reaction to the joke.

"Don't you like your miniature switches?" Angelee teased.

"The big ones were too obvious, so we made them tiny." Aimee qualified the description.

"I can't believe you girls!" Daddy said. "Sending your brother unwarranted tokens of misbehavior! Tsk! Tsk! Tsk! Just think of the raucous that would have erupted in the barracks!"

"You have to be creative!" Aimee said as she took a stick from the box. "See, you can make your own matches...or whittle the end for a toothpick."

Drew suddenly yawned.

"So, our gift is boring you?" Angelee teased.

"Sorry, but we drove non-stop. Four-hundred and fifty miles make for a long trip!" Drew defended himself.

"You can have a rest after we finish here," Mommy said. "We've got cinnamon rolls and coffee cake for breakfast."

Paper tearing, teasing, and squeals of delight filled the next half-hour. To make sure nothing was left unopened, and nothing was hidden amidst discarded paper, Angelee and Aimee collected and folded the wrapping paper and ribbons, sorting what could be reused later from the unusable remains. The rescued wrap was stacked neatly into a pile, to be stored in a box later.

While the girls cleared the clutter, Mommy and Aunt Milly had gone to the kitchen. The aromas of coffee, hot chocolate, and cinnamon rolls, wafting from the kitchen, set empty stomachs rumbling. The Tilson brood eagerly regrouped at the dining room table.

Chatter at the breakfast table included the trip from Georgia to Indiana, the condition of roads from one state to the next, and what 'the boys' hoped to do while on leave.

"Mommy, Olivia, and I agreed we'd get together tomorrow. I can start getting things ready for dinner if you want." Angelee suggested.

"Thanks for offering," Mommy said. "But you don't need to rush. Just come down when you're ready."

"Are you sure you don't mind if I go over to Sonya's?" Aimee said.

"Of course, we don't mind Mee-Mee." Mommy smiled. "We've got plenty of time before dinner tonight. Drew, go on up and get some sleep. I know you need it!"

"Not fair!" Alistair protested. "He promised to tell me about Bootcamp."

"You're not the only one who wants to talk to him." Daddy admitted. "But your big brother is exhausted. I'm sure he'll reserve some special time for you tomorrow. Right now, let's go examine that new erector set."

Since everyone else seemed preoccupied with other things, Angelee rose from the table, taking her plate and teacup to the kitchen. Collecting her pile of gifts from the parlor she went upstairs. Angelee indulged in a hot bath and shampooed her hair. Afterward, she dressed in a well-worn, favorite blouse with three-quarter sleeves underneath a corduroy jumper dress. She pulled on woolen socks and slid on her flannel slippers. Clipped barrettes held her hair away from her face with a ribbon creating a high, loose ponytail, allowing her heavy mane to dry.

Refreshed and comfortable, Angelee sauntered down the stairs to the ever-warm kitchen. It was impossible to resist nibbling on another piece of coffee cake since no formal lunch was being served and dinner was to be in the evening.

Smashing the last of the crumbs onto her fingers, she licked them off before placing the empty plate into the sink.

****

Potatoes pinged against the enameled, tin bowl as she counted out potatoes to peel. She was coming out of the pantry when Aunt Milly joined her.

"I thought I'd get started on the potatoes. There's going to be a lot of mashed potatoes in this pot." Angelee pointed to the stew-pot.

"I just can't get over your brother surprising us like that." Aunt Milly marveled. She took onions from the drawer in the Hoosier cabinet and collected celery from the icebox. "So, I guess I'll have to make more dressing."

"Do you realize we have sixteen people at our Christmas dinner table—that's if you include baby Louis," Angelee remarked. "I'm glad Daddy bought that twenty-five-pound turkey from McIntire's farm."

Touching her fingertips, while saying each person's name, Aunt Milly counted silently. "I just hope we don't get any more unexpected dinner guests, although we will probably have more than enough food. It's more a question of, where do we sit everyone."

Angelee picked up the paring knife and began peeling the first potato. "Maybe Mee-Mee and I could sit in here with Alistair and Bart."

"I have an idea that might work," Mommy said. "Was that the doorbell?"

"I think so." Aunt Milly said. "We'll know in a minute—if one of the boys answers it!" She quipped, referring to Daddy as 'one-of-the-boys."

"Look who's here!" Daddy declared, ushering in the evening's first guests. "Nori and the family."

"I hope there's enough room for one more?" Nori asked, hugging everyone.

"You mean your early Christmas Surprise?" Mommy asked, knowingly.

"Yes!" Nori enthused, her eyes sparkling with tears. "And I finally told him about the baby."

"Elnora Hanson! Only now?!" An astonished Aunt Milly asked.

"I didn't want him to worry while he was gone. And I'm pretty sure 'it' happened right before he left in August."

"I hope you reassured him that we are taking good care of you and the little ones," Mommy said.

"I've told him about Angelee finding me in a puddle of tears and how all of you have been helping me and the children."

"You were working too hard, especially trying to take care of the children and keep up the job at the sanitarium. I'm glad you listened to Andrew's advice to quit the washing dishes at night-time." Mommy said.

"I wasn't sure how much Jasper's Army pay was going to be. Besides, a little hard work never hurt anyone. Speaking of hard work, that's quite a pile of peelings you've acquired." Nori pointed at the peelings Angelee had collected.

"All potato skins. There's going to be mashed potatoes and an apple-and-sweet potatoes casserole." Angelee put the pot of potatoes on the stove to cook.

"What can I do to help?" Nori asked, pulling a clean apron from the drawer.

"Will you peel some apples for me?" Mommy instructed. "Plus, I think it's time for a fresh pot of coffee," Mommy said, placing the coffee pot under the faucet to fill it. "What's the weather like?"

"It's kind of grey out—trying to snow." Aimee volunteered, entering the kitchen from the back door and allowing a refreshing blast of cold air to follow her.

"You're back sooner than I expected," Mommy said.

"Caroline's cousins were in town with them. It was pretty crazy over there; I decided I preferred our crazy. Plus, I wanted to be here when my Christmas surprise arrived!"

"*Your* Christmas surprise?" Mommy and Aunt Milly asked simultaneously.

Daddy chuckled softly, poured himself some fresh coffee, and left the kitchen.

"Yes! M. Torrington will be here later with the surprise."

"Aimee Rochelle, did you invite him for dinner and not tell us?!" Mommy said.

Aimee suddenly looked sheepish. "Well, I did tell him that he would be welcome to join us if he decided that Home Lawn's Christmas dinner didn't appeal to him."

"And what did he say?" Mommy pressed.

"The invitation was appreciated and wanted to know what time to come over."

"Truth be told, what's one more? We always have leftovers." Aunt Milly observed. "Are those pumpkin pies ready to come out?"

Mommy, closest to the oven, peeked into the cooker. "Not quite—about ten more minutes."

"Since I'm here, Mommy, go sit in the salon or go upstairs for a rest," Aimee said.

"That's right, Mrs. Tilson. There are plenty of cooks here. It's all under control." Nori seconded.

"Nori, you are one to talk! You should be resting too!" Mommy, face flushed from the oven heat, had light shadows under her eyes. "I must admit, I am feeling tired. Babies..." She smiled. She untied her apron and removed it. "I will go up for a nap—I was up very early. Nori, get out of here and go spend some time with Jasper"

"Please let me help!" Nori pleaded.

Aunt Milly reviewed the menu, the progress of each dish—from turkey and dressing to pumpkin, mincemeat pies, and persimmon pudding. "Emileah is right. Nori, the girls, and I have everything in hand. With all this help, and getting an early start, I think our feast will be ready a little after five o'clock.

Aimee, will you go get Drew for me?"

Aimee obliged, returning with Drew in tow.

Aunt Milly instructed Drew to shift the table in the dining room. "Your mother suggested that we position the table diagonally across the room. We'll have more space, especially with the extra table leaves in."

Drew recruited Alistair, Jasper, and Bart to shift the partially set table and adjust the seating. The dining room tables received special attention with fancy Holiday embroidered table cloths, matching napkins, and special china.

Cheerful chatter filled the kitchen as Aunt Milly's crew cleared away and cleaned while keeping an eye on the cooking and baking.

"You know, it's nice to have a day off from cooking tomorrow." Aunt Milly mused. "Seems like we should cook before Christmas—and not have to cook on the day!"

"It is ironic, isn't it?" Angelee responded to her Aunt's remark.

"With so many people, maybe we won't have too many left-overs!" said Aimee.

With the food cooking, and the dishwashing caught up, Aunt Milly, Nori, Aimee, and Angelee sat around the table, each with a needlepoint or knitting project. They chatted about sewing patterns, projects from prior years, and other Christmas memories.

As the culmination of cooking came close to its orchestrated climax, the sewing was put away. Angelee went upstairs to wake her mother and notified the remaining family to wash hands and prepare for dinner.

The doorbell rang.

"I'm sure that's Mr. Torrington," Aimee said, dashing to answer it. "I'll go."

As anticipated, Mr. Torrington arrived, carrying a large object wrapped in brown paper. Aimee took it, placing it in the salon.

"We're just about to eat," Aimee advised.

There was a clamor as sixteen people came into the dining room. They stood around the table, holding hands while Daddy said the prayer.

Ting! Ting! Ting!

Daddy gently tapped the side of his drinking glass. "The women have certainly outdone themselves. But I believe we should remember—especially because we have Jasper and Drew home—that this is not a feast because of the food. It is a feast because we are celebrating love—the love of family. More importantly, we are celebrating the source of love, our Savior, God with us. Merry Christmas!"

There was a chorus of "Merry Christmas".

"Now let's fill out plates so we can eat!" Alistair implored!

And so, they did.

Tuesday, December 25^{th,} 1917
Unveiling

"We're glad you could join us, Steffken. Aimee forgot to mention it to us until this afternoon." Mommy winked at Aimee. "As you can see, we are hardly short of food."

"It is kind of you to make room for me. Aimee has been working very hard on this gift for you, Mrs. Tilson."

"He has been teaching me the right techniques!" Aimee explained. "I thought it only fair that he gets to see your reaction!" Aimee added.

"I thought we'd opened all our presents!" Alistair remarked.

"This one is especially for Mommy and Daddy!" Aimee qualified.

"It gives us something to look forward to after we've eaten too much of this delicious Christmas meal!" Daddy said, eyes twinkling.

"I gotta make the most of it!" Drew said, leaving the table to fill his plate again at the sideboard.

"Can you top mine up too?" Jasper asked, lifting his plate towards Drew.

"Anyone else, while I'm at it?" Drew asked, as he sat his full plate back on the table and took Jasper's.

No one else was so inclined.

"Daddy, does Drew have to help with dishes since he's home on leave?" Angelee asked. "He shouldn't have to do any chores, since it's Christmas and he only has a few days."

"Did you put her up to that?" Alistair asked, giving his older brother the eye.

"No, I did not." Drew mockingly furrowed his brow at his younger brother. "And I have every intention of keeping the tradition of 'men-only' dishes duty. I need to move around a bit. But I'm not starting clear up until we see this mystery present for Mommy and Daddy."

"Now, now, let's not rush everybody," Mommy said. "We have all evening."

"I suggest that we take a break between the main course and dessert." Daddy said. "Then Mommy can unwrap whatever it is that Steffken has delivered."

The idea was unanimously accepted. Nearly half-an-hour later napkins were folded and laid on the table.

Standing, Daddy theatrically waved him arm in the direction of the parlor. "Let us repair to the salon."

"Oh My! Such formality." Mommy rejoined. "I shall do as you bid."

"These little ones need some soap and water first!" Nori said.

Angelee smiled and shook her head at her father's silliness and the messy children.

Though wearing bibs, Bobby and Jilly wore crumbs and smears of food like clown make-up on their round faces. Louis attested to his enjoyment of the fare; food smeared in his hair; hands gooey from grasping tidbits of tasty vittles; the bib proved useless. The children were directed upstairs to the bathroom for a clean-up. Angelee assisted Nori, helping the older children to wash their hands and faces while Nori deftly stripped Louis, gave him a quick sponge bath, and redressed him.

Ministrations to the little ones complete, she took Bobby's and Jilly's hands and led them downstairs. Nori followed right behind her with Louis on her hip.

The content of Aimee's gift was already known well to Angelee, haven been asked by her sister to play an important part in its production.

Every available seat was taken, while Alistair and Bart sat on the floor. The packaging paper crackled softly while Aimee lifted the present and placed it in front of her parents, settled on the love seat.

"I'm hazarding a guess that this is a painting of some sort," Mommy said, observing the shape of the object.

Mommy fiddled with the string until Daddy pulled out his pocket knife and deftly cut through it. Mommy pulled the paper away, and her eyes grew wide. Aimee had purposely situated the offering so that her parents would be the first to behold the subject matter.

Still holding the top of the frame, Mommy covered her mouth and tears filled her eyes.

"Aimee..." Daddy's voice choked. "I'm speechless."

"Perhaps I should turn for all to see?" Steffken asked, coming to stand by Aimee.

Daddy nodded, removing his glasses and wiping his eyes.

"It's a portrait!" Aunt Milly cried.

"Did you paint yourself as well?" Nori asked.

"She painted it all," Steffken replied. "She has captured her sister and Mademoiselle Olivia very well. In truth, Mademoiselle Aimee has proven to be the hardest working and most talented student I have ever had."

The gold scrolled frame enhanced the vibrant colors and delicate brushstrokes, of three girls on a couch, their hands in their laps. Leaning towards impressionism, Aimee had captured the likenesses of Angelee wearing rose, seated in the middle; Olivia, outfitted in periwinkle and sitting on her right; and Mee-Mee herself, attired in russet and situated to Angelee's left. The background was a muted green, with only the arms of the couch showing.

Aimee, cheeks flushed with pleasure and excitement, remarked. "Making sure I was keeping my head positioned correctly while looking in the mirror was enough to give me more than one headache. And of course, working the changing light was almost torture. Mr. Torrington pushed me to try things I had not done before. I surprised myself."

"Looks like I'd better start preparing for Aimee to attend Herron Art Institute after she graduates next year." Daddy stated proudly.

Indianapolis's growing and thriving artistic community benefited from patrons, such as John Herron, who had bequeathed the financial resources to establish an art museum and art school. The Italian Renaissance Revival-style, limestone building had been built about a mile north of the circle on Pennsylvania Street.

"What about the Art Institute of Chicago?" Aimee asked flippantly.

"Well, I can see Aimee's future education is going to be a topic of hot discussion, maybe even debate!" Aunt Milly chimed in.

Angelee found herself sighing deeply, the temptation to envy her sister pricking her mind.

"What was that sigh about?" Nori asked, leaning closer to her friend.

"Aimee's gift is so obvious—everyone knows she wants to be an artist. And Olivia is following her desire to become a nurse. I feel like I'm in the world floundering for some sort of direction or purpose for my life. Maybe I'm just feeling a bit sorry for myself."

"Angelee, you are so good with children. Maybe you have a calling or purpose is working with them. You know, there are times when others can see what we are good at. But we don't. Even when they say something, we don't or won't listen. Have you thought that you aren't giving consideration to people's input because you want to 'hear it directly from the Lord'?"

Nori's question both peeved Angelee and pricked her conscious. "I don't want to think it about right now. I don't want to steal Aimee's thunder."

They had kept their voices low, to not bring attention to themselves while the others marveled at Aimee's accomplishment.

"It's going to take a bit of thinking to find just the right place to hang this lovely painting," Mommy observed. She gently pulled Aimee down on her lap.

"I'm too big for this Mommy! And I don't want to hurt the baby!" Aimee made a verbal protest but did nothing to resist her mother's lap.

"I'm fine," Mommy said. "You're also one of my babies. I want to show you how much I love you—and how much your gift means to me."

"Is it time for dessert yet?! Alistair lamented.

"Yeh! Can we get the dishes done so we can get pie and cake?" Bart added.

"Are you nuts?" Alistair elbowed his friend. "Why did you ask about washing dishes?"

"Cuz it's what your dad calls pro'col!" Bart retorted.

"That's pro-to-col." Daddy chucked his correction. "And I think you've got the right idea, Bart. Come on men-and-boys; all-hands-on-deck. Aimee, thank you for giving us a part of your heart. We will always treasure it."

Aimee shifted from her mother's lap and onto the spot her father had just vacated. "Thank you, Daddy."

Angelee looked down at Jilly in her lap. Even amid family and friends, she felt alone, lost, and restless. She had never imagined that she would have such feelings on Christmas Day. Once again, this Christmas was very different than any she had experienced previously.

Wednesday, December 26th, 1917
An Admission

The post-Christmas Day let-down was tempered with the pleasure of enjoying new clothes and books. The focus on Christmas Day activities now unnecessary, Angelee decided the opportunity was ripe to pick and organize selections for the Saturday morning reading sessions. With everyone home during the day, the large home provided no quiet corner. Nor did the house afford access to the new children's books that had recently arrived at the library.

Bundling up warmly, Angelee escaped her rowdy abode, making for the enforced quiet of the limestone building with its book-loaded shelves just blocks away.

Fair skies meant no snow or sleet. However, a scarf protected her face from the freezing temperatures. To stave off the seeping cold in the breeze, Angelee trotted along the paved sidewalks, quickening her blood flow, her puffing breath steaming the air.

At nine o'clock, as Mrs. Johnstone opened the library door, Angelee was the first to pass through. Finding a place to sit in the watery sunlight coming through a window, she hung her coat on the back of a chair before browsing through the titles in the young readers' section.

Immersed in planning for the first quarter of the year, Angelee was sorting through the assortment which she'd pulled from the stacks and had spread out on the end of a table. She liked the idea of doing projects with the children, concentrating on prioritizing the order in which she wanted to read the books. Topics like Epiphany, St. Valentines, the birthdays of Abraham Lincoln and George Washington, plus stories about Raggedy Ann and Raggedy Andy were possibilities on her list. As she read through the books, she assembled a list of questions for the children to answer.

"Is children's literature that fascinating?" A friendly, familiar voice murmured in her ear.

"Lord have mercy!" Angelee gasped, flinging her pencil into the air. Her hand covered her heart, and she took a deep breath.

He chuckled softly. "Mustn't laugh too loud, here in the library."

"You enjoyed that too much, Pauley Alexander!" Angelee hissed, yet smiled despite the startle.

"I truly didn't intend to do that." Pauley indirectly apologized while retrieving her pencil.

"Let's say I believe you, that you didn't purposely set out to make me jump. I have to ask what did you intend to do?" Angelee challenged.

"Hmmm, let me see." Pauley held up one finger. "To ask what time you might be finished today…"He held up the second finger. "To ask you if you'd like to go to lunch with me when you are;" He held up his third finger. "And to ask you if I could walk you home afterward."

Angelee acknowledged his questions with a nod of her head.

"So, that is a yes…to all three?" Pauley teased.

Angelee grinned irrespective of her resolution to remain serious. "You are an opportunist! However, I was simply acknowledging your questions." It felt wonderful to be with someone she knew well enough to appreciate his games, his humor, his way of thinking.

"I see. So, what are the answers?" Pauley persisted.

Coyly Angelee laid a finger to the side of her face and pretended to think about the invitations.

"Well, I have a question for you. What did you mean by going to lunch with you: to the White Star; or following me home and eating turkey sandwiches; or maybe going to your house?"

"That was four questions." Pauley parried.

"No, that was one question with three qualifying phrases that followed." Angelee giggled.

"I see." Pauley pretended to be exasperated. With a deep sigh, he replied. "Well, Mischievous Maiden, I was inviting you to the White Star."

"Then, I accept your invitation." Angelee affected innocence. "And yes, you can walk me home after that."

"You certainly know how to put a man through his paces." Pauley smiled broadly.

"But after boot camp at Fort Harrison, and your time at Fort Oglethorpe, you should be well-practiced."

Rolling his eyes and shaking his head, he crossed his arms. "Let me tell you something; crawling through mud, shooting at targets, and marching for hours is child's play compared to negotiating with the female mind." Pauley taunted.

"If we weren't at the library, I'd find a way to make you regret that last remark!" Angelee shot back.

"You have such fire in your eyes when provoked." Pauley's all-knowing smirk was accompanied by a taunting wink.

Irked by his self-assurance, Angelee consulted the clock on the wall, which indicated that it was fifteen minutes past eleven o'clock. "I shall expect you to come for me at twelve-thirty this afternoon."

Pauley chuckled. "Yes, Ma'am. I shall report for duty promptly." He saluted her.

She saluted back. Pauley finished the salute, turned in a military manner, and marched to the door. Pausing in the doorway, he turned and winked at her. Angelee waved back.

With a smile on her face and in her heart, Angelee returned to her task of preparing for the Saturday morning reading group.

Mrs. Johnstone stopped as she walked by. "Do you think we'll get many children tomorrow afternoon for the special reading group?"

"I have a feeling that many mothers will be glad to bring the children tomorrow. There's no snow for sledding, and it's pretty cold out. So, I have a feeling that there will be a touch of cabin fever going around."

"On the list, you've put *Old Mother West Wind* for tomorrow. Any changes to that?" Mrs. Johnstone inquired.

"No changes; I read it last April and I think the children will like revisiting it," Angelee confirmed.

"I'll let you get on with things." Mrs. Johnstone concluded and headed back to the office.

Angelee returned the books to the front desk, knowing that Mrs. Johnstone preferred the library staff to reshelve the books. Satisfied with her decisions, and the completed task. Angelee was shrugging into her winter coat as Pauley came into the library.

"Has it warmed up any?" Angelee inquired, picking up her satchel.

"It's a few degrees above freezing now. If the wind doesn't blow, the sun has a little heat." Pauley informed her.

They left the library and walked across the square to the restaurant. The main lunch crowd, minimal though it was, had finished by the time they arrived. Finding a seat was easy, and Pauley guided them to a back corner.

"Are you ashamed of being seen with me?" Angelee teased Pauley.

"No, but I do want some privacy. And the harder it is to be seen, the more we can talk uninterrupted."

"That sounds rather serious."

Pauley helped Angelee out of her coat and held the chair for her as she sat. Removing his coat, he draped it over the back of his chair and sat down. He leaned forward, resting his forearms on the table.

"Angelee, I only have a few days, and I want to make the most of the opportunity to see you as much as I can."

"It's not easy, is it; with your family wanting you there as well," Angelee observed.

"I know Mom and Dad understand. I don't think the twins understand. They've barely left my side since I arrived." Pauley reached across the table and took her hand.

"Hello, you two." Kim, the waitress, stood by them with a pen and order pad in hand.

They sat back and smiled at Kim.

Angelee ordered a pot of hot tea and Pauley ordered coffee.

Within five minutes Kim was back with the drinks and took the rest of their order.

"As I was saying, Lucy and Lori have not wanted to let me out of their sights since I got home. Mom and Dad have had to threaten punishment if they didn't go to bed last night." He chuckled.

"So, how did you escape today?" Angelee cracked a wide grin at the thought of the twins.

"I had to barter all the way: if they let me see the people around town I wanted to see, they would have my undivided attention this evening. Just so you know, they demanded to know if 'people' included you."

"Nosey little ladies, aren't they?" Angelee cackled at their audacity.

"It's just that they have my best interest at heart," Pauley said.

"Are you sure it isn't more a case of, they're young and selfish and don't want to share you?"

"That too!" Pauley acknowledged. "Thanks for the Christmas gifts. I like that scarf you sent to me."

"I knitted it myself," Angelee said. "I had to sacrifice several hours of reading to do that."

"This young man has a great appreciation for your sacrifice. By the way, I have something for you as well." He pulled up the side of his coat and reached into an inside pocket, withdrawing a rectangular box. He handed the five-inch-by four-inch item, wrapped in brown shipping paper to her.

"Thank you, Pauley. Am I supposed to open it later or do you want me to open it now?"

"By all means, open it now." Pauley encouraged.

The brown paper carefully pulled away revealed Christmas gift wrap. Being less careful, she tore away the colorful paper to find a blue box. She lifted the lid of the box and gasped when she saw the hand-carved doll inside. "Pauley, where did you get this?"

"One weekend, when Drew and I were on leave, we went to Chattanooga. We'd been around town, looking at the sights. We got to visit The Read House Hotel and tried a Coca-Cola. It was too expensive to have lunch there, so, we wandered down to the riverfront. When we got hungry and we stopped in a small cafe. In the corner of the room, an older gentleman was sitting there whittling. He had some samples of his work; you know dogs, cats, babies, boats, etc. Some of the babies and other people figures had clothing. We got to chatting with the man. He'd been a carpenter but injured his back. Now he made a bit of money carving these toys and figures. His wife made the clothes. When I saw that one, it reminded me of you and I just had to buy it."

Gently removing the doll from the tissue, Angelee thoroughly examined it, admiring the way the hair had been given the texture of lines, and carved in such a way that the little lady had permanent curls, with a part down the middle. The eyes had been sculpted evenly, complete with pupil and eyelids. The nose and lips had been shaped in relief. These features were painted—yellow hair, brown eyes, and red lips. The doll's hands were mitten-shaped, without detail. The feet were flat-bottomed and rounded on top. The simple navy shift was covered with a cream-colored apron. "Oh, Pauley, she is beautiful. She'll have a special spot on my shelf with the others."

"I didn't have enough money to buy a boy to go with her. But I got his name and address so I can make a special order. I wanted to buy some for Lori and Lucy—and maybe Mom."

"Does he take special orders?"

"Yes, and he has started teaching some of the local youngsters to carve and whittle as well. He would like to set up a gift shop and workshop. He hasn't been able to raise the money to do it."

"Do you think he could make it work once the upfront costs were covered?" Angelee speculated.

"Maybe, because he says he makes just enough to keep buying more supplies. The problem is, Gus can't charge for the work he does, because he hasn't got a business. He's allowed to take donations. His wife keeps a roof over their heads by cooking and cleaning at the restaurant. The owner is a friend."

"Well, let's start praying God will give him a miracle and he can open his own business."

"Angelee, I love your generous heart."

She felt herself blush. "Thank you." She replaced the doll into the box and then added it to her handbag. "I will always treasure it."

"Being away from you underscores for me that you are the woman I want to come home to," Pauley said. "I try not to think about leaving again on Saturday night. And not knowing when we'll be shipping out makes life even more frustrating. All we hear is rumors and supposition. So, we just keep training, and work as hard as we can."

"I must confess, I've missed you more than I expected."

"I'm glad to hear that!" Pauley took her hand. "So how are things with Mrs. Parkham? Is she still pushing for Wellesley?"

"No, we came to an understanding. She accepted that I needed to make my own decisions. I explained that my place is here, at least until I have that 'I was born to do this' revelation. I keep getting an inkling that I'll know soon. Mrs. Parkham and Cameron were with us for Thanksgiving; he truly dotes on her."

"Cameron, eh? Do you think he was part of her agenda for you as well?" Pauley speculated.

"Really! Pauley, what does it matter if he is? What she hopes for has nothing to do with Cameron's feelings for me—or me for him! But Cameron is my friend. It's true, I was guarded with him, to begin with. But he is kind and funny, and genuinely likable."

"Do you think you could be falling in love with him?" Pauley persisted.

"Pauley! Why are you acting so jealous?! He is my friend—nothing more. Just like you're my friend. And I can't imagine my life without you. But I can't tell you what my feelings are right now. I don't know what to expect of falling in love, being in love. It doesn't seem right to explore what might develop in the future since you're away and leaving for France soon."

"I'm sorry Angelee. I was badgering you. Jealousy does niggle at me sometimes. Yet, you're right, it isn't fair to push you to say something before you're ready. Maybe I should take you home now. Unless you want to walk on your own." Pauley started to rise from his chair.

Reaching across the table, Angelee put her hand over Pauley's. "Don't rush off."

Pauley sat down again.

Angelee nodded agreement. "Ever since high school graduation, I've been pressed into situations that have made me take responsibility for my own decisions. I'm learning that being compliant makes me vulnerable to other people's expectations and desires. I think I was lulled into a false sense of security by always following the rules. Go to church, go to school, do your homework, obey your parents, and stay out of trouble. There is a degree of merit to that. But I think I'm beginning to learn that when you have to resist something you don't want or fight for what you do want, that is when life begins to have real value."

"Like King Solomon wrote; 'God gives wisdom, out His mouth comes knowledge and understanding." Pauley encouraged her. Pauley leaned back in his chair, while still holding her hand. He relaxed, smiled. "I'm not trying to rush anything. But I do want to talk freely with you—maybe dream together. Who knows how long this war will drag on, or how long I'll be away? So, let's just try to enjoy the time we have together. In the meantime, I think I'd better pay the bill and walk you home. Looks like we are being a nuisance by sitting her so long."

Angelee stood up as Pauley went to the cash register to pay Kim. By the time he'd finished and come back for his coat, she had wrapped up with her coat, hat, scarf, and gloves.

The courthouse bells chimed at two o'clock as they left the restaurant and headed towards the Tilson home. Freezing temperatures precluded a slow ramble home for the pair. Otherwise, Angelee might have put her arm through Pauley's in a companionable manner. Making her eyes water, a sharp breeze tugged at the edge of her scarf.

"Wish I'd brought my car," Pauley remarked ruefully. "I could have gotten us home faster and out of the cold."

"That would have felt like a luxury," Angelee observed, shoving her hands into her coat pocket.

Brisk footsteps carried them across the square to Washington street. Conversation ceased as they concentrated on traversing the brick sidewalks along Washington street, maintaining as much body heat as they could.

Arriving at the red brick domain, they skipped up the steps and entered the house. Angelee savored the warmth that greeted her face as she pulled off her scarf. Shrugging out of her coat, she hung it on a hook, draping her hat and scarf over the top of it. Pauley loosened his scarf but seemed undecided about removing it.

"What are you doing this evening?" Pauley asked.

"Olivia and I are getting together," Angelee said. "Why?"

"There's a basketball game at the high school tonight-- Bloomington," Pauley mentioned Martinsville's greatest rival. "I wondered if you'd be interested in going."

"In all the years you've known me, have I *ever* been interested in basketball?" Angelee laughed.

Shrugging, Pauley laughed. "Guess that ruins my excuse to spend time with you instead of the twins."

"I thought I heard your voices," Mommy said, coming down the stairs. "I'm glad I caught you, Pauley."

"Why's that, Mrs. Tilson?" Pauley cocked his head, smiling at her.

"I was on the phone with your mother a bit earlier. We've decided to have a going away evening for you and Drew."

"Are you sure a party is a good idea?" Pauley asked.

"We agreed it would be just our two families," Mommy informed him.

"That sounds wonderful. Maybe I'll bring over our new Monopoly game. And of course, Snakes and Ladders." Pauley suggested.

"Good idea. We decided to do it tomorrow night because you'll be leaving on Friday." Mommy said.

The grandfather clock chimed two-thirty. "I promised the girls I'd be back by three o'clock, so I'd better get going," Pauly said re-wrapping his scarf around his neck.

"Thanks again for lunch," Angelee said. "I guess I'll see you tomorrow night."

Pauley gave her a quick hug, and let himself out the door.

"Mommy, would it be okay if I invited Olivia for tomorrow evening?" Angelee asked, following her mother into the kitchen.

"Of course," Mommy said, sitting down at the kitchen table, rubbing her stomach. "Would you please fix me a cup of tea?"

"Of course. Do you want a cookie or some toast as well?" Angelee asked, placing the kettle on the stove and lighting the gas ring.

"How was your time at the library?" Mommy asked.

A grin creased Angelee's face, knowing her mother really wanted to ask about her lunch with Pauley. "Very productive. I've picked out books for the children that will take us up to Easter. And before you ask, I had a nice lunch with Pauley."

The kettle sang, and Angelee poured the steaming, bubbling water into the porcelain teapot, where the black tea leaves swirled as the pot filled. She added sugar into the two cups she'd set out, deciding to join her mother.

"Am I that obvious?" Mommy chuckled.

"No...but I know how you think. Now, Aunt Milly—she *is* that obvious, blunt even." Angelee nodded adamantly setting the tea tray on the small round table and took the chair across from her mother. Pouring the amber liquid into the china cups, Angelee inhaled the scent of the orange pekoe. She pushed one cup towards her mother and then stirred her tea to dissolve the sugar.

"Mommy, is there something wrong with me? I feel so confused about so many things."

Mommy lifted the cup and took a tentative sip, testing the temperature of the drink. She smiled compassionately at her daughter. "Did Pauley say something that makes you feel befuddled?"

"Most girls my age would be pleased to be courting and thinking about marriage. But I just feel like I'm not ready. Is it wrong to feel like I need to discover my own purpose first?"

"No, Gee-Gee, it isn't wrong. Part of the problem is that we are affected by our emotions. The paradox of our feelings is that we can feel more than one thing at a time."

"Can you give me an example?" Angelee asked.

"Our emotions are a bit like the weather on a Spring day. One minute the sun is shining, spreading its warmth. Suddenly the temperature drops, black clouds roll in, the rain comes down in sheets, with lightning and thunder. You feel hot, then chilled. You are filled with awe at the power of the wind, startled by the boom of the thunder. The sky turns a peculiar color, and suddenly you see a tornado on the horizon. Fear and panic affect your thinking. Only a few minutes ago, you felt safe. Instantly you have to decide where to hide from the storm. You're still amazed by the beauty of nature's power while feeling helpless to stop it. After the storm is over, you come out from your hiding place, to find that your home is undamaged. You feel relieved, thankful. But then you see that two doors down a family's home has been demolished. Your heart is filled with sorrow at their loss. You feel overwhelmed by the downed trees, the other homes that have broken windows, damaged roofs. You're confused. Why would God protect your home, but allow so many others to be damaged? With your emotions convoluted by the event—relief, guilt, compassion—you can be left speechless, stunned, dismayed. Your emotions didn't cause the storm, but the violent weather did make an impact on your emotions."

"I guess I see what you mean; what we feel is changeable. But what does that have to do with me finding my purpose?" Angelee furrowed her brows, tilting her head as she looked at her mother.

"In the last six months, you've had several events thrown at you that have made your head spin. Without realizing it, God has provided you the opportunity to be guided by His Spirit and your understanding of His principles provided in the Bible. Paul wrote that those who seek to please themselves will never know God's plan and purpose. As long as you seek to please Jesus, the truth will provide peace during any storm."

"You're talking about growing in my relationship with Jesus, and being more like him, aren't you? I know God wants us to grow into His character. But somehow, I feel like I'm not hearing Him, and what He wants me to do."

"Angelee, I'm going to tell you a secret. There are times that even when we do know, it doesn't make your life any easier. Not to discourage you; but once we know, the devil will use all kinds of things to distract you."

Angelee finished the last of her tea, sighing, she set the cup onto the saucer.

Mommy also finished her tea, her cup rattling as she put it on the saucer. "Okay, the good news is this: once you do know the direction God has for you, it also serves to make you resolute. Now to get back to your desire to find your calling; once again you aren't wrong.

"Remember Rev. Matthias's sermon about love and marriage?" Mommy continued.

"Yes, he spoke on that on the Sunday before Valentine's day," Angelee replied.

"That's right. Rev. Matthias made the point that God had Eve to be a *suitable* helper for Adam. By knowing God's blueprint for your life, it will help you recognize the man you are meant to be with."

"First of all, by keeping God first in your life, our Heavenly Father will make sure He leads you to a man who also puts Christ first in his life. Next, your life's mission will match or tie in with his life mission. Let's say that a young woman has been musically inclined. She has studied piano and guitar all her life. She feels led to move into the city and start a music school; by teaching students who can afford to pay, she earns money to teach children who can't afford fees.

"During this time two Christian men have shown an interest in her. One of them is a city resident, an accountant. The other one is a farmer. The accountant isn't musical himself but loves attending the symphony. He is financially successful and admires the young woman's vision of a music school. The farmer is also successful. But he wants a wife who will help him on the farm. While the young woman has a deep appreciation and affection for them both, her passion and purpose help her choose the like-minded man for a husband."

Companionable silence filled the following moments. Mulling over her mother's words, Angelee tipped the teapot up, sharing out the remaining tea into their cups. This unanticipated conversation with her mother gave her a new perspective. She wondered what else she should look at differently?

Standing up to clear away the dishes, Angelee said. "Thanks, for the reassurance, Mommy. I still need to think about what you've said."

Looking up at Angelee, Mommy replied. "Just remember this, Gee-Gee. Emotions come and go, but we don't need to let them control us. Faith empowers us to get through any and every storm. Over a lifetime, we are constantly relearning that lesson. You're doing just fine."

Stepping around the small table, Angelee kissed her mother on the cheek. "I'm going over to Olivia's now. Mrs. Biers might invite me for dinner tonight. Is it okay if I stay and eat with them?"

"Sure. Make the most of your time with your best friend." Mommy consented. "I think I'll walk that way with you. I need a walk."

"Meet you at the door and help you bundle up!" Angelee said.

"Very wise—even if I am only going around the block," Mommy said.

Friday, January 18th, 1918
Children's Clothes and Toys

The remaining winters days of 1917 provided below-freezing temperatures and only a few flurries of snow. While the winds blustered outside, the Tilson and Bannister families enjoyed the final night before Pauley and Drew took the train back to Fort Oglethorpe, Georgia. Though daylight increased by minute increments, the evenings were still short.

Right after the new year, the Daily Reporter reported that the war department was preparing to rush troops to Europe. National Guard members from Martinsville, who were training at Camp Shelby, Mississippi, enthusiastically received the news. Troops who rated highest during their recent inspection were to go first. The question upmost in each man's mind was, "When do we go?" The answer was ambiguous— 'soon'. As for Drew, Pauley, and Jasper, they had been shipped out upon their return to Georgia.

Snow began to fall the second Friday in January 1918. Not flurries, but a proper storm. The sun made an effort to breakthrough, but the high-stacked, black-bottom, snow-laden clouds refused to give territory. By evening the wind had picked up, even more, seeping into every tiny crevice and minuscule crack of every home and business. Homeowners and janitors fought to keep buildings heated. Overnight the storm ramped up into a blizzard.

The Daily Reporter blazed a three-line headline proclaiming
"THE WORST BLIZZARD OF THE YEAR GRIPPED THE COMMUNITY FRIDAY NIGHT."

People awoke to find thermometers reporting minus twenty degrees. Although Saturday meant no schools were in session, mothers refused to let their children play outside for fear of frostbite and chilblains.

Farmers, county road maintenance drivers, police officers, and others of like employment, faced nature's arctic conditions. City postmen trudged through knee-deep snow, while rural mail carriers refused to venture out, as the danger of drifts and uncleared roads proved too high.

To make matters worse, coal was an expensive commodity. Shortages were caused by fuel companies directing sales primarily to industry rather than to the general public. Miners were on strike, wanting the right of union representation. To conserve fuel, Daddy moved the family into the salon for the duration of the cold snap. This meant using one fireplace, rather than trying to heat the whole house.

The Saturday, January 12th, issue of the *Daily Reporter* notified the community that all church services were canceled. Monday, the paper printed stories about drifts sweeping across the state making train and interurban transportation nearly impossible. Telephone lines were also affected by the wind, weighty ice cycles, and high banks of white. However, people in town were able to make local calls if they were patient.

Angelee took to wearing two pairs of socks, and two sweaters over her warmest wool dresses.

An average of three inches of snow fell daily over the next seven days. Undeterred by the challenges presented by the snow and frigid weather, Home Lawn Sanitarium proceeded with their celebrations for the grand opening of the new addition and other improvements. The newspaper story provided an itinerary of each evening's guest speakers and entertainment.

Professor Claude Michelon spoke on Thursday evening; presenting an illustrated lecture of the war, using photos recently taken on the Western battlefront in France. Having missed an opportunity to see his presentation the previous June, Angelee bundled up and made the short trip across the street to join others who had braved the elements to hear him.

Friday morning Angelee sat in the salon, looking out the front window, watching new snow accumulate of the exiting piles. She pondered the previous evening's illustrated lecture, most specifically Professor Michelon's appeal for clothing, especially for orphans. Heart aching for them, she wanted to find a way to help them.

As was her childhood custom, Angelee fiddled absent-mindedly with a small toy in her dress pocket. Pulling the figure from her pocket, she looked at it affectionately-- a friend she always had with her. A thought flashed through her mind.

Professor Michelon had encouraged people to include note cards with the clothing, which in turn would be sent on with the apparel. What if she could find a way to make a pocket-sized-toys for each garment she collected and sent them to the children? They would receive a small toy of their own, to keep. Making enough dolls or cars was a task beyond her ability. Who could she ask to help her do it?

"Are you contemplating what to wear to the Home Lawn dance tonight?" Aunt Milly's question broke into Angelee's train of thought, making her jump.

"Oh!" Angelee jerked, startled. "No, just thinking!"

"Here it is a Friday night, with an invitation to this evening's grand dance. Don't tell me you're going to miss it? I'm sure several young men would delight is guiding you around the dance floor."

"Even though we live just across the street, I still don't fancy the idea of getting out if I don't have to."

Despite herself, and her close relationship with Aunt Milly, Angelee found herself blushing. "Aunt Milly, you're being coy, and teasing me."

Aunt Milly grinned and couldn't repress the chuckle. "Maybe. But tell me, what were you so lost in thought about?"

"I was just contemplating an idea to help the war orphans." She handed the calico-covered wooden peg, with its painted face, to her aunt. "You know I've collected my 'pocket toys' since I was four or five. And it occurred to me that lots of the orphans will have nothing—not even their own clothes, let alone a toy. But what if I could make a bunch of these and send them with the children's clothing, we collect for Professor Michelon? Not only would they be getting dressed, but they'd be getting a small toy that would belong to them."

"That's a great idea!" Aunt Milly agreed. "But there are thousands of children. You can't possibly provide that many—especially by yourself."

"Oh, I know you're right." Angelee sighed. "The idea just occurred to me—including the notion of recruiting a group of people to make them. Maybe it could be done in conjunction with Professor Michelon's clothing drive for the widows and orphans."

"I do have a suggestion. If you decide to carry this through, then why don't you get the school children involved. Maybe teachers in town will allow the children in their classes to make these little characters as part of their art classes. We would do a session here on Saturday mornings in the salon." Aunt Milly offered.

Angelee's eyes widened as she looked at her Aunt. "That is a really good idea! Thank you."

Aunt Milly gave the figurine back to Angelee. "You don't want to lose your inspiration."

****

That evening Angelee and Aunt Milly sat at the dining room table, discussing the clothing and toy project. The conundrum of how to afford buying all the materials needed to make tiny toys for the children of Belgium and France came up. Besides the local churches, letters were written to many of the prominent businesses in town requesting their help.

Crumpling her third piece of paper, Angelee closed her eyes. "Pheeewwwww!"

"I'm getting tired too. I think we've done enough for one night." Aunt Milly said, taking off her newly acquired glasses and pinching the bridge of her nose.

"It isn't just being tired. I thought I'd write to "Papa Biers--but that seems so silly. I can just hear Olivia telling me; 'Just go next door and talk to him.' But I guess I'm also struggling with exactly what I should ask him for."

"What do you mean?" Aunt Milly put her glasses back on.

"I know we'll need crates for all the items we collect. But how many? Should I ask him to help with transportation to Indianapolis? Will he be willing to build crates instead of barrels? And you know his company make all kinds of things. I'm wondering if he'd be willing to have his workers make some small shapes that we could use to make toys."

"Since you can't go see him now, let's stop for now. There isn't anything else we can do. Your parents and Aimee will be home from the dance soon. I'll make a pan of hot chocolate for all of us. We can work on this tomorrow."

Angelee looked at the clutter on the table—envelopes heading for tomorrow's post, blank stationery, notebooks with lists of names and resources, ink bottles, and pens. Nodding her head, she said, "You're right, enough for tonight. Maybe the managers at Old Hickory will also donate some clothes pegs for our toys."

"Good thinking." Aunt Milly began collecting paper and envelopes to put away. "We need to do a lot more praying to make a difference. Do you mind taking over here? I'll go get things going in the kitchen."

Angelee nodded and organized the materials before putting them away. Just as she was putting the writing paraphernalia into the desk, a blast of frigid air coming through the glass-fronted door signaled the arrival of the dance attendees. The cold air chased the heat up the stairs and spread into the parlor and salon. She heard stomping feet, trying to remove snow from shoes, while they crowded into the small doorway. Angelee went to help them unbundle. Scarves were unwound from faces and neck, coats were shed and hung on the coat rack. "Good timing!" Angelee said. "Aunt Milly is making hot chocolate in the kitchen."

"Oh perfect," Mommy said. "I know it was a short walk, but I feel frozen to my core."

"You should have come, Gee-Gee! The band was marvelous." Aimee enthused. "I danced with lots of guests, and even waltzed with Mr. Torrington a couple of times."

"While you were dancing, did you manage to talk to anyone about the children's clothing drive?" Angelee prompted her sister while leading the party-goers into the kitchen.

"Yes, actually." Aimee grinned. "a few people want to donate money to help with the shipping costs."

"On top of that, I spoke with Mr. Kennedy." Daddy said. "He is more than happy to allow the facility to be a collection point. That way the clothing can be examined, laundered by the staff, if necessary, before being sent up to Indianapolis."

Angelee threw her arms around her father's neck. "Oh Daddy, that is wonderful."

"Have you realized just how big this project is going to be?" He asked.

"No, I suppose not. That's why Aunt Milly and I have been making lists of people to contact. This is going to be a committee-sized job."

"Come on, everyone, hot cocoa is ready." Aunt Milly ladled the steaming drink into waiting mugs. "We've written several letters already—inviting ladies from the different churches to come for an afternoon tea party. If we can recruit a team, then we can organize ourselves, and try to determine what needs to be done and who is the best one to do it."

"Did you know that Gee-Gee wants to make clothespin toys to put in the children's clothes pockets?" Aimee volunteered.

"Does she?" Mommy looked at Angelee and raised an eyebrow.

"Maybe we can't put them into the pockets, but we can send them along with the donations and ask them to distribute them along with the garments," Angelee said.

"But just how many toys do you think you can make?" Mommy gently challenged.

"Well, it wouldn't be just me making them. Aunt Milly suggested that I ask the schools if we can have the children make them as art projects. And I'm sure we can get some other groups together to make them."

"But that doesn't answer my question…how many do you propose making?" Mommy pressed.

"What's more, how are you going to pay for the materials?" asked Daddy.

"I know it would be impossible to make enough toys for all the orphans in Belgium and France…. because there must be thousands, if not hundreds of thousands of them. But I suppose if I guess, I just need to decide the number I think is achievable, and work hard to get as much help as I can. I thought I'd talk to Mr. Patton at Old Hickory Furniture and of course 'Papa Biers.' They might be willing to contribute the clothespins or short dowel pieces for us to make the toys."

"Well, you're going to need paint and fabric to actually dress them, give them faces and such." Aimee expounded.

"Well, I'm sure if we tell the different quilting and knitting circles in town about what we want to do, they would step up to the challenge. After all, the pegs are small and most women I know have all kinds of remnants from their sewing or knitting projects." Aunt Milly said.

Angelee finished her hot chocolate and took her cup to the sink. Taking out the washing-up tub from under the sink she added some soap flakes to it. Lifting the filled kettle of boiling water from the back burner of the stove, she poured it into the tub. After adding cold water to cool it a bit, she plunged her cup into the soapy water. "I have a feeling I may not sleep much tonight. I just want to start right now."

The others brought their empty cups on the cabinet top where Angelee automatically picked them up and washed them.

"To be honest, it appears to me that you and Milly have begun." Mommy expostulated. "You have a stack of letters to drop off at the post office tomorrow. Right now, jot down any ideas that you've not already recorded. You can climb in bed with a clear mind, say your prayers, and go to sleep."

"I'm proud of you Gee-Gee." Daddy gave her a one-armed squeeze. "You're blessed to have an Aunt that likes to get roped into your ideas. I think you're on the right track. But expect some opposition. When you have a worthwhile project, the devil uses circumstances and people get in our way. The important thing is to make up your mind before you start that you will finish your goal."

"Thanks, Daddy." Angelee rinsed the washed cup with the last of the water from the kettle. "I just have to figure out the specifics. That way I will know exactly what I need and who to talk to."

Refilling the kettle and placing it back on the stove, she turned on the gas and lit the burner with a match. "All those requiring a hot water bottle, please bring them. This pot will be boiling soon!"

As Angelee dried the cups and cleaned the hot chocolate pan, the others went upstairs to change for the night. Waiting to fill the rubber containers, Angelee reviewed her thoughts. The simple idea had grown into a challenge that was both exhilarating and formidable.

She made her way upstairs, delivering the bottles wrapped in towels. Thinking sleep would evade her, she climbed into bed. Expecting to toss and turn, she curled up and pulled the blankets tight. The heat emanating from the hot water bottle seeped into her body, relaxing her; the warmth lulling her into slumber.

Saturday, January 26th, 1918
Let Go of The Fear

Two weeks had passed since the blizzard. January days passed with unrelenting cold and snow. Daily flurries might progress to snow showers, adding additional inches already carpeting the ground.

With the national coal shortage, and industry nationwide still hampered by mounds of snow, the federal government ordered companies to close for a week. In Indianapolis, the businesses that did manage to open, were closing at four o'clock in the afternoon. Some companies extended the weekends to include Mondays. Theaters, schools, churches all remained closed.

In Martinsville, the three theaters, a couple of department stores, and some factories closed their doors to conserve coal, in compliance with federal dictates. Mrs. Johnstone called Angelee, informing her that there would be no reading sessions on Saturday mornings, as the library was also closed.

Though Alistair was a serious-minded boy and curious, he was also bored easily; he had lots of energy but no way to expend it. And being shut in for a day was just tolerable. The second day he was annoyed by the enclosure. On day three, Aunt Milly and Angelee had wrapped him up with extra layers and sent him outside. He promised them a snowman. But within five minutes the sub-zero temperatures had forced him back inside. Simply for something to do, he helped with cooking meals. His reward for good behavior— baking his favorite cookies with Aunt Milly supervising.

Nature's enforced shutting-in of the town's residents, served to limit Mommy's charitable activities. Angelee, Aunt Milly, and Aimee enforced extra rest since the baby was due in eight to nine weeks. Although Mommy grumbled, protesting that she was not an invalid, she was quick to acquiesce.

Saturday morning, while eating breakfast, Angelee brought up the subject of her toy project.

"Mommy, with all this time on my hands, could I use some of our clothespins to make some dolls?" Angelee asked as they sat in the salon.

"Sorry, Gee-Gee, but we haven't got many to spare—maybe half-a-dozen. Most of them are old, grey, and weather-worn. They wouldn't make good toys."

Angelee sighed and crossed her arms. Knowing her mother was right, it didn't make her feel any less miffed.

"How about making some hanky dolls?" Aunt Milly suggested. "I have lots of fairly new handkerchiefs you could use."

"I've got lots in my drawer as well," Aimee added.

"I'm not sure how to make them." Angelee faltered, although interested.

"Go get your sewing baskets and meet me back here." Aunt Milly directed the girls. "Your mother and I will teach you."

Alistair, sat on the floor by the fire, assembling a tower with his erector set.

"Hey, Young Man. Do you still have that bucket of buckeyes?" Mommy asked.

"Yeeuup! Why?"

"We would like to buy them from you."

"Really?" Alistair's eyes lit up for a second. Suddenly frowning, he tiled his head, suspicion written across his features. "But what do you want them for?"

"Tell you what," Mommy began her barter. "Go get them and you can watch me use one. If you don't want to sell them, we won't argue."

Leaving his construction project, he joined the girls going up the stairs.

Heavy velvet curtains hung between the front door entrance and the salon blocking the cold air. Pulled together they kept the large room well heated. Passing through the curtains, they climbed the stairs; Angelee shivered, goosebumps rising on her flesh.

"Brrrrrr." Aimee chattered, right behind her. "I'm glad we don't have to go out."

"Hurry up!" Alistair commanded. "The faster you move, the warmer you'll be!"

The girls collected their sewing kits, dug the flowered cotton handkerchief squares from their chest-of-drawers, and hurried back downstairs. Coming out of their room they encountered Alistair with a bucket full of the brown, shiny buckeyes.

"Come on girls, I want you to sit either side of me." Aunt Milly invited.

"Put your bucket here, and sit with me." Mommy guided Alistair. He quickly obliged and sat on the edge of his chair.

A piece of wadding lie on the table beside a stack of handkerchiefs and a basket of let over ribbon and lace.

Settling down, the tutoring session began.

"First, thread your needles with some strong thread. You'll need it to make the head." Aunt Milly said.

"Next, pick up the handkerchief and tie a knot in the top two corners. This will be the arms."

"Like this?" Alistair asked. He had made the knots close to the middle.

"Your knots are good, but they are too close to the middle. And don't make them too tight." Aunt Milly advised.

"About a third of the way from the edge," Mommy added.

The knots, tied and adjusted, Aunt Milly continued. "Now, we could use the wadding, but we thought they might be better with the buckeyes. Between the two knots—which will be the arms—tuck the buckeye under the edge of the hanky. To make it permanent, take your needle and thread and sew around the buckeye."

The room remained quiet, as they concentrated on gathering the neck together and making it secure.

"Now, if we loosen the knots, to move them back towards the middle, we can make the arms longer. It will look better. And let's sew the edges of the top of the dress together."

Alistair's tongue stuck out as he came to terms with the needle and thread.

"All that concentration and effort has worked," Angelee said mirthfully.

Five dolls lay on the table, each with little personal touches.

"Now then, Boy-Two, you see what we have in mind for your buckeyes. Are you interested in selling?"

"How much?" He quizzed.

"How about 10 buckeyes for a nickel?" Mommy proposed, winking at Angelee.

"Well, …it's for a good cause." Alistair mused. "So, I suppose that would be okay."

"Better get counting, so I can pay the right amount." Mommy laughed.

While the Buckeyes were being counted, Aimee spent a few delighted moments stitching eyes, a nose, and a mouth with embroidery thread. Mommy showed them how to tie knots on the bottom corners to form a little boy doll.

By noon the little group had made about two dozen handkerchief dolls.

The grandfather clock struck twelve-thirty.

"Are we having lunch today?" Alistair chirped.

"Let's go make some grilled cheese," Mommy said. "I need to move around a bit."

"Do you think we should put this away for now?" Aimee asked.

"I want to keep working." This from Angelee.

"There are only two hankies left." Aimee protested.

"I've been thinking, we could cut twelve-inch squares and hem the edges," Angelee said. "I've got a couple of old petticoats I can rip out at the seams. I'm sure that fabric would work."

"It's up to you. But I'm going to do something else after lunch. I'll help you move things down to the end of the table."

After lunch, Mommy settled down on one of the make-shift beds for a nap. Aunt Milly sat at the end of the table writing letters. Nestled in an over-stuffed armchair, Aimee's beloved sketchbook took her attention. Daddy, who had struggled across the street to see the few Home Lawn patients, was now home and in his office doing paperwork.

Angelee retrieved the petticoats from her bedroom and settled at the opposite end of the table from Aunt Milly. Carefully unpicking the seams, she pondered her future. Angelee had spent much time trying to discover her life's purpose. She couldn't help but think about other women she knew who seemed to be drawn to vocation. Her Aunt Milly followed the call to foreign missions; Olivia healthcare. Her mother's mission went beyond the family; providing hospitality at home and working with a local group of Christian ladies who provided charity to the local poor. Mrs. Parkham had an aptitude for business and finance development.

The thing was, serving others, in the way her family and friends did, was not to the exclusion of marriage and children. Olivia hoped and dreamed of marriage and children. Mrs. Parkham was a widow.

"Four weeks," the thought went through her mind. Four weeks had passed since Drew and Pauley returned to Fort Oglethorpe, Georgia. Daily praying for their safety, she often jotted notes to herself for her journal and letters to 'the boys.'

Looking up from her work, she saw through the window that snow was falling again. Large lacey, icy crystalline flakes swirled about, before settling on the frozen ground and snow-covered bushes. She always liked snow, because it made the earth look fresh, clean, at times even fascinating. The recent blizzard had left her amazed and humbled.

Looking over at Aimee, she asked. "What are you working on, Mee-Mee?"

Aimee smiled, turning the sketchbook around for her to see.

"Is that *Timmy Chitter*?" Angelee grinned, hopefully.

"It is!" Aimee flashed a grin.

During the Christmas break, Angelee had been struck with a flash of inspiration. She invented a character, a little Harris Sparrow, whom she named Timmy Chitter. She'd asked her sister to create some pictures of Timmy Chitter to show the children. At the next reading group—whenever that might be—she'd invite the children to write a story about him; then they would share the stories next time the group met.

"You know, Mee-Mee, this summer you could come to the library with me and you could show the children how to draw birds and flowers and such." Angelee teased.

"No small children for me! I'm going to be an artist—like Gertrude Partington Albright. However, I could teach you! Then you can teach the children. You have a gift working with little people."

"How can you say that? After what happened in Louisville? I wouldn't trust myself to be alone with children—at least not without another adult!" Angelee protested.

"Gee-Gee, that was years ago. And we were just children ourselves. Nobody blamed either us for what happened." Aimee protested.

"We need to talk about that day," Mommy said, sitting up on the bed. "I never really got the full story."

For years Angelee had suppressed incident, relegating it to the back of her mind. The temptation to leave the room and go to her bedroom was strong. But the rest of the house was just too cold. Although she could make an excuse to go to the kitchen, she knew it would be running away from something. It was time to face that memory.

Mommy got up from the bed, walked over to the table, and taking Angelee by the hand, Mommy led her over to the couch next to the fireplace. Aunt Milly and Aimee joined them on the sofa.

Mommy continued holding her hand, waiting. Taking a deep breath, Angelee began the story of her cousin's betrayal and the toddler's accident. The ache in her heart triggered tears as the memory replayed in her mind.

As a child she had not been able to overcome the shock of seeing the blood, the little boy laying on the floor, possibly dead.

Praying hands comforted the girls.

"Angelee, you mustn't blame yourself for what happened anymore," Mommy said softly.

Angelee rocked; her sobs deepened. "I don't blame myself." She garbled. "But I was terrified."

Reaching for Aimee's hands, she clasped them. "I'm so sorry, Mee-Mee. I'm so sorry. You must have been scared as well."

Aimee squeezed her hands. Angelee sensed her sister's weeping. Wrapped in Mommy's and Aunt Milly's loving arms, she opened her heart and mind to Jesus.

As the recollection unfolded, something in her mind shifted. Not only had she allowed fear to crash in waves over her heart, but she'd also been carrying hatred and resentment of Hedda since that day. To let go of the fear, she needed to forgive Hedda. Hedda's betrayal had been irresponsible, and manipulative. But Angelee needed to see her own sin—anger, bitterness, judgment. To grasp the resentment now would result in keeping her tied to Hedda forever. In this safe place of truth, she purposed to absolve Hedda. Quickly repenting, she exhaled deeply, pushing the grudge, out of her spirit and soul.

The picture of the memory changed again.

As if watching herself from a distance, Angelee could see that she had done what she knew to do; and God had honored her actions. The boy was fine; his injury was not her fault.

"Let go of the fear, Angelee. Let go of the fear. Trust Me." The Holy Spirit instructed her.

The burden in Angelee's heart dissolved, the crying dissipated. With another deep sigh, the fear was dispelled. Peace in her heart grew; understanding grew as the revelation came. By avoiding being alone with children, especially vulnerable ones, she was not preventing an accident. She was, in fact, trying to avoid the fear. That fear had been chained to her hidden sin of hate. Through contrition, and praying for the one who'd used and offended her, she was released, finding peace and victory.

Could it be that trying to elude the anxiety and fear of bad consequences, was the reason she couldn't hear God's voice, leading her to discover her life purpose? It also meant that she didn't want to be responsible for discovering the root of her fears, facing her personal sin.

What if Fear had kept her from considering all kinds of possibilities—like working with children?

At that moment she admitted to herself that she truly enjoyed working with children, especially young ones.

Trusting God meant she could let go of fear. It was a choice to face doubts, things by which she felt threatened—no matter how hard. God was with her forever, even to everlasting. She didn't have to trust herself but put her total confidence in Jesus.

Angelee looked up and smiled directly at her sister.

Aimee squeezed her hands again and smiled back. "Wow! I had no idea you were scared. You acted so bravely. And because you were, I decided to be brave too. All I had to do was what you said. I ran my fastest to get help. It took me a long time to forgive Hedda for her deception. I think I was too angry to be afraid."

Angelee leaned forward and hugged her sister. Then she sat back, looking at her mother and then her aunt. She was so thankful for women who knew how to pray.

"Thank you for that. I know it will make a difference." Angelee said.

"Darling Gee-Gee, you were braver than you think," Mommy said. "You didn't run away. You didn't collapse on the floor crying. You didn't see it at the time, but by acting on what you knew, you became a leader that day. I am sure God will provide more opportunities for leadership in the future."

"I hope it's a long time in the future!" Angelee half-joked.

"Oh, I don't know…" Aunt Milly remarked drolly. "You've already started a miniature toy factory. Surely others will join in on your adventure."

"You have a point!" Angelee concurred. "Speaking of doll production, I think it's time to get back to my seam ripping."

"Alistair, it's time to stir up the fire and add some coal," Mommy said, as she picked up her knitting.

The youngest Tillson, who had become enthralled in a Meccano building kit, looked up from his handiwork. "Are Gee-Gee and Mee-Mee okay?"

"Yes. Now please see to the fire." Mommy said.

With a light heart, Angelee stood up and went to wash her face. Then she would get back to her labor of love—toys for orphans.

Grey clouds blanketed the sky, although blue could be seen in the occasional break in the sailing nimbus layers. Days of constant cloud cover, freezing temperatures, and threats of snow or freezing rain had become wearying. Blustering, frigid wind toyed with Angelee's skirts as she stood in front of the Interurban station, waiting to meet Olivia, arriving on the morning train. Saturday was usually a busy day for traveling to and from Indianapolis. Women loved going shopping in downtown Indianapolis, while friends and students came to Martinsville to visit. Angelee looked forward to a few hours with her best friend.

The train car rode along the rails, powered by the electrical charge through an overhead cable. It pulled into the station, parking in between the terminal and the Eslinger Hotel. Once stopped the few commuters braving the weather moved closer to board. The steward opened the train doors, assisting the disembarking passengers.

Angelee remained back from the others, waiting. Her patience was rewarded seeing Olivia step down and wave her heart lifted, a broad smile crossed her face. Returning the wave, she walked toward her best friend.

Olivia carried a single case for her weekend visit. Freezing gusts played havoc, causing Olivia's scarf to flap wildly. She quickly grabbed it with her free hand. The suitcase dropped to the ground and the girls hugged.

"Come on, let's go over to the White Star. I'm buying you lunch." Angelee told her friend.

"That sounds great!" Olivia said, bending to pick up her suitcase.

"Oomph!" Angelee grabbed the handle first. "Wasn't expecting that! Let's get this into the car."

"I'm so glad you brought the car! Carrying that suitcase was a fight in these gales! I tried to pack light." Olivia laughed. "But that case is always heavier than I'd like it. There's a chemistry test on Monday, so I've got to study this weekend."

"I've been spoiled living around the rich and catered for! We're driving a block away to the White Star!" Angelee half-teased. "So, which do you have more of, books or clothes?"

"Books, of course!" Olivia replied, climbing into the passenger seat. "I've plenty of clothes stashed at home. It will be so good to see Oma, Opa, and Mommy, and Daddy."

A few minutes later, Angelee parked the car in front of the favorite eateries. They entered and took a table far away from the door, out of the chilling wind.

Once seated, Kim, the waitress came and took their order. Returning with two cups and a coffee pot, she filled their cups and left.

"I'm looking forward to this," Angelee said. "We've got so much to catch up on."

"How's the clothing drive going?" Olivia jumped to ask the first question.

"This month has rushed by! You know, Daddy said I should expect difficulties. I've had so many surprises since I got involved with this."

Olivia sipped her black coffee. "Like what?"

"I've been shocked by some people's hard-heartedness, to be honest. All I can think about are the children without parents; some who may have even seen their parents killed. You would think that anyone would want to help them. I was at Toners store last week, a woman came up to me and told me that there enough poor children and orphans in America and I should be trying to help them."

Olivia shook her head. "So selfish and narrow-minded. I guess some people just can't put themselves in another person's position. You wrote to me about the toy-making. How is that coming along?"

"I couldn't understand the attitude of the school commissioner and school board." Angelee continued. "It seems that the domestic science classes are already involved with projects to provide orphans with all kinds of other supplies. The teachers and administrators felt my project would be a distraction and interfere with their program, or compete with theirs."

"Really? Why couldn't your idea just be incorporated into their program?" Olivia commiserated.

Angelee shrugged. "I guess they didn't want to be bothered. On the other hand, I must say, I've also seen surprised by the generosity of other people. You know the ones who are most against the war, yet provide help to those affected by the war. Like Mr. Clark, the owner of the Auto Company. A couple of weeks after we announced the clothing drive, he stopped me while I was doing errands. He said he was a strong believer in helping orphans and widows. He said he would provide a truck and driver to collect the donations from the various collection points in town and drive them to the depot. I had been wondering how I was going to get the donations from the churches and other collection points. Suddenly God answered my prayers."

"That's wonderful." Olivia enthused.

Kim arrived with their sandwiches and refilled their coffee cups. "I hope you're saving room for pie."

"Of course!" Angelee confirmed.

"I'm thinking about cake," Olivia said. "Kim, is there is any of Mrs. Smith's lovely, white coconut cake available?"

"Same for me, if there is!" Angelee added.

"Yes, there is. Good choice, by the way." Kim finished scribbling the order on her pad and left.

"Now fill me in on the news about things at Butler." Angelee encouraged.

"There's talk of some new buildings. I heard Butler acquired some property from an investment company. I guess that means the university is growing."

"Have you thought any more about joining a sorority?" Angelee inquired.

"I'm not interested. I just want to concentrate on getting the best possible grades. I need a good grade point average to get into Nursing school."

Kim returned with two pieces of cake and a coffee top-up. "Enjoy!" She smiled and went to her next customer.

"What's the latest from Drew and Pauley?" Olivia asked, taking a bite of the white cocoanut confection.

"As you know, Drew isn't one to write much. He generally writes a letter to the whole family. As for Pauley, his last letter perplexed me."

"Now that's curious. What left you bewildered?"

Angelee sighed, opened her handbag, pulled out an envelope. "I'll let you read it yourself."

Olivia took the light blue paper parcel and removed the hand-written pages. Reading the content and lifting her eyebrows as she returned the letter to Angelee.

"I'm sorry, but I don't see what's bothering you," Olivia responded. "Obviously he can't say exactly where he is—like that would mean anything to you. But you know he's working near a field hospital and helping out the Red Cross."

Angelee extracted the missive, skimmed the pages until she found the exact spot.

"It's here. *'Last week we met a very charming young lady, whose name is Esme Roussel. She is learning English quickly and enjoys flirting with all of us in the unit. This feisty girl is also doing her best to make us improve our French. Should our company receive orders to relocate to a new assignment, it will be difficult to leave her behind. At least on my part, for I have fallen in love with the adorable red-head.'*

"Before he left for the Army, Pauley professed to love me. Then in this letter, he writes that he has fallen in love with the adorable red-headed Esme. I want him to be happy…but…" Angelee shrugged, confusion clear in her eyes.

"Angelee, I think you're reading too much between the lines. Remember the year Mr. Hartley came to teach at the high school. Besides being handsome, he was kind and funny. Both the faculty and student body 'fell-in-love' with him. Since Pauley says she is popular with the whole unit, it's probably the same situation. But I don't think it is Pauley's feelings that are confounding you. It's your own. You need to examine your heart and see what's in there."

Frowning, she put the letter back into its paper cover. "What do you mean?"

Olivia pushed the empty cake plate to the side of the table, rested her hands flat, and leaned forward. "Gee-Gee, either you feel only friendship for Pauley or you feel something else. Simple friendship would mean that you would be pleased, excited even, that Pauley has potentially found his true love. Or, you are actually in love with him yourself—and return the feelings he expressed before he left to enlist."

Angelee pursed her lips as she considered Olivia's observation. "So, it would be like this. If you came home one weekend and told me you'd met this handsome doctor, I, of course, would be thrilled for you. And if my brother, Drew had written about a Red Cross nurse to whom he took a fancy—once again I'd be excited. If I loved Pauley purely like a brother, I might suddenly feel relieved that he'd found someone else to focus on."

"So, do you feel relieved? Are you feeling jealous? Could you be feeling protective? Or are you actually in love with him and need to acknowledge it to yourself?" Olivia gently quizzed.

"I don't know, to be honest," Angelee replied, almost whispering.

"Don't look so upset!" Olivia patted Angelee's hand. "I'm not the one who needs an answer. And certainly not this minute. *You* need the answer—and you can take as long as you need to figure it out. Regardless of any feelings, we still have to entrust Drew and Pauley into God's care."

Angelee smiled back at her, nodding her head. "I'm glad you're my best friend. It always helps to talk to you."

"I just wish we could see each other more often." Olivia mused.

"See, you know how to be my best friend as well. I'll just pay the bill and then we can go."

"Oh, the luxury of being driven home!"

Sunday afternoon found Angelee sitting on the edge of her bed, pondering what to do next and how to spend the afternoon. The childhood habit of napping was tempting. How easy it would be to flop over onto the pillows and sleep—forgetting about the war, the unmade toys, the business of collecting clothes, and most of all, Pauley's ambiguous letter. The issues would still be there, to be faced once she awakened.

'Be pragmatic.' She told herself. 'One-thousand clothespins are not going to become toys by magic.' She remained sitting admitting to herself that it was beyond her ability to assemble that exceedingly large number of toys by herself in just two weeks.

Aunt Milly and she had coordinated with ladies from several churches around town and established a deadline for the clothing to be collected, sorted, and organized into shipping cartons, on Saturday, 2nd March. The barrels and boxes would be loaded onto the trains and taken to Indianapolis to Professor Michelon's headquarters, The Paris School of French, on North Meridian Street.

Rising from the bed, Angelee took a seat at her desk. Taking Pauley's latest letter from the drawer, she removed the multiple, hand-written pages from the envelope. His words of praise for her clothes-gathering project brought a smile to her face. But the paragraph in the middle of the letter continued to nag at her. Not only second-guessing Pauley's feelings for her, but his letter also had her second-guessing her own feelings about him.

Was Pauley "in love" with Esme, just as he was "in love" with her? Could that be possible? She supposed it was possible—maybe on some level. But during this morning's sermon, Pastor Matthias had read Jesus' words, "No man can serve two masters..."

Any other time she would have been impatient to write to Pauley, sharing her thoughts and the news around town. Now she hesitated. Was she being silly, reading more into the short sentences than was actually there? Of course, she could ask him to tell her more about Esme. That was the best thing...just be honest, direct. After all, they had known each other all their lives.

"*Search your own heart.*" The Holy Spirit whispered.

The Holy Spirit's prompting reminded her again of Olivia's challenge. It was no use speculating on what was going on in Pauley's heart and mind. Rather, she needed to explore her reaction to Pauley's short mention of Esme.

Opening the drawer again, she took out her journal. Today, she would write a letter to God, an outpouring of the unexpected emotions that were distracting her. She wanted to stop the thoughts riding a merry-go-round in her head. Angelee turned the pencil in the sharpener, preparing to make the best use of time, paper, and lead.

Not wasting any time with grammar or spelling, she scrawled across the blank page the first thoughts that came to her.

"Why does this always have to be about me? Why can't I make this about Pauley and Esme? But I do have to ask myself, why am I upset about his feelings for the Red-headed charmer? What exactly am I feeling anyway?"

She looked up, staring, unseeing, out the window. Although fair, dissipating snow, barren trees, and dark clouds contributed to the bleakness inside her heart. As the evening drew in, dusk deepened the shadows.

Examining her emotions, she squirmed, shifting in her chair. What was she afraid of finding? Up until Pauley's correspondence about Esme, she had taken her life-long friendship with him for granted.

Pauley had always been around. The impact of Pauley's confession of love for Esme brought home a new understanding. If Pauley brought Esme with him when he came home from the war, Angelee's relationship with him would change irrevocably. She would have no legitimate reason to have unlimited access to him.

Reading newspaper reports and letters from Drew and Pauley, images of the battered French countryside, the responsibilities of driving the wounded from field hospitals to transport trains, and encounters with the French locals had filled Angelee's mind. She never envisioned that those encounters with the locals could lead to relationships and romance. While she knew such things did happen, she'd never imagined it would happen to Pauley.

Re-reading the page, she found herself interpreting Pauley's words as almost flippant; saying he'd fallen in love with a feisty flirt. Well, that was one thing she had never imagined Pauley falling for, flirting. Especially since the 'vixen' was flittering her attention on the whole unit.

If Pauley's heart was broken by a French coquette, Angelee would be very angry. She only wanted the best for her friend. She challenged herself. Was she willing to see him make life with another woman if that was best for Pauley? Facing that question scared her.

From the desk's bottom drawer, Angelee took her high school graduation album out and laid it open on the desk. Turning the pages, she stopped at the photo of Drew, Olivia, Pauley, and herself.

Could Pauley—dependable, familiar, resolute Pauley—be so fickle as to fall in love with someone else in just a week? That just didn't seem possible. But then, on a war battlefield, perspectives changed. Maybe Pauley was taking Angelee's last words to heart— that all she felt was affection born of comradeship.

Angelee sighed and shifted in her chair again. Her thoughts turned to Cameron Parkham. Since he'd arrived in Martinsville, she'd found him to be kind, funny, generous, and industrious. He'd been a patient driving instructor, especially attentive to Alistair during the process. Mrs. Parkham frequently encouraged Angelee to keep company with Cameron, subtly hinting her approval of their association. Inevitably, this made Angelee strongly suspect that Mrs. Parkham's motives were to match-make.

Initially, at Mrs. Parkham's insistence, Cameron had been her responsibility, guiding him around town and making introductions. Mrs. Parkham explained that it was only logical since Angelee had been raised in the town and knew the community well. Though annoyed with the arrangement, Angelee found that Mrs. Parkham's nephew did not make a nuisance of himself. Thankful for his consideration, Angelee began to relax around him.

Now, how did she view him? More than an acquaintance, she conceded. Cameron was older, with more sophistication. Pauley's friendship was deeper, born of long-time affiliation. The problem was rather like trying to weigh the difference between strawberries and apples. Both could be sweet, a pleasure to be with.

What kind of a husband would each man make? No, that wasn't the right question. Could she see herself as a wife to either of them; to neither of them? What was God saying about this?

The instruction was, *"Examine your heart"*. Angelee sensed that phrase indicated that the truth she needed to embrace existed already. She needed to be courageous enough to face what was really in her heart.

Finally, she admitted she was jealous of Esme. She couldn't imagine her life without Pauley in it. Confronting the truth, she admitted to herself that she loved Pauley Alexander Bannister—and she was also in love with him. Writing down her swirling thought had served to awaken her heart to the verity of her heart's desire.

Wonder, awe, and joy welled up inside her. Now that she knew her own heart, she would have to trust that Pauley had not had a complete change of heart himself.

The storms of January had relented; the snow began to dissipate. However, for some of the mounds around the countryside, it would be months before the drifts disappeared totally. Though coal was still in short supply, temperatures had risen enough for families to enjoy full use of their homes.

"Is this a party for one, or can anyone join?" Mommy came from the kitchen, a cup of tea in her hand.

Angelee sat working at the dining room table. The day before she and Aimee had spent a couple of hours painting on faces, shoes, and even hair on the clothespins. Now that they were dry, it was time to add arms and costumes.

"I'll take all the help I can get." Angelee smiled up at her mother

"I take it these are for dresses?" Mommy asked, fingering the three-inch squares and circles.

"Yes, and that paper is the pattern. You can cut some of those out if you want to." Angelee suggested.

Mommy set about cutting out a few dozen circles of calico and gingham.

"I suppose I should contribute some of my sewing skills to this venture." Aunt Milly quipped as she came into the room.

"Only if you're feeling inspired." Angelee grinned. "We've got a whole village of miniature people to make."

"I am so thankful that we recruited the sewing circles from all those churches. I think each church took 100 clothespins." Aunt Milly said.

"Which leaves the other 500 in my lap." Angelee sighed. "My biggest concern is getting these done in the next two weeks."

"It is too bad that the schools couldn't help." Mommy commiserated.

"I know. And it doesn't help that Mrs. Parkham has bought some new rental property here in town. She's been having me go with Cameron to collect rents."

"Is that why you were so late this last week?" Aunt Milly asked.

Angelee nodded. "New account books had to be set up. Mrs. Parkham's been teaching me how she wants it done. There's so much to do. By the way, where's Aimee this evening?" Angelee inquired.

"Oh, she said that M. Torrington was giving her another lesson. She and Jilly Atherton went over to his studio."

"Which do you think she prefers, milk-paint" Mommy nodded in the direction of the peg-toys, "or oil paint?"

"Obviously, oil paint." Laughed Aunt Milly. "That girl is a darling, I just hope she doesn't get her heartbroken."

"What do you mean?" Angelee asked. She'd been so wrapped up in her own dilemma, she hadn't been paying much attention to Aimee.

"Your aunt and I think that Aimee is harboring some deep feelings for M. Torrington. There is an age difference, so I have a feeling that he might genuinely like her, but not recognize how serious her feelings are." Mommy replied.

"Have you talked to her about it?" Angelee asked. In a few weeks, Aimee would be seventeen—old enough to think herself in love.

"I haven't found the right way to approach it. I don't want to discourage her, but I also don't want to treat her like a child. I keep praying that the right opportunity will present itself—and keep an eye out." Mommy said.

"She's been a real sport to help me with this project. I know she's got her own things to keep track of, homework, girls' choir at school, and her art lessons."

"Since she isn't around, how about we plot her birthday party? It's only a few weeks away." Aunt Milly suggested.

"We've got plenty of time…five, six weeks!" Angelee said.

"Still, it's a good opportunity," Mommy said. "How many of these circles do you want?"

"As many as you can stand to cut out!" Angelee laughed.

Birthday planning monopolized the conversation as the work on the toys progressed. Eventually, conversation dwindled as the women's concentration focused on the meticulous crafting of the dolls. Angelee hummed softly, enjoying the pleasure of creating.

"It's nice to hear you humming," Mommy said, cutting out a circle. "I haven't heard you do that much lately."

Angelee bent pipe cleaners into round hands, then looked up her mother. "Yesterday afternoon I did some soul searching. You know that last letter I received from Pauley; he mentioned someone named Esme. The description was cryptic, at best. It bothered me when he said he'd fallen in love with her. It seemed peculiar that he'd profess to love me, and then write those words about someone else."

Angelee looked from her mother's soft smile to her Aunt's grinning face.

"Don't smirk, Aunt Milly! I had to ask myself what I was afraid of. Facing the truth is the only way to conquer fear. And the truth is; I woke up and realized I've fallen in love with him."

Mommy stood, holding out her arms to her oldest daughter. Eagerly stepping around the table, she snuggled into her mother's hug. The bond between mother and daughter deepened. As Mommy released Angelee, she found Aunt Milly waiting for a hug as well. That hug communicated what was beyond words.

The cords of love strengthened among herself, Mommy, and Aunt Milly; formed with the memories each of them cherished. The moment each of them discovered she'd fallen in love, and the joy of being in love and the years of loving husbands. Angelee found courage and comfort to face the unknown future because these women provided examples to follow.

Bong! Bong!

"Goodness—nine-thirty already! Time to pack this production line up!" Angelee quipped. "I'm sure we are all going to be busy tomorrow."

Mommy kissed her good night, heading towards the stairs to go up to bed. Aunt Milly took the empty teacups back to the kitchen before following Mommy upstairs. Angelee tidied up the dining room, turning out the gas lights as she went up to bed herself.

Completion of the "orphan project" loomed only one week away; Angelee wished she could afford to skip the Saturday morning reading group to work on doll making. Yet, she couldn't let Mrs. Johnstone down. Not that this day was special in any way. Under Angelee's oversight, the Children's Story hour had progressed from once a month to a weekly activity. Therefore, she felt it was her responsibility to keep the commitment she had made to the children—even if it meant at the expense of the toy-making project.

Angelee quashed her anxious thoughts about the unfinished toys. The truth was, she had not made a promise to Professor Michelon, or anyone else, about providing play-things for the orphans of Belgium and France. Thankful for the help of the women's groups from the various churches, she was going to be able to send at least a few hundred instead of a thousand. Unless help came from someone and somewhere else.

In the meantime, Angelee got washed, dressed, and went down to eat her breakfast.

"M-o-r-n-i-n-g..." Aimee yawned, sitting down at the dining room table, still dressed in her nightgown and robe.

"Good morning to you too!" Angelee smiled at her sister, as she spread blackberry jelly on her toast. "You're up early for a Saturday."

"Oh, well..." Aimee sipped coffee and said. "Ummm...that is so good."

"Was it the coffee that woke you?" Angelee prodded.

"Oh...no." Aimee took another swallow of coffee. "I wondered where you were keeping the paint for the clothespins. Thought I'd experiment with a new style of painting."

"All the paint is in the box on the floor in the utility room. I appreciate your help Mee-Mee." Angelee said, digging the boiled egg from its shell as it sat in the egg cup.

"My pleasure." Aimee sighed. "But as good as this coffee is, I think I'm going to go back up to bed for half-an-hour. After all, it is Saturday." She left the table and returned her cup and saucer to the kitchen before trudging up the stairs to their room.

Angelee laughed at her sister's antics as she cleared away her dishes from the table. After donning her coat, scarf, hat, and gloves, she left the house.

The February day was clear, and the forecast predicted temperatures around freezing. After the brutal blizzards of January, the clear skies that allowed the sun to heat the atmosphere created a merry heart.

The cold air invigorated her, removing any remaining vestiges of sleep. Humming she scampered up the limestone steps and entered the library, removing her outerwear as she descended the stairs to the public room. Laying her garments aside, she began organizing the room where the children would be gathering mid-morning for the story.

Mothers accompanying children, between the ages of four and ten, arrived within minutes of each other, settling into the semi-circle of chairs.

"Good Morning Everyone!" Angelee greeted the group. "It's nice to see that the weather hasn't kept you away."

Since the January storms, this was the first time the group had reassembled; much to Angelee's delight. As she expected, numbers were down. Not everyone knew that the activity had resumed. Having focused on the orphan work in previous weeks, she had missed seeing the local children and interacting with them.

"Is everyone settled?" Angelee grinned at the five mothers and the seven children.

Seven bobbing heads assured her that she had their limited attention.

"Good. Our story today is 'The Dutch Twins.' It is written by Lucy Fitch Perkins." Angelee showed the book cover, with an illustration of a boy and a girl in Dutch clothing.

As she read the book, she asked the children questions and patiently waited for their answers. Since the group was so small, she finished earlier than usual. This provided her with the time to read the second book, 'The Japanese Twins'. At the end, she allowed the children to carefully handle the books and ask their own questions.

The chimes from the wall clock announced it was noon, and time to dismiss the group. Angelee assisted the mothers in bundling up the youngsters in coats, scarfs, ear-muffs, mittens, and hats.

Mrs. Morgan stopped in front of Angelee as she stood up. "Miss Tillson, I am SO glad we could resume this today. The children have been getting irritable because it's been too cold to play outside for very long. Obviously, you have a gift for working with children. Have you considered becoming a teacher? I just thought I should mention it to you."

"Thanks for the vote of confidence." Angelee giggled, feeling embarrassed. "It has never crossed my mind." The truth was, it had crossed other people's minds, who lost no time in making the suggestion to her.

Mrs. Lambert joined them, holding the hands of her two girls. "I wasn't trying to eavesdrop, but I overheard what Mrs. Morgan said. I think she's right, Miss Tillson. Maybe you don't realize it, but you don't just read to the children. It's like watching you give a little lesson and make sure they understand what you're showing them."

"I might as well crash this party as well." Mrs. Gardener chimed in. "Last time we came, Mark said the cutest thing. 'Mommy, I wish Miss Tillson was my teacher at school. She makes things easy to understand.'

Then Alan added in, 'And she's way prettier than Mr. Ford.'"

A burst of laughter filled the room. "I have to agree with Alan." Added Mrs. Morgan.

"I think it's hardly fair to compare a man and a woman," Angelee observed. "But you three have given me something to consider. When I have time, again."

"How is the clothing drive coming?" Mrs. Lambert asked.

"Very well. The collection is next Saturday. We need to get the boxes and barrels to the Vandalia Station by early afternoon so it can be loaded onto the afternoon train. Besides the clothing, a couple of the churches have done fundraisers to help cover the cost of shipping to Indianapolis."

"You've worked very hard on this." Said Mrs. Gardener

"Not just me, lots of people have—my Aunt Milly, all the different ladies from the churches. It has certainly been God at work in the community."

"Mommy, I'm hungry! I want my lunch!" Mark Gardener complained.

"Well, better not keep the young man from his food." Angelee smiled down at the freckle-faced boy.

"Thanks again for this morning. It has been a wonderful break." Mrs. Lambert said as she directed her daughters towards the stairs. "Hope to see you next week."

The other mothers thanked her as well and left Angelee to stack the chairs away and tidy the room.

"I heard laughter." Mrs. Johnstone said as she joined Angelee. Angelee regaled the librarian with the anecdote from the Gardener children, who in turn chortled.

All the while Angelee restored the public room to order, she thought about the women's remarks. She thought her way of interacting with children was natural—like any person would. But her thinking had shifted. Instead of being resistant, irritated by the suggestion of being a teacher, she was willing to consider that her resistance was fear-based. Not ready to invest any time in examining that idea, she concentrated on getting home and working on creating more clothespin soldiers, dolls, and airplanes.

Within seconds of entering the house, Angelee's ears were met by music from the Edison phonograph player, laughter, and chatter. It was easy to see that the salon was a bee-hive of activity. She wasn't sure what all the industry revolved around.

She pulled off her coat and but was unable to hang it up. All the coat hooks were holding at least two coats. Just as she was about to take it upstairs with her, Aimee appeared, grinning like a Cheshire Cat. "Surprise! Welcome to the party!"

"What are we celebrating?" Angelee asked, bemused by the noise and commotion.

"It isn't so much a celebration as an initiative. Go up and change into your old clothes, then come down and join us. Mommy and Aunt Milly have dinner under control."

"But…I don't understand!" Angelee said, clearly puzzled.

"Go get changed and when you come back down, I'll explain." Aimee gave her sister a gentle shove towards the stairs.

Rather than argue, Angelee did as she was directed. Her stomach rumbled, and she longed for lunch. Her curiosity was greater than her hunger. In only a few minutes she'd changed into her old, comfortable house dress.

She lightly ran down the steps and entered the salon. The armchairs were pushed back towards the walls. Several card tables with folding chairs were lined down the middle of the room. Toy-making paraphernalia cluttered the tables. Angelee quickly counted twelve young people who were certainly having a great deal of fun but also accomplishing a great deal.

Angelee stood for a moment, mouth agape. Finally, she managed; "What's going on?"

"Simple—I recruited some unemployed elves. You know, Christmas is well over and so I thought they'd appreciate some honest work."

Angelee couldn't help but laugh. "Seriously, how did you do this?"

"I bribed my Sunday School class with lunch!" Aimee winked. "Some of them commandeered their boyfriends."

Aunt Milly came in with a tray of drinks. "Hello, Gee-Gee. Like the impromptu factory?"

"I'm astonished....and thankful. Did you suggest this to Mee-Mee?" Angelee asked.

"No, she asked me if I'd help by providing a meal if she could get a group together. I said yes, and here we are." Aunt Milly held the tray so Angelee could take a glass of tea.

Turning back to her sister, hugging her long and hard, her throat grew tight as tears slipped down her cheeks. "Thank you so much, Mee-Mee! I'm overwhelmed! I was so worried that I'd end up with a bunch of clothes pegs and left-over paint because I couldn't get the dolls done. Have you counted how many you've done?"

"No, but you can start doing the inventory and packing them into the shipping boxes properly. We've just been dropping them into a basket here on the floor."

Angelee looked around the room again. A window screen lay across two chairs situated next to the fireplace. On it lay rows of painted wooden pegs. "Wow, looks like you've been a task-master."

Aimee just shrugged. "Not really. Mommy is the one who organized the assembly line approach. I wanted to start dressing the pegs you'd already painted. But she told me that if we painted the bare clothespins first, they could be drying while we dressed the ones that were already dry."

"That drying rack is so clever," Angelee said, looking at it, arms crossed, shaking her head. "I'm not sure I would have thought of that."

"Alistair came up with that. He was here for several hours too. But Bart came over and asked him to spend the night."

"It's time to eat!" Aunt Milly announced. "Everyone, finish what you're doing and go wash up."

Angelee headed toward the dining room, her arm slipped through Aimee's. "I am so looking forward to whatever it is that

Mommy and Aunt Milly have made for lunch. I need something to fill me up."

"No problem there!" Aimee volunteered, with a laugh.

On the sideboard was a feast of soup, sliced bread, cold luncheon meat, cheese, pickles, and cut vegetables covered the sideboard. A small table from the kitchen had been brought in to hold bowls, plates, and cutlery. Once assembled, Daddy asked the blessing. The group squeezed around the lengthened family table.

Chatter covered the school closures because of blizzards, coal shortages, and severe cold. The teenagers shared stories of older brothers, uncles, and cousins who were either in Camp Shelby, Mississippi, or France. During the course of the meal, Aimee also informed her sister that her friends had agreed to come back during the week to help finish the toys and help pack them for shipping.

For Angelee, a miracle had happened. The project for the clothing and the toys would provide children across the ocean with a bit of comfort and hope. They would know that people, whom they had never met, did care about them and their needs. This thought warmed her soul, just as the food had satisfied and warmed her body.

Friday, March 1^{st,} the hard work of the clothing and toy drive culminated at Vandalia Train station. Angelee and Aunt Milly oversaw the loading of boxes and barrels, before boarding the train themselves to accompany the contributions to Indianapolis. Angelee had taken the day off from working for Mrs. Parkham, who had insisted that Cameron accompany them to help with the delivery.

Associates at the Paris School of French on North Meridian Street had arranged transport from the train station. As Angelee signed off on the paperwork, documenting the delivery to the school, she felt relief, joy, and pride. Pride in her community, who had invested time, talent, and practical resources to make a difference for the orphans in Europe.

Two weeks had passed. The Saturday reading group was canceled. Unexpectedly, a civic group had reserved the use of the library community room. While Aunt Milly and Aimee had gone into town to shop, Angelee was enjoying a rare Saturday morning at home sewing.

The fair day provided sunshine through the windows. In the quietness, as Mommy read, Angelee's nimble fingers pricked the fabric and pulled the thread taut to create a perfect tuck. Uniform, tiny pleats were the foundation for the smocking designs, creating fullness as well as beauty for the nightdress she was making for the new baby.

Neither of them realized how quickly the morning had passed.

"Ka-bam!" The front door banging shut sounded like a minor explosion, startling Mommy; who jumped and nearly dropped her book.

Automatically jerking, Angelee pricked her finger. "Ouch! Great! Now I'm bleeding!" She quickly pulled her hand from the material to prevent blood from staining the white flannel. She laid the fabric on top of the open sewing basket.

"Mommy, when's lunch?" Alistair demanded, his heavy boots clomping as he walked into the room. "I'm hungry."

"What time is it?" Mommy said, her hand still resting over her heart. "I've totally ignored the clock chimes."

Angelee looked at the clock on the mantel. "Oh, it's after twelve-thirty. I guess you would be hungry."

Mommy shook her head and laughed softly. "He's always hungry!"

"Come on, Growing Boy!" Angelee said. "I'll fix you some lunch."

"Thanks, Gee-Gee."

Mommy gave her a thankful smile.

"I'll put it on the table when it's ready Mommy."

Angelee instructed Alistair to hang his coat up, then come to the kitchen. He was gone for so long she began to wonder about how hungry he was.

"I'm here now," Alistair announced. "I thought I'd give you time to get it ready."

"Do you mean, you thought you would just show up and get to eat?" Angelee raised an eyebrow at him. "And when did I become your slave?"

"Well, I knew you'd be fixing lunch anyway, so what does it matter?"

"My goodness, you're developing a bit of an attitude these days. It just so happens that you get to help me with making our lunch. I was helping Mommy in the kitchen when I was eight. And I don't mean helping myself to the cookie jar!"

"That's not fair! Why do I have to start helping with cooking?"

"Because you like eating. And at some point, you will appreciate knowing how to stack up some sandwich fillings on bread. So, to start with, let me see your hands. You were gone long enough to take a bath...so they had better be clean."

Alistair proffered his hands, turning them over for her to inspect both sides. He rolled his eyes while she gave them exaggerated scrutiny. After a few seconds, she gave her approval.

"Okay, first things first, you get the bread and I'll get the leftovers from last night," Angelee ordered.

Alistair got the bread from the bread box and put it on the worktop.

"Now then, we are going to play a game!" Angelee said. "I'm going to ask you ten questions. If you get five or less correct, then you have to help me make cookies for my Sunday School class. But if you get at least six right, then I will bake your favorite dessert for tomorrow's dinner."

"How come we have to play this stupid game? I want lunch!"

"Because you took so long to come down, I had time to think about it."

Alistair sighed and crossed his arms. "Okay, let's get this over with."

Angelee was careful not to laugh out loud. Of late, Alistair had started to become moody, stubborn, and challenging family rules. Recently, witnessing one of his more demanding moments, Angelee had seen him actually go to bed without his dinner rather than back down. Mommy had explained that he was trying to become his person. It was a challenge for him to no longer be a baby, yet wanting to be independent. Right now, she wanted to turn the moment around, to make it fun for him.

"Doesn't having your own, personal dessert sound good?" Angelee asked.

"Is that one of the questions?" Alistair asked, suspicious.

"No, but it suddenly occurred to me that maybe, since you are such a clever young man, you would like to pick your prize."

Alistair put a finger on his chin, considering possibilities. "Hmmm...okay. If I win, then you have to make a double batch of sugar cookies for my scout troop."

Angelee folded her arms across her chest and tilted her head to the right. After a second, she said. "Fine. Here we go. Question number one, you have a whole loaf of bread and need to make five sandwiches. To get ten pieces of bread, how many times do you have to cut the bread?"

"That's easy, ten." Alistair spouted out the answer without thinking.

"Sorry, that's wrong. If you make ten cuts, you'll have eleven pieces of bread. So, the answer is nine."

"That's not fair! You made this too hard so I won't win." Alistair complained.

"It is fair. It's only the first question—which you didn't take time to think about. Now slow down and I'm sure you're going to get the rest correct."

"We're going to put some ketchup on our sandwiches today. From what is ketchup made?"

"Tomatoes." Alistair crowed triumphantly.

"See, not too hard," Angelee reassured. "Now then, true or false, the only thing that can be pickled is cucumber."

"Oh, that's false. Mommy pickles onions…and eggs…and even green tomatoes." Alistair suddenly seemed to be having fun.

"From where does butter come, from a plant or from a cow?" Angelee challenged.

She began cutting the homemade loaf of bread, showing him that they could work and also talk.

Alistair picked up the sliced bread and sat them to the side. "Let me think…from milk…so a cow. Hey! You know what, butter could come from a goat too! Goats give milk."

"Now that is good thinking, Alistair. It's good that you made that observation. You get a bonus point for that."

Angelee finished cutting the bread. "See, I made nine cuts, because I now have ten slices."

Alistair nodded.

Angelee took the left-over ham from the icebox. "Now, spread out the bread in a row. While I carve the ham, you take it and put it on five slices of bread."

"You're stalling, Gee-Gee. What's the next question?" Alistair prodded.

Angelee chuckled. "How many eggs are in a dozen?"

"Well, that's a stupid question! Twelve, of course."

"Okay, Mr. Know-it-All, how many are in a baker's dozen?"

Alistair shook his head in disbelief and rolled his eyes. "A dozen…twelve…I just said."

"Gotcha! A Bakers' dozen is thirteen. Haven't you noticed that when we order a dozen donuts, we are given thirteen?"

"Thirteen!? How come?" Alistair protested.

"I don't know. But it's a tradition that bakers give out thirteen donuts when you order a dozen." Looking at the sandwiches, Angelee paused. "Alistair, will you get out the jar of bread-and-butter pickles from the icebox?"

"Do you know how many ounces are in a cup?" Angelee asked.

"Wait a minute…" Alistair went over to the cupboard, opened it, and took out a measuring jug. "A cup is eight ounces."

"Hmmm…now should I consider that cheating?" Angelee said, raising an eyebrow.

"No. You didn't say I couldn't look for the answers."

"It's true, I didn't say it was a test. Nor did I say it was a 'closed cupboard' game. And, you did figure out how to find the answer. Okay, I'll give it to you."

Alistair jumped up and down excitedly.

"So tell me, what do tomatoes and potatoes have in common?" Angelee asked next.

Alistair started giggling. "They both have 'toes'!"

Angelee couldn't help but laugh too. "That is *not* the answer I was looking for. It is correct, and it is an answer. But not the correct answer. Think about it for a minute. And put some of those pickles on top of the ham while I cut some cheese."

Alistair set about taking the round pickle slices from the jar and putting them on the ham. He was holding his tongue out in concentration.

"I think I know." He said eventually. "They both grow from the ground."

"That's right, they're both plants." Angelee put the cheese on the sandwiches. "Okay, Little Man, I think that's enough questions in this game. I've asked eight, and you only missed two. But you also got that bonus point for goat's milk. That means you win. And I owe the troop two dozen cookies. Would you consider helping me put the icing on?"

"I suppose. Yeh, it's a deal." He stuck out his hand to shake. "If I can lick the bowl!"

"Great! Now then, will you go tell Mommy lunch is ready? I'll go get Aunt Milly and Aimee."

Alistair headed toward the living room. Then he stopped and looked at Angelee. "You know, Gee-Gee, you'd make a great teacher. You make it fun to do things and learn." Then he turned and went on his errand.

Angelee plated the sandwiches, stored away the meat and condiments, and took the meal into the dining room. Alistair's words were amusing, bringing a smile to her. She didn't take his remarks seriously—let alone take them to heart. He was just her younger brother, what did he know? But she'd made a promise, and after lunch, she had sugar cookies to bake.

Saturday, March 29th, 1918
An Easter Baby

A general restlessness pervaded the Tilson household the week leading up to Easter. Mommy's moodiness became more pronounced; tearful one minute and laughing the next. Although the Saturday morning house cleaning had been accomplished thoroughly, Mommy wandered around the house organizing pillows, moving books, re-dusting shelves, and re-pinning doilies on the back of the sofa and easy chairs. A small, niggling back-ache compounded Mommy's restiveness.

Aimee's new Easter dress needed hemming, and Angelee volunteered to pin it up.

After lunch, the two girls retreated to their room to work on the project. Aunt Milly joined them, embroidering a pillowcase while they chatted.

Aunt Milly explained Mommy's urge to organize and clean had a name, 'nesting.' It was an innate behavior, the subconscious' way of preparing for the process of labor and giving birth.

"I just hope she has it by Sunday or on Tuesday," Angelee said.

"Me too!" Aimee chimed in.

"Why ever for?" Aunt Milly asked.

"Because Monday is the first of April. And I don't think anyone would want a birthday on April Fools' Day." Aimee explained.

"An Easter baby would be wonderful!" Angelee said.

Mommy, coming upstairs with a load of newly folded diapers, walked into the girl's room. "I heard that." She puffed. "If this baby is a girl, and she is born on Monday or after, it would be appropriate to name her April."

Angelee jumped up and took the baby clothes from her mother. "I'll put these in your room. Is your back still aching?"

"Yes, and seems to be getting worse. Well, it's more than a niggle now. But then, it's all a part of the process, I guess. I think I'll sit here for a few minutes."

"Good idea!" Aimee said. "You know Mommy, April might be applicable, but somehow that just doesn't sound right."

"I agree." Aunt Milly chimed in. "It would be justified, but it would also be boring."

"I can tell you one thing; this baby is way too active to be boring!! Now if you'll excuse me, this little one seems to be doing headstands on my insides." Mommy grimaced, applying pressure to her stomach, attempting to shift the baby into a better position.

Angelee had not made it out of the room. She walked over to her mother, placing her hand under Mommy's arm to help her up.

Mommy stood up slowly. "Phew!"

Following Mommy out into the hallway, she nearly stumbled as Mommy stopped abruptly and straightened up a bit. Angelee continued to support her.

Angelee wondered why there was the sound of water puddling on the floor.

"Oh, Mercy!" Mommy exclaimed. "What a mess! I certainly wasn't expecting THAT to happen now!"

Hearing Mommy's outburst, Aunt Milly and Aimee came running.

Angelee continued to look at the puddle on the floor, which in turn made Aunt Milly and Aimee followed her gaze.

"How'd that puddle get there?" Aimee said.

"Your mother's water broke. Mercy Yes, Emileah!" sputtered Aunt Milly. "Rather silly on your part to not expect it. You've been nesting for a few days now."

"Of course, I've been expecting it to happen!" Mommy retorted. "I meant I wasn't expecting it this exact moment. No going back now."

"Angelee, where's your Dad?" Aunt Milly asked, taking charge of the situation and issuing orders.

"If he isn't at Home Lawn, he's probably at the church getting ready tomorrow's sunrise service."

"Right. Aimee, get Alistair, and go over to Home Lawn. If your father isn't there, then send Alistair over to the church and you come back here."

Aimee knocked on Alistair's bedroom door and pushed it open. "Alistair, come on. I need your help to find Daddy."

Clambering on the stairs and the sound of the front door slamming testified of their departure.

"Angelee, let's get your mother into the bedroom and help her get changed. I'll start getting the bed ready."

"Should I ring Dr. McCormack as well?" Angelee asked.

Like a metronome, Aunt Milly tilted her head side to side as she contemplated her answer. "Yes, go ahead and call."

"Shouldn't I be the one answering that?! You're acting like I'm not here." Mommy complained.

"Well, do you want her to ring Dr. McCormack?" Aunt Milly countered, guiding her into the bedroom.

"I'll wait till Andrew gets here and see what he thinks. I wouldn't say that I am having any immediate contractions." Mommy said. "Milly, will you unbutton me?"

"What do you want me to do Mommy?" Angelee asked. She smiled, finding it a bit strange hearing Mommy refer to Daddy by his given name.

"Well, right now, help Milly get the bed changed. I've put the rubber sheet in that drawer."

Angelee did as her mother asked, and began pulling the quilts and sheets off of the bed. They proceeded to place the birthing sheets onto the bed along with towels. The pillows, thumped and plumped, were arranged on the bed, ready to support and comfort.

"Do you want to lay down, or walk around?" Aunt Milly asked.

"Actually, I'm going to sit in my rocker for a while."

"I'll be back in a bit," Angelee told them. "I'll just clean up the mess in the hall."

"Gee-Gee, do you know what Aunt Milly meant by Mommy's water?"

"I'm not sure myself. But will you help me?"

The water was beginning to turn the floorboards white. Angelee found old rags from the cleaning cupboard and mopped up the water. Murphy's Oil Soap filled the air with pine scent as Angelee washed the floor and rinsed it. Aimee followed behind drying with another rag. Deciding it should dry completely, Angelee left waxing the spot until later.

She went back to her mother's bedroom for more instructions.

"Aunt Milly, can you tell us what you meant by Mommy's water breaking?" Aimee blurted. "I asked Gee-Gee, but she wasn't sure."

"I'm still here!" Mommy elicited their attention. "I believe I'm the one who should explain that."

"But we didn't want to bother you. You have enough on your mind."

"Nonsense! Now then, when a woman is pregnant, the baby inside her grows in an amniotic sac, which is full of fluid. It protects the baby and allows it to move. When it's time for a woman to give birth, the sac breaks and causes the woman to go into labor."

"Did it hurt?" Aimee wanted to know.

"No, but I did feel a strong pressure when it gave." Mommy took a deep breath and fidgeted in the rocker.

"Are you okay, Mommy?" Angelee asked, observing her mother's furrowed brow and measured breathing.

"What I'm feeling is normal. I do wish you two would stop fussing. I've done this before, you know! And it will probably take hours."

"I barely remember Aimee being born. But Drew, Mee-Mee, and I weren't here when Alistair was born." Angelee supplied tentatively.

"Angelee, I would appreciate it if you'd organize some food for this evening. Just things to make sandwiches, cookies. People can eat when they get hungry. Then if you can keep Alistair occupied, that will be great."

"I came as quickly as I could." Daddy came into the bedroom, closing the door behind him. Alistair's explanation was a bit sketchy—something about 'Mommy and broken water.' But the gist was more than enough for me to understand."

"Yes, and these two have been fussing like mother hens," Mommy complained.

"I'll just go and boil some water..." Angelee said. "...for a pot of tea. And I'll start supper."

"I'll come with you, Gee-Gee." Aimee volunteered.

"Thanks, Girls."

The first action, lay a spread on the sideboard so that people could eat when they wanted to. Keeping Alistair pre-occupied involved making sure his homework for Monday was completed. Baking cookies passed another hour. Aimee was persuaded to join them for card games and eventually a board game.

When they had settled down to play backgammon, Alistair surprised them.

"I know we're having a new brother or sister. But I wish we were getting a puppy instead."

"Where did that come from?" Aimee gasped; her eyebrows raised.

"Instead?!" Angelee glared at him. "Alistair, babies aren't something that you can swap for something else—like a puppy?"

Alistair dropped his head and mumbled unintelligibly under his breath. Then he shrugged. "Well, maybe I mean as well as a baby."

"Getting a puppy isn't a bad idea, but you'd better wait for a while before you bring the topic up with Mom and Dad. Maybe around your birthday."

"But that's August!" Alistair sulked.

"I know, but we need to get used to having our new brother or sister here. And in the meantime, you can show Daddy that you're old enough to have a dog. For the moment, you take the first turn." Angelee directed, pointing toward the game.

The sun passed through the sky towards the west, the late afternoon became evening and evening into the night. Angelee took the occasional moment to say a prayer for Mommy and the new baby.

As the pink dusk darkened to purple, Daddy called Dr. McCormack. Upon arrival, he headed straight up the stairs to see Mommy.

Before going to bed, Angelee prepared a pan of hot chocolate for Aunt Milly, Dr. McCormack, and Daddy. Although she and Aimee would have loved to stay up, there was nothing practical to be done.

The clattering bell of the alarm going off at five-thirty o'clock Sunday morning startled Angelee awake.

"Hey, Gee-Gee, turn off the alarm! I just got to sleep!" Aimee moaned.

"Sorry. I set it early, so I could go to the Sunrise service." Angelee explained, making sure the jangling stopped properly. She sat up in bed, wondering if the baby was born.

Aimee pulled the blankets up over her head, then suddenly flung them back down and sat up. "How's Mommy? Is the baby here yet?"

"Let's go see." Angelee stood, pulling on her housecoat.

Aimee collected her housecoat from the closet door, shoving in her arms as they crossed the hall.

Angelee knocked softly on the door. It opened a few inches, Aunt Milly sticking her head out.

"Please, may we have a progress report?" Angelee gave Aunt Milly a pleading look.

"Please..." Aimee folded her hands as if in prayer.

Dark shadows smudged Aunt Milly's eyes. She stepped into the hallway to give the girls a briefing. "Unlike Alistair, this baby is in the correct position. Your mother is doing well. We are all getting tired. But I'm pretty sure the baby will be here soon. Are you going to sunrise service?"

Exchanging a short look, Angelee and Aimee, simultaneously looked back at Aunt Milly and shook their heads.

"I thought you wouldn't. Then go downstairs and make us a pot of coffee and a pile of toast. And keep praying—your Mommy needs the strength."

The outside sky had turned to a deep blue-grey, with a hint of red brightening the skyline. Downstairs Aimee took out the bread knife and collecting the bread from the bread box. Angelee was busy grinding a fresh bunch of coffee beans.

"The sun is already rising. I wonder who is heading towards the church now." Aimee speculated.

Still groggy from the short night's sleep, Angelee offered. "I checked the newspapers, and it reports that sunrise is about six-thirty this morning."

"Well, we'll soon know whether we have a new sister or a new brother," Aimee said.

A plate of buttered toast sat on a tray, next to a pot of freshly brewed coffee. A second tray with cups, plates, a jug of milk, a bowl of sugar, and the butter plates was prepared for the upstairs crew.

"Look Angelee, it's turning pink outside." Aimee held back the lace curtain.

"Let's get this up there. I bet the coffee will be at that perfect temperature to drink." Angelee turned and lifted the first tray.

As they entered the dining room, the sound of a baby's squall filled the house. A new member of the family was making him or herself known.

"What about this?" Aimee asked.

"Forget them! They can go up later!" Angelee blurted, heading toward the stairs.

The girls sat the trays on the dining room table.

"What's that sound?!" Alistair met them on the landing.

Their parent's bedroom door opened and Aunt Milly met them in the hall. "It's a girl, a sweet little girl."

"Another Girl?!" Alistair groaned. "I wanted another brother."

"How's Mommy?" Angelee asked, concerned.

"Tired, of course." Aunt Milly said, wiping a tear from her cheek. "But she is fine."

"Now we have to find a name!" Aimee reminded them.

"Enough time for that!" Angelee said. "Let's go see Mommy."

Daddy and Doc McCormack came into the hallway. "Is there any coffee or food going?" Daddy asked, running his hand through his hair.

She hugged her father quickly. "It's on a tray in the dining room. You and Doc McCormack can help yourself."

"Remember kids, your mother has been working hard all night. So, don't stay too long." Doc McCormack instructed.

Holding Alistair's hand, Angelee hurried into the room and looked at her exhausted mother. Although Mommy's hair had frizzed out, and she had dark circles below her eyes, there was a sparkle. The baby, wrapped in a towel, still covered in blood and wax, lay mewling in her mother's arms.

Aunt Milly came back into the room. "Do you want me to take her and clean her?"

"Just let us rest here for a few minutes. Go have some coffee." Mommy replied, content to see her newest settling down.

"Okay, but I won't be long." Aunt Milly said.

"Well, Alistair, there's your new baby sister," Angelee said.

"She's so tiny. How can she be so loud, when she is so small?" Alistair looked askance.

"It is a mystery, but it means she's healthy," Mommy explained.

"We'd better left Mommy rest," Angelee observed.

Kissing her mother on the forehead, and stroking the baby's cheek, Angelee led Alistair from the room. Aimee protested about leaving her mother so soon but had no choice. Doctor McCormack revived by the coffee and toast, went back into her parent's room, closing the door behind him. Apparently, to give Mommy and the baby a final examination before he left.

Angelee wrapped an arm around Alistair's shoulders. "Poor Alistair. First no puppy and now no baby brother."

"And she doesn't even have a name." Alistair lamented.

As they came out of the bedroom, Daddy mounted the last step. He was carrying a cup of coffee.

"Just be glad your mother is fine. And Little-Girl will have a name soon enough." Daddy said, ruffling Alistair's hair.

Angelee hugged her bleary-eyed father.

"Happy Easter, Daddy! I know it seems unrelated, but 'He is Risen'."

"He is risen indeed!" Daddy re-joined. "The Lord has been so good to us. Your mother did splendidly, all very straight forward. I'm just thrilled."

"I wish we could get a telegram to Drew. He'll want to know."

"It is unfortunate that Drew isn't here. Once Mommy and I realized that the baby was going to be an Easter Day baby, we thought about possible names that would be appropriate. We thought maybe Lazarus if it was a boy. Your mother remembered that one of the Russian princesses was named Anastasia. We now have another princess, so we are naming her Anastasia Helene."

"What does it mean?" Aimee asked.

"Anastasia means 'resurrection' and Helene means 'light' or 'shining one'; her name means 'Resurrection Light."

"How beautiful!" Angelee said. "I like it."

"Me too!" Aimee chimed in.

Aunt Milly came to join them. "I've just put the baby in the bassinet. I've told Emileah to get some sleep as well. It's been a long night." She yawned.

"I think we should all go to bed. All of us are worn out." Daddy said.

"But we just got up," Angelee said.

"How did you sleep?" Daddy persisted.

"I just tossed and turned all night. I finally fell asleep when Gee-Gee's alarm went off." Aimee stated.

"It was the same for me," Angelee said.

"Okay, everybody to bed. We'll get up in a couple of hours." Even Alistair was agreeable to more time in bed.

Angelee doubted that she would go to sleep. But the knowledge that Mommy and Anastasia were fine gave her such peace of mind that she fell asleep almost immediately.

News of Anastasia's birth spread quickly through the Christian Church congregation. The ladies from the church provided meals for the family for two weeks following her arrival.

Alistair found having a baby in the house perplexing. He didn't understand why babies had to cry all the time. What was even more mystifying to him was Mommy's ability to identify Anastasia needs just by the way the baby cried. As the days passed, despite her annoying dribbling and smelly diapers, he admitted she was pretty— for a baby. He even confessed to Angelee that being an older brother wasn't so bad.

"Besotted, that girl is!" Aunt Milly said. "I never thought I'd see Mee-Mee taken with anyone or anything more than her drawing and painting. But she never misses an opportunity to cuddle that precious baby."

"Well, I think Anastasia is going to be a bit confused when she gets older. She won't know which of us is her mother!" Angelee laughed.

"You could be right." Aunt Milly laughed. "Are you going to walk to church today, or ride with your parents?"

"I think I'll walk. Mommy said she wants to start taking longer walks so she can get back to walking into town."

"I know your mother misses walking, but being an older mother does seem to require longer to recover. I'm going to ride along with them. I'll see you at church."

Aimee trotted down the stairs and joined Angelee. "I'm ready, let's go!"

The girls crossed the porch and skipped down the steps. Angelee pulled at the back of her short spring coat.

"The sunshine feels so good!" Aimee said. "Look, daffodils are coming up in Mr. Foster's garden."

"And some crocus as well. Spring is certainly trying to show her face." Angelee observed.

"I just wish I could capture those exact colors when I'm painting." Aimee sighed wistfully.

"Mee-Mee, just lately I've had a feeling that a change is coming," Angelee confessed.

"What a silly thing to say! We just had a big change—Baby Anastasia. And you just mentioned that it's springtime."

"But I don't mean the weather, or in our family. I just feel like I'm on the edge of something—me personally."

"What makes you say that?" Aimee cocked her head to one side.

"I can't put my finger on it. Do you know what it feels like when Christmas is coming? Maybe something that you asked for, someone else has gotten for you as a Christmas present. Even that explanation is wrong...but it's the best I can do."

"You mean when you've made a list; you're pretty certain that someone will buy it for you—but you're just waiting for Christmas to find out for sure."

"Yes, like that," Angelee confirmed.

"Well, as Daddy says, 'When the time is right, the answer comes.' And sometimes when you don't expect it." Aimee said. "We're here. See you after Sunday School."

As Angelee entered the hall, a family friend stopped her. "Miss Angelee! You're just the person I was hoping to talk to."

"Good Morning Mrs. Clifford. How can I help you?"

"First of all, congratulations on the addition to your family. How is your mother coping?" The merry woman's face beamed at her.

"Oh, Mommy is getting lots of help. Right now, we keep encouraging Mommy to look after the baby while we take care of everything else. But you know Mommy, she loves to be up and about. Anastasia is an easy baby."

"That is good news. I'm sure you're learning a lot! What I wanted to talk to you about is...well it's more of a call for help. You see, we have decided to start a Brownie group. The little sisters of the Girl Scout troop have been asking us when they can join. The other night we —the leaders I mean—were meeting to discuss it. We realized we had more than enough little girls to make it worthwhile. But we need a couple of more leaders. One of the other leaders, Mrs. Guilford, says she often takes her children to the reading groups on Saturday mornings. She says you're wonderful with the little ones. She suggested you as a possible Brownie leader."

"My goodness, Mrs. Clifford. I've never done anything like that before! I wouldn't know where to begin."

"Don't worry about that!" Mrs. Clifford said, bright blue eyes sparkling behind her wire-rimmed glasses. "To begin, you can assist. One of the other ladies, who has been working with the older girls, will be taking charge of it. And you'll catch on soon enough."

"When would you need to know?" Angelee hesitated.

"Now, I'm not trying to talk you into anything. Here's what I suggest. The next Girl Scout Meeting is Friday. Come here and observe. Then you'll get an idea of what to expect. You can decide after that."

"That seems fair enough." Angelee consented. "What time on Friday?"

"The troop meets at seven o'clock, in the basement here."

"Keep in mind, Mrs. Guildford, I'm more of an inside kind of girl. Don't the scouts spend lots of time outdoors and camping?"

"Being an inside person is no problem. I think you'll enjoy it. The girls will be doing all kinds of projects. I find that I learn all kinds of things while I'm teaching them! Must go, don't want to be late for my class."

Angelee hurried to her class, feeling ambivalent about Mrs. Clifford's request.

Giggling and excited squeals carried through the evening air as Angelee walked towards the church. A few girls, between seven and ten years of age, chased each other. The sing-song chants mingled with the smacking of jump rope on the pavement.

The organizational meeting for the new Brownie troop would soon require that they quit their games and gather in the basement of the Christian Church.

Ruefulness rose in her mind; Angelee began to question her motives in entertaining the idea of becoming a Brownie Scout leader. Skulking around the corners of her mind, the old doubts and fears of supervising children without another adult's assistance tried to creep back into her mind. Internally, she addressed them. *"Fear, I recognize your lies. Get out of my mind right now!"* immediately dismissing them.

It was true she enjoyed reading to the children at the library group. She enjoyed working in the Sunday school. Girl Scout Troops were known to go camping, build fires, go for nature hikes, and such like. An occasional picnic at Blue Bluff was her idea of "roughing it." Would she be expected to take girls, some barely school-age, out into the forestry for rambling around? Outdoor sports and other pursuits had never appealed to her.

"Angelee Giselle Tilson, what have you gotten yourself into?" She muttered to herself, crossing the street and marching up the steps. "Maybe nothing...you've not made any promises to anyone."

A clanging bell called the girls into the church. Angelee was surrounded by chatter; from the little girls entering the church with her, and from the basement, where mothers and other helpers congregated. The enthusiasm of the others changed Angelee's misgivings into ambivalence. The problem lies in not knowing what skills she needed to be a Brownie leader. Even more daunting was the thought of a gaggle of girls following her into an unfamiliar, wild environment with creepy-crawly creatures.

Four little ladies ran up to greet her.

"Hello, Miss Tilson." A girl with wispy blond hair took her hand. "We're so excited you're going to be our troop leader."

The blond girl's friends nodded enthusiastically.

"Just a minute Sally-Jane, don't get too excited. I haven't decided to do it yet. I came because Mrs. Clifford invited me." Angelee tried to defer.

"But we need yooouuuu!" Argued blue-eyed Gail, whose over-long bangs fell into her face.

"I'm pretty sure that some of your mothers might help out," Angelee reassured them. "Even if I don't become a leader,

From the front of the room, Mrs. Clifford clapped her hands attracting everyone's attention.

"Come on girls--ladies. Please sit down. It's time to start!"

Sally-Jane pulled Angelee along, insisting Angelee sit with them. Angelee smiled, enjoying their affection. The idea of disappointing them lodged in her brain, like a small stone in her shoe. Yet, committing to something because she felt obliged was equally unpleasant.

Angelee made the effort to listen to Mrs. Clifford's presentation objectively. Being a leader would require time to develop ideas for projects so that the girls could earn badges. That in turn would require time to obtain the materials and prepare them for each meeting. The girls would meet each Friday, readying themselves for a week-long camp experience in the summer. They were not able to officially meet as a Brownie Troop until later in September when the next school year started. Which, in turn, meant that they could not join the official Scouts' summer camp. However, because of the girls the interest, Mrs. Clifford felt they could begin meeting anyway. This also meant that the leaders would have time to get some training from other leaders from currently active troops.

When she had finished explaining, Mrs. Clifford allowed the other potential leaders time to ask questions. She even allowed some of the youngsters to make inquires.

Following the official business, the girls delighted in serving the adult ladies tea or lemonade with pieces of cake at the end of the meeting. Observing, but not contributing to the conversation, Angelee's was even more irresolute. She'd thought the evening would produce a clear answer—enough information to make an easy decision. The interaction with the girls, her friendship with Mrs. Clifford, and the other mothers, plus the benefits of the program provided a strong incentive to say yes to making the commitment. Yet, an indefinable feeling within made her hesitate.

The first one ready to leave, she interrupted Mrs. Clifford's clearing-up efforts to talk for a few minutes.

"Mrs. Clifford, I'm sorry, I can't give you an immediate answer. I promise to let you know on Sunday."

"Well, I am surprised." Mrs. Clifford remarked, bafflement in her eyes. "You know most of the girls already and they love you. You have a natural ability to work with children and young people. I don't know what's holding you back."

"Thank you for your vote of confidence. But I don't think it's wise to make a hasty decision. I have some very mixed emotions, to be honest. I want to think this through." Angelee insisted.

"Knowing your own mind is important." Mrs. Clifford conceded. "So, I will talk to you Sunday."

Angelee left the church mulling over the meeting. As she walked home, the thoughts about Pauley and Drew's welfare danced in the shadows in the back of her mind. It had been weeks since she'd had a letter or postcard from either of them.

A Memorable Decoration Day

"I know it's Decoration Day, but are you sure you want to go to the cemetery?" Mommy asked. "That rain is making it pretty nasty out there." Mommy sat at the table, holding Anastasia in one arm while eating toast with her free hand.

"Don't you think it's important to observe Decoration Day?" Angelee replied. "Especially this year—since we just entered the war in Europe. It must be bittersweet to the members of the Grand Army of the Republic and Women's Relief Core who come to put flowers on the graves. I want to support them."

Angelee referred to the Civil War veterans and their wives and families who annually performed the solemn act of decorating the resting places of those who died in battle.

"Besides the rain isn't that heavy." Angelee rationalized. "There isn't to be a long program, just the placing of flags and flowers. I'll go to Mrs. Parkham's from there."

Angelee finished her coffee then took her dirty dishes to the kitchen. She tugged on galoshes and collected her raincoat and from the hall closet. As a rule, she wouldn't bother taking an umbrella with her; but today she would be standing outside, as well as walking.

The light drizzle didn't warrant raising the umbrella as Angelee took the fifteen-minute walk to Hill Dale Cemetery. Near the entry gate, a parked car served as the meeting point. Next to it was a flat-bed truck, containing the wreaths, bouquets, and miniature flags. Angelee made her way to the group and joined the line for grave decorations.

The overcast skies suited the somber occasion. Women's Relief Core members, equipped with lists of the final resting places of Civil War soldiers, directed participants along the rows to make sure every deserving plot received a floral tribute. Having received the information about which burial spot to attend to, Angelee started down the grassy path. Rain-softened, uneven ground gave underneath her step, causing her to lose her balance. Certain of falling, Angelee pressed the wreath close to her body.

"I've got you!" A warm, familiar voice said.

She felt a steadying hand take her elbow, helping her to regain her balance. She turned to look at her rescuer.

"Thank you, Cameron. I thought sure I was going to be laying my face on a grave instead of this wreath."

"How fortunate for me that I get to be your knight in rusty armor!" Cameron teased, his eyes twinkling.

"Don't you mean I'm the lucky one?" Angelee replied, feeling her face grow warm.

"Actually, I think it's the wreath that benefits the most." Cameron chuckled.

Angelee laughed softly. "You're right. I see you have some flags to place as well. I think we should get on with it. It feels like this drizzle is turning to proper rain."

"Angelee, would you join me for a cup of coffee when we're finished here. I'd love to catch up with you." Cameron smiled warmly, his gaze hopeful. Cameron had just returned from a three-week trip to Boston and New York.

Large drops of rain began to patter. Angelee took the umbrella from the crook of her arm and opened it. It was large, and she lifted it to protect both of them.

"I'd enjoy that. But I've promised your Aunt I would come to work straight after I finished here." Angelee hesitated. Crouching down, Angelee lay the wreath on the grave, then gave a short salute. "Thank you, Jasper Gowans, for giving your service to our country."

Cameron planted the flag next to the wreath on the grave. They stood silently for a few minutes. Angelee prayed for the protection of all the American boys fighting in a foreign land and a quick resolution to the war.

The rain continued dancing on the umbrella's black canvas.

Pointing toward the line of vehicles along the road, he said. "Tell you what; I'll drive you to Aunt Marceline's. And if we stop for a coffee along the way, I'm sure she won't mind."

They trod through the drenched grass, feeling the spongey soil give beneath their feet. Angelee sighed in relief when they arrived at Cameron's Cadillac. Climbing into the front passenger seat, she lowered the raingear, paying particular attention to avoid the canopy top.

"I wish the day were clear," Cameron said, climbing behind the steering wheel. "I would be tempted to kidnap you for a drive." He started the car and eased onto Columbus street.

"Guess I'd better thank the Good Lord for sending us liquid blessings!" Angelee remarked flippantly. "However, that offer for coffee is very tempting right now."

"Besides your company, the only thing that could make it better is a nice piece of cake...or pie...or some sort of nibble..."

"Oh great!" Angelee laughed. "It's bad enough you're enticing me with a hot drink. But food along with it...that is just plain devious."

The wind blew rain underneath the canvas car-top during the drive into the town square. Cameron pulled into a parking spot in front of the White Star.

"Come on! I know it's May, but this rain has given me a chill." Cameron said, opening Angelee's door.

Only a few steps from the door, they left the umbrella in the car. It was mid-morning, and the restaurant was half-full. Divested of damp coats, Angelee and Cameron claimed a table.

"So, what would you like?" Cameron said, using his handkerchief to wipe his face.

"Just coffee. I had breakfast before I went to the graveyard." Angelee shrugged her shoulders, an unexpected shiver running down her neck and spine.

"Coward..." Cameron teased. "Mrs. Smith's cinnamon rolls are perfect with coffee."

"You go ahead." Angelee deferred. "I am content with the coffee."

"Are you sure you don't want an early lunch?" Cameron persisted.

"I'm fine, really." Angelee insisted. "But, tell me about your trip. Where did you go?"

"There was nothing overly exciting. Just business for Aunt Marcheline in Boston. Then I visited some friends in New York. Although I must say, I kept thinking I would have enjoyed showing you the shopping, theatres, and restaurants. I've decided that I want to ask Aunt Marcheline if I can take you with me on my next trip."

"Me? Whatever for?" Angelee jerked her head back, blinking.

"Why is that so difficult to consider?" Cameron leaned towards her, his mood becoming serious. "You know about the different businesses my Aunt has. Wouldn't you want to see them in person?"

"I've never thought about it. When I started working for your Aunt, I didn't think I'd be doing this job beyond one summer. This is my third year already, and I'm still working for her. She's been very generous and kind. My parents convinced me that going to work in the tomato canning plant would be a bit like cutting off my nose to spite my face. For me, it's just a job I keep doing because I have a genuine affection for your aunt."

"But don't you think going to New England would be a nice vacation? A chance to see someplace besides Indiana?" Cameron pressed.

"I suppose." Angelee considered, then shrugged. "I guess I've just never been interested in traveling. Did your Aunt put you up to this?"

"My idea, totally. However, when I mentioned it to her, she was delighted."

"But why do you suddenly want to take *me* to Boston?" Angelee asked, puzzled by his persistence about the idea.

Cameron leaned back in his chair. "One of the things I like about you, Angelee, is how unassuming you are. There are several reasons I want to take you East. To expose you to the beauty of Boston, and for you to see first-hand some of the places you've read about in books. I enjoy watching your face when you discover something new. Plus, you are easy to be with—no ulterior motives. You may not know this, but according to society papers, I'm regarding as one of Boston's most eligible bachelors. That makes me a target for all kinds of female attention.

"When I'm with you, I feel like you see me—not my famous name, my bank account, and business portfolio. I can relax and share things with you. Do you know, I find myself telling you things I've never told anyone before?"

"Oh, my goodness. I had no idea." Unsure where to look, and suddenly feeling shy, Angelee dropped her gaze to her lap, and reaching into her pocket, fiddled with her tiny doll, Mildred.

Cameron gave her a one-sided grin. "No, from your reaction, I can see clearly that you didn't. I value our friendship, Angelee. I suppose I was hoping that you'd be excited by the idea of time away in a new environment. That, in turn, would provide the opportunity to discover if we could be more than friends."

Angelee felt the heat rise up her neck and her cheeks began to burn. Automatically, she placed her cool fingers on her heated face. "Cameron, I'm flattered. But I really don't know what to say."

"Flattered...and embarrassed. I apologize—it was not my intention to make you so uncomfortable. It's clear now that you've never entertained any thoughts of romance towards me."

"Cameron, ...I've been totally oblivious to your feelings. I'm sorry." Angelee murmured. She took a deep breath, to gather her wits. "I need to tell you, in the last few weeks, I've discovered that I'm in love with Pauley Bannister."

Cameron looked down at his hands for a moment. Looking up he said. "Thank you for being honest with me. I just hope I've not ruined a good friendship. One that I truly value."

"I'm sorry your feelings have been hurt," Angelee said.

"I am disappointed. But now I know where I stand." Cameron said. "Let me pay the bill. I'll take you to work now. I'm sure Aunt Marcheline has a full list of things for you to do."

"No doubt! And thanks for the coffee." Angelee said.

Cameron left payment on the table and rose. Angelee rose as well. Cameron helped her into her still damp coat. They were silent as the left the restaurant, and even on the short drive to Mrs. Parkham's.

As Angelee was about to leave the car, she turned to Cameron. "Thank you, Cameron. If you're sure it isn't too awkward, I'd like to continue being friends."

"I'm okay Angelee. Now, off you go. We'll make plans for the weekend. Okay?" Cameron reassured her.

"Maybe a movie?" Angelee suggested.

"Sounds fun. Talk to you later."

Angelee climbed out of the car and ran through the rain. Today would indeed be a Memorial Day to remember.

No alarm went off on Monday, the 3rd of June. Mrs. Parkham had insisted that Angelee have the day off to celebrate her birthday. Although Olivia would not be home for a couple of weeks as she finished her second semester, they had planned to celebrate later in the month.

Angelee snuggled in the bed, enjoying the morning breeze easing through the open window. Accustomed to rising early, she'd been dozing off-and-on.

A knock on the door brought her fully awake. "Come in!"

Angelee pushed herself up in bed. The door eased open, revealing Mommy and Aunt Milly, who sat the bed table on Angelee's lap.

"Birthday Breakfast in Bed is being served." Aunt Milly cheerfully declared. "Any thoughts about turning nineteen today?"

"I haven't been awake enough to think about it!" Angelee yawned. "However, I'm sure there will be no dramatic events this year!"

"Shall we stay, or should we allow you to eat your breakfast in peace?" Mommy asked.

Angelee looked at the French toast, bacon, and coffee. "Oh, please stay."

Mommy sat down on Aimee's bed, and Aunt Milly sat at Angelee's desk. Stacy nuzzled at Mommy's front, whimpering to be fed.

Angelee closed her eyes to say a short prayer over the food. When she opened her eyes, the baby was nursing quietly.

"How can we make today special?" Aunt Milly asked.

Angelee savored the perfectly hot coffee. "Well...I don't know. I've had my sleep-in and now breakfast in bed. Olivia's still up at Butler...Drew and Pauley are still away..."

"I would have thought that we'd have news from them more recently.... maybe they're in a situation where they can't write." Aunt Milly offered.

Though unspoken, knew that neither she, nor the others, wanted to think about what those circumstances might involve.

"When I talked to Mrs. Bannister, she said that her last letter from Pauley was the end of February," Angelee remarked, sighing. "He's always on my mind. I can't imagine how his mother feels."

"I can," Mommy said. "That's why we need something to take our minds off of our worries."

Angelee finished the syrup-sweetened French toast and savored the last bit of bacon. "Thanks, for doing this. I can't think of anything special I want to do or anything I want. But I'll think about it while I take a bath. Where's Aimee this morning?"

"M. Torrington has decided to go to the artist colony over in Nashville for the summer. So, Aimee has gone over to his place to help him pack up his studio. She's very sad about it, but is putting on a brave face." Mommy explained.

"Wow! This is a bit of a surprise." Angelee observed. "Guess we do need a distraction for all sorts of reasons."

"Would you like to invite Cameron over for supper tonight?" Aunt Milly asked.

"As nice as he is, it just isn't wise. Last Thursday he asked me to consider having a romantic relationship with him. I told him that my heart belongs to another."

Aunt Milly nodded her understanding. "I'll take this back down to the kitchen. You go take your bath and think about possible 'party ideas.'"

Mommy lifted Stacy onto her shoulder, patting the baby for burps. "I'll leave you now too. Enjoy your bath."

After a warm bath, she dressed in a simple, spring dress. A silky warm breeze hinted at the warmth and bright light streaming in the windows showed a sunny day outside. Plaiting her blond curls, she considered how to spend the day. Aimee was likely to be gone all day. The possibility of taking a walk on her own didn't appeal to her. Maybe Daddy would let her borrow the car for a drive to the country.

Tying the end of her braid, she sat down at her desk. A short pile of books sat on the edge of her desk, her Bible on top. She lifted the leather-bound book, embellished with her name on the front, and laid it next to her right hand. The journal, which had been lying underneath it, was taken next, and she turned it to the page marked with a ribbon.

Her writing started at the top of the page, with the day and date. *"Today, as I turn nineteen, I have decided that I will use this coming year to read the Bible all the way through. However, I am not going to start in Genesis. Since certain books appeal to me more than others, I will start with those I am most familiar. Although I've grown up in a Christian family, I am not proud of the fact that I have only read a few of the sixty-six books. From those few, in some instances, I've selected only passages or certain chapters. I have decided to start with Romans."*

The resolution and goal for the year written down, Angelee pushed the journal to the side of the desk and opened her Bible.

"Jesus, I love you. I've always read the Bible for church; you know during Sunday school class. I want to know You better. Please, speak to me today. Amen." She prayed.

Commonly taught that Paul had written Romans as a letter, Angelee decided she would read the epistle from beginning to end, in the manner Paul had intended it.

With no-one and no task requiring her time or attention, Angelee allowed herself to become absorbed into The Apostle's instruction, encouragement, and challenges. An uncommon peace seemed to fill the room. Angelee felt as though she was the only person in the world.

Unexpectedly, a passage in chapter twelve became enlightened, like a spot-light focusing on the words.

"And having gifts differing according to the grace that was given to us, whether prophecy, let us prophesy according to the proportion of our faith; or ministry, let us give ourselves to our ministry; **or he that teaches, to his teaching***; or he that exhorts, to his exhorting: he that giveth, let him do it with [a]liberality; he that rules, with diligence; he that shows mercy, with cheerfulness."*

Memories from the last several months began to flood her mind: the mothers at the library saying she would be a good teacher; Alistair saying that she made learning fun; the invitation to become a Brownie leader because she could teach children.

She read the verses again.

This time different words lit up:

*"And **having gifts** differing according to the grace that was given to us...".*

In her heart and mind, she heard the Holy Spirit speak. *"This is what you've been asking about. This is what I've been speaking to you, but you've not been hearing me. Teaching is your gift. Now you know My plan for you. Pursue a teaching certificate."*

Angelee's heart sang. Previous experiences now became a whole picture. She grabbed her fountain pen, pulled the journal to the center of the desk. She felt it imperative to record how the words in the Romans had seemed to jump off of the page. The direction and confirmation of her purpose also had to be noted down. Angelee's intuition defined the message as a birthday gift from God the Father.

Now that celebration seemed possible, she could barely wait to share her news with her family.

Closing the books and restacking them, a barefooted Angelee, bounced down the stairs, looking for her mother and Aunt.

Humming softly to herself, Angelee circled the dining room table, laying plates at each place. So excited about the discovery of her purpose and talent that she'd been giddy for two days.

Monday evening's celebratory meal included the Hanson family, whom Mommy invited, as well as M. Steffken Torrington. The conversation at her birthday dinner on that Monday evening centered on which college she should attend. Even now as Angelee thought about the joking, teasing, and unsolicited recommendations, she laughed out loud.

Indiana University was in Bloomington, easily accessible by train. The teachers' college at Indiana Central University at Indianapolis had a celebrated reputation. However, Butler University was the strongest contender; Drew and Pauley had studied there before signing up for the Army. Olivia was currently completing her first year of courses there. Butler was also affiliated with the Christian Church.

Angelee collected the cutlery from the sideboard drawer and started to round the table again. "I need to do that."

"You need to do what?" Aimee asked, walking onto the room.

"Huh, did I say out loud?" Angelee replied. "I was just thinking that I should write to the colleges for information on the fall term. I'm sure some of the organizational skills I learned with Mrs. Parkham will be an asset."

"Does she still hint to you about going out to Massachusetts, and becoming a 'Wellesley Girl?'"

"Oh, yes. She can't help but allude to the 'beneficial experience of being a Wellesley graduate.' She tries to pretend subtleness, but I know her too well. However, I do know she is glad that I've decided on a future. At least in terms of studying at college."

"What about Cameron Boyer-Parkham?" Aimee grinned slyly and winked.

"What kind of stupid question is that?" Angelee asked, hands-on-hips.

Aimee giggled at her sister's askance expression. "Steffken told me that at one point, Mrs. Parkham was resolutely set to match-make between you and her nephew. She wanted to make sure she could hang on to you." Aimee slowly shook her head in mock chastisement. "But you just refused to cooperate with any of her 'schemes and plans'."

Angelee picked up a cloth napkin and threw it at her sister. "You, Little Sister, are naughty!" Laughter spilled from the girls, filling the sun-lit room. "I hope Alistair is on his way home. Daddy won't wait lunch on him."

"Ever since he missed lunch on Saturday two months ago, he's made a point of being back in plenty of time."

"It's a hard lesson, not getting anything to eat because you're late for lunch. But it isn't a lesson he's had to have twice." Angelee agreed.

They heard the back-door slam shut. "Well, Alistair is home!"

As the family gathered to sit down to a lunch of cold meats and salad, the doorbell rang.

"I'll go." Angelee volunteered, the chair tilting awkwardly as she jumped up. She grabbed it and pushed it back properly before going to the door.

She saw a man's silhouette through the curtain. As she opened the door, she recognized Floyd Smithers, the Western Union messenger. Since the war had started, a telegram usually brought news of the soldiers fighting in France. The sight of a Western Union man triggered immediate dread.

"Hi, Miss Tilson. I've got a telegram for Dr. Tilson," he said.

"Can I sign for it?" she said, reaching for the clipboard with trembling hands.

Floyd handed it to her. She signed her name and handed it back.

The young man handed her the envelope.

"Wait a minute and I'll bring back your tip," Angelee instructed.

Carrying the yellow and brown envelope into the dining room, she handed it to her father. "It's a telegram. Do we have a tip for Floyd?"

Daddy reached into his pocket, took out his folding coin purse, and procured the tip. Angelee delivered the coins and hurried back.

Silence met Angelee when she returned to the room. Daddy's brow was furrowed as he stared at the page, as though he couldn't comprehend the words on it. All the color had drained from Mommy's face; her eyes shiny with tears. Aimee's mouth hung open, and Alistair's head hung as stared at his plate—not eating. Aunt Milly, as white as Mommy, blinked back tears.

"What is it, Daddy?" Angelee asked.

"Sit down Angelee." Daddy said, and handed her the page. Angelee read the message.

'We regret to inform you that it is officially reported that your son, Andrew M. Tilson, medical Corps of the 10th Field Artillery, was wounded in Action May 27th.

Major Frank C. Robinson, Medical Corps, War Department.'

"It can't be possible." Angelee vocalized her thoughts. "He isn't infantry. Drew's a medic."

The concise, but sparse, missive reported Drew as wounded. But what did 'wounded' mean? Was it from a bomb? Had he been shot? Had the ambulance he was driving, or riding in, crashed? How badly was he wounded? Drew wasn't dead...the telegram said wounded. But could he die from his wounds?

Another thought surfaced, adding to Angelee's tangled thoughts. Were Pauley and Drew together when Drew was injured? If they were, was Pauley hurt too? Where were they? What could be done to find out? How come there wasn't more information in the government communique?

Only the previous Sunday Angelee had spoken with Mrs. Bannister, inquiring about any news from Pauley. But Mrs. Bannister reported that she had not heard from Pauley for weeks. Angelee wondered if she should contact Mrs. Bannister now. The hall clock struck twelve-forty-five. Realizing that she needed to return to work, there was no time to pay a visit down the street.

Angelee trudged back to Mrs. Parkham's home to finish her afternoon hours. Numbness created a mental fog, and she developed a headache trying to concentrate on her work.

Angelee thought of Drew frequently in the following hours. Not knowing how seriously he was injured chaffed her peace of mind. Had he been taken to a field hospital? If his injury wasn't bad, would he be patched up and sent back to duty? The not-knowing left her restless. The bigger question was Pauley.

Later, following the family's evening meal, Angelee walked to the Bannister home; vacillating between anticipation and dread of seeing Mrs. Bannister.

Angelee stood at the front door, debating inwardly whether or not to ring the bell when the door suddenly opened.

"Hi Angelee," a little-girl voice came from behind.

Angelee jumped then laughed nervously. "Oh! Hi Lucy! How are you?"

Lucy sighed and shrugged her shoulders. "I'm sad. Everybody at our house is."

"Why's that?" Angelee asked, her stomach tying in knots.

"We got a letter today. But Mommy can explain it better than me."

Mrs. Bannister had come to the door. "Angelee! I thought I heard voices. Please come in."

"Hello, Mrs. Bannister." Angelee followed her into the living room. "Lucy was just telling me it's been sad at your house. What's wrong?"

Mrs. Bannister gestured toward the love seat, inviting Angelee to sit.

"We got a telegram from the war department." Mrs. Bannister smiled bravely. She swallowed hard and tears gathered in her eyes.

Angelee felt her heart race.

"It seems," Mrs. Bannister said. "Pauley has been listed as wounded in action." Mrs. Bannister dropped her head. "It's hard to know what to think. There are so many questions."

" We got the same message about Drew. We've no idea what the situation is, only that he was wounded on the twenty-seventh of May."

Mrs. Bannister lifted her head. "When did you hear?"

"Today, at lunchtime. Although most of us lost our appetite once the telegram arrived." "Oh, Angelee! We got our news about the same time." Mrs. Bannister commiserated. "When I read it, it was like all the air had been sucked from my lungs."

"I felt the same way." Angelee agreed.

"How is your mother taking it?"

"Mommy is stoic at the moment. I think she's determined to be strong—for the rest of us."

The women sat quietly for a few minutes. Mrs. Bannister broke the silence.

"When the shock finally wore off, I reminded myself that Pauley was injured, not reported missing...or dead. I reminded myself to be thankful for that."

"It's just so frustrating, not knowing how seriously they're wounded." Angelee lamented.

"That and not knowing how to find out anything more." Mrs. Bannister said.

"Mrs. Bannister, I have no idea whether or not Pauley and Drew were together when they were hurt. But if they were, I'm sure that at some point we will hear from one, or both, of them. If I hear anything, I'll let you know."

"Thank you Angelee. I'm sure we'll hear something eventually. Either the army will contact us again, or maybe someone from the Red Cross. In the meantime, I'm hanging onto God with every prayer I have."

"I know you're right." Angelee gave her a half-hearted grin. "We are not alone in this."

Mrs. Bannister nodded, understanding that Angelee meant God, each other, and many other friends.

"I'm sure Lucy and Lori will be wanting your attention soon, so I'll go home now."

Angelee stood and walked toward the door. Mrs. Bannister followed her.

"Angelee, thanks for coming by." Mrs. Bannister opened her arms.

Angelee readily embraced her. "You're welcome. We both love him, you know."

"Yes, I know. And I'm glad you do." Mrs. Bannister replied.

"I'll see you soon." Angelee released her.

As she walked home, alone in the quiet night, Angelee let the tears roll down her cheeks. Every step was a prayer. Regardless of how frightened she felt about the future, how powerless she felt, Angelee knew that God was present with her and present with Drew and Pauley. She refused to give up hope.

Setting her cup and saucer on the crocheted placemat, Angelee sat down at the dining room table. Lost in her thoughts, she distractedly smoothed down the tablecloth. Having left the brown manila envelope from the Butler admissions office on the table before getting the coffee, Angelee now picked it up and pulled out the pages.

Unnoticed by Angelee, Mommy sat down across from her, holding two-month-old Stacie. "Are you leaving for work soon?"

Angelee jumped, her hand smacking the table.

Mommy chuckled softly. "Sorry."

"Oh, that's okay." Angelee looked at the wall clock. "I was just looking over these forms and thinking about my to-do list for the day."

"Don't dawdle, you don't want to be late for Mrs. Parkham."

"Actually, I've asked her for the morning off. I'm going to the high school administration office because I need at least three copies of my high school transcript. Daddy said that I should apply to IU and Indiana Central as well, to make sure I can get into at least one of them."

"What else did Butler want to go with your application?" Mommy asked. She placed Staci on her shoulder, firmly patting the baby's back, encouraging her to burp.

"They want letters of recommendation: two from teachers— which will be former teachers in my case. A third letter needs to come from someone who knows me, but isn't a teacher and isn't a family member. Mrs. Parkham said she would write that one for me. She teases about doing it under duress because she will miss me. But she's truly proud of me."

"Have you thought about who to ask to write the teachers' letter?" Mommy asked.

"An interesting thing happened Saturday. You know that Aimee and I went to Phelps's drug store. While we were shopping, Mrs. West, the high school history teacher came in. When I explained to her about applying to college to become a teacher, she asked if there was anything she could do. I asked her if she would write a letter of recommendation to the colleges for me. I was so excited when she said yes." Angelee picked up the instruction sheet in front of her. "But I've been reading this again. I just realized that they want TWO teacher recommendations, not one. While I'm at the high school I'll ask the school secretary for some help."

Stacie whimpered, squirming in her mother's arms. "Well, now that she's no longer hungry, she needs a dry diaper. And probably a nap." Mommy stood up. "I'll pray for you to find the right teachers."

Angelee refolded the papers, replaced them into the packet from the college. Draining the last of the coffee in her cup, she pocketed the envelope, and carried the cup and saucer to the kitchen.

Powerful sun heated the day, even before noon. A linen parasol shaded Angelee as she walked the twenty minutes along Washington then turned onto Jefferson streets to the high school. Though there were no classes during the summer break, the school office remained open. Angelee took the stairs up to the first floor and walked into the office.

The clacking of typewriter keys being pounded flowed into the hallway, confirming the presence of at least one secretary.

"Good morning, Miss Tilson. It's good to see a different face around here." Mrs. DeVore remarked. "What brings you in?"

Taking it from her pocket, she showed the letter to the grey-haired, bespectacled sturdily-built woman. "How much is the fee for three copies of my high school transcript?"

Mrs. DeVore quickly scanned the page and handed it back to Angelee. "Since it has to be for official purposes, we are charging five cents per page. It will take a day or two to type them up for you."

Angelee opened her reticule, extracted a coin purse, and counted out the coins before laying them on the countertop. Replacing the purse, she pulled the strings of the larger handbag to close it. "I was also wondering if you could help me with something else."

Mrs. DeVore, busily collecting the money, smiled. "What is it?" She placed the payment into a money collection box.

"As you read, I need two teacher's recommendations. Mrs. West has already agreed to write one for me. I was wondering if you know Mrs. Louis's address?"

"Oh, I am sorry. Even if I gave you the home address, it would not be any good. Mrs. Louis and her husband have gone to California for the summer. They aren't due back until a couple of weeks before classes start."

"Oh." Angelee absorbed this bit of information. After she thought for a moment, she made a second inquiry. "Do you know if Mr. Martin is still in town."

"Let me think...yes, I believe he is in town. But I think I heard his wife suffered a stroke week before last. This is probably not a good time to ask him."

Angelee dropped her eyes to the floor, sighed, and pondered who else to consider asking. "I had Miss Simmons for home economics. Do you know if she's around?"

"Now there's a story. She went to Chattanooga to visit her parents. While she was there, she met up with a young man she'd known since their school days. He was about to ship out, so they got married. She's moving back to Tennessee to live with his parents while he's in France."

"Mercy! That was fast! She probably won't have time to think about writing references." Angelee conceded. "Can you think of anyone else I could ask to write a recommendation for me?"

"I tell you what, as I'm looking through your records, I see if any of your former teachers are around." Mrs. DeVore responded.

"Can you come back on Thursday morning? Your transcripts will be ready by then. And I may have a couple of names of people you can contact."

"Thanks for your help, Mrs. DeVore." Angelee turned to leave.

"You're welcome. Oh, by the way, have you heard from your brother lately?"

"No, we haven't. We keep hoping we will hear from the Red Cross or get another message."

"Why? What's happened?" Mrs. Devore's eyebrows drew together.

"We received a telegram, informing us that he'd been wounded in action. We've heard nothing since. All we can do is pray...and keep contacting the Red Cross."

"Oh, I'm so sorry. I had no idea. But I will keep you in my prayers."

"We'd appreciate it. And thanks again for your help."

Angelee's mind whirled with memories of walking these halls with Olivia, Drew, and Pauley. Now she wanted to follow in their footsteps to college; specifically, to Butler University. But to accomplish that goal, she needed another teacher's recommendation.

Angelee skipped down the stairs and out the school's propped-open doors into the mid-morning heat. Glad for the extra shade from the parasol, Angelee admired the view of homes lining Jefferson street. Young poplars, sycamores, and oaks looking like tall sticks protruding from the ground, promised summer shade in the coming decades. As she walked towards home, the astringent scent of freshly mown grass wafted past her.

Through her mind ran the teachers that had written recommendations to colleges for her friends and older brother. Some of them were teachers for classes she had not taken. Besides getting into college, Angelee knew she needed confirmation of acceptance in order to find a room in a recommended boarding house near the campus. It would be ideal to stay in the same rooming house as Olivia. However, in her last letter, Olivia had said that the house had a waiting list of women hoping to procure a room there.

Along the sidewalk leading up to her own front porch, golden daisies and blue lavender bloomed, perfuming the warm air. Discouraged because she couldn't identify a second referee, and any further action being stymied, Angelee trudged up the steps. Closing the parasol, she dropped into the swing and just sat. Absentmindedly she sat the swing in motion, the chain squeaking.

"So, why are you out here brooding?" Aunt Milly asked as she walked out the front door.

"Because it's too hot to sit inside and brood." Angelee quipped. "Just frustrated because I thought once I knew what I was supposed to do with my life, I thought everything would just fall into place. But it hasn't." Angelee explained her current dilemma.

"I know just want you mean. But strangely enough, there are times when the path that should be straight-forward is a road with unseen curves and side roads. I know from experience."

"I know you do." Angelee gave her aunt a wry smile. "But the strangest thought popped into my mind while I was sitting here."

"And what was that?"

"That verse in the Bible, where Paul writes: 'in everything give thanks...'. With so many people applying for admission to colleges, and just a set number of rooms in boarding houses, I am afraid that

I'll miss the cut-off dates for getting accepted for college this fall. Thanking God once I'm accepted into school and have a place to live seems logical. But to be thankful when nothing is going according to plan? That seems crazy, silly."

"Yes, I can see it seems upside down to be thanking God before you get the answers we want to our problems. But Thanksgiving isn't just about being grateful. When we choose to tell God, 'Thank You', our hearts are saying to God, Who is our Father, 'I trust You.'. With every challenge we face, God is allowing us to use our faith more deeply. Praising God when we get what we want is expected, normal. But when we give Jesus honor and adoration while we are waiting and hoping for the resolution to our problems, we are using our faith, and growing stronger."

"I guess right now I just have to do what I *can* do and refuse to give in to the fear of the future."

"Steps. Each task that God guides us to do requires us to do it one step at a time. It's like when Joshua led the Israelites across the Jordan river; the waters didn't stop flowing until the priests actually stepped into the water. God makes a way at the right moment. You're collecting the information you need, and when you need the recommendation, the right person will come forward. But brooding isn't going to help in any way."

"You're right, I know. But the more I think about getting into college, the less time I have to think about Drew and Pauley."

Aunt Milly nodded appreciatively. "All of us are worried about them. All the unanswered questions haunt us. I refused to be pessimistic though. Until I'm told otherwise, I am choosing to believe they will return home."

"I am hoping for that too." Angelee agreed. "Mrs. Parkham wasn't expecting me this morning. But since I don't have to do any other errands, I'm going to go to work."

The swing rocked softly as she stood. Kissing Aunt Milly on the cheek, she set off to work.

Life's rhythm of work, rest, play and Sunday worship carried Angelee through the weeks of June and July. Twice a week she wrote letters to Pauley and Drew—never knowing if those hand-written communications found their way to the recipients in France. Her missives regaled the young men with stories of funny incidents involving children at the reading sessions, updates of Anastasia's growth, and her own struggle to be positive regarding her hope of going to college.

As the first week of August rolled onto the calendar, the papers reported temperatures in the 90's. Lush green gardens were thriving with produce hanging in abundance from bushes and vines.

Mommy and Aunt Milly rose by six o'clock each day, to fill Ball jars with green beans, pickled cucumbers, blanched and peeled whole tomatoes, and corn cut off of the cob. On Saturdays, Angelee helped process the food and watch the water-bath canner as it boiled for hours.

"We'll have no problem filling the pantry this year," Mommy said, sweat trickling down the side of her face. She wiped her forehead with a dish towel, then stuck it back into the waistband of her apron.

Angelee picked up another cucumber to slice. "Why don't we cut these length-wise, so they'll fit nicely on a sandwich?"

"I've never thought about it before. We could try it." Mommy shrugged her shoulders.

Angelee sliced the green, knobby vegetable into strips before placing them into a large crock. "Mommy, I saw an article in the Indianapolis paper for the State Fair. It's starting on the 31st. What do you think about maybe going up for a day? There's a train we can catch from here and it goes to the Fair Grounds."

"If the heat gets worse, I don't think I could keep Stacie cool enough. Talk to Daddy about it. He might take you and Alistair and Aimee. Or if he isn't willing, Milly would you be interested in going."

Mommy peeled an onion and began slicing it, before adding it to the cucumbers.

"I think a day away will do us some good." Aunt Milly said.

"You're right. But I want to go someplace that isn't crowded or hot." Mommy agreed. "By the way, Angelee, did you have any

⌐ getting in touch with Mr. Edwards?" Mommy swiped at the ⌐ rolling down her face and then her forehead again.

"He replied to my letter and I received it last week. He said that he sent the reference letters directly to the colleges, which is what I asked him to do. Latin wasn't my favorite subject, but I worked hard, so he remembered me. But I have no idea as to whether I will hear from any of the colleges in time to start there this fall."

"Didn't you say that the first semester begins on the 17th of September? There's still plenty of time for you to hear."

"Six weeks doesn't feel like enough time when I think about trying to find a boarding house. But I just keep reminding myself that God knows what I need and He is more than able to sort things out." Angelee popped a slice of cucumber into her mouth.

"I suggest that you start making a list of the things you want to take with you, like your clothes, special books. By organizing your thoughts and ideas, you're exercising faith."

"I guess that's a good idea." She agreed to Mommy's reasoning.

"Have you discussed it with Olivia? She could tell you what you'll need."

"We've chatted about it off and on. She thinks that her landlady will be happy to have me. A couple of the girls that stayed in that house graduated in June. Olivia told her about me. But to be honest, I'd feel a lot better if I knew for sure I've been accepted."

"It may be another month before you get that confirmation," Mommy said. "And once you get that letter, you'll look back and think that you wasted a lot of time fretting."

"This brine is ready." Aunt Milly interjected. "Let me pour off that water, so you can fill the jars."

Angelee lined the glass containers up. The vinegar's pungent smell wafted through the kitchen while the woman packed the vegetables into the jars, and Aunt Milly poured the brine over. Lids and rings were screwed on, fingers protected with potholders.

"Hello! Anybody home?" Olivia's voice floated from the open kitchen door.

"Come on in!" Mommy called.

"Should I put on an apron?" Olivia said, walking into the hub of activity.

"Thanks for the offer, but we are ready to put these jars on the stove to boil. You two need some time together. Gee-Gee, get your apron off and go spend time with Olivia. Your Aunt and I will clean up the mess here."

Angelee pulled the apron over the top of her head and hung it on the hook. Then she and Olivia headed toward the stairs. As they reached the foyer, Angelee heard the mailman whistling and the letterbox lid drop.

Taking the few steps to the screen door, she pushed it open and reached into the black metal box. She lifted out a small stack of letters. Turning, she went back to the kitchen.

"Look Mommy—it's from the Red Cross." Angelee held the blue envelope out towards her mother.

Mommy was sitting at the table, nursing Stacie. "Open it for me, will you?"

Angelee put down the other letters, and slit the foreign document open with a table knife. Mommy took it from her and unfolded the pages. While she read it, Angelee examined the rest of the mail—letters from friends, one from her grandparents in Kentucky. But there was no letter from any of the universities. So she left them on the table.

"The letter is from a ward nurse," Mommy explained. "Let me read it to you."

Dear Mrs. Tilson,

My name is Sybil Robinson. I am so sorry it has taken me so long to send this letter. But the field hospital is rarely quiet. A few weeks ago, a convoy of ambulances were on their way from the field hospital to the trains, which take the wounded to the coast. From there they are taken by ship back to England. The German fliers seemed to ignore the Red Crosses on top of the ambulances—and dropped bombs as if they were rain.

The drivers did their best to evade the bombs and were most valiant. Because of their efforts, many lives were saved. Later, it was reported that no vehicles took a direct hit. However, the explosions caused some of the ambulances to turn over. I had the privilege to attend to the causalities.

Your son, Drew, was one of the drivers. He suffered broken bones, lacerations, and a terrible concussion. He did require surgery on his legs to reset the bones. The medication for pain helped him to rest. After a few days, he was transported on the train to the ferry. I do not know which hospital in England he was sent to. However, I wanted to send word that he was now safe and on the mend.

He is unaware that I have written to you. But I wanted to ease your mind and heart. Let's pray this war ends soon—so that we can all be reunited with your families.

God bless you,
Sybil Robinson, RN, Red Cross

Relief spread through Angelee's body, causing her knees to buckle. She sank onto a kitchen chair, as did Olivia.

"Thank the Lord!" Aunt Milly said.

Mommy dried her eyes and smiled. "Yes, indeed—Thank You, Lord."

"Hey! What's everybody crying about." Alistair's voice broke through the solemn moment.

"We just received a letter about Drew," Mommy informed. "He was hurt pretty badly, but was sent to a hospital in England."

Alistair, standing next to Aunt Milly, threw his arms around her waist, nearly knocking her over. "Did she say if he was coming home? Do you think he'll be home soon?"

"We don't know. The nurse just explained how he was injured, and that he was sent to England. She wanted us to know he was okay." Mommy said, shifting Stacie onto her shoulder for a pat. "And for that alone, I am thankful."

"We all are." Angelee joined in. "Come on, Olivia, let's go get some ice cream to celebrate!"

"Great idea!" Olivia smiled and clapped her hands. "The perfect way to celebrate good news."

Sunday, August 11th, 1918
Drew Comes Home

Angelee awakened without the aid of a ringing alarm clock. The thought of yesterday's post brought a smile to her face. She hoped for an acceptance letter from Butler would arrive today.

Angelee thrust her arms from under the covers and stretched. A delicious breeze puffed the lace curtain out, as it came through the opened window.

"You remind me of a cat with all that stretching." Aimee yawned, peaking over her covers.

"What woke you up?" Angelee asked, reveling in performing wrist and ankle circles, her toes tautly pointed.

"Don't know," Aimee replied.

"Well, I recently learned that stretching is the body's way of getting the blood pumping faster. All that faster blood to the brain makes it easier to wake up. I'm getting up and going for a walk."

"Why would you want to do that?" Aimee opened one eye to observe her sister.

"Now that I know for sure I've been accepted to Butler; I've only got a couple of weeks before my classes start. I just want to savor these days here at home before the big move."

"Really?" Aimee had closed her eye and rolled onto her back. "It isn't like Martinsville is going to dry up and roll over into the White River while you're gone."

"If all you're going to do is grumble, turn back over and go to sleep while you can. The new Sunday school classes start this week, and you've got to decide between joining the choir, being in a Sunday school class, or helping someone else run theirs."

Aimee groaned. "Why did you have to remind me? And don't think I don't know that you're hinting about taking over your former class!"

"Mee-Mee! Have I ever suggested that you take over my class—or teach Sunday school for that matter?" Angelee chided her sister.

At that point, Aimee threw back her covers and rolled out of bed. Standing with feet shoulder-width apart, she intertwined her fingers, then slowly raised her arms above her head and raised onto tip-toe.

"Now who's practicing cat stretching?" Angelee teased.

Returning to flat-footed standing, Aimee turned and stuck her tongue out at her sister. She traipsed across the floor. "Beating you to the bathroom!"

Angelee grunted and called after Aimee. "Just don't doddle!"

Aimee laughed, sticking her head back around the bedroom door. "Appropriate to me…but don't you mean don't dawdle!"

Laughing at herself, she sat up on the side of the bed, she looked out her window. Within two weeks the view from a different bedroom window would be in front of her. She hoped there would be a room in the same house as Olivia.

Waiting for her sister to return, Angelee picked up her hairbrush and set to work taming her blond tresses. The previous Sunday had been her last day to teach the group of children Bible stories. Tomorrow she would begin organizing her wardrobe to take to Butler, as well as books, photographs, and other personal things.

When Aimee returned, Angelee took her turn in the bathroom, relishing the warm water on her face and arms. To tame her frizzing hair, she smoothed it down with a damp comb. Finishing her ablutions, she returned to her room and got dressed.

Others of the family were beginning to rise as Angelee unlocked the front door and left the house. At the bottom of the steps, she hesitated a moment, considering whether to walk east or west. East invited more strongly, and she moseyed along, stopping occasionally to imprint images on her mind. The morning sun filtering through the branches above her head; the smell of roses and lavender from flower beds.

She'd gone only four blocks when she felt a sudden sense of expectation grab her attention. Though it had never happened previously, Angelee heard a kind voice in her mind. She knew it wasn't her own thought. The voice instructed. "Go home. Go home now."

So taken by the unexpected experience, Angelee immediately changed direction to return home. Though urgent, she felt no foreboding.

Curiosity grew stronger with each step. Why would an inner voice suddenly compel her to return home? Being a Sunday there would be no mail delivery. Everyone else in the family was either still sleeping or just rousing up from the night's slumber. Yet, she was compelled to obey, her walk turning into a run.

At the corner of Washington and Grant Streets, Angelee could see a car parked on the street outside her home. The car was unknown to her, making her even more curious. From inside her home, she heard raised voices.

Rushing up the steps, Angelee shoved the front door open. Several voices talking at once emanated from the living room.

"What's all the commotion about? Whose car is out front?" Angelee asked, raising her voice to be heard.

"It's Andrew!" Mommy declared, pivoting away from the rest of the family circled him.

"He's home!" shouted Aimee, jumping up and down.

Involuntarily her hands flew up to cover her mouth, her throat tightened and tears began streaming down her face. Though only a few seconds passed, they felt like long moments. Then she flung herself into her brother's arms.

Just the relief and pleasure of having him home bubbled up in tears and laughter. Then the babble of questions from everyone wanting to know the circumstances of his injury and his return home.

"TWEEEEEEEEETTT!" Daddy's sharp, shrill whistle filled the air, bringing the group to immediate attention. "Now then," Daddy said. "Let's make some coffee and sit down and let Drew explain everything just once."

"But what about church?" Alistair said.

"Very good question." Daddy replied. "I believe God will understand if we stay home today to celebrate your brother's surprising return."

Alistair, in his serious-minded way, nodded his head and smiled. "I want to hear all about the planes and tanks and stuff like that."

"Come on, Angelee, let's get the coffee pot on." Aunt Milly said. As she turned to follow her aunt to the kitchen, she heard her mother give instructions.

"Alistair, you can ask Drew all the questions about machinery later. Right now, take his suitcase up to your room. Wash your face and get dressed; you can come down and talk to him while I take care of Stacy, and the girls fix breakfast."

Alistair pulled himself up tall, giving his mother a salute. Turning on his heel, he tugged the suitcase up, mastering its weightiness, the lumbered up the stairs to accomplish his task.

Having made their way into the kitchen, Angelee took the largest coffee pot from the cupboard while Aunt Milly collected the coffee from the pantry. "I have a feeling that even Alistair will be allowed coffee today."

"No doubt," Angelee replied, smiling and filling the pot with water.

"And it's a morning for cornflakes. Cereal is the fastest thing we can get on the table."

She sat the enameled coffee pot next to Aunt Milly, who placed the center basket with the ground coffee into the pot. While Aunt Milly placed the pot on the stove, Angelee went to the dining room and opened the hutch. Her mind raced with the same few questions, revolving like a spinning top. While she desperately wished the tasks in front of her would distract her attention, the automatic habit of setting the dishes around the table was not enough to quiet the mixture of anxiety and relief.

Placing the last bowl at the end of the table, Angelee took hold of the chair back. Steadying herself, a great sob wrenched from inside her. Throughout the rest of the house raised voices and laughter celebrated the return of the eldest child.

Eyes closed, weeping out frustration and hope, Angelee was unaware of anyone entering the room, until she felt a hand on her shoulder.

"I know what you're thinking." Mommy murmured in her ear.

Angelee turned; Mommy embraced her, comforting her.

"Gee-Gee, go ask your brother if he knows anything about Pauley."

"I am so happy that Drew is home. I just don't want him thinking I don't care about what he's been through."

"Remember, your brother loves Pauley—just like a brother. He knows you're in love with his best friend. He'll understand that you need to know about Pauley."

"Go wash your face before you see your brother." Mommy released her, giving her a little shove.

Angelee went to the washroom, splashed cold water on her hot, tear-stained face. When she felt better, she found Drew in the family room, with six-month-old Stacy resting happily on his lap.

Drew shifted in the armchair and began bouncing Stacy on his knee.

Angelee sat down in the chair next to him. She smiled and said, "I'm so glad you're home."

"It's wonderful to be home. You don't have to ask--Pauley is fine. We're both pretty beaten up, but we're still in one piece. He is due on the next ship home. Please keep praying—but stop worrying!"

Angelee stood, lifting Stacy onto her hip so Drew could get up more easily. She then hugged Drew, with Stacy squealing between them.

"Come on then, let's go get breakfast," Angelee said. Together, they joined the rest of the family in the dining room.

Thursday, August 15th, 1918
Pauley's Surprise

August sunshine blinded Angelee as she climbed off the interurban, returning from a trip to Indianapolis. Together with Daddy, Angelee had journeyed up to Indianapolis by train, then taken a local tram to Irvington. Their purpose, to register Angelee for the first semester classes at Butler College.

"I'm glad the walk is only about five blocks," Angelee said, using her handkerchief to wipe a trickle of sweat from her forehead before it dripped into her eyes. "It's been a long trip and I'll be glad to get home. Then I can walk around in bare feet!"

"That's fine for you, Gee-Gee. But your old dad has to go visit his patients at Home Lawn." He'd removed his straw hat to also wipe his brow. "But I'm going to have a glass of iced tea before I go."

"Hey, you two!" Drew grinned at them, sitting in the front seat of the family car. "Thought I'd come to get you; save you that walk."

"It's pretty bright out in this heat." Daddy admitted. "Sometimes a half-mile can seem like a long way."

"What a blessing!" Angelee enthused. "It's been a taxing day—mentally and physically."

"Well, I hope you're not too depleted…because…there is a surprise at home. Which is the reason I've driven over here to pick you both up."

"So now my brother is being a hero with ulterior motives." Angelee grinned, having settled in the back seat.

Daddy, hat replaced, sat in the front seat with Drew.

"Of course! But I'm sure you'll appreciate me even more once you've seen the surprise." Drew teased, putting the car into gear and after checking for pedestrians and other cars, pulled into the street.

"Are you going to ask me about the classes I signed up for? Don't you want to hear about what's been going on at Butler?" Angelee quipped.

"Aren't you even curious about what the surprise might be?" Drew countered.

"Nope! You'd only side-step any questions I have. Plus, it's less than a five-minute ride to the house."

"Point taken." Drew chuckled, turning the car onto Graham street and parking.

"I hope your mother has some nibbles because I'm hungry!" Daddy said, having taken off his jacket while on the train, now collected it from the seat and draped it over his arm. "Thanks, son, for the lift. It's much appreciated."

"I agree," Angelee said, exiting the car. "Now to get inside and get my shoes off!"

"By the time you see what's going on inside, you'll forget all about your feet!" Drew hinted.

The heat of the day was beginning to wane. Instead of the front door, they walked to the back of the house to enter the kitchen door. As she pushed the door open, she could hear laughter and chatter from within the house, causing Angelee to conclude that the surprise had something to do with guests. Despite the anticipation of discovering who might be visiting, Angelee had had enough of shoes. She sat down at the work-table and immediately loosened the shoe strings and yanked off the offending, leather high-top shoes.

"I can't believe you!" Drew laughed. "You must be desperate!"

"Yep! I just want to feel some cool linoleum on my feet so I can cool down. Walking around in this heat is more than a little tiring." Angelee stood and sighed with pleasure as the cool flooring absorbed the heat of her still-stockinged feet. Collecting her shoes, she stood up. "I'm sure that the surprise will wait while I go upstairs for a quick change."

"I suppose I could wait..." A voice came from the dining-room door. A voice Angelee had not heard for too long. "But I really *don't* want to."

"Pauley." A whisper escaped her lips. The shoes clattered onto the kitchen floor. "Oh, Pauley!"

Joy gushed through her being, escaping as sobs. That same energy released her from the momentary stupefaction. Merely steps apart, they met in the middle. Angelee threw her arms around his neck. Pauley lifted her off the floor for a long embrace. Setting her back onto her feet, he kept her in his embrace. Resting her head on his chest, she felt his tears drop on the top of her head.

"If you want to, you can kiss her son." Daddy encouraged.

Angelee blushed but raised her face in hope.

Pauley smiled at her, his blue eyes shining. Lowering his head, he placed his lips on hers. Like a man who had been stranded in the desert and was tasting water again, his kiss was slow, savoring, and appreciative.

"I'm so glad you're home," Angelee uttered when the kiss ended.

"Thank you for all your letters. They meant so much." Pauley said. "Now, come with me. There's someone I want you to meet." He released her but took her by the hand.

As they walked through the dining room, the parlor, and then into the salon, Angelee battled fear. After the kiss he had just given her, she did not doubt his love for her. But who was he so attached to that he had to introduce her as soon as he was home?

Mommy was sitting with four-month-old Stacy in her arms. Sitting on Aunt Milly's lap was a little girl with copper hair and large green eyes. She was wearing a light blue frock. In her hand, she held a bouquet of Black-eyed Susans.

The little girl slid from Aunt Milly's lap and ran to Pauley. With an effort, he lowered himself and put his arm around her tiny waist.

"Angelee, this is my newest little sister, Esme." Pauley began the introduction.

"Oh...so you are the Special Lady Friend. Hi! I'm Esme De Vos and I'm six years old." Esme thrust the flowers toward Angelee.

Suddenly Angelee understood how this charming child would captivate the heart of those who met her. She squatted down, accepted the blooms of gold and black, then shook Esme's hand. "Esme, it is lovely to meet you. Thank you for these." Angelee nodded toward the flowers. "You can call me Angelee. By the way, your English is very good."

"Merci! Pauley and his friends were teaching me very much English." Esme cocked her head to the side. "Pauley said that I must learn. To live in America, I must speak the English. And..." Looking coyly at Pauley, she continued. "he said if I bring the 'Susan's', you will, of course, like me."

Angelee looked at Pauley. "Did he *really* now?"

Pauley gave Esme a loving smile. "Miss Esme is very truthful. I will explain later."

Angelee wobbled, lost her balance, and landed with a thud onto her bottom. Laughter rang out in the room, Angelee laughing the hardest. All her anxiety about the unknown Esme was for nothing. The "Little Lady" was a child.

Angelee rose from the floor and took a seat on the sofa. Pauley sat next to her and took Esme on his lap.

Throughout the rest of their visit, each time Angelee looked at Esme, she couldn't help the laughter that bubbled out of her heart.

"Why do you laugh at me?" Esme asked, her eyes brimming with tears.

"Oh Mon Petite, I'm not laughing at you. I'm laughing at myself. You see, I thought you were a grown lady, and that Pauley wanted to marry you."

Esme widened her eyes. "Ooohhhh...! Hey, how do you know French?"

"We have a friend, M. Torrington, who is from Belgium. So we have learned a bit of the language from him." Aimee explained.

"I should like to meet M. Torrington," Esme said.

"And you shall. Not right now, but we'll make sure that we have a big party so you can meet him. Now then, Mon Petite Marionette, we must go home to Mommy and Daddy." Pauley announced. "And I need to rest."

Esme slid from his lap, crossed the room to kiss the cheeks of Mommy, and then Aunt Milly in turn. Returning to Pauley, she remarked. "Okay, I'm ready!"

"Esme, it has truly been a delight to meet you," Angelee confessed. "You must come again soon."

"Oh yes, s'il Vous-plaît." Her emerald eyes twinkled. "You are most lovely."

"As are you!" Angelee stood up, shaking out her skirt.

Grimacing, Pauley braced himself against the arm of the sofa and slowly rose. "Still have a bit of recovery to do."

Angelee walked them to the door and out onto the porch. "There's so much to catch up on. I wish you could stay longer."

"I do too. But we got into town early this morning, so both of us are worn out. Do you mind if we make it for tomorrow?"

"No...and yes...you know what I mean." Angelee raised her gaze to his hazel eyes.

"Of course." He replied, taking one step down, making him eye-level. "Are you working tomorrow?"

"Yes; I finish at 4.00 o'clock," Angelee answered.

"How about this? I'll pick you up from Mrs. Parkham's. We'll go for a drive out to Blue Bluff and take a walk. Then we can come back into town, have supper at the White Star. Sound good?"

"Sounds perfect." Angelee agreed.

"May I come too?" interjected Esme.

Pauley chuckled. "Sorry, I need some time with Miss Angelee by myself. But maybe we'll take you out another time."

Holding Esme's hand while she stood next to him, Pauley slipped his other arm around Angelee's waist and gave her a lingering kiss. "That will have to hold you until tomorrow."

Angelee sighed and smiled. "See you tomorrow."

Hugging herself, she watched the tall, brown-haired man and the tiny red-headed girl walk down the street.

Her spirit lifted her prayer to her Lord. "Heavenly Father, thank You so much for bringing him back home—to his family—and to me. And thank You for Esme too."

When she could no longer see them, she turned and went inside.

Upon Angelee's decision to seek her teaching certificate, Mrs. Parkham had agreed to the hiring a new assistant--a bright young man out of business college, Samuel Booker.   Although the decision to hire had been Mrs. Parkham's, it was Angelee who was tasked with training Samuel in the methods Mrs. Parkham preferred. That Friday, Angelee had her hands full answering Samuel's questions, while also trying to attend to Mrs. Parkham's immediate needs.

But the anticipation of her evening with Pauley made the day drag. There was so much to discuss; questions about him filled her mind, as well as the many things she had discovered about herself during his time away.

At exactly four o'clock she packed up her work for the day. Samuel was left to ask Mrs. Parkham any questions. She skipped down the steps to Pauley. Leaning against his Underslung Scout, he was dressed in cream linen pants, a matching vest, and a pin-striped shirt. She flung herself in his arms and they both laughed. He kissed the top of her head.

"Come, Miss Tilson, let's go play and enjoy this lovely afternoon." He had released her and then opened the car door for her.

"This has been the longest day! I hope it starts cooling off soon. Even with the windows open, Mrs. Parkham's office has been almost unbearable. There's just not been any air moving."

"The good news is that the heat of the day is over. Once we're out of town, I can speed up and you'll feel plenty of moving air." Pauley left her side of the car and walked to the front to crank the engine. The car fired on the first attempt and hummed rhythmically.

Though she wanted to hold his hand, Angelee knew Pauley needed both hands to drive the car. However, they would arrive at the Blue Bluffs within fifteen minutes. Then she would certainly hold his hand while they walked along the trails.

Pauley looked over at her. "Happy?"

"More than just happy...I'm in ecstasy!" she called out over the sound of the engine.

The strands that had escaped from her chignon flapped in the wind as the car passed from the edge of town, northward to the local resort.

Angelee took in a deep breath, relishing the feel of the air against her face and forearms. Once past the edge of town, the road curved around the hills. Trees on either side of the road shaded the tarmacked surface. Though the temperature had topped ninety degrees a couple of hours earlier, and the humidity was wilting, Angelee's delight at being with Pauley again rendered the discomfort of August's heat insignificant.

Pauley guided the Scout off of the tarmac onto a gravel road, the entrance of the Blue Bluff Resort. Countless other vehicles had created tracks in the rocky surface. The summer was the busiest season for the Boy Scout encampments and vacationing families keen to use the cottages. A designated parking area came into view.

"Do you think we'd turn heads if we suddenly wanted to attend one of the dances out here?" Pauley asked as he parked the car.

"Of course,...and set tongues wagging about how we've become 'worldly'." Angelee laughed. "But I suppose that after what you've seen, dancing would be a celebration of life—not a sin to be avoided."

"Yes, I've seen a lot. But let's go find someplace cool we can drink this lemonade that Mom sent." He pulled a thermos from underneath his seat. "I shouldn't put this under my seat. It might roll out and affect the clutch or accelerator. In other words, it's dangerous."

Angelee turned and alighted from the car. "Oh no! I was in such a hurry I left my hat at the library."

"Hold this, while I get a blanket." Pauley handed her the flask. "We'll find a bit of shade, so it won't matter too much."

Along with a small draw-string bag, he took a summer blanket from the back of the car and they started toward the picnic area.

"Remember when we were here last? We met Glen Tincher."

"Sure, it was a different world then. At least for me. We knew the war was happening but had no idea what it was really like." Pauley observed.

An area of mown grass underneath a stand of Poplar trees afforded a practical place to lay the blanket. They sat down in the shade and Angelee opened the metal bottle. From the cambric bag,

Pauley removed two enameled drinking cups. Angelee filled both of them.

When Pauley had his cup, Angelee held it up and said, "To coming home!"

Pauley clinked his cup with hers. "To coming home."

"There's so much I want to know, so much for both of us to say to each other. I don't even know where to begin." Angelee said, pouring the lemonade into the cups.

Taking one of the cups from her, Pauley tipped the cup for a drink of the well-sugared but tart liquid. "Mom is set on spoiling me." He chuckled.

"I noticed the chipped ice she added." The drink both cooled and refreshed her.

"Do you know why I brought you out here?" Pauley asked.

"Because it is a bit cooler than in town?"

"No, because there are so many people around that I can't give in to the temptation to take you in my arms and kiss you till your head swims." His eyes twinkled.

Angelee felt the heat rise. "Just when I was beginning to cool down!"

The laughed, glad for the opportunity to flirt.

"France, Esme, how you got injured; Pauley, I have so many questions. But I don't know where to start. So, tell me the first thing that comes to your mind." Angelee instructed, gazing at him closely.

Pauley grinned. "The first thing that comes to mind...is how beautiful you are. You were always on my mind."

Angelee rolled her eyes and shook her head. "Thank you for the compliment. But tell me about how you were injured."

"It's still hard to talk about." He lifted his hand and traced the side of her face. "But I know you need to know. I can't believe it's been almost five months since I was near the battlefield. It was so awful, Angelee. I've never been so dirty in all my life."

Pauley took time to tell her about the relentless noise of the bombs falling, shells exploding, and gunshot. Besides the noise, there was the mud from Spring thaw and rain. Mixed in the struggle against never-ending bombardment there was bad weather, foul food, and lack of sleep, intensified by the infestations of cooties, lice, and mice. It wasn't uncommon to share sleeping quarters with rats, as they were primitive—abandoned sheds, pieces of board lying on the ground. Near areas of the front, it was the worst, trying to drive the ambulances through muck or deep potholes caused by explosions.

"Amidst all that horror, we seemed to find things to keep our spirits up. Letters from home were the biggest boost. I was thankful that Drew was with me. We depended on each other a lot. We prayed, all the time. Not only for our safety but for everybody back home."

Angelee, who had taken Pauley's hand, stroked the back of his hand with her thumb. "I just kept writing to you and Drew because I hoped that they would get to you. Even after we learned that you had been injured. No one notified us about how badly you were hurt. Or even where you were."

"I couldn't write for a while because I was blinded by mustard gas," Pauley said. He grew quiet, remembering.

"How did it happen?" Angelee gently inquired.

"Drew and I were driving with a line of other ambulances toward an ambulance train station. It had been raining, so the mud was thick and sticky. We were bumping along, with patients in the back. German planes had been harassing us, at first just flying low, over the convoy. They were known for using shells with gas. Wearing a gas mask was almost useless against the mustard gas, but Drew and I decided that we were going to use them anyway. They might use some other gas.

"The pilots had made several passes above and beside us. Suddenly there was an explosion near the front of the line. It wasn't a bomb from the plane, but a shell from a cannon. The ambulance in front of us was thrown up into the air. When the shell detonated it created a large hole in the road. I jerked the steering wheel, trying the avoid the vehicle crash-landing in front of me. The force of the turn catapulted our ambulance, making it roll when it hit the crater in the road.

"Being trapped underneath the steering wheel, I bounced against it, breaking a couple of ribs and one of my collar bones. When the ambulance flipped back to an upright position, I was thrown against the seat and broke one of my shoulder blades. The impact must have also knocked me unconscious because the pain brought me back. The impact knocked my gas mask off, so I inhaled some of the gas. I found out later we were in an area that was still affected by the use of mustard gas. It had been used a couple of days before, but it lingers. My eyes began to burn, I was blinded by tears and started vomiting.

"Drew was thrown free. The wounded soldiers in the back were thrown around like rag dolls."

"Did you have a whiplash too?" Angelee asked.

"Probably, but the pain in my chest and back was so intense all I could do was try to breathe slowly. It was excruciating to take a deep breath."

"What happened next? How did you get help?" Angelee busied herself pouring more lemonade.

"I don't know how it happened, but the ambulance driver behind me managed to stop, which prevented a block-long wreck! He jumped out of his cab and ran to see how badly I was hurt. I told him to check the soldiers in the back. It was only a few minutes and other drivers and medics were transferring patients from our truck into the other ambulances. Then they checked on Drew and helped me. All the occupants of the first ambulance were killed. There was certainly chaos; since some people gave up their gas masks for the wounded. Men crying in pain, others crying as a result of the residual mustard gas, coughing, and everyone who could, working as quickly as possible.

"Once we were on the road again, I passed out again. When I woke up, I found myself on the hospital train, on my way to an English hospital."

"Did you think you'd be sent back to France? After you got better?"

"Drew and I had discussed it before the attack. We knew that some men had injuries that healed well enough for them to return to the fighting. But after the attack, we both had to recover from the blisters in our throat, sore and sticky eyes, and of course our broken bones. Even now, there are times when my eyes feel irritated."

"Drew told us about his having blisters because the mustard gas got onto his uniform. But thankfully he wasn't as badly affected as some me who had been in the initial attack. And he says his leg hurts sometimes, like when there is a storm moving in."

"Yes, the other drivers got him off the ground as quickly as possible. He was in so much pain that he didn't care that they stripped his clothes off him. One of the medics realized that he'd been laying in a contaminated area, so he put on gloves and got Drew out of his uniform as quickly as possible. That prevented him from having worse injuries. Some of the men I saw had horrible yellow blisters.

"We were taken to a casualty clearing station and assigned to a ship to England. I had a difficult time settling down in my mind; I was worried about Esme. I couldn't come back home without her. Every time I thought of her, I'd think about the twins. What would happen to them if they lost Mom and Dad?"

"Is that why you got home after Drew?" Angelee asked.

"I began bothering the Red Cross workers about her. It was a struggle to write letters with a broken collar bone and a broken shoulder. I began dictating letters to a volunteer, who would pass them on to the Red Cross. I even wrote to my commanding officer, telling him I would commit AWOL to find her—once I was released from the hospital."

"I have to confess; I was jealous of Esme." Angelee chuckled. She picked a dandelion and fiddled with it.

"Really? Of Esme? But why?" Pauley looked at her incredulously.

"I had no idea she was a child. In your letter, you called her "Little Lady." You said she was charming. It never occurred to me that she was younger than the twins."

"I know it was like dropping a bomb when I brought her home to Mom. But I had no idea that she would be a "tiny" surprise for you." He laughed.

"Anyway, I asked God for a miracle, to find her and let me bring her home with me. Drew was a big encouragement, writing letters to other guys in our unit. My C.O. remembered Esme and thought it was a good idea to give her a real home. An orphanage is not always the best place in the world. Between our bunk-mates, our commanding officer, and the Red Cross volunteers, Esme and I were reunited."

"I would have loved to be a fly on the wall when you took her in to meet your parents." Angelee mused.

"She was asleep in my arms. The twins were in bed, which is was the best for Esme. They would have overwhelmed her with all their energy. I told Mom that Esme would be happiest to sleep in my bed, and I'd sleep on the floor. They weren't too sure about it at first. But they also realize that she would be less fearful if I was near when she woke up.

"After I put her to bed, I went downstairs to talk to my parents. I apologized for bringing her home without waiting for their answer."

"They knew she was a child?" Angelee shifted her position to be more comfortable.

"I wrote to them from the hospital, telling them I was okay. My letter explained her situation and that I wanted to bring her home. I joked about Lori and Lucy wanting a little sister. I was shipped back to the US before they had time to reply. I asked them not to tell anybody until they gave me an answer. But in my heart, I just knew I simply could not leave her behind."

"I have a feeling it's going to be a big adjustment for everyone," Angelee remarked.

"She's been through so much already. I want her to get used to our family and feel like she belongs." Pauley said.

"Are you officially discharged now?" Angelee asked.

"Yes, I was after I arrived back in the States and released from the hospital," Pauley explained.

"So, what now? Are you going back to college?" Angelee threw the wilted flower aside.

"I've been thinking about it, and I'm going to go back to Butler in January. It will give me a few months to get Esme settled. If I try to go in September, I'm afraid she'll feel abandoned. But if I wait until January, then I can take her up to the college, so she can see where I'll be."

"That's a good idea. And, you can bring her up with you when you come to see me!" Angelee cheerfully instructed. "I'm moving up a few days before classes start next month."

"I had no idea you decided to go to college." Pauley cocked his head to one side. "If you wrote to me about it, the letters haven't caught up with me yet."

Angelee told him about the experiences she'd had that led to her decision to become a teacher.

"I'm so proud of you. You'll make a great teacher." Pauley laid down and put his hands behind his head.

"I hope so."

"Angelee, can we come to an understanding?" he asked, eyes closed.

"About what?" Angelee said, tickling his nose with a piece of grass.

"I want to finish college and go to law school. You want to get your teacher's training. I know it's a long time to wait. How would you feel if I said I think it's best if we finish our education and then get married?"

"Is that an indirect marriage proposal?" Angelee challenged him.

"Not intentionally. I do want to propose properly. However, I guess I just want to make sure you aren't going to run off with someone else before I'm in a position to do that."

"I couldn't do that Pauley. There was an opportunity while you were away. Life without you in it seems impossible. Our parents are sure to agree that we should get our education out of the way and then move forward. So, even though it will be very difficult, I am willing to agree."

"Now that you know my story, and we've made a very sketchy plan for the future, shall we do for a walk before we drive back into town and have supper at the White Star?"

"I'm hungry now! Let's forget the walk!" Angelee asserted.

Pauley slowly arose. Angelee had quickly jumped up, collecting the empty cups to put into the bag. While Pauley shook out the blanket and folded it, Angelee picked up the thermos bottle. Before she took a step, Pauley pulled her to himself.

"Fine, we'll go to eat now! But first, kiss me." Pauley ordered.

Angelee yielded to his request, her hands still holding the drinking utensils, she wrapped her arms around his neck. He smiled, then lowered his head and gently, slowly kissed her.

"I love you, Angelee. I know your prayers helped to bring me home."

Tucking the thermos under her arm, and carrying the bag in her hand, she took his and they started down the road, into the future.

Angelee stood by the window, taking in the view from the top floor of Boston's Copley Plaza Hotel. The view included the expanse of park lawn across from the broad street. The sheer curtains danced with the incoming breeze.

Pauley, smelling of shaving soap and bay rum, slipped his arms around her waist. "Good morning, Mrs. Bannister." He nuzzled behind her ear.

"I love hearing you say that." Angelee turned in his arms, wrapping her arms around his neck.

Pauley leaned down, his lips slowly tasting hers. Angelee, enjoying the freedom of being a newly married woman, responded eagerly.

"If we keep this up, we won't get out of this room." He said, ending their kiss.

"Would that be so bad?" Angelee replied, with a teasing grin.

"I thought you wanted to attend a service at the Old North Church. We may not get another chance to see the place where Paul Revere reportedly sent the 'One if, by land, two if by sea' signal."

"You're right, I do. Guess we will have to resume this later."

"Since we're on our honeymoon, shall we take a cab to the church?" Pauley offered.

"What a lovely idea." Angelee agreed, sitting down to put on her shoes. "Although, it is quite walkable. Let's save the cab for our trip to Mrs. Parkham's."

"I thought she was sending her driver for us." Pauley reminded her.

"Of course,...so let's take a cab to the train station tomorrow morning," Angelee suggested.

"Good thinking! Let's go have some breakfast before we go to church." Pauley said.

Collecting her handbag, she met him at the door. Leaving the room, they held hands as they walked to the elevator.

The elegantly decorated restaurant was on the ground floor. Seated immediately by the hostess, they ordered coffee. A waitress brought menus with the coffee and glasses of water.

"Can you believe we've been married a week already?" Angelee said, draping the napkin over her lap.

"After waiting for five years, it seems like a blink!" Pauley agreed. "A lot has happened in the last two months."

"It boggles my mind. I finished my first year of teaching. You, along with the class of 1923, graduated on the 6th of June from the Indiana School of Law."

"That was just three days after your twenty-third birthday!" Pauley grinned, remembering the celebration.

"We were so wise to give ourselves a month between the end of the school year and the wedding."

"It also gave me time to get our house painted and move in. And of course, we moved your stuff in the week before the wedding. It will be nice to return and have it all organized."

"And I can actually stay at night, instead of going back to my parents." Angelee agreed.

"I'm glad we're spending the rest of today with Mrs. Parkham. She is being very generous to us."

"Even if I disappointed her," Angelee said ruefully.

"On that note, I can honestly say, you have not disappointed her."

"How can you say that when I refused to attend Wellesley? And even though I became a teacher instead of her companion/assistant?"

"I can say that because she told me. When we were in the solarium at Home Lawn…"

"At our reception?" Angelee wanted clarification.

"Yes, she took me aside and told me that she was very proud of you; especially fact that you dared to stand up for yourself and follow your heart. She says that she loves you like a daughter."

"I had no idea." Angelee sat, pondering this bit of information. "She truly is a special friend." Wiping a tear from her cheek.

"I think that's why she's organized this soirée this afternoon. She wants to show you off to all her friends and family."

"You know what surprises me most? She made the reservations at The Copley instead of asking us to stay in her home."

"I think she knew we'd want our privacy, and the freedom to roam Boston at our leisure."

"Like I said, very generous and considerate."

"Indeed. Now then, are you finished? We don't want to be late for the service."

"As lovely as all this has been, I'll be glad to go home tomorrow."

"Me too—since I start work a week later."

"Are you sure you can branch out into family law working with Mr. McKinlay?"

"Yes, because there are lots of changes going on with adoption laws now."

"Esme has been a real inspiration for you, hasn't she?" Angelee grinned, as they walked toward the church.

"In many ways. But then she has been for you as well. You've been very diligent in raising support for the orphans in Europe."

"Just because the war has been over for a few years, doesn't mean they don't need help. The American Legion appreciates all the contributions to help support the children in France. And I'm glad I found a way to continue to be involved."

"We are a good team, Angelee. But then, I always knew we would be. Look, the church is right here. What a great way to start our last day in Boston."

"And prepare for the days ahead."

Acknowledgments and Gratitude

The following are the people to whom I owe a big thank you.

To Father God, for giving the gift of writing.
To Jesus Christ, for His Special obedience to the cross and purchasing my salvation.
To the Holy Spirit, for dwelling in me and guiding me daily.

My Dad, who was a master storyteller. My mother, who always believed in me, supported and encouraged me. They are now part of that host of witnesses who have gone before us.

My husband, John, who has believed in me, encouraged, nagged, and supported me in many ways to make this project happen.

Youth With A Mission, 1994 School of Writing Staff—who provided a foundation of understanding of the "how" and "why" of effective written communication. They are Merry Puff Hoffmann, Janice Rogers, Pam Warren, and James Patrick Shaw.

Donna Fletcher Crow, author, and teacher—who taught at the School of Writing in 1994, teaching us principles of fiction writing and character viewpoint. She is now a friend. Check out her work at https://www.donnafletchercrow.com/

Intercessors and encouragers—all of the people who have faithfully prayed for me over the years as I have pursued the dream of completing this book. Without their prayers, I could not have done it.

Critiques:
- **Carol Burkes:** A special thanks to her, for reading and sending a detailed edit and helped make this story the best I could make it.
- **Sheila Faye Mansker Davis and Karen Jeannine Wickliffe:** Dear and faithful friends, who provided feedback by e-mail.
- **Tracie Williams**: who made brought significant errors to my attention so I could correct them; and encouraged me to use Grammarly.
- **Judi Marsh and author Mari Howard:** Association of Christian Writers members, who provided input in the early days of the rewrite. To see Mari's fascinating Mullins Family Saga, check out her work at https://hodgepublishing.co.uk/
- **Wendy Collins**: Neighbor, creative mind and great listener. Who helped keep me focused and listened to my plotting and character conundrums.
- **Heather Reed Powell** Special thanks to my lovely step-daughter who helped edit the back-cover copy and find appropriate public domain artwork for the cover.

Joanne Raetz Stuttgen and Curtis Tomak for their wonderful Postcard History Series, specifically *Martinsville* and *Morgan County*. The books are great for research, as well as very entertaining. You can find these books from Arcadia Publishing, at www.arcadiapublishing.com

Online publishing: Christine Draper, friend, mentor, and author. Check out her children's books and tutorial books on Amazon. https://www.amazon.co.uk/Books-Christine-R-Draper/s?i=stripbooks&rh=p_27%3AChristine+R+Draper

Permission from Martinsville Daily Reporter for allowing me to use the information listed in the archives.

References:

[1] Quote taken from report in Martinsville Daily Reporter, Friday, September 7th 1917; Article entitled, So Long Boys, Good Luck

[2] The Indianapolis Star, Indianapolis, Indiana; November 13 1917, Tuesday, *Medics with Go to Dixie Camp*, Page 15

[3] Letter taken from The Indianapolis Star, Indianapolis, Indiana; Wednesday, December 5th 1917, pg. 5, in the article "Hoosier A.W.O.L. at Camp Shelby

About the Author: Dalletta was born in Bakersfield, California, and raised in Martinsville, Indiana. She has worked as a barber, receptionist, and administrative assistant. She has a passion for missions and missionaries, serving five years collectively with Youth With A Mission. She lives in England, with her husband, John, and miniature Yorkshire terrier, Maisy.

Website: https://dallettaolenareed.com/
E-Mail: MaisysMom@dallettaolenareed.com

Printed in Great Britain
by Amazon